EDGE OF DISASTER

A NOVEL

LYLE A. WAY

CREATION HOUSE
A STRANG COMPANY

EDGE OF DISASTER by Lyle A. Way
Published by Creation House
A Strang Company
600 Rinehart Road
Lake Mary, Florida 32746
www.creationhouse.com

This book or parts thereof may not be reproduced in any form, stored in a retrieval system, or transmitted in any form by any means—electronic, mechanical, photocopy, recording, or otherwise—without prior written permission of the publisher, except as provided by United States of America copyright law.

Unless otherwise noted, all Scripture quotations are from the Holy Bible, New International Version. Copyright © 1973, 1978, 1984, International Bible Society. Used by permission.

Scripture quotations marked KJV are from the King James Version of the Bible.

Cover design by Rachel Lopez

Copyright © 2008 by Lyle A. Way

All rights reserved

Library of Congress Control Number: 2008937330

International Standard Book Number: 978-1-5979-492-1

First Edition

08 09 10 11 12 — 987654321

Printed in the United States of America

Acknowledgments

A number of family members and a new friend at Texas Tech University worked closely with me during the writing of this novel.

I want to thank my wife, Darlene, who tirelessly came to my rescue as I bellowed for help when a cantankerous computer expressed a mind of its own.

Legions of thanks are due to my daughter, Brenda Riffle, who joyfully edited my work and helped proof galleys. She patiently endured my wailings when she removed some of my most beloved words.

I stand in awe of my son, Mark, who provided the intricate details involved in receiving foreign wire transfers of dollars into the United States since the tragedy of September 11, 2001.

I must also express my deep gratitude to K. Wyatt McMahon, Ph.D., Postdoctoral Research Associate, Department of Internal Medicine, Texas Tech University Health Sciences Center, Lubbock, Texas. This dear friend took hours of his valuable time to explain the properties of bacteria and how they might apply to this work. He made the tour of his lab fun and very informative. His insightful and helpful comments on my first few drafts gave great assistance and encouragement.

I must offer my heartfelt thanks to my pastor, Andy Wood. He kept encouraging me to keep writing even when I felt like quitting. His positive and upbeat attitude is quite contagious, making it impossible to be discouraged while in his presence.

Finally, I would be remiss if I neglected to acknowledge and thank my good friend, Jesus, who always responded to my pleas for help and insight. Any good ideas were His!

Introduction

Historical note: Cyrus the Great was the founder of the Persian Empire under the Achaemenid dynasty. He was born in the year 590 BC or 576 BC; there seems to be some uncertainty as to which date is correct. He reigned from 559 BC to August 530 BC where he died in battle fighting the Massagetae along the Syr Darya. An alternative account from Xenophon's Cyropaedia contradicts the others, claiming that Cyrus died peaceably at his capital.

During his twenty-nine year reign, Cyrus fought against some of the greatest city-states, which resulted in the Persian Empire becoming the largest kingdom ever known up to this time.

Cyrus played a very important part in Jewish history. He is mentioned 23 times in the Old Testament, the first being in Isaiah 44:28 to Isaiah 45:6 where God calls him by name and says that Cyrus is "His shepherd!" This portion of scripture was written a century and a half before Cyrus's birth, and it is important to note that no other gentile has ever been given the title "anointed."

Cyrus was known for his religious tolerance; allowing conquered nations to continue to worship whatever god they chose. It is reported that he believed in the equality of man, abhorring the common practice of slavery. This seems to account for his willingness to allow the Jews to return to Israel. In just one year after he defeated the Babylonians he issued the famous proclamation which allowed the Jews to return to their country and rebuild the temple. This proclamation is recorded in the book of Ezra, Chapter 1:

"This is what Cyrus king of Persia says: 'The Lord, the God of heaven, has given me all the kingdoms of the earth and he has appointed me to build a temple for him at Jerusalem in Judah. Anyone of his people among you-may his God be with him, and let him go up to Jerusalem in Judah and build the temple of the Lord, the God of Israel, the God who is in Jerusalem. And the people of any place where survivors may now be living are to provide him with silver and gold, with goods and livestock, and with freewill offerings for the temple of God in Jerusalem.' "

Interestingly enough, only two tribes accepted the king's offer, Judah and Benjamin and the priests, which were the Levites. Cyrus also provided these pilgrims with money, protection and all of the gold and silver items taken from the temple.

Cyrus built the city of Pasargadae as his capital. His tomb lies in the ruins of this city, which is now a UNESCO World Heritage Site.

Pasargadae: Spring, in the 30th Year of Cyrus's Reign

Through the large open windows, a refreshing spring breeze was bringing into the palace the fragrance of new growth. Cyrus longed to be outside, riding around his kingdom and watching people busy with spring planting.

The great king was seated on his throne trying very hard to concentrate on the report that was being given by his Treasurer Mithredath. The dull, but important, report reiterated that taxes received would be sufficient to recruit and train men for his army. He was increasing the size of his armed forces in preparation for the upcoming war with the Massagetae. A true warrior king, he loved battle and conquest but was bored with the details necessary to prepare for battle. One thing he did know, all of the logistical support cost money, lots of money. These funds came from tribute paid by conquered kings, and some wealth came from goods captured in battle. He had been careful, however, not to bankrupt a conquered nation or city-state. He made these inhabitants a part of his empire and treated them with a surprising amount of respect and freedom. He tolerated their religious beliefs and allowed

INTRODUCTION

them to worship whatever god they wished. He felt this tactic was proper, and he was proud of his plan to keep the people satisfied and happy to be part of his empire.

Cyrus's mind wandered back to the second year of his reign and the strange events that took place during that time. He had defeated the Babylonian King Nebuchadnezzar and had inherited a very sensitive problem. The Babylonians had brought the Jews from Judah and Samaria back to Babylon as slaves. Now, after many years, these people were assimilated into the greater population with many Jews having forgotten their true heritage. Cyrus demanded that any royal records concerning these people and the one God that they worshipped be read to him. Not particularly religious himself, Cyrus was perfectly willing to let people worship the god of their choice, which kept conquered people quiet and peaceful. But these Jews confused him! Some of them worshipped their God with great fervor while others seemed to take no notice of their traditional God, whose name was Yahweh. He found it interesting that they would never pronounce that name. Those who didn't recognize Yahweh went about their daily life as if the gods of Babylon were perfectly fine with them.

During the following months, dreams began to haunt him. His soothsayers and magicians were unable to advise him on how to stop them. In these dreams he saw heavenly beings around a great throne located in a beautiful room. A cloud of light surrounded the throne, preventing him from seeing the one seated there. A voice from the throne proclaimed that He was the God of heaven, and it was His wish that Cyrus let the Jews return to Jerusalem. Not only was Cyrus to release them, but he was to give them money for the trip and send troops to protect them. The same dream disturbed him night after night. In the mind of the great king, there could be no other answer; this had to be instructions from the God of Heaven. After pondering for many days, he decided to allow any Jew who wished to go to Jerusalem to make the journey. He couldn't help smiling to himself as he remembered the look on his treasurer's face when Cyrus told him that he needed money to send with these people and to pay for troops necessary for their protection.

"Excuse me, your highness, but I must have misunderstood, fool that I am. You need money for what?" Mithredath stammered. His elegant green satin robe made a swishing sound as he quickly turned back to face the king.

"I am going to allow any Jew who wishes to return to their homeland to leave Persia, and I need money to pay their expenses, including funds to pay for the troops they will need for their protection. It will require a huge caravan to move the people and their belongings, and the journey to Jerusalem is long and dangerous."

"But sire, why would you want to do these things? It will set a dangerous precedent to others who may demand the same privilege." The treasurer, like all of his kind, disliked surprises and always tried to avoid them.

"I don't agree. Those living under our rule seem content to live their lives in Persia. The God of the Jews, who is the God of Heaven, spoke to me in my dreams and gave me these instructions," Cyrus replied confidently.

"Does his majesty worship this god?"

Cyrus thought for a moment and then added, "I'm not sure. I believe in the truth of the dreams and what was said to me."

The beleaguered treasurer glanced around the room with a slightly frantic expression on his face, pleading with his eyes for some support from the officials who were gathered in the room. No support was coming, so he finally resigned himself to do what the king wished when Cyrus interrupted his retreat. "There's another thing I need you to do."

"Yes your majesty."

"Give the Jews all the gold and silver treasure that was taken from their temple by Nebuchadnezzar. Provide them with a complete inventory of what we are giving back to them. And be sure that this decision and the inventory is copied and placed in my historical records."

Mithredath seemed to stagger ever so slightly. "Give them

Introduction

ALL of the treasure AND an inventory?"

"Yes, and remember the historical record. That is my order!" The king's rugged face had such a determined look that there could be no argument.

"Yes, great king. It shall be done." The treasurer hurried away, wiping perspiration from his face as he shuffled down the palace hall. He had known that allowing foreigners to have their own gods would be trouble some day. Well, now this trouble had become reality.

Cyrus's thoughts were abruptly interrupted when Roshti, the commander of his military forces, stepped forward to comment on the readiness of the army. He wanted to proceed with the planning for the battle with the Massagetae. The king's son, Cambyses II, joined them. Cyrus was very proud of Cambyses. He was proving himself as a very capable leader of men in battle. Some day, he will succeed me on the throne! he thought to himself. The king leaned forward in anticipation of good news about his forces. He was eager to return to battle.

August, in the 30th Year of His Reign

Cyrus the Great was eagerly anticipating the upcoming battle. As aides dressed him in his battle gear and armor, his mind was already planning new conquests. He was confident that this battle with the Massagetae would be a short and decisive victory. Next, he would lead his army against that great and ancient nation, Egypt!

He had been planning for the conquest of the Land of the Nile for months. Several times his generals reminded him that he needed to focus on the battle they were about to enter. Egypt would come soon enough. But this mysterious land kept capturing his thoughts. He remembered the reports from travelers and merchants detailing the incredible wealth they witnessed when they travelled south. The country boasted of immense natural resources including gold, silver, lead, iron, and enough wheat to feed the world. Cyrus could not keep from dreaming of the power he would have if he controlled a large part of the world's wheat and other grains. Gold and silver brought him great wealth, luxury, and power. But, he thought, Everyone has to eat! What if Persia controlled most of the world's wheat and countries had to purchase it from his kingdom to get the food they needed to survive?

His daydreaming was interrupted by his generals entering his war tent, urging him to please hurry. The enemy had an army that appeared to be much larger than their spies had led them to believe. They were camped along the Syr Darya, northeast of the headwaters of the Tigris River. The weather could not have been better with clear skies and a slight, cooling breeze. That old thrill of impending battle rushed over him. He could almost hear the horrible noise of battle, the clash of iron on iron, sword upon shield, cries of pain, the sound of death! War horses snorted and pawed the ground while others pulled clattering chariots over the rough ground.

Cyrus wore a purple tunic under golden armor. His head was encircled by a simple gold band. His black hair and beard glistened with the mixture of perfume and honey that had been combed into it earlier by his servants. Tall, muscular, and bronzed by the sun, Cyrus the Great was an imposing figure of strength and power. He was a natural leader of men, and when they saw him emerge from his tent, a great cheer went up as they raised their swords in salute.

As king, Cyrus felt it was his right and his duty to lead his men into battle. His war chariot was pulled by a matched pair of white stallions, well trained and fearless. He loved these animals and spent time talking to them as he stroked their great necks. He considered them "kings" of their breed and lavished them with special food. This food was specially delivered to them from Pasargadae, regardless of how far away they might have been during any campaign.

His generals and commanders were not as happy about their king leading the battle as he was. His dress, his chariot, the two white horses all shouted "King" to any enemy soldier that saw him. He was, without doubt, a perfect target for archers and spearmen. Because of this, he was always surrounded by a defending wall of soldiers, on foot and on horseback. Every possible precaution was taken to keep him safe. But, he was king! And as king, he would often order his men to get out of his way so he could join in the battle. He imagined his sword swinging in a great arch, inflicting terrible injuries and death. This was what he intended to do today. His great ego would allow no other course of action.

Years ago, Jewish priests had shown him an ancient parchment that contained the words given to their great prophet Isaiah more than a century before his birth. The great God of Heaven had called him by name, Cyrus, and had called him God's shepherd or servant. Surely this God would lead him to another victory. He would lead, he would fight, and he would kill for his Persia, his empire!

The battle raged for hours with first the Persians winning, then the Massagetae. The destruction was terrible and the noise was deafening. The grass slopes were littered with the fallen bodies of soldiers from both armies. Cyrus was sure of victory and took chances that were risky and dangerous. He moved his chariot perilously close to the front lines while his sword inflicted terrible wounds and death. Suddenly, with a faint "swish" that he heard plainly even while surrounded by the roar of battle, an arrow struck him in the throat, tearing an artery into several pieces. Blood spurted from the wound like a great red fountain. His bodyguards, frantically trying to defend him, did not see him fall. Finally, the alarm went up, and his men rushed to his aid. But, it was too late. Cyrus the Great was seated on the floor of his chariot in a pool of his own blood. He was carefully carried from the chariot and gently laid on a bed of cloaks that were hastily taken from his men. His most trusted general, helmet off and tears coursing down his cheeks, tenderly cradled his king's head on his lap. He bent down close to Cyrus's mouth when he noticed that the king seemed to be trying to say something. Softly, the great king whispered, "O God of Heaven, remember me."

Bandages were applied, surgeons summoned while bodyguards formed a solid wall of humanity around their fallen king. Then he was gone! This amazing life was over. The man who had formed the largest empire ever known had been struck down by an unknown archer, with a single arrow.

The battle raged back and forth for hours, but the Persians were finally victorious. This grand victory was joyless because their great king had fallen. An honor guard was quickly formed, and a cart draped with purple cloth. The royal pair of white stallions led the silent procession, slowly pulling the cart carrying their beloved master. The soldiers marched in silence all the way back to the capital city of Pasargadae.

Thousands of women wept and tore their clothes demonstrating their mourning. A great funeral takes time! This funeral took many days. Each ceremony was more elaborate than the previous one. Many speeches were given to groups of people who tried to listen but were tempted beyond their ability to resist drinking from an ever-flowing supply of free wine. Presiding over all of these events was one of the king's sons, Cambyses II.

Ambassadors from all of the Empire's regions came to pay their respects while they privately wondered who would become king. Government officials were conducting secret meetings in the palace to quickly and quietly decide that very issue. Cambyses met with all of the generals, satraps, and governors of the Empire. Pouches of gold were distributed to the generals while promises of increased power and wealth were made to the satraps and governors. Everyone was in agreement. When an appropriate time of mourning had passed, Cyrus's son, Cambyses II, would be crowned king and leader of the Persian Empire. Construction had already begun on a grand tomb that would provide a chamber of rest for the great king's body. A golden coffin along with golden furniture and other items the king would need in the next life were placed in the tomb. Cyrus the Great was ceremoniously placed in the coffin which was positioned in the tomb with great fanfare. Inside, by his coffin, an epitaph was printed on a golden plaque which said:

"O man, whoever you are and wherever you come from, for I know you will come. I am Cyrus who won the Persians their empire. Do not therefore grudge me this little earth that covers my body."

His wife, his two daughters and both of his sons were present and shamelessly displayed their grief and sadness. The tomb was sealed, and the ceremonies ended. People struggled back to their homes and their mundane daily lives while in the palace King Cambyses was already planning a military campaign against Egypt. A new company of advisors, religious priests, and military bodyguards were brought in to take their place in this new administration. Cyrus the Great was now part of history!

Chapter One

At the University of Tehran, Arastoo Faridoon had just finished teaching his afternoon class in economics. Arastoo (which is the Persian form of Aristotle) was very young to be a professor, but in everyone's mind he was a genius. He was the professor of Economics, Mathematics, and Political Sciences. He possessed the rare combination of the good looks of an ancient god and the photographic memory of a chess champion. His piercing gray eyes seemed to be able to penetrate into a person's soul. He was tall, muscular, and had a bright, ready smile that dazzled everyone. In addition to this very god-like mixture, he was blessed with the gift of being a spellbinding orator. No student ever wanted to sneak a nap in his classes; they hung onto every word that he said.

The professor was very popular on campus and enjoyed a large following of students that truly believed he was the greatest man in the country. This following had not gone unnoticed by the religious clerics that governed the university. They secretly observed his every move, trying to detect anything that might threaten their power and control. They watched and waited, ready to react to any evidence that Arastoo was a danger to them. Most of these clerics were radicals who had never attended any university, nor had they had much theological training. They were placed in positions of authority at the university, as well as other key locations throughout Iran, to keep an eye on all academic and political areas that were important to the Supreme Leader, Ayatollah Bahman Khodadad. The Ayatollah, as Supreme Leader of

Iran, was the ultimate power behind all things religious and political. The clerics were his eyes and ears as well as being his enforcers, when necessary. Because of their lack of education, they viewed all professors with suspicion and jealousy, particularly Faridoon. This made them very dangerous fellows indeed.

Professor Faridoon (Faridoon is a Persian name for king) was on his way to meet a hand-picked group of students at an off campus location. Before going to the meeting with the students, Arastoo arranged to meet with a mysterious stranger privately in a small outdoor café. The street noise and casual conversation in the background made it a good place to hold a quiet, confidential meeting without the danger of being overheard. The stranger, who rarely smiled, was dressed in an extravagant suit. On his feet he wore Italian loafers with leather so soft it could have been used for gloves. Tall, slender, with a dark complexion, he was remarkably handsome; his eyes were hidden behind trendy Oakley sunglasses.

Arastoo thought back to the first time he had met this strange man. The man had walked unannounced into his classroom several weeks ago and shocked him by saying that he was going to make Arastoo one of the most powerful men on earth. Of course the professor thought the man was either mad or joking. However, the man was neither mad, nor was he joking; he outlined a definitive plan showing how he was going to bring about this transformation of Arastoo from a professor to a new world leader. Arastoo was told that details would be given to him when it was the proper time; until then, he was to go about his daily routine until given further instructions. Now, weeks later, it was beginning!

"Well, professor, is our plan on schedule?" the mysterious stranger asked softly.

"Yes sir. I'm meeting with some of my most trusted students in just a few minutes. May I be so bold as to ask, how will we be able to gain the support of the Ayatollah Khodadad

Chapter One

and the Assembly of Experts? Their religious power over our nation is immense. Without the Ayatollah's support, along with the Assembly's, I fear we are doomed to failure," Arastoo said through pursed lips.

"You need not worry about gaining their support. Ayatollah Khodadad and I have been friends for many years. I'll be meeting with him in just a few minutes to go over the details of our ultimate goals. I'm certain he will be extremely pleased because our goals are also his desires. As far as the clerics who make up the assembly are concerned, they will follow my suggestions. Remember that I am somewhat of an expert on religions. Through the years, I have started many of them all over the world. Some have millions of followers." The man held Faridoon spellbound in his gaze and continued, "Are you sure that you have enough trustworthy people to set the plan in motion? What about the Revolutionary Guard?"

"I feel very confident that there are plenty of disgruntled men who will do our bidding when the time is right. We also have high ranking Army officers ready to respond when the order is given. However, I am not so confident about the Parliament. Can you provide some help in persuading leading members to join us?" Faridoon asked.

"I can influence many of them to come around to our way of thinking. Remember, this is my plan! I am not going to let it fail!" *Strange*, Arastoo thought, *he just said it was 'our' plan.*

"Indeed, sir! Thank you! I'm ready to fulfill my role in this great venture that will strike a fatal blow to our most hated enemies!"

"Very good! You are a very charismatic speaker, and I know you will be successful when you address the students. I'll be following your progress very carefully. If you have any problems, I'll be available. I have a number of my agents placed in strategic areas around Tehran who will alert me if something goes wrong, but I am trusting that you will make sure that there will be no reason for me to be concerned." He looked into Arastoo's eyes with such intensity that the professor had to stifle a small shudder.

"Remember, time is of the essence," the man said as he rose to leave. Anyone watching would see a very confident, handsome man getting up from a business meeting. What they would not see, however, were his eyes, nor would they be close enough to note a very faint odor of sulfur as he left.

The professor paid the bill for the coffee that neither one had touched and left the café. Falling in beside him as he walked quickly down the sidewalk was his constant companion who had waited for him just outside the café. He was a six foot, nine inch giant of a man named Shaheen, which means peregrine falcon in Persian. This fellow would have been a great linebacker for the Green Bay Packers. His very dark complexion was magnified by the blackness of his hair, beard, and eyes. Eyes that testified to the danger that lurked within. He never smiled and spoke only to Arastoo. His wardrobe consisted of black robes similar to what clerics wore. The one exception to the color of black that made up his persona was a glittering gold Rolex watch that he wore on his right wrist. Students and friends of the professor secretly wondered about this fearful looking giant that was always near him, but none dared to ask any questions.

Arastoo and Shaheen walked quickly to a small warehouse located in the market district. The giant was watchful to verify that they were not being followed. Inside, the professor found over one hundred young people, all of whom had been warned to be careful when coming to the meeting. It was important that they not be followed to the warehouse. Should they have the slightest suspicion of someone following them, they were to try another route or not attend at all. This, of course, gave these young people the intoxicating excitement that all youths have when they are part of something big, secret, and powerful.

The oppressive heat of summer had not yet arrived, and

Chapter One

the shade provided by the large building made the temperature bearable, almost comfortable.

Arastoo took his place in front of the group, held up his hands to quiet them, and began to speak so softly that everyone had to strain to hear his words.

"My dear young friends, I have asked that you join me here to put before you a plan that I believe will change our country and the world forever, but I need your help! Because of the flawed policies of the present government, our great land has become a pariah to most of the world. President Niloufar's all consuming effort to create a nuclear weapons program, with his open threat to use these weapons against the United States and the state of Israel, is a hopeless plan that is bound to fail. Because of this, the rest of the world believes that we are insane, dangerous, or just plain STUPID! This has accomplished nothing except to have nuclear warheads atop thousands of missiles aimed not at the former Soviet Union, but at us! It is a foolish plan that if carried out, will bring certain annihilation."

"What do we gain if we explode a nuclear weapon over a great city or over that country's farm land? Oh yes, there will be thousands, if not millions of people killed, but what about the land, the buildings, and the infrastructure? They become useless for hundreds of years—absolutely good for nothing. This is not the time for a small nation such as ours to decide that we will be the bullies of the world! In the name of all that's good, this is the time for us to use our intelligence to make this a great nation, not to use weapons to threaten others!" He had to pause because of an eruption of applause."

Smiling, the professor continued, "Many of you do not know that I am a man of the land. I was born on a small farm in the northern part of our country. I have worked the land, along with my parents, to make a small living. I am familiar with blisters because I know what hard manual labor is like. I also know what it is like to be ignored by our government except at tax time." More applause and cheering stopped him again.

"When you work the land, you love the land, and you want to protect it!"

"After years of hard labor, I was given the opportunity to come to this great university. I worked in a café as a waiter in the evening and studied until early in the morning. Years later, after more hard work and intensive study, and with the help of many friends, I finished graduate school. Then, something magical happened; I was given the opportunity to become a professor!"

"After I became part of the faculty, I was horrified to learn that this great institution of higher learning is not run by academics, but by uneducated, mean-spirited men who want to use your intelligence to further their warped ideas of world conquest! My friends, when you overhear these men talking, it becomes clear that they are not proud of you or your potential, they DESPISE you! You are a tool to be used by them and their superiors; nothing more."

The room exploded with cheers and applause and shouts of "Yes!" and "It's true!" It took several minutes for the noise to subside so he could resume speaking. Arastoo was ecstatic! He had the crowd right where he wanted them. This university professor was now convinced that these young people would do his bidding; they would serve him when he called on them to rally around the great cause he was about to present to them. He was sweating and shivering at the same time. Adrenalin was pouring through his veins, filling him with incredible power. *This was wonderful!* he gloated to himself.

Looking around the room into the expectant eyes of these young Iranians, Faridoon continued, "When I first arrived here, I became acutely aware of my destiny. I conducted exhaustive research to learn as much as I could about my ancestors. Going back through time, generation after generation, I discovered something so astounding that my

Chapter One

life has been changed forever! An unseen force seemed to be guiding me as I pored over ancient records. When one door was found locked, another opened to my inquiry. Finally, I discovered an incredible truth that I want to share with you today. I AM THE DIRECT DESCENDANT OF CYRUS THE GREAT, AND I INTEND TO RESURRECT THE PERSIAN EMPIRE FROM ITS GLORIOUS PAST AND REMAKE IT INTO A NEW GLOBAL EMPIRE!" He was shouting with emotion, caught up in the excitement of the moment and the impact of his own words.

A tremendous roar exploded from the crowd, so loud that Arastoo began to fear that people on the street would hear the clamor and call the authorities. He raised his arms requesting silence, and when he once again regained control, he continued.

"As you know, the great Cyrus unified our country twenty-five centuries ago. He became king and formed the largest empire that the world had ever known—the PERSIAN EMPIRE! As king, he was a fair and benevolent leader who treated conquered peoples with respect and tolerance. Cyrus allowed each conquered nation or city-state to worship their own gods, according to their customs. He did not impose his religious beliefs on others, unlike our government today, which has set as its goal the forcing of all nations to follow Islam. Our government uses political influence or the use of violence, by supporting terrorism, to achieve their objective. Their cry is 'believe as we do or die!' I believe this strategy to be foolhardy and destined to fail!"

Now the students were standing and cheering. Arastoo could feel the power he had over these young minds, and it was intoxicating!

"Much of the world stands against us. The United States and Israel are currently ready to deploy missiles to destroy our nuclear facilities when they believe the danger is too great. What madness! What will become of us when the missiles come? What will become of our beautiful land when a mushroom cloud hangs over it in the sky?"

The room was engulfed in a deafening shout of "No!"

"We must not let this happen to us, to our homes, or to our families. STOP THE MADNESS!" he shouted.

Everyone was on their feet shaking clenched fists in the air. Once more Arastoo raised his arms to quiet the crowd.

"What you may not be aware of is the fact that the great Cyrus was a friend of the Jews! He allowed them to return to Israel to rebuild their temple. They hailed him as a great leader and friend. Did you know that he is mentioned twenty-three times in the Jewish Old Testament? Another astounding bit of information I learned is that the Jewish God called Cyrus His servant, and said that he was 'anointed.' He was the only non-Jew to ever be given that title."

"But, what is our government doing today? President Niloufar has sworn to destroy Israel and wipe it off the map. This strategy forces the United States, Israel's ally, to defend them. Who do you think will win that confrontation?"

Arastoo's delivery was passionate. On some points he was nearly shouting; on others he nearly whispered. He used his hands as points of emphasis, stabbing the air to make a point, palms out as if pleading for understanding.

"Now, my friends, to the reason I have called you here. I believe that you all are intelligent, industrious, and, hopefully, loyal to me."

Another roar went up, with shouts of "Yes" and "Arastoo" drowning out the professor.

"I have a plan that will improve this country and alter the way the world perceives us. It is my goal to re-establish THE GREAT PERSIAN EMPIRE and make it the leader of the world! To do this, I must be elected PRESIDENT! You will be my ambassadors, my cabinet, my advisors, my foot soldiers. We need followers in the Parliament and in the Council of Ministers. The government must be persuaded to

Chapter One

hold an election. Then the people of Iran need to vote for me when the time comes, and it will come soon. This is how I am counting on you for your help and support. Our political campaign will take thousands of workers, and I need you to help recruit them."

"Some of you, and others that will join us, will go to other countries to pave the way for the Empire to expand by forming new alliances. Soon, very soon, THE WORLD WILL BE OURS!" He shouted and raised his hands in a victory salute while sweat poured from his face. He knew this audience was his!

The room erupted in applause and cheering! The students rushed the platform, straining to touch him. They chanted his name over and over, and for a moment he feared they might try and raise him to their shoulders. These young men and women were obviously willing to pledge their allegiance to him and promised to give their life, if necessary, to help accomplish this wonderful dream.

Shrewdly, Arastoo had insisted that this group include women. He knew that women, who had been suppressed by men in an intolerant religion all of their lives, would respond with passion and commitment when given the chance to experience freedom and a sense of belonging. Now, these women were bursting with pride and determination to serve Arastoo and Persia!

Half an hour later, he was finally able to quiet the crowd enough to continue speaking. His piercing gray eyes moved over the group, making contact with nearly every person. He smiled and waved. *How easy they were to motivate!* he mused.

"Thank you, thank you so very much! I am humbled by your trust and faith in me and your willingness to work with me in this adventure to make Persia the greatest of all nations. But you must understand that it will take hard work, and some of it will be dangerous. A few of you may even lose your lives.

But if so, you will not have lost it in the name of an old man's dead religion that began thousands of years ago, but in the name of a new and great Persia!"

"Our plan starts now! You will soon be contacted regarding what your role will be. We must confront our government and the military they control. This plan, of course, must be completely secret. Let caution be your constant companion! Some of you will work with student activist organizations; others will work with conservative opposition groups and newspapers. When the campaign begins it is imperative that we control all of the media."

"Many of you will be sent overseas to implement the most important part of our plan, which will soon lead to our CONTROLLING MUCH OF THE WORLD!"

Applause and cheering once again drowned him out. Their voices were nearly hoarse from cheering and shouting, but it didn't stop them.

"What we cannot accomplish by using missiles and bombs will be accomplished through diplomacy. Yes, I said diplomacy. There are other details of the plan which I cannot share with you now, but you will learn about them when they have been put in place. You are the brightest and the best that our great Persia has ever produced. I know that with you supporting this great endeavor, WE CANNOT FAIL!"

They roared their approval! Everyone was pounding someone else on the back. Arastoo waited; then resumed speaking while thinking to himself, *This must be how a god feels!*

"We have a sea of oil beneath our great land. Nations with oil thirsty economies from all over the world are anxious to buy this black gold from us. We will use their money to finance our grand expansion. Ironic, isn't it? Their own wealth will bring their downfall, economically and politically, and make us the greatest power on earth!"

"Oh, just one more thing. We are going to build refineries

Chapter One

to make gasoline for our own country's use. No more waiting in long lines to buy foreign gasoline. THAT'S CRAZY AND IT'S GOING TO STOP! NOW, GET ON YOUR CELL PHONES AND I-PHONES AND RECRUIT YOUR FRIENDS TO JOIN US IN THIS HISTORIC ADVENTURE!"

The room erupted again. There was laughing, crying, singing and praise for Arastoo. His eloquence, confidence, even his hand gestures had captivated them. They were now his, to do with as he saw fit. He smiled, waved, shook hands, and hugged everyone who came close enough. *Yes, Professor,* he thought to himself. *You have them! And wouldn't they be surprised to know that you learned the techniques for speaking to a crowd and controlling their thoughts from the great master, Adolph Hitler!*

He had worked for weeks, reviewing every newsreel of Hitler's speeches to the German people. He studied his body language, the gestures he made with his hands, his facial expressions, and the way he paused for effect. Many of these speeches have been lost to the public for years, but his "special" friend had made them available to him.

Finally, late that night, he was able to leave the oppressive heat of the warehouse, and walk down cool, moon-lit streets. Shaheen appeared from the darkness and fell in beside him.

"It went well, my friend. We are ready to begin and you must have those that have already been recruited put our plan into motion immediately. It is time for the first step. I am trusting that you will take care of it tomorrow."

The menacing giant gave a slight bow and disappeared into the darkness.

Unseen by either of the men was a slight movement in the shadows. Someone was following them at a very safe distance. Whoever they were, they were very good.

After he was a good distance from the warehouse, Arastoo flagged a taxi and was taken to his apartment. He was pleased with the way the night had gone, but he was also exhausted and spent. There was no doubt that this was just the beginning and there was still so much to be done, but he reveled in the victory he witnessed tonight.

Grabbing a sandwich and a glass of milk, he wolfed down his food and went to bed. Sleep avoided him, though. The sequence of events that needed to happen for the implementation of the plan kept rolling over in his mind. He had to get a staff right away, and thousands more people needed to be recruited and interviewed. Money was no problem since financing was being taken care of by the man he met with earlier. This rather aloof person, who had recruited him some weeks earlier, seemed to have inexhaustible resources. Arastoo shivered just a little as he thought of this mysterious and obviously very powerful man whom he now followed and put so much trust in. For reasons of his own, this secretive man was helping Arastoo satisfy his enormous ego and ambition. He wasn't sure just who this man was, nor where he came from, but he instinctively knew that this was not the time to inquire into his background. One thing was sure; this foreigner commanded great power and demanded complete loyalty, loyalty that the professor was glad to give in order to pursue his own selfish goals.

As he lay in the darkness, he allowed himself to dwell on his ancient ancestor, Cyrus, and what that great man had accomplished. He wanted to be exactly like the great Cyrus; he wanted to be KING OF THE NEW PERSIAN EMPIRE and lead it to become THE MOST POWERFUL EMPIRE ON EARTH! He had never shared with another soul his secret ambition.

Finally he slipped into a dreamless sleep.

Chapter Two
Fall, 2007

The driver pulled the cab over to the curb at 1719 South Burlingame. From the street, the place looked like a nineteenth century plantation, protected by huge magnolia trees with giant blooms and an assortment of shade and evergreen trees. The manicured lawn accentuated the red brick, two-story family residence which proudly displayed two grand porches encompassing the entire length of the building. White railings and windows completed the picture-perfect architecture which could have easily been displayed on the cover of any *Southern Living* magazine. Scattered about the property were small cottages that were of the same design and color of trim but were nearly covered with ivy. These little cabins appeared to have been designed to welcome the occasional traveler with warmth and comfort regardless of the length of stay. A very small brass sign placed on a rather forbidding rock wall, which was completely covered with ivy, said, "The Brothers Clinic and Seminary." The second line made the point very clear; it said "Private."

From the back seat, Tuck surveyed the grounds with rheumy, bloodshot eyes that were having a great deal of difficulty focusing on anything. The cabby coughed to let him know that he wanted his money so he could be on his way. Fumbling in his shabby camel hair jacket, he tried to locate his wallet by patting every pocket, but he had no success. This caused him some measure of panic! Crumpled in one of the jacket pockets he found a slip of paper that read 1719 South Burlingame, Charlottesville, Virginia. *Charlottesville?* He wondered to himself while experiencing the worst hangover ever endured by a human being. *How did I get here, and for heaven's sake, why am I here?*

Tuck finally located a crumpled twenty and handed it to the guy at the wheel, who was glaring at him without pity. His suitcase was beside him on the seat, and he valiantly attempted to pull it with him as he struggled out of the cab, which immediately drove away. He was swaying slightly, but he was standing upright on the driveway, which Tuck considered to be a major victory. There was a forbidding looking black wrought iron gate that he had not noticed before, which prevented him from walking any further. Tuck swore quietly and thought, *They're trying to keep me out before I even get in!* He felt like he was going to be sick, so he quickly glanced around to see if anyone was watching. Stumbling into some bushes that were close by, he wretched a few times until the bile descended once again into his innermost parts. His mouth tasted like the inside of a bat cave. Forcing his bleary eyes to focus on both sides of the gate, he finally located what appeared to be some kind of a call box. The fool thing seemed to be moving before his eyes, and he knew from experience that when things began to move like that he couldn't catch them unless he closed his eyes for a minute. This short respite worked well enough for him to find a button and push it. A velvety sounding voice with a Southern accent asked him for his name.

"Aristotle Tucker," he stammered. *Tuck to my friends*, he thought to himself.

As if by magic, two unsmiling young men in dark suits with red ties appeared and proceeded to unlock the gate and begrudgingly pulled it open. One of the guards took him by the arm and half dragged him up the driveway while the other guy grabbed the suitcase that he had abandoned, closed the gate, and followed them. Tuck did not like anyone touching him and resisted half-heartedly, but that got him nowhere.

"Now, now Mr. Tucker, let's not be difficult," the man clutching his arm said as he squeezed just a little harder. There obviously was a great deal of muscle under that suit coat, so

Chapter Two

Tuck stopped struggling and walked along as best he could. He thought he was going to be sick again. What a mess! What a hangover!

The struggle up the steps to the porch was almost too much for him. The young fellow kept his body moving straight to the front door, which opened, again, as if by magic. They entered a large, comfortable looking room with couches and stuffed chairs scattered about. Tuck lunged for the nearest chair, but the vise-like grip continued to guide him towards a beautiful mahogany desk. *This must be the reception area, and that beautiful blond young woman must be the receptionist.* Tuck was rather pleased with himself that he had figured that out.

"Mr. Tucker, welcome. I'm Valerie."

"Of course, who else could you be?" Tuck muttered. "Can I sit down?"

"There is no need to sit now; we're taking you straight to your room so you can rest for awhile. All arrangements have been made. You'll start treatment tomorrow morning, bright and early," she said sweetly. He didn't like her accent.

"Treatment! What treatment?" Tuck yelled. "What goes here?"

"Mr. Tucker, don't you remember? The company sent you to us for treatment since we are the finest rehabilitation facility in the country. We take care of lots of government employees who are struggling with drug or alcohol abuse. You'll stay here until you feel better and the doctors are convinced that you can get back to work. I'm sure you're going to be very comfortable here," she said as she smiled again.

"Rehabilitation! You mean you're going to dry me out?" Tuck looked around frantically for a way to escape, but he couldn't see anything that looked promising. The two guards appeared bigger and stronger than he remembered when he first met them at the gate.

The conversation was over abruptly. The men each grabbed

an arm and pulled him down a hall and through what Tuck believed was a locked door. The hall was painted in muted pastel colors that seemed to make it quiet but failed to make him feel calm or welcome.

His room was rather plain, but nice with pleasant, semi-modern furniture. The walls were painted the same pastel shade as the hall. Adjacent to the living room, there was a bedroom containing a king-size bed which seemed to be beckoning to him, promising the sleep that he craved. Attached to the bedroom was a stark white bathroom with a small shower. The walls in this room were altogether too institutional according to his way of thinking.

"There are pajamas and a robe in the closet. I think you should get right to bed and get some rest. Treatment starts bright and early in the morning." The guard grinned at his jab at Tuck who didn't look as if he would be alive in the morning! "Good night Mr. Tucker." The door closed, and they were gone. He sat on the bed and held his head in his hands. *How did I get in this mess?* He wondered to himself. *I'm a good agent and a good journalist! I've served my country well! But look at me now, I'm just a drunk! Oh, dear God!* He slumped over on the bed and was immediately asleep.

Back at the reception desk, the beautiful young woman and the two men were having a cup of coffee.

"Man, if that's what we've got protecting this country, I'm buying some Chinese war bonds! What a stinking mess he is!" The taller of the two men said.

Valerie replied, "I dunno, I kind of feel sorry for him. The word I got was that he's been in some real nasty places doing undercover work. He constantly risks his life and what does he get for it? The work turns him into an alcoholic. It makes me feel very sad!"

The tall one liked Valerie and wanted more than anything to keep talking to her. But she had made it very clear in the past that she wanted nothing to do with anyone working on

Chapter Two

staff. She kept her private life to herself. *Too bad!* He thought. *She was a real beauty and nice too!* They both left to resume their guard duties.

Chapter Three
January, 2008

In the cold, early morning hours after the warehouse meeting, an old, dust colored military CH-47 Chinook helicopter was flying very low and very fast. There was no doubt that this bird was evading radar. It was flying in the Dasht-e Lut desert region, heading towards the small town of Mashhad. The chopper landed on the outskirts of the town in a cloud of dust, and was met by a small group of military men from a nearby outpost. They jumped into the chopper and unloaded a large bundle, wrapped in blankets. The bundle moved and made strangling noises. A huge man dressed in black jumped down from the chopper and joined the men as they carried the bundle and unceremoniously dumped it in the back of a deuce and a half. The soldiers clambered into the back of the truck, which suddenly roared to life and headed out into the mountains towards the Turkmenistan border.

Not one soul said anything as they bounced around trying to keep warm while holding onto their seats. Cautiously, the men shot glances toward the giant who sat on the floor near the front of the truck. He ignored them completely. These were fighting men who had experienced battle and been in perilous situations. They knew instinctively that this man was dangerous.

After an hour of growling over the sand and rocks, the mysterious mission came to an end as the old troop transporter ground to a halt in a cloud of dust and grit. Jumping down, the men grabbed the bundle and threw it on the ground, where it emitted a howl of pain and abusive swearing. The giant

Chapter Three

jumped from the truck and ripped the blankets off the bundle. The startled soldiers yowled and turned as if to run. They immediately recognized the man on the ground; he was THE PRESIDENT OF IRAN!

"What in the name of Allah is happening? This is President Niloufar! We can't treat him like this!" one of the soldiers growled as he struggled to stand at attention. Two of the men started to bring their rifles to the ready position.

From the folds of his robe, the huge man in black produced a Glock 25 Safe Action automatic, which he pointed at the soldiers. He gestured at them to drop their rifles and pick up the president, who was swearing like a camel herder, demanding that he be released.

"You fools! You idiots! What do you think you are doing? Release me at once or I will have you all shot!"

"But your highness, what are we to do? This man has a pistol aimed at us," one of the men whined.

The men wanted to obey their president, but feared the deadly looking automatic and the man that held it. The driver of the truck jumped down to join them, but he was completely unaware of what was happening in the back. He was a slight and frail man who hated military life. He hated the threat of violence even more, and when he understood what he was seeing, he became sick and threw up all over the back wheels while holding onto the side of the bed to keep from falling.

Shaheen growled and pointed the gun menacingly at the group, indicating that he wanted them to pick the leader of Iran up and bring him with them. Trudging through the sand was desperately hard work but carrying their heavy burden made it all the more difficult. They were quickly covered with sweat and dust, and as all foot soldiers do, began to complain. A sinister glance from the giant in black put a stop to their grumbling, and they moved on in silence.

They soon came to a dry wadi that had a deep crevice shaped much like a ragged cave. Shaheen motioned the men to move to the edge of the chasm. They had to use great care to keep from slipping and falling into the dreadful hole. The president was no longer belligerent and issuing commands. He was now filled with terror and began pleading for his life.

"Listen to me!" the president cried, "You can have anything you want in this world, just don't leave me here!"

Shaheen, breaking his normal silence, grunted a guttural, "Shut up!"

"Please, you can have anything..." A single shot from the Glock put a .380 slug in the president's head, and he fell lifeless into the cave-like opening. All of the soldiers screamed and began to beg for mercy, but there was no mercy to come. The automatic spat out lead death to each of them, and they all fell into the same pit. Tromping near the edge of the wadi, the giant was able to dislodge a good quantity of sand and rocks that fell into the crevice, partially sealing the improvised tomb. There was always the possibility that a wandering nomad might stumble upon this newly created grave, but Shaheen felt that the risk was small enough to be acceptable.

The black robed killer returned to the truck and started the long, uncomfortable journey back across the desert to Mashhad, where the ancient Huey helicopter stood waiting. Finally, the truck approached the chopper sitting quietly where they had left it. The pilot was sleeping in the back of the machine to get out of a cold breeze. Arastoo's companion walked up to the helicopter where the pilot was snoring loudly. Anyone close by would have heard the snoring cease abruptly. Mysteriously, a fire started and rapidly consumed the entire helicopter and its contents; a military truck could be seen lumbering out of sight.

In Tehran, the president's disappearance was beginning to be suspected, and rumors were circulating around the city. What was noticed by student groups and some in the press was the fact that many clerics were not to be found anywhere around the governmental buildings. They were also absent from

Chapter Three

the university. This was very strange indeed, but it didn't bring about any loud outcry of public concern. These black robed religious zealots were disliked, or even hated, by most people, especially by younger Iranians. It was commonly known that many of the clerics, while haranguing the public to hate the West and the luxuries the Western people enjoyed, were wealthy and corrupt themselves. Stories of alcohol abuse and the fondness for young women quietly circulated throughout the city.

Stranger still, the elite Revolutionary Guard was not in the capital. They were rumored to have been deployed to a secret military exercise in Tabriz, in the northern part of the country. Continuous flights of old C-130 Hercules transport planes were ferrying them rapidly out of the city.

Governmental officials were becoming suspicious of the events that were rapidly taking place. Members of Parliament were demanding to know why the Guard was moving out of the capital. Generals from the army and air force were summoned while police forces from all over the country were placed on alert with instructions that any intelligence issues were to be forwarded to the president's office immediately.

Finally, the news could no longer be contained. A public state of emergency was declared and the people of the nation were notified by radio and television that the president was missing. Vice President Bahram, whom most people had never heard of, assumed control of the country, urging everyone to stay calm and attend to their daily duties.

The Supreme Commander of the Army, General Parvin, was summoned to the president's office. After being announced and ushered into the room, he noticed that Vice President Bahram was seated behind the huge, ornate oak desk, talking on the telephone. Ending the phone discussion, Bahram slammed down the receiver and turned to face the general.

"General Parvin, what in the name of all that is holy is going on? People are disappearing all over the place, and the Revolutionary Guard has been ordered away from the city. Did you order them out of Tehran?" the vice president shouted. His mousy face was beet red.

"No sir, I did not issue such an order. I am trying to track down who issued the directive as we speak. Has there been any news about our beloved president?" Parvin asked.

A very large, rotund man, Parvin was sweating profusely. He wiped his forehead with a large, white handkerchief that was already damp and did not provide much assistance in controlling the large droplets that kept falling on the president's desk.

The vice president looked at the general with disgust as he watched a small puddle of sweat form on the beautiful desk. Bahram was not tall, but he kept himself in good physical shape. He was disgusted by the general's appearance. *This is an example of our military?* he asked himself.

"Do you mean to stand there and tell me that you have no idea what is happening and who might be behind this loss of our president, some of his cabinet, and most of the cleric contingent in the city?"

"I have not been able to find out any information as of yet, but I have my best men working around the clock to get a handle on this crisis," grimaced Parvin.

"Well, general, you had better do a lot better than that if you want to keep your job and avoid the firing squad! I am holding you personally responsible for this mess. You are supposed to have this country under control! Now get out of here and find out what is happening, and I mean find out right away!"

He dismissed the general with a contemptuous wave of his hand. General Parvin scurried out of the room while thanking Allah that there was a chance he might still be alive tomorrow if he could just find out what in the world was taking place and who was causing this mess.

Chapter Four

Thousands of miles to the west of Tehran, Aristotle Tucker was in the Brother's Clinic library reading every newspaper he could find. After several weeks of therapy, good food, and exercise, he was back in the land of the living. He had survived many days of painful withdrawal and more than a few horrible visions that he never wanted to see again. The need for a drink was slowly leaving him although he still found himself glancing around whatever room he was in, hoping someone had left a bottle of anything lying around!

The news reported from Iran filled him with several unanswered questions, questions that he wanted answered. While working at the CIA, he had been assigned to the Iranian section the majority of the time because of his ability to speak Farsi and Persian fluently. He was also considered to be an expert in Iranian politics. He knew who the power brokers were as well as being extremely familiar with the people who were the leaders in the opposition student and political groups. Much of this knowledge had been gleaned from covert operations that utilized his journalistic skills as good cover. Because of what he liked to call his 'swarthy' complexion, he had always been able to walk around Tehran nearly unnoticed.

There did not seem to have been a coup d'état in Iran since the vice president had taken control of the country peaceably when the president disappeared. The military appeared to be taking orders from the civilian government, and there did not seem to be any great amount of population unrest. It was strange—everyone seemed to have a "wait and see" attitude.

Man, he wanted to be back to work with all of this

excitement happening. The truth was, however, he was not sure that the company would take him back because of his personal problems. He had just learned that he didn't even have a place to live. A notice came in the mail stating that the landlord in his apartment building had cleared out all of his stuff and put it in storage because of his ignoring the rent.

No job, no home, no money, what a mess he had made of his life. *How had this happened?* he kept asking himself. He had had everything going for him. He had a degree from Stanford University in journalism and a minor in foreign languages. He had a great job with the Central Intelligence Agency; well, he used to have a great job with the agency! He once had respect from his peers. He even had some investments that were doing pretty well. That and the retirement plan from the company; his future had looked awfully bright!

But now! *Great Caesar's ghost*, he whispered to himself, *his life seemed to be over!* All of this could be blamed on abusing alcohol. Oh sure, he told himself that he needed to fit in with the guys, so he had to take a drink once in a while. But, "once in a while" had turned into keeping a bottle of "Uncle Jack" in his desk drawer and having six or seven drinks after work.

Tuck walked out of the library and wandered down a hall that he had just discovered. In fact, he hadn't even noticed it before because he was so absorbed in his problems. The hall had the same paint scheme that was dominate in the rest of the clinic public places. After several weeks, it looked more institutional than ever. He passed a mirror and was surprised at his reflection. *Dear God!* he murmured to himself. Looking back at him was a middle aged man with a dark complexion and thinning black hair, who was nearly six feet tall, that is when he didn't slouch. Once muscular, he now seemed thin and undernourished. However, a protruding belly told of fast food and lots of beer. Well, at least that was getting smaller with the exercise program they had him on.

Because of his swarthy complexion, the agency had often

put him in Arab countries to work undercover. He had a gift of being able to blend into the surroundings and not be noticed. This had proved to be an invaluable gift that had saved his life on many occasions.

He snorted and charged down the hall, anxious to get away from that mirror. As he stumbled along, he noticed a small room with a door open. Curious, he strolled in, trying to look as if he didn't have a care in the world. He was startled to learn that this was some kind of little church or chapel. The walls were covered with dark, expensive looking wood panels. There were wrought iron chandeliers hanging from a very high ceiling, which held little lights resembling candles. *Not much light in here*, he thought. Straining to get accustomed to the dark, he noticed wooden pews with scarlet covered cushions. The carpet contained the same scarlet hue. There were what he assumed to be Bibles in racks on the backs of each pew. Candles were burning at the foot of a large wooden cross that was hanging about ten feet from the floor. *Must be a Catholic chapel*, he thought to himself.

Embarrassed, he turned to slip out quietly, but he stumbled and fell against a pew, letting out a grunt when he hit the edge of the seat. *Clumsy fool!* he raged to himself.

Just then a slender young man, who probably was in his thirties, rose from where he had been kneeling in the front pew. Tuck was startled because he didn't know anyone else was in the chapel. *Boy, am I losing it*, he thought. *If he were an assassin, I would be a goner for sure.* The man began to walk up the aisle to where Tuck was standing. His brown hair was shoulder length, and he wore a short, well-trimmed beard. A casual white polo shirt with tan slacks made up his very normal looking wardrobe. But then Tuck noticed that this guy was wearing brown sandals and no socks. *Great!* Tuck thought. *A hippie!*

"Please excuse me." He was smiling broadly and held his hand out to greet Tuck. While shaking hands, Tuck could not help but notice this young man's eyes. They were dark brown, but there was something more than just their color. They seemed to be bursting with friendliness and concern.

As they shook hands, the young man said, "Hello, I'm Abisha, Abisha Davidson."

"Of course you are!" Tuck responded sarcastically, not knowing why he was being so rude. *Maybe he really was depressed like the doctors were telling him*, he thought. "I'm Aristotle Tucker. My friends call me Tuck."

"Well then, hello Tuck. I'm proud to call you my friend. I know I have a funny name. Abisha means 'God's gift' in Hebrew. I guess that's why I like to spend time in here. I do volunteer work here in the clinic. Is there anything I can do to help you?"

You have got to be kidding! Tuck blustered to himself. *A Jewish, hippie volunteer! What's next, an Israeli fight song?* Pulling himself together, he asked, "What in the world is a Jewish volunteer doing in a Catholic chapel?"

"Oh, it's not Catholic. All Christian faiths are welcome here. I like it; it's a really good place to be alone for a few minutes and pray. Do you pray Tuck?"

Ignoring the question, Tuck nearly exploded. "But, you're Jewish! You shouldn't even be in here!"

"Half Jewish," Abisha corrected him. "Just on my mother's side of the family."

"Well, whatever! Glad to meet you, but I've got to get going; I've got some time to waste!"

"Tuck, did you have something you needed to talk over with the Lord while you were here? I'm sorry if I interrupted you."

"Nah, to tell you the truth, I'm not sure there is a God. I haven't seen any sign of a loving God in the world I live in, or used to live in that is." He needed to get away from this guy; Tuck was beginning to feel nervous.

"I know how you must feel. The world you work in can

be brutal."

"What do you know about my world?" Tuck was immediately suspicious.

"I know you work for the government, or you wouldn't be here. This clinic is for civil servants from all over Washington. This city can be a brutal place to live and work," Abisha said as he casually slouched against a pew. His eyes never left Tuck's for a second, and his face reflected genuine concern.

Tuck made a living reading other people's faces. He had to admit that he was disarmed by this guy's smile and friendliness. This was probably a truly nice guy!

"Well my man, I have got to get out of here. Religion makes me nervous!"

"Me too, Tuck!" Abisha replied. "See you later."

As Tuck walked back down the hall in the direction of his room, he realized that he had to meet with some counselors in a few minutes. These so-called experts in their white coats have probably never been exposed to anything more dangerous than standing in line to get tickets for a Redskins game! These were the same guys that were telling him how to handle problems without liquor or drugs. One of them even told him to "BE A MAN!" Tuck had tried to get over the desk and smash his face in, but the other doctors in the room grabbed him and forced him back in his chair.

This place was getting him nowhere. He felt that his drinking problem was now under control. He desperately wanted to talk to his old boss at the agency to see if he still had a job. This was going to be a little difficult since the rules did not permit contact with the outside world. No big deal! He had been in this same situation many times. No matter what, tonight he was going to get to a phone and make some calls.

Chapter Five

In Tehran, the country appeared to be running fairly smoothly, but there was an air of confusion and uncertainty that affected everyone. All ambassadors had been called home to be briefed with what information the government possessed, which wasn't much. The official explanation that was released to the press, and what these ambassadors were told to convey to the officials in the country where they were stationed was that the president was taking a short vacation. The military was on high alert and were very visible all over the country, except the Revolutionary Guard, which was noticeably absent. This elite fighting force had not been seen nor had there been any news disclosing their whereabouts for weeks. All intelligence services were also on high alert with orders to get every agent working leads that might suggest that a foreign government was behind this crisis. So far no evidence had been unearthed; in fact, the agents were reporting that other countries seemed to be as much in the dark as Tehran.

Vice President Bahram had called a cabinet meeting and was in his office preparing his remarks. He paused for a moment, pencil poised in his hand above a sheet of paper. A thought had just occurred to him, one that had been pushed aside due to the stress of current events. Now, however, he began to think that the president was probably not going to be coming back. What did that realization mean to him? He didn't have to think long. *This is my chance to be president!* he thought to himself, smiling broadly as he gazed at the ceiling. *It couldn't be better! This office is being handed to me on a silver platter. I'd be a fool not to grab the office before some*

Chapter Five

other politician gets the same idea.

Just then an aide knocked on the door and came rushing in without waiting for permission to enter.

"Mr. Vice President, you need to turn on the television right away. There is some kind of a demonstration near the university."

"What the..." he said, startled. He couldn't find the stupid remote control and began cursing loudly. The aide ran around the desk and grabbed the remote control from the desk where it had been hiding under a pile of folders. He impatiently pushed the button, and the screen burst into life. What Bahram saw made his chest grow tight, and he experienced a sudden attack of anxiety. There were hundreds of demonstrating students holding up signs and marching down the center of the street. Traffic was blocked, and even more frightening to the vice president, the people on the street were cheering, waving and joining in the march with the young demonstrators.

"What are they doing?" Bahram stammered.

"They're marching!" the aide responded without thinking.

"You stupid son of a camel, I know they are marching! What are they marching about? What do the signs say?" he stuttered as some spittle began to run down his chin.

"Please forgive me, sir! I believe it is some kind of a political rally. The signs say 'We want Arastoo,' and 'Faridoon for President.'"

"Arastoo Faridoon, who in the name of Allah is that?"

Just then the door to the office burst open and some of the cabinet members poured into the room. The men were shouting and pushing and shoving; they wanted to get as close to Bahram as possible.

"Have you seen the march?" they shouted. "Have you seen what the students are doing? Do you see the signs?"

"Shut up you fools! Of course I see it. Get control of yourselves! Go back to the cabinet room, and I'll be right there. Parvin, you stay here!"

General Parvin seemed to shrink inside of his massive uniform. He knew that somehow this jerk was going to blame him for the demonstration. He lowered his considerable bulk into a beautiful red leather chair that was positioned in front of the desk. He could see that the vice president had now worked himself into a rage. *Maybe he'll have a stroke*, he thought to himself.

"Are you going to sit there and tell me that your intelligence people had no idea that this demonstration was even possible?" Bahram asked. "Is everyone asleep over at your headquarters? Is anyone competent over there?"

Parvin seethed with his own rage and sprang to his feet. "You dare ask that of me? Who do you think you're talking to, one of your girlfriends? No one even knew your name before our glorious president disappeared! So, just shut up and let's try to get a handle on what is happening."

He was surprised at his own boldness and didn't care what this idiot thought about anything. He loathed the man and considered him an incompetent fool.

The vice president was stunned. His face turned beet red, and he began sweating profusely. He sat in his chair and stared at the general, unable to believe what he had just heard. He had always fooled himself into thinking that no one knew about his visits to various beautiful young women around the city. He had been careful when and where they met, and he had bribed his driver to gain his silence. How could this halfwit possibly know about these trysts, unless… *That's it, he has had me followed!* He cleared his throat and forced himself to speak calmly.

"All right, general, perhaps I spoke too hastily. But you must agree that the government needs to move in quickly to get this situation under control before it grows too big to handle. It has been my experience that these things can have a momentum all their own; then who knows what will happen?"

Chapter Five

Bahram was now placid. He was obviously trying to become a leader in the general's eyes.

"I agree. Now, if you will excuse me, I must get troops on the street to break up these demonstrations. I'll position intelligence people on the streets with instructions to find out who the ring-leaders are."

He got up and walked to the door, then turned and spoke with a slightly sinister tone in his voice. "I'm glad that we agree on what must be done. Good afternoon!"

Bahram nodded, bowed slightly, but did not speak. When the door closed, his anger could no longer be contained. He grabbed everything he could lay his hands on and threw it against the wall and the door the general had just closed. His swearing could only be described as a terrible scream and was heard both by the departing general and the cabinet members seated around the table. If they had taken the time to look at the general, they would have noticed a smile appear on his face as he walked swiftly through the room.

"My God, what was that all about?" one member asked.

"I don't know, and I don't want to know! Let's get back to work on our plans to squelch these demonstrations," another said.

One hour later, the USS Gato, an American attack submarine settled her 278 foot length on the sandy bottom of the Gulf of Oman. Her officers and enlisted men immediately began preparing her secret electronic intelligence gathering gear to perform the work she was designed for. The Gato's patrol in the Atlantic had been interrupted, and she was rerouted to the waters off of Iran.

Overhead, a United States spy satellite was being repositioned to enable it to intercept more electronic data from Iran, destined for stations around the world. The United States, already on alert because of Iran's desire to construct nuclear weapons, was now very interested in the recent developments in this dangerous country and wanted every piece of information it could glean from the airwaves.

Both of these intelligence gathering platforms were already sending television images of the student demonstrations back to the Central Intelligence Agency, the National Security Agency, and the Pentagon, where analysts were poring over every second of video.

Chapter Six

In Dover, Delaware, Darren Sorrois, a very expensive attorney specializing in international law, filed all of the necessary paperwork with the appropriate state offices to form a new, privately held corporation named the Nuhoma Corporation. The corporation was formed to conduct business in the trading and transportation of commodities.

A storm was threatening as Sorrois took a taxi back to the Residence Inn by Marriott and went directly to his room. He was exhausted and suffering from jet lag. During the last week he had been jetting from Macao to Dubai, and then to the British Virgin Islands, finally ending today in Dover. While in Macao, he had set up a company that would be conducting business offshore. Darren had chosen to form the company there because the laws of the country allowed it to remain secret and its ownership remain anonymous with a very high level of privacy protection. There are no taxes, no accounting requirements, and perhaps the most important advantage, no auditing and no reporting to anyone.

Darren went directly to the little bar in his room and took out a miniature bottle of Cutty Sark. He didn't bother with a glass. He downed the drink directly from the bottle and reached for another one. The alcohol tried, but was unsuccessful, in calming his fertile brain. He couldn't stop thinking about what he was involved in. There could be little doubt that he had been used to set up shadow companies all over the world to shield someone from the prying eyes of governments or regulating agencies. That usually meant the drug cartel or petty despots in third world countries. There was no doubt in his weary mind that money laundering was the purpose for this world wide tangle of companies.

Sorrois was middle aged, and he felt that he was reasonably physically fit. Now, however, his body ached from the travel and the stress of the work that had taken him around the globe. He absent-mindedly turned on the television, where all of the news channels were focused on the demonstrations in Iran. He didn't care about student marches in Iran, so he kept surfing the channels trying to find something soothing to watch. *Rats!* he thought to himself. He couldn't get his mind under control. Darren was now convinced that he had to get out of this job that almost certainly would lead him into peril! People who need the kind of legal protection he had been setting up were often were dangerous!

Finally the booze was beginning to take some effect. Yes, he was making a ton of money for doing the work he had been given, but was it worth it? He had a family to think of, three little kids in school and a wife who thought he was the greatest person she had ever known. Calmer now, he began planning a way to escape the entanglement of this mess. The only person having any contact with the people running things was their representative, a young man who used the name of Jim Holdson.

There was a knock on the door. He swore to himself, angered by the interruption he lumbered to the door. He didn't feel like talking to anyone; he needed to be alone and allow his trained attorney mind time to analyze his options. He opened the door and found Holdson leaning casually against the doorframe. Not waiting to be invited in, the well dressed young man pushed past Sorrois and walked into the room, seating himself in a comfortable chair. He was not smiling. His eyes locked on Darren's while motioning him to take another chair. Sorrois had formed a real dislike for this babysitter's arrogant attitude.

"How did everything go?" the serious looking man asked,

Chapter Six

taking out a small notebook.

"No problems to speak of, just a few *i*'s to dot and *t*'s to cross. Call your bosses and tell them the job is finished. I'm heading back to New York tomorrow. If they need me, they can reach me at my office," Sorrois replied nervously. He rubbed his face with his hand, trying to keep from looking at his visitor, whose eyes never looked away.

"By the way, if your clients want me to do anymore work for them, I'm afraid I'll have to decline. I've just got too much other work to take care of. You know how it is. Now, if you'll excuse me, I need to take a shower; it's been a long day."

Holdson stood up and hovered over Darren who was sliding down a little in his chair. The look in his eyes made Sorrois shiver involuntarily.

"There seems to be a little misunderstanding, Darren. My people are not in the habit of letting employees dictate their terms of employment. They will inform you if and when they want to terminate your services. In the meantime, I'm sure you will want to be available for any other assignment offered. You understand that we are on a very tight schedule." He leaned over Sorrois until he was at eye level. "Now, go freshen up while I make some calls. Then we'll go have some dinner." His smile was anything but friendly. He spotted the empty whiskey miniatures standing on the side table.

"I see you've been drinking. Our company takes a very dim view of alcohol. I'm sure you will want to refrain from drinking while you're working."

Jim moved across the room as he took his RAZR cell phone from his pocket and started making his calls. He went into another room and closed the door. Sorrois rose slowly from his chair and watched the other man until the door closed behind him. *My God*, he thought. *What have I got myself into?* As he moved to the bathroom, he defiantly grabbed another little bottle. He didn't care what it was, but that hotshot was not going to tell him what he could or couldn't do.

As he entered the bathroom, he slammed the door in another display of independence.

In the other room, Holdson was talking softly into the RAZR.

"We may have a problem. Our attorney thinks he doesn't want to work for us anymore. I think he's been adding things up and doesn't like what he sees." He was quiet as the person on the other end finished speaking. "Yes sir. I'll take care of it tonight."

Half an hour later, the two men were walking through the lobby when they stopped to ask the elderly man on duty at the desk his recommendations for the best restaurant in town.

"If you want good steaks and prime rib, you'll want to go to the Angus, on 8th Street."

"Thanks, my friend," Jim replied. "That's just what we'll do. Goodnight."

"Goodnight," the clerk answered merrily. "Enjoy your dinner!"

They went outside and hailed a taxi that was waiting just down the street from the hotel. As they got in the back, Sorrois was overcome by a feeling of foreboding. He thought that maybe it was the booze, but he couldn't shake the feeling. The two men rode through the streets of Dover in silence.

After ten minutes, the cab pulled up in front of the restaurant. Jim paid the fare and charged in the front door completely ignoring Darren. He ordered a booth and a perky teenager who said her name was Sandy guided them to their seat. She took their drink order, which was water, and hastily left, leaving them to look over the menu.

"What looks good, Darren?"

"Oh I dunno. I'm not very hungry. I think I might just visit the salad bar."

"You just want the salad bar! Are you crazy? You can't just eat salad in a steak house!"

"Well, that's all I want, okay?" His voice was a little higher

Chapter Six

than normal.

"Sure, get what you want. No need to be so cranky!"

Darren left the booth and made his way towards the salad bar, which was crowded with people standing in line holding their plates like obedient children. As he began to fall in line, he happened to look up and spot an "Exit" sign at the rear of the room. Suddenly, not knowing why, he knew that he had to escape, and this was his chance. He charged to the back of the restaurant and out the door that he found just past the restrooms. He burst out into a shadowy and dirty back alley, which was wet from a rain shower. The single bare light bulb that hung above the door threw out almost no light; it merely made the shadows deeper and more sinister looking. Darren turned into the gloom and began to make a run for the street. He slipped on the wet asphalt, and starting to fall, he stumbled into someone. Mumbling apologies he looked up and was horrified to see the darkened face of – JIM!

Darren panicked! How could Jim have known he would try to escape? He must have been waiting for him! This was a trap, and he had fallen for it hook, line and sinker! Jim's face was hidden in the darkness. If it had been possible for Darren to see Jim's face in the dim light, he would have seen that his eyes were cold and pitiless. A weak cry of alarm escaped from his dry and raspy throat.

"What's the big hurry, Darren? There's no salad out here. You go through the wrong door?" Jim sneered with the very faintest hint of a smile on his lips. "You afraid I was going to ask you to pick up the check?"

Sorrois was in danger, and he knew it. He looked frantically around, hoping someone would pass by on the street, or come out of the restaurant. No one did. Jim moved slowly toward him. In the meager light, Darren saw the glint of steel in the young man's right hand.

"Hey, wait a minute. For God's sake what are you doing?" he shouted.

"Oh, it's not for God's sake, my friend." He chuckled, amused at his cleverness. "I'm just taking care of business."

A guttural, animal-like moan escaped from Darren's throat. The sound pleaded for both help and mercy, but it was interrupted by the long steel blade penetrating the right ventricle of his heart. He fell forward and grabbed his assassin by the arms. It was almost as if he might find safety there. Blood was spreading over the front of his shirt, and as he slipped to the ground, Darren uttered the last sound of his life, "Why?"

The young man bent over and wiped his knife on the fallen man's jacket. He took his handkerchief and began wiping his hands while walking down the alley toward the street. Moving casually, he took out the RAZR, pressed the speed dial button, and announced, "The problem has been taken care of."

Closing the cell phone, Jim hailed a passing cab, climbed in, and was gone.

Chapter Seven

The street demonstrations continued every day for a week. As the weather grew warmer, these rallies were now growing larger and were becoming more vocal. The name of Arastoo Faridoon was recognizable to nearly everyone in Iran. The state-controlled media refused to cover the marches, but there were just too many private video cameras and cell phones in the country to stop information from getting out to the public.

Shahi Edaroz, the minister in charge of all media in Iran, was beside himself with fear. He had just hung up the phone after taking yet another angry call from the furious and threatening vice president. This was the third call today, and the minister knew that he was helpless in preventing private videos from being shown around Iran.

Just then, there was a knock on his office door, which quickly opened without his giving them permission to enter. Two people sauntered into the room. One of them was a young man, who had the good looks of an actor, or a Greek god. Standing beside him was a pretty young woman wearing designer glasses with her blonde hair pulled back in a very tasteful bun. The woman had an air about her that suggested that she might be a computer geek, one that had little patience for anyone who did not possess the same interest. They smiled and offered to shake hands, but the minister roared at them, "Get out of here, you fools. Who do you think you are coming in here like you own the place?"

The couple boldly continued to approach him until they stood almost on his toes. Still smiling, the man said, "Good afternoon, minister. We have a request to make. Will you allow Arastoo Faridoon to broadcast a speech to the people of Iran?"

The minister was instantly enraged. His eyes bulged, and his face turned almost purple in color.

"What? What did you say?"

Once again the man spoke, carefully, slowly and softly. "Mr. Faridoon wishes to address the nation regarding his ideas for our future. Will you broadcast his speech?"

"Are you insane? Do you know what would happen to me if I did such a thing?" Edaroz looked as if he might be close to stroke level.

"Well, I'm afraid you are in a very difficult situation." The beautiful young lady leaned down to look directly into the beleaguered civil servant's eyes. "You see, we're going to make sure that Mr. Faridoon's speech is broadcast with your permission or without it. The people of Iran deserve to hear what this great man has to say!"

"What are you babbling about? Faridoon, who is he? I've never heard of him!" The minister tried to control himself. For the first time this portly, middle aged man, who had made his living at the public trough, noticed that there might be some danger in this confrontation. These people were young, strong, and very determined looking. Drawing from courage he didn't know he had, he lunged for the intercom and tried to call for help. Unfortunately, the woman was faster than he was, and her hand slammed down on his wrist with the force of a blacksmith's hammer. He yelped with pain and tears formed in his eyes, blurring his vision enough so that he did not catch the deadly, fanatical look in her eyes.

The Greek god was still smiling, but his smile contained no humor.

"I'm afraid that we may have a misunderstanding. Mr. Faridoon is the man that the people of this country want as their president! Haven't you seen the demonstrations? Surely

Chapter Seven

even a FAT BEAR like you doesn't hibernate all the time." Somehow during the insults, a small caliber automatic had appeared in his hand.

Immediately upon seeing the pistol, Edaroz realized that his time on this earth might be drawing to a close. Sweat was soaking his shirt. His hair was wet and hanging down over his eyes. He knew that his life depended on his next words.

"I couldn't broadcast the speech even if I wanted to. There are soldiers stationed in the broadcast area of every television station and in the editor's office of every newspaper. They would never allow such a thing to happen," he stammered, thinking that he might have discovered his way out of this mess.

The young woman spoke again, this time barely above a whisper. "Other people in our movement have been assigned the task of compromising the security at the places you mentioned. What we need from you is your signed, written approval of the broadcast. We wouldn't want to do anything illegal, now would we?"

She handed him a copy of the form he used for authorizing broadcast and newspaper articles.

"All you have to do is sign the paper; we'll take care of the rest." She slid the paper over to him, took a pen from its holder, and positioned it in his hand.

The long time civil servant became indignant when he saw the form. He exploded, "How did you get this form? I'll have you...!" the pistol pushed against his forehead abruptly stopped his tirade.

"All right, I'll sign the paper, but you'll never get away with this!" He grabbed the paper from the desk and hastily signed his name.

"There, now get out of here!" He gave a meek pretense of still being in charge.

"Excuse me," the young lady said sweetly. "But there is just one more thing. Send an email to your staff stating that this broadcast order has been approved by you."

Edaroz hesitated, so she forced him out of the way and positioned herself to operate his computer.

"I'll be happy to take care of that for you," she said.

Her hands were a blur as she typed. In seconds she had it finished. She smiled broadly as she clicked on the 'send' icon. Instantly, every person on his staff and those in charge of the media were notified of the upcoming broadcast. He was frightened and wondered what fate awaited him. Surprisingly, they gathered up their papers, ready to leave. Both of them smiled at Edaroz, and the god said, "Thank you very much, minister. You have been very helpful. There may be a place for you in the new administration." Then they were gone.

Edaroz collapsed in his chair and began to mop his face with tissues that were in a desk drawer. He had to think. The last comment of the man gave rise to a small amount of hope. Perhaps he might survive after all. But, how in the name of the blessed Allah, was he going to explain this to the vice president, who was already in a permanent rage. Slowly, he began to draw on the eternal survival instinct of every civil servant around the world. Somehow, no matter what administration is in power, the bureaucrats always remain.

His hands were shaking as he poured some water from a carafe that rested on the corner of his desk. He involuntarily glanced around as he opened a desk drawer and took out an unlabeled bottle that held Chivas Scotch whiskey. Mixing his drink, he drank greedily and waited for the alcohol to make its way to his brain. There must be a way of escape! But, for the life of him, he couldn't think of what to do or who to call. He had no desire to call the vice president. He almost vomited when he thought of the reaction the news of what he had done would have on the man who was so positive that he would become the next president.

He poured himself another stiff drink, settled deeper into his chair, and began to whimper quietly to himself.

Chapter Eight

All of her life, Dorri Golnessa had been victimized by religious men. She was an extraordinarily beautiful young woman for a girl of fifteen. In spite of her past, she loved life and went about her household duties with a cheery, sunny attitude. Her mother loved her and watched over her carefully to protect her from the world as best she could. They laughed and enjoyed being together when doing even the most tedious tasks. Neighbors thought that the Golnessa family was surely a happy family.

However, there was a deep, dark secret that tarnished this "happy" family. Her father, Zhubin! He was a fanatical believer in radical Islamic religious ideas. He dominated his family with vicious cruelty. Like many ignorant and selfish men who followed radical elements of this religion, he ignored whatever parts of the Koran that he chose not to agree with. He was an alcoholic and obtained whiskey through the underground black market. When he drank, he became mean and belligerent, taking his rage out on his wife, Shideh. The whole family watched the beatings in terror because they knew that the pain would soon spread to them. The four children, including Dorri, had lived with this violence all of their lives. Somehow they survived.

On the night of Dorri's fifteenth birthday, the evening air was comfortably warm. The dark sky held millions of bright points of light. A beautiful full moon lit the countryside with soft, muted light. Zhubin had become drunk early in the evening, muttering obscenities and leering at his horror-filled family through half closed eyes. He was a dirty man by nature, but tonight the odor from his filthy body permeated the room. His black, scraggly beard was filled with spittle, particles of food, and whiskey.

Suddenly, he tore off his robe, and began to weave around the house half naked. Flopping onto a chair, he roared at Dorri to come over to where he was seated. Terrified, she backed away until she found herself up against the door of the bedroom. This ugly, filthy drunk lurched toward her and pounded her forehead with his giant fist. Stunned, she fell through the door onto the bed. He charged into the room and fell on her while continuing to beat her with both fists. She screamed and cried, begging him to leave her alone.

"Please, father, please don't! You're hurting me! Please, mother, help me!" she screamed again and fought for her life.

The alcohol in his brain made him slow and clumsy, but deadly. He ripped at her clothing while pulling her closer. He forced his mouth onto hers. The stench of his breath and the mind-numbing terror she felt caused bile to rise in her throat, and she spit vomit all over him. This involuntary reaction to fear probably saved her life. He lurched away from her while trying to wipe the sickening mess from his face. She was quickly able to get to her feet. Insane with rage and hatred, this horrible, beast-like man produced a knife from a belt that encircled his bloated belly. There was no doubt what his intentions were. The man, who should have been her protector, was now a predator.

"Too good for me, are you?" he slurred. "Well, my pretty, I'll make sure that you're never good enough for anybody else!"

He charged her with the force of a bull, knocking her against a dresser, causing it to overturn and fall on her as she cowered on the floor. She couldn't take her eyes off of the knife; all of the light in the room seemed to be focused on the steel blade. Closer and closer he staggered, jabbing the knife at her face. Zhubin was now snarling like a vicious carnivore. His

Chapter Eight

face was a hideous and contorted mask! He swung the knife, and it tore through the flesh on Dorri's face leaving a path of blood and cut flesh from her forehead, down over her left eye; biting deeply into her cheek. She screamed and screamed until the sound from her throat became a low, guttural groan! She believed that she was about to die, but she continued to struggle, desperately trying to live. The weapon once again tore through the air, striking her just above her left ear. Oddly enough, Dorri did not feel any pain from this latest attack. She just felt a strange sensation as the blade moved through her flesh.

Suddenly, Shideh was standing behind the husband she was cursed to live with. The hatred she felt for this brutal, drunken, monster raged through her as she swung a large cast iron pot towards that evil head. The blow made a sickening sound as it struck just behind his right ear. He dropped in a crumpled heap, covered with sweat and Dorri's blood!

Shideh gathered her bleeding, crying little girl to her bosom, gently rocking back and forth while she tried to calm her with loving words. She did her best to stop the bleeding, but the gashes were too deep. She knew that she had to get Dorri to a doctor quickly, or it might be too late to save her life. As she looked into Dorri's face, she was overcome with the sickening realization that this once beautiful little flower would forever be horribly disfigured!

The frenzied trip to find the doctor, the pain as he put antiseptic on her wounds, and the searing sting of the needle as stitches bound her flesh back together brought Dorri to the point of collapse! These things were nothing like the pain she would later feel when she looked at her image in a mirror. Her sobbing produced no tears, just shame, embarrassment and hatred. The moaning sounds that came from deep within her were the sounds of a wounded animal, primal and pitiful.

Remarkably, Zhubin survived the attack from his wife. He was mean and moody and continued to drink heavily, but strangely he offered no further threat to the family. When he first saw the damage his brutal attack had caused on his beautiful daughter, he laughed at her!

Dorri, no longer a bright and happy teenager, was consumed with hatred and the desire for revenge. She wanted to kill this animal who had ruined her life. Strangely, her wish to see him dead was fulfilled when Zhubin abruptly died a week later. The burial was swift as is the custom in this part of the world. The family was present, but no one mourned. No one else attended the burial because this vicious man had no friends.

A few weeks after the death of her father, Dorri was seated at the table with her mother. Her face had now healed, but the scarlet scars that disfigured her face revealed the horror she had endured. The other younger children were outside doing their best to entertain themselves with broken, second hand toys. As the two women chatted with mother-daughter talk, there was a knock on the door. Dorri answered and found the doctor that had treated her standing outside. Avoiding looking directly at her, he bowed slightly. For the rest of her life she would have to endure the cruel stares and the embarrassed averting of eyes. He handed her an official looking paper.

"This is the official death certificate. Your mother will need this so she can get on with the rest of her life. You will notice that I have put down that Zhubin died of natural causes." He smiled slightly, looked into Dorri's eyes for a moment then turned and walked briskly away. She closed the door and took the certificate to Shideh.

"What is this?" she asked.

"It's the certificate of Father's death. It says that he died of natural causes. What does that mean?" Dorri inquired.

The smile that spread across Shideh's weathered but still pleasant face was the first sign of new life. She got up and went out the backdoor and pulled something from under a potted flower. Sunshine streamed into the room through the

Chapter Eight

open door, filling the room with light. The sounds of the street pushed their way into the house, sounds that meant normal life and possibly some hope of happiness. Returning to the table, this mistreated mother looked around slyly then showed her daughter what she had retrieved. In her hand she held a small glass bottle containing a clear liquid.

"What's this?" Dorri asked, taking the bottle and holding it up to the light.

"That, my sweet, is a bottle of strength for the weak, courage for the timid! It has been used by our women ancestors since ancient times. It has now been used by me to save our lives!"

Dorri stared incredulously at her mother. Suddenly she knew the truth. POISON! Mother and daughter fell into each other's arms while weeping quietly. After a few minutes, the tears stopped, and these two battered women vowed to remain silent about the truth until they reached their own graves. This mute but sure retribution, yearned for by abused women from the distant past, had given them freedom.

Ten years later, after proving herself to be an exemplary student in upper school and then at the university, Dorri Golnessa was awarded the position of head of the Bio-Chemistry department. She had the reputation of being a genius in this field of study.

Suddenly, without the courtesy of prior notification, she was unceremoniously transferred to the Ministry of Agriculture. The office assigned to her was small and rather dingy, with the walls plastered with an institutional light green paint. Small windows did little to dispel the feeling of gloom that invaded this place. Her laboratory, though, was equipped with many fine instruments which pacified her somewhat.

She was furious with the powerful religious men who had obviously inflicted this on her. She sat at her desk and wondered, angrily, why she had been transferred from her beloved university to this dingy, government backwater!

Dorri loved research, and the university setting had been perfect for her work. Having an academic career gave her fulfillment and a freedom that was virtually unheard of in the Iranian culture dominated by male religious zealots. Her investigative research into the very foundation of bacterial life brought her and the university worldwide acclaim. She relished the attention she received from universities around the world. Dorri was flattered by the offers she had received from Massachusetts Institute of Technology in Cambridge, Massachusetts, and Oxford University in Oxford, England. These great learning institutions had offered her wonderful opportunities to continue her research and tempted her with nearly unlimited budgets.

But, the clerics and even the Supreme Leader himself had determined that it was not proper for a woman of her abilities to leave the country and live alone in the western culture that they despised. Any honors that she might receive would be obtained in Iran, and the Islamic Nation of Iran would garnish most, if not all, of any publicity or honors.

Now, this latest affront to her ego had placed her in the position of being lost in a world of unimportant and faceless bureaucrats. It seemed like her promising career was about to be declared dead! This professor, who had not cried since she was fifteen, now allowed a tear to escape from her eye and slowly trace one of the scarlet scars down her cheek. Dorri, suddenly realizing that someone might see her, grabbed a tissue and dabbed at this small display of her vulnerability.

Just then, the door to her office was flung open and a gorgeous looking man swept in with the aura of a movie star. She slowly rose to greet this intruder who was rushing toward her as if he were a long lost friend. He looked familiar but she couldn't fix a name to the face.

"Are you Dorri Golnessa?" The intruder asked, being careful not to stare at her disfigured face.

"I am Dorri. Who are you, and what do you want of me?"

Chapter Eight

She was immediately sorry for sounding so brusque.

"I'm Arastoo Faridoon. We are professors together at the university. I have heard marvelous things about your work. May I sit down?"

"Sure, have a seat," she said warily. "Faridoon! That names sounds vaguely familiar."

"Maybe you read about the name in history class. He was a king in Persian legends." He laughed as he sat back and watched her reaction.

Dorri couldn't help smiling at his explanation although she was sure that wasn't where she had heard the name. Arastoo smiled back at her and couldn't help thinking to himself; *She must have been a beautiful woman before her father carved up her face!*

Suddenly, she recognized him. "I know who you are; you're the one the students are demonstrating about."

He smiled again, nodding his head shyly. "You've got me!" he exclaimed.

He stood to shake her hand, and she responded by taking his hand lightly in hers while looking into his eyes. It was completely unreasonable, but she immediately trusted him. *Why is he here to see me?* she wondered to herself.

"Well, Mr. Faridoon, why have you come all the way out to this desolate government wasteland to see me?" she asked.

"Dorri, I have heard a lot about you and the work you're doing in the composition of various forms of bacteria. Can I impose on you by asking that you give me a brief, and simple, thumbnail sketch on where you plan to go with your research? And, please remember that I will not understand very much of what you tell me, so as the former American President Bill Clinton's campaign manager once said, 'Keep it simple, stupid!'"

Dorri had a great laugh at that comment. It was the first real laugh she had enjoyed for ages. "I'll do my very best. My research is in the basic makeup of bacteria and how that primary composition might be altered. As you might guess, the world is not holding its breath waiting on the results of how to change bacteria. I, however, hold a deep belief that we might be able to do wonderful things with this knowledge. The size of crop harvests may be increased or the whole field of medicine could be changed! We might even be able to eliminate the common cold! Now THAT, Mr. Faridoon, would really be an extraordinary discovery!" she laughed again as she finished speaking.

Arastoo was leaning forward on the edge of his seat. He ignored her little joke and asked her, "What has to be done to make this become a reality? What technique would you use to make these changes?"

"Well, it is just a theory, you understand, but I believe that it may be possible to change the DNA itself. This would change the very design of the bacteria cell. We would, in fact, be creating NEW LIFE! Think of it as if I was a computer hacker, and I could 'hack' into the DNA and change it into any form I wished. You may or may not know that there are three main forms of bacteria: Spherical (cocci), rod-shaped (bacilli), and spiral (spirilla). Some bacteria cause diseases, such as pneumonia, tuberculosis, and anthrax, while others are necessary for fermentation, nitrogen fixation, and so on. Bacteriology is a science important in food processing, agriculture and industry. So, if we can alter the bacteria into a new 'life form' designed to do a specific job for mankind, it would be a monumental discovery! However, there would also have to be extensive testing to be confident there are no unwanted or dangerous side effects."

She paused, trying to gauge his understanding of what she had been saying. Arastoo was lost in thought and did not hear her when she asked him, "Why is this very dull subject of any interest to you?"

"What?"

"I said, why does this interest you?"

Chapter Eight

"Forgive me, I was miles away. I'm going to share something with you, and you have to promise me that it will stay just be between us. Okay?" His eyes locked onto hers.

"I guess so, although it sounds just a bit ominous."

"Great! Can we go somewhere and get a cup of espresso or something? Government buildings make me nervous. There are too many ears hidden behind too many doors. I know of a little café where we can go and be reasonably soundproof!"

"Sure, let's go. It will be good to get out of here for awhile. Lead the way." She rose to follow him. Her curiosity was now piqued.

Dorri rose to follow him while removing her stark white lab coat that is the universal uniform of all scientists. She was alarmed to remember that she was not wearing the hijab head covering in a man's presence. If this error were discovered, she would have been severely punished by Clerics. She wondered why her visitor had not mentioned it. She put on the appropriate coverings that the Revolutionary Government deemed proper for women. She hated the ugliness of what she was forced to wear.

They walked out of the building into the bright sunshine together, giving the casual observer the impression that this properly dressed young couple was on their way to some special event. That observer would have no way of knowing that this couple possessed the ability to change the very balance of power in the world!

Dorri did not notice that a great bear of a man dressed in black robes was listening intently to a very handsome man wearing expensive sunglasses just outside of the building. They nodded to each other, and the man, dressed as if he had just stepped out of a man's fashion magazine, turned and walked away. The bear followed Dorri and Arastoo as they walked to the corner and hailed a cab. They climbed in and were whisked away while the giant grabbed a cab of his own, following them downtown.

None of the four people had noticed a student lounging on a bench reading a newspaper. He watched them intently, his eyes hidden by dark sunglasses. He made some notes in a little book, folded his paper, and walked to a corner bus stop. He waited for a particular bus, climbing aboard after it growled to a dusty stop. It is doubtful that anyone watching would have noticed that the young man slipped a piece of paper into the hand of the bus driver as he paid his fare.

Chapter Nine

The weather was unpleasant when Tuck was released from the Brothers Clinic. The low, brooding clouds and scattered rain showers gave the day a cold, melancholy feeling, a feeling of sadness. With a lot of apprehension, Tuck called his old boss, Herb Worthington, at the agency's Iran section, to see if he still had a job. The secretary that answered the phone recognized him immediately.

"Hi Tuck, how in the world are you doing? It's good to hear your cranky voice again. What can I do for ya?" He could hear the annoying clicking of the gum she always chewed with gusto and an open mouth!

"Hi Sally, good to hear your voice, too. Can I talk to Herb?"

"Sho nuf!" she laughed. She loved to make people think that she was a Southern belle, but he knew she was from Idaho.

The phone clicked signifying that that the call would be secure, and Herb Worthington came on the line. "Well, I wondered if we would ever hear from you again. How are you feeling Tuck?"

"I feel really good. Lots of rest, exercise and a good diet mixed in with no booze. I'm a new man!"

"That's great, Tuck, the new man part, I mean. You had us worried."

"Yeah, me, too. Herb, I'm calling to see if I still have a job. I'm pretty much down for the count if I don't get a paycheck pretty soon. What do you think, can you still use me?"

The line was silent for what seemed like an eternity. Then

Herb said, "To tell you the truth, Tuck, I could use you right now, but it will be really tough to get you back in the ballgame. The boys upstairs don't like security risks. Here's the skinny, Tuck. Everyone's pretty much given up on you and would like you to disappear into history."

"I know and I can't say I blame them for thinking that way. But I really believe that I've got this booze thing whipped. I'm begging ya, Herb. Please, give me another chance!" The bile was rising in his throat as he pleaded for his job back. He hated begging, it made him feel cheap and rotten, and it destroyed what little pride he had left!

"Tell you what, Tuck, ole boy. Come in and see me. Let's talk this thing through and see if we can't get you back into harness. I'll get your identification approved so you can get back in the gate. Drop by Friday, at say, eleven o'clock."

"Okay, Herb. Thanks for the opportunity to at least talk with you. I'll see ya Friday."

Hanging up the phone, he walked aimlessly down the hall of the clinic. It would be a few hours before all the paperwork would be completed. He was shaking a little and needed to think. Without realizing it, he walked into the chapel. When he was inside the quiet room, he smiled to himself and sat down in a pew. *What is it about this place that keeps drawing me in?* he wondered to himself. He did enjoy the peace he felt in this little chapel. Somehow, it made him feel better.

"Hello again, Tuck." a voice behind him said.

Tuck nearly jumped out of his skin. He turned around and yelped, "What the…? Oh, it's you, whatever your name is! Are you trying to give me a coronary? What's wrong with you? Why are you always sneaking around in this place? Don't you have a home?"

Abisha laughed quietly. His voice was soft and somehow comforting. "I'm not sneaking around! Why are you always interrupting my prayers? Is that what you came in for Tuck, to pray?"

Chapter Nine

"Nah, I'm not into praying. I came here because it's quiet and restful and look what I get. What was your name again?" Tuck tried snarling, but he was, in reality, glad to see this kind young man.

"Abisha Davidson. Say, congratulations. I hear that you will be leaving soon. Are you going back to work for the company?" he asked, smiling broadly.

"Not sure, but I hope so. I burned a lot of bridges with my drinking. I may be out on the street begging at bus terminals!" Tuck teased, but he didn't say how true that statement might turn out to be.

"That's not going to happen. You're too valuable to the company for them to give up on you. Look at all of your experience in Iran," Abisha replied.

"How do you know so much about my experience? Does the administration of this place blab everything they know?" Tuck tried to sound angry, but failed.

"Don't worry; I'm not a security risk. I do quite a bit of counseling. People seem to like to talk to me, so I hear a lot of things. I do know that you are a good man who has done a great job for his country. I also know that you tried to drown the stress of your work in alcohol. That's what got you in trouble. Why don't you try something else that could help you with your problems? Why not ask God to help you?" Abisha asked. The smile was gone, replaced by a look of genuine concern.

"You've got to be kidding! I told you that I don't even know if there is a god. The things I've seen done to people in the name of God would turn your hair white, so I don't think that's the road for me." He got up to leave. This guy was starting to make him nervous.

"You're right about all of the awful things that have been done in His name, and He is deeply hurt. But I know that He is interested in you, Tuck. But, He is a true gentleman and will not force Himself on you. When you're ready to talk, He's ready to listen!" As he rose to leave, he reached out and put his hand on Tuck's shoulder.

"Yeah right! We'll be best buds!"

"That would be good." Abisha said. "I'll see you around."

"I doubt it. I get out of this place of happiness in just a few hours," Tuck said as he walked out of the chapel.

"You never can tell. See you later." Abisha returned to his seat and continued with his prayers.

As Tuck walked away, he caught himself whispering a prayer. He would never admit it, but he said, *God, if you are really there, I could sure use a hand. I need to get my old job back, but I've done some pretty stupid things. Funny,* he thought. *I kind of feel better.*

Friday, at the appointed hour, Tuck walked out of the bright sunshine into CIA headquarters in Langley, Virginia, and proceeded to the security check in area. He presented his identification to the uniformed security officer guarding the entrance. This officer was a no-nonsense professional who examined the photo on the card closely, comparing it to the rather nervous man standing before him. He checked the name on the identification card, then looked at a sheet of notes on a clipboard. The officer looked at Tuck with a non-committal scowl and motioned him through the metal detector. Tuck was as nervous as any foreign agent would be entering into this super secret building.

Now, he was about to meet with his boss and discover if his career was indeed finished. He was weighed down with stinging pessimism, which actually caused him to slouch as he shuffled along the marble corridor towards the collection of offices that were under the umbrella title of "Iran Section."

As he walked into the glass offices, he was greeted warmly by friends and colleagues. He shook hands with many and endured numerous poundings on his back. Tuck stood straighter, and his face brightened considerably. He smiled and

Chapter Nine

answered the standard questions about how he was doing and how he felt.

Finally, after running the gauntlet of well-wishers, he made it to Sally's desk.

"Hey Tuck! Sho nuf is good to see ya! I'll tell the boss man that you're here. Be just a minute. Sit down and take a load off!" Sally gushed as she went to a glass door, knocked, and went in. He could see Herbert L. Worthington, nicknamed Lucky, seated at his desk, with reading glasses perched on the top of his head. Herb was middle aged and physically fit, but his hair was completely snow white. The sleeves of his plain white shirt were rolled up to the biceps, announcing that he was hard at work. His right forearm displayed the eagle, globe and anchor tattoo that proudly proclaimed to the world that he had been in the Marine Corps. Marines always say, "Once a Marine, always a Marine," and that is what defined Herb: his experiences in the Corps!

He had a pleasant face dominated by a large Roman nose and two large ears that extended from the side of his head like small billboards. He smiled and waved for Tuck to come in.

"Gee, Tuck, it's great to see you. You're looking pretty good considering the shape you're in!" he laughed. He loved teasing Tuck about being out of shape. He motioned for Tuck to take a seat in a dark green leather chair.

There was a moment of awkward silence, which Tuck broke by asking, "What do you think, Herb? Can you still use me?" He closed his eyes as he waited for an answer, fearing what that answer might be.

"Have you had any time to read the papers?" Herb asked while his eyes examined Tuck closely.

"Not much, what with therapy and everything, but I have tried to read as much about Iran as I could. Looks like something big is brewing over there."

"You got that right! President Niloufar has disappeared from sight. Some of us believe Arastoo Faridoon is a power hungry college professor of all things!" Herb shot a glance toward the ceiling to emphasize his disbelief of the events in Iran.

"Got much on him?" Tuck asked. He suddenly felt like he was part of the team again.

"Yeah, we have a little file on him. He seems to be a brilliant professor in mathematics, political science, and economics. Hasn't been there very long, but appears to have a huge following of students. They seem to think that he is the Messiah! Sorry, wrong religion! Anyway from what we hear, he is a spellbinding speaker who can really control a crowd. The demonstrations on the streets are huge but well organized. Other than that we don't have any information on what is really going on behind the scenes. We've got to get the number of people who are on the ground beefed up, pronto! Oh, and another thing, the Revolutionary Guard has disappeared from sight. No one seems to know how that happened or what it means. But, it makes sense that someone wanting to become president would have to get those boys out of town!"

Tuck listened carefully but said nothing. Finally he looked Herb directly in the eye. "Put me in there, Herb. I might be able to get a handle on this thing. I still have lots of contacts who may not want to talk to some of your guys. I've got no ties here; don't even have a home. I've been as low as a man can go, and I can tell you that I don't want any more of it. Please, Herb, give me another chance. I won't let you down!" Tuck pleaded.

"It won't be easy, my friend. I need to clear this with the suits upstairs. And quite honestly, you're not their most favorite spook right now!"

Tuck looked at the floor while his hands caressed the soft leather arms on the chair. "I know, I know. I appreciate your going to bat for me. When will I know what they decide?"

"Come back this afternoon, say three o'clock. I should know something by then." He stood as he finished speaking,

Chapter Nine

indicating that the interview was over.

Tuck stood up, shook hands, and turned to leave, but stopped, embarrassed. He mumbled, "Herb, can you lend me a few bucks to get a cab and something to eat? I'm busted." He was too ashamed to look Herb in the eye.

"Sure, Tuck. Sorry, I didn't think about money. Here." He placed a handful of bills in Tuck's hand then turned abruptly away to hide the tears that had suddenly blurred his vision.

Herb cleared his throat and said, "Don't count yourself out just yet, my friend. There's always hope. And, quite frankly, I need you over there to get me some good, accurate information. See you in a few hours."

Aristotle Tucker walked out of the office not noticing that one of his shoe laces was untied. He was at the lowest point of his life and it hurt, it hurt badly! *So it's come to this*, he thought, *begging money from a friend. Dear God!*

He was sweating as if he had been sitting in a sauna. He knew that the rest of his career rested on the shoulders of the man he had just left. Everything was now out of his control. All he could do was wait!

Chapter Ten

The cab brought Arastoo and Dorri to the back of a little sidewalk café near the university. His handsome face was now known by nearly everyone in the country, so they decided to take a little table in the back of the café that was obscured by the dim light. With brick walls on two sides, their privacy would be assured. Dorri noticed that in a short time a giant in a black robe came in and sat at a table a short distance from their own. Blessed with a near perfect memory, she remembered seeing him at the agriculture building and asked Arastoo who the man was.

"His name is Shaheen. He has made it his life's work to take care of me. He is a trusted friend who kind of acts as my bodyguard," Arastoo replied.

"Bodyguard? Why do you need a bodyguard?" she asked.

"Well, bodyguard and butler rolled into one. Sometimes the crowds get a little overwhelming." He eyed her casually, but in reality he was studying her intensely.

"Makes sense; should have thought of it myself. What did you want to discuss with me? You have made me very curious."

"I am going to present something to you, but I am afraid there will not be a lot of time for you to think about it. The plan I am going to propose will have a direct and vital impact on Iran, and on the entire world. It will place our beloved country in the position of a world leader, second only to the United States, and even that may change. Are you up to it?" Arastoo spoke quietly, but she heard every word.

Chapter Ten

Dorri's pulse began to beat a little faster as her mind whirled with the information he had just shared with her. She leaned forward in her chair, elbows on the table with her jaw cupped in her delicate hands. She needed to see his eyes! Men had hurt her before, and she was not going to let that happen again if she could help it. When her eyes met his, it was as if he could see into her soul. This frightened and thrilled her at the same time. She quickly made up her mind. Whatever this plan was, she wanted to be a part of it.

"Okay professor, I'm in! Let's hear your plan," she said somewhat jauntily.

Arastoo wasted no time. He gave her a brief history of the dangerous policies that President Niloufar had put in place by threatening the United States and Israel. He painted a terrifying verbal picture of the consequences of nuclear war and the devastation that would make Iran a radioactive wasteland for hundreds of years. Those who survived the initial blasts would probably die horrible deaths due to cancer, just as the victims of Hiroshima and Nagasaki had suffered at the end of World War II.

After nearly twenty minutes he switched gears, becoming more animated as he talked. He spoke about winning the world through economics not missiles. Then he arrived at the real reason for this meeting and why he needed her expertise in order to accomplish the fantastic goal he had shared with her.

"Dorri, will you really be able to hack into the DNA of bacteria and create something new? And if you believe you can, when could you accomplish it?" His eyes glistened brightly. He was now so intense that there didn't seem to be enough air in the room.

She thought through everything carefully before answering. "Yes, I believe I can do it, and I think it could be done fairly soon. However, there still would need to be a great deal of testing with rats and mice to determine if the new bacteria might be dangerous to humans, either by handling the grain, or by ingesting it. I was awfully close to a breakthrough at the university until the government in all of its glorious wisdom decided to move me!" She spat out these last words with obvious disdain. "The Ministry of Agriculture does not have the new and updated equipment I had at the university. If you want me to complete my work, I would need to move back on campus."

"No good! Security would be impossible. You need to stay at the Ag Ministry. I'll make sure you have everything you need and that it is delivered immediately. When can you get started?" In the dim light, she could not see the small sweat beads forming on his upper lip.

"I need all of my lab equipment including the electronic microscopes. I will also need all of my research files. Have your guys gather all the records they can find. No wait!" she interjected, "I need to be there to show them exactly what I want brought over to the institution! I am also going to need a larger workspace. Can you combine the lab with other offices to give me more room?"

"Done! Anything else?"

"No. I'll get back to my apartment and get some clothes and other personal items. I think I'm going to be living at the office for awhile."

"I'll have my friend give you a special cell phone which will enable you to reach me anytime or anywhere," Arastoo got up to leave. On impulse, he bent over and kissed her on her scarred cheek. This both startled and frightened her because public displays of affection were forbidden, but it also had the desired effect on her. She would do whatever he asked!

As he started to walk away, Dorri touched the sleeve of his shirt and whispered, "By the way, what is it you want me to do?"

He turned, looked intently into her eyes and said, "I want you to create bacteria that will destroy both seed and mature

Chapter Ten

grain and leave no trace of what caused the destruction. I need this within a couple of weeks along with plans to safely transport the bacteria anywhere in the world. Can you do it?"

She replied without thinking, "Destroy the world's grain and starve people? How is that any different than using bombs?"

The professor had a serious and determined look on his face. When he answered Dorri, he spoke with such passion that she was taken aback!

"We want to establish our empire without war and all the destruction that goes along with war. If we can control commodities from the world's largest producers, we can distribute food supplies to third world countries. But to make this work, we have to destroy surplus grain and drive commodity prices ever higher. Iran will then become the market basket of the world! We'll be feeding them, not killing them! They will want to join our alliance to assure they receive a constant supply of grain, at a cheap price. To help them even further, we intend to supply them with oil, also at lower than market value. In exchange for these goods, we will ask them to send us their raw materials as payment. This will give us control over additional markets in the world; thus we would gain the power to have the world's most powerful economies dependent on the Persian Empire! Diplomacy will bring others into the fold, and our empire will be the largest the world has ever known!" His eyes were blazing with passion as he added, "Dorri, you are the key to our success. I am depending on you to be a moving force for our country! Will you help me?"

Nothing in Dorri's life had prepared her for such a tremendous opportunity. She actually would be impacting the world! She had no illusions about how great her responsibility would be, though. Could she really do it? She was just a Muslim woman in this stifling, backward nation! What would it mean for other women? Would they gain freedom and respect? She doubted that her efforts would make that much of an impact on the status of Third World women, but it would not hurt to try and make a difference.

All of these questions raced through her brain. She was less sure than she was a minute ago, but in her heart she knew she was willing to take this chance.

Arastoo turned to leave. As he walked out, he nodded to Shaheen. His friend rose from his seat and walked over to Dorri. She noticed his eyes were fierce and cunning as he handed her a cell phone and then left without saying a word. Just being so close to the quiet giant caused her to shudder involuntarily. She had too many things going through her mind to realize that the phone was brought to the meeting. They knew that she would agree to do what Arastoo wanted!

Chapter Eleven

After leaving Dorri, Arastoo went immediately to the school of public broadcasting at the university. He traveled in a car that was heavily guarded by the military. Never again would he be able ride in public transportation!

Arriving at the studio, he was pleased to find all preparations had been finished. The staff at the studio was upset by these strangers invading their facilities. Camera crews from the nation's television stations demanded space and more electrical connections. And if that wasn't enough, all of Iran's radio stations were scrambling for their share of podium space for their microphones. The print media was much more docile requiring only that they would be seated where they could see and hear everything that the professor was going to say.

Now, everything was in readiness for him to present the most important speech of his life. He was startled as he noticed the well dressed, handsome man in sunglasses, standing in a far corner of the room. Their eyes met, and the man nodded ever so slightly and motioned him to come over. Arastoo was nervous about his speech, and this interruption of his train of thought was unwelcomed. He looked around to see if his movements were observed, then quickly walked over to where his benefactor was standing. The stranger got right to the point, speaking in a low voice knowing that with all the background noise, no one would be able to hear them.

"Do you have your speech ready?" The man who was shrouded in mystery asked.

"Yes, and I need to get in there right away," Arastoo turned to leave but was stopped cold by a vice-like grip on his arm that halted his retreat.

"Young man, don't you ever walk away from me again! If you do, you will cease to exist!" the man hissed.

The professor was visibly shaken by these words. He could barely see past the sunglasses, but what he saw caused a chill to run up his spine. The eyes that glared at him seemed to glow!

"Now, Arastoo, I want to make sure that some things are emphasized in your little talk!" There was no doubting his sarcasm. "Have you included the information about the major religions starting wars?" he asked, still holding Arastoo tightly in his grip.

"Yes, it's all in there, just like you wanted."

Leaning forward until their eyes were level with each other, the man said, "I want you to put special emphasis on the things done in the name of Christ! His followers are weak and detestable, and it is important that you offer proof as to why people should want nothing to do with Him! Got it?"

"Yes, I've got it! Now please, I must go!" he bleated. He struggled slightly to get out of the restraint holding him.

"Be precise, and remember, emphasize the important points with gestures and by the inflection in your voice. Don't disappoint me!" He smiled and released Faridoon's arm and disappeared back into the shadows.

Moving quickly away, Arastoo took his place at the podium, straightened his shoulders and waited for the signal that they were on the air. He was trying to regain his composure. He was furious at the way he had just been treated. *Remember the gestures indeed!* He fumed to himself. Cameras were trained on the news anchor from the most popular Tehran television station. He cleared his throat and began speaking as the director motioned for him to lead off the program.

"Good evening. We are interrupting all broadcasts across the nation so that we can bring you this historic event. As you know, over the past few days street demonstrations and marches by thousands of people have been calling for a change

CHAPTER ELEVEN

in our government. The man that many believe will be able to bring about this change is Professor Arastoo Faridoon from Tehran University. Mr. Faridoon has requested this time to speak to the nation to explain his plan for our nation's future. Here now, for the first time on nationwide television, is Professor Faridoon, Professor!"

Arastoo smiled into the cameras and began speaking softly. Engineers frantically turned up the gain on the microphones so he would be heard.

"Good afternoon! Thank you for allowing me to enter your homes or businesses for a few moments. I must tell you that all of the demonstrations have been very gratifying, and quite frankly, just a little embarrassing," he lowered his eyes shyly. "Politics have always been of little interest to me," he lied. "However, certain recent events have impressed upon me that perhaps I might be able to offer some hope in these troubled times."

The audience noticed that he was impeccably dressed with no jewelry of any kind showing. They quickly grasped the fact that he was speaking without visible notes. People in the studio gasped and looked at each other with disbelief. He was not using the Teleprompters! Arastoo was relaxed and comfortable. His smile inspired confidence and trust. He truly was in his natural element.

"I am just as concerned as each of you about the mysterious disappearance of President Omid Niloufar. Nationwide searches have proved futile. Everything possible has been done to find our leader, but all has failed! Sadly, we cannot remain in the state of limbo any longer. The world will not tolerate a political vacuum. Foreign governments will use this confusing time to their advantage. And, sadly, there are radical groups here in our own country who would like to gain power and push us even farther back into the past. I hope you will agree with me that it is vital that we get our government back in operation quickly."

"I must tell you honestly that I think the policies of President Niloufar were both wrong and extremely dangerous. It is ludicrous for a nation the size of Iran to threaten the world's superpower, the United States and its ally, Israel. We are spending billions of rials to develop nuclear weapons and platforms to deliver them. And this spending has caused the annual inflation rate to rise so high that our currency has little value! You are reminded of this every time you go to the market or when trying to buy gasoline, what there is left of it!" He chuckled just loud enough to make sure it was heard by his listeners. "Here's a novel thought, maybe this is money that could have been spent to make life a little more enjoyable for all of us. Maybe some of it could be used to BUILD A REFINERY and make some more gasoline!" He was forced to stop speaking as the studio audience was laughing and cheering. After a few moments, he continued, "And what do you think would happen if the president decided to launch those missiles? What do you think the United States would do? Do you think that they would just sit and wait to be destroyed? You're all much too intelligent to believe that. Some of the missiles that were aimed at the Soviet Union are now aimed at US!"

His voice was now rising, and his hand gestures stabbed the air for emphasis. All over the country, people were watching and listening. Most were nodding their heads in agreement with what was being said, especially the part about the high inflation and not having enough gasoline.

"This is a great land. Too great to be destroyed by the thinking of a mad man! I have an idea that can protect us from such foolishness and guarantee we will become a world power at the same time. I believe we should go back to our roots, to our ancestors from our glorious past for the course of action we should take." He paused for effect and looked around the studio to gauge the reaction of the crowd. People were hanging onto every word he was saying. He smiled to himself. *He had*

Chapter Eleven

them! He knew he had them, and he liked it!

"As you know, many people have demonstrated their wish that I run for the office of president. I have never wished to enter the political arena," he lied again. "But I am first and foremost a patriot. I love this country and am committed to giving my life, if need be, to return it once again to the status of a great nation, rather than being a little nation acting like a big bully kicking sand in the face of other countries."

"Therefore, today I am asking the Parliament to authorize immediate elections for the office of the president of Iran and ask them to place my name on the ballot!"

The studio erupted into wild applause. People at home or in their offices jumped up from in front of their television sets and laughed and pounded one another on the back. Traffic throughout the nation was at a standstill. The honking of horns turned the streets into a cacophony of mechanical notes. No business was conducted except hospitals and emergency rooms.

A few minutes later, he was able to continue. "My friends, if I am elected your president, there are several things that I will do immediately. One is to stop asking for war and begin to win friends by diplomacy!" He had to stop speaking once again due to the cheering and applause in the studio. Cars continued blowing their horns on streets in every town in the country.

The professor, who now had the country eating out of the palm of his hand continued, "Another goal is to…" he paused again for maximum effect, and then shouted, "REVIVE THE GREAT PERSIAN EMPIRE! Not by military might, but by friendly diplomacy. No longer will we threaten the world with a fist holding nuclear missiles. Instead, we will extend our hand in peace and goodwill. Our empire will be formed by making alliances with other nations. We will seek friends, not create enemies!" He gave another pause to allow the audience to regain control of themselves. Never in his life had he felt so elated!

He began again, "The details of this plan will be explained later. But, from the moment that I am elected, if I am elected," he looked directly into the camera and smiled his most engaging smile, "we will all be PERSIANS!"

He extended both arms into the air and waved, and thanked them for their adulation. People were ecstatic, laughing and crying and jumping like kids!

He eventually continued, "There is something else that you should know. I'm afraid some of you will not like this idea, but I believe it is essential in achieving the goals we have set for our future. If you remember history, you will remember that the first man to form the Persian Empire was Cyrus the Great. He conquered by war, yes, but that was what was required to build a nation in those days. But, he did something else that was phenomenal! He allowed people in the nations that became a part of the Persian Empire to worship whatever god they chose! Isn't that incredible? What tremendous wisdom this great king possessed!"

"Down through the centuries millions of people have been killed, maimed, or made orphans in wars that have been fought in the name of Allah, God, or Jesus. Islamic radicals have started wars in an attempt to force infidels to embrace Islam, or die. Some choice, huh! The Jews invaded what is now known as the Holy Land and wiped out entire nations in the name of their God. In the Middle Ages, the Inquisition tortured people in order to force them to become Christians. The Crusades were waged against Muslims in the Holy Land, all under the banner of the cross, representing the Prince of Peace, which is what some people call Jesus."

"Religious wars do nothing but fuel old men's hatred for each other. Well, my brothers and sisters, a new day dawns. There will be no state religion in Persia. No longer will we demand that people worship as we dictate under the threat of death! Instead, we will worship at the altar of...MANKIND!"

CHAPTER ELEVEN

He was shouting at the top of his voice, with arms extended, symbolic of an embrace.

The studio was suddenly silent as were the streets outside of the building. People were so stunned they couldn't speak. Older men began to shout and shake angry fists in the air. But the young people were a different story. They were tired of generations of being strangled by the rules of an ancient set of laws; they were also stunned, but for a different reason. This man was offering them freedom! Freedom to live and worship as they chose if they chose to worship at all! They would be free to be like the people in the West. There was careful applause, then it steadily increased to cheering, and finally young people began to dance in the streets. This was, indeed, a revolution!

Arastoo smiled and waved at the television cameras; then he quickly left the studio. While being rushed out, he glanced in the shadows to see if the mysterious man who had guided his campaign and provided unlimited amounts of money was still there. He absent-mindedly rubbed his arm where the terrible grip still left an impression. He wished he knew who the man was, but he was somewhat relieved to discover that the shadows were empty.

This new national hero was escorted to his apartment under heavy guard to await the aftermath of his speech. Exhausted and soaked with sweat, he prepared to take a shower. He did not hear what took place on the air after he left the studio. A member of Parliament was interviewed by reporters to get his reaction to the speech.

"I am permitted to tell you that the Parliament and the Supreme Leader himself have authorized an immediate national election for president. On the ballot will be Vice President Bahram and Professor Faridoon! This special election will take place as soon as ballots can be prepared. We feel that our country cannot go without a leader any longer. It is the will of the people!"

In Langley, Virginia, and in the nation's capital, many government people had also watched the speech from Iran, and most were troubled! Tuck was in Herb's office at CIA headquarters where they had heard Faridoon for the first time.

"He's a charismatic speaker, Tuck!"

"You're right if they let him live! He'll probably be a magnetic leader that the people will follow down whatever road he chooses," Tuck replied.

"Well, start growing your beard right now. I'll have your papers, money, and special equipment ready for you in forty-eight hours. We've got to find out what's going on over there!" Herb stood and shook Tuck's hand. "Be careful, old friend; that place is still a nest of vipers!"

"Thanks, Herb, for everything. I know you went out on a limb for me, and I promise I won't let you down." He turned and strolled out of the office with a new spring in his step, but his shoe was still untied!

Chapter Twelve

In the little western Iowa town of Sioux Center, a white Cadillac Escalade pulled up in front of the Des Moines Central State Bank of Sioux Center. The bank's façade was of solid brick and marble construction that was intended to give depositors a sense of permanence and security. Inside the lobby, the visitor was greeted with light colored marble floors and a number of mahogany desks with brass lamps shielded by green glass shades. Mahogany paneling had been used to make the teller cages, which were open and inviting. Glass walled offices were lined neatly along the side wall. A huge vault of grey steel located behind the tellers conveyed the message that this huge metal room was impregnable. The vault's giant round door that stood open allowed the visitor to peek inside and wonder how much money was deposited there. Tall windows welcomed in the light from outside and made the lobby feel warm and comfortable.

A short, slightly rotund, white haired man wearing glasses with lenses as thick as Coke bottles got out of the Cadillac and walked into the bank. He was not wearing a hat, so he shaded his eyes from the bright morning sun with his right hand. He walked with the roll of a seaman who has just come ashore and still needed to get his land legs. A pleasant woman conservatively dressed in a dark grey business suit met him just inside the door.

"May I help you, sir?" she asked while smiling. She had seen him exit the Escalade and formed an opinion that this man was probably very successful.

"Thank you very much. May I speak to your president, please?"

"Certainly. May I tell him your name?" she was still smiling.

"Elias Windgate. Here is my card," He handed her a white business card with dark gold embossed letters that said, Elias Windgate, Vice President, Nuhoma Inc., Des Moines, Iowa.

They walked to a slightly larger office that was also encircled by glass, located near the back wall. The still smiling woman held the door open for him to enter, then announced, "Mr. Ebbits, this is Mr. Windgate. He would like to visit with you for a few minutes."

Windgate, a very detailed man, didn't remember saying anything about needing just a few minutes, but he let it slide. The sign on the desk said Victor Ebbits, President. Ebbits rose and came around the desk while extending his right hand. He was very tall and nearly bald with a pale face that had been fairly handsome in days past. Smiling broadly he shook Wingate's hand and said, "Hello Mr. Windgate, I'm Victor Ebbits. Please have a seat. How may I help you?"

"Thank you. I represent the Nuhoma Corporation that is headquartered in Des Moines. We are in the process of setting up offices in a number of cities around the Midwest, and Sioux Center is one of those cities."

"May I inquire as to the type of business you are in?" Ebbits asked, still smiling. Windgate noticed that he had an irritating habit of continually nodding his head.

"Nuhoma is a new company that is in the business of buying, selling, and trading commodities. We also are investing heavily in bulk transportation equipment and to a lesser degree, buying and selling of farm machinery."

"That's very interesting! I'm sure you will find our little town a wonderful place to do business," Ebbits said. His head was still nodding as if he was agreeing with some unheard dialogue.

"How can we at State Bank be of service?" Ebbits asked as he began to rub his hands together in the universal sign of

Chapter Twelve

someone eager to make money. He was able to refrain from licking his lips.

"We will want to open a business checking account. Another thing we will require is the ability to receive wire transfers of fairly large sums of money from Des Moines and that these transfers are handled with complete confidentiality!" He stared at Mr. Ebbits who now looked like a bobble-head doll.

"Both of those items can be handled immediately and under the strictest confidence. I'll have Mrs. Knapp sit down with you and record all the necessary information. Everything should be in order by tomorrow morning."

"Fine. If you don't mind, I like to know whom I will be doing business with, so may I meet the person who will be handling the wire transfers?" Windgate said with just a hint of a smile.

"Mrs. Knapp will be handling those transfers for you. Let me call her back in." He dialed a number and spoke into the phone.

She arrived instantaneously, almost as if she had been transferred by wire. "Please come with me Mr. Windgate, and we'll get the necessary paperwork started."

He stood, shook hands with the president who was still smiling and nodding, and followed Mrs. Knapp to her desk. She was very efficient and soon had all of the information she needed to establish a checking account.

"Mr. Windgate, will you be receiving any funds from international sources? If so, you should know that there are a number of security safeguards that have been put into place by the Department of Homeland Security in an effort to intercept and stop the transfer of funds between suspected terrorist organizations around the world and any financial institution within the United States." She looked at him over a pair of Ben Franklin replica glasses.

"That's very interesting, Mrs. Knapp. What will be required

in order for me to receive U.S. dollar wire transfers into our account with your bank?" Windgate inquired.

"First, you will need to direct U.S. dollars into the country through a correspondent bank of the remitting international bank. The correspondent bank must be located here in the United States, preferably a nationally chartered bank in New York City. That bank will then wire the funds to you here at our bank. There are, of course, long established banking laws that govern all incoming and outgoing wire transfers. The rules are very strictly enforced, but you are likely very familiar with these rules given a man of your stature in the international business community," Mrs. Knapp said without emotion.

"Nuhoma already has that set up with the Western Nations International Bank in New York. In anticipation of transferring sizable amounts internationally, my company has sought, and received, a bank memorandum from the Office of Foreign Assets Control, or OFAC. That memo contains all the necessary language which supersedes all previous memos relating to incoming and outgoing wire transfers. Further, the memo contains the unique encryption coding germane to all messages transmitted via the SWIFT communication system. I will forward a copy to you and your president so if any transfers in question do occur, they will be honored and also kept confidential." He gazed intently at her as she wrote herself notes.

"Yes, thank you. But I'm afraid it will be necessary for OFAC to send their memo directly to us for our files. That would be most helpful," she said thoughtfully. "This is very interesting. I have never seen anything like the memo you described. I can't imagine how difficult it must be to get that done!" She looked at her customer with a good deal more respect.

"It's not that much of a problem. You just have to hire expensive lawyers with international banking experience. Quite frankly, I'm glad the government is careful. We sure

Chapter Twelve

don't want terrorist money going in and out of our country, do we? Do you have everything you need to get the account setup?" His smile was friendly, but unfortunately, she did not look into his eyes. They were hard and unfeeling.

"We have all the information we need. Thank you for coming in; it has been a pleasure to meet you and we look forward to a long and successful business relationship. I know I speak for everyone here when I wish you much success," She shook his extended hand and smiled her somewhat humorless smile.

"Thank you. You have been most kind. Good afternoon." He got up to leave while checking his watch. He had an appointment with a realtor in half an hour. As he went outside, he breathed in the brisk, almost spring-like air. This was shaping up to be a great day!

When he was in his Caddy, he called a number on his cell phone. The person answering did not say anything except to repeat the phone number. Windgate said, "The bank's online, and we will be ready to receive funds tomorrow if necessary." He listened for a minute then hung up. As he drove away, he did not see that the president of the bank and Mrs. Knapp were standing at a window watching him leave. They both seemed a little nervous.

The same event that had just taken place in Sioux Center took place in Oskaloosa, Iowa. Other bank meetings were held in Garden City, Kansas; Bismarck, North Dakota; Aberdeen, South Dakota; and Quincy, Illinois. The staff working for Nuhoma had been instructed to accomplish their tasks quickly since the headquarters wanted the ability to make wire transfers within days. Everyone working for the company was brand new and did not really understand what the rush was all about, but, glad to have a high-paying job with what looked like a thriving new company, they got busy. When each one reported to the office that a bank was in place, they heard a simple, "Good. Come to Des Moines right away. We're going to give you extensive training on how we want you to approach farmers and get contracts to sell their grain directly to us."

The vice presidents received this information with a little surprise. Most of them had never seen a farmer, let alone negotiate to buy their crops. This was going to be interesting. The women were quietly thinking about what kind of shoes they would need.

In the Westin Hotel in Chicago, Dakota Winters was pouring over stacks of commodity brokerage firm brochures. A graduate of Princeton University with a degree in Economics and Financial Planning, she felt like she was going blind from reading all of the materials before her. Not only was it her job to find a broker to make trades on the Chicago Board of Trade, but the company wanted another broker to work in the Kansas City Board of Trade. She had worked for Nuhoma for only a few weeks and had found them to be hard task masters who paid a high salary.

She was finally ready to select brokerages. It was her opinion that the big name players were more interested in churning the account to produce more revenue for them than they were in making their customers prosperous. They also had a much higher overhead; countless account executives demanded enough money to keep them in thousand dollar suits and six figure bonuses.

Her choice for Chicago was going to be the Woodson House Brokerage firm located on the south side. She had checked references and found a rather impressive client list. A few calls produced favorable comments. The founder of the firm still made trades daily and put in countless hours conducting market research. They were small and hungry, but successful. Woodson had a ten year history of making their clients substantial profits. Nuhoma's legal department had checked the company to make sure they were registered with the proper institutions and that there were no suits pending against them.

Chapter Twelve

In Kansas City, Dakota decided to go with a relatively new firm, The Commodity Geeks. This little business was just beginning to make a name in commodity trading. Small and lean, this group had only a few employees, but all of them were computer geniuses who used the internet to track commodity prices and trends around the world. Their uncanny track record proved that their innovative ideas were beginning to pay off in the market, and their customers were making money, a lot of money! After her due diligence was completed and the lawyers signed off on the Geeks, she was ready to hire them to represent Nuhoma. She knew that this recommendation, as well as the one in Chicago, held a lot of risk for her. If things went sour, she knew that she would be on the street very, very quickly!

Dakota made the decision to go the Woodson House firm first thing in the morning and set up both stock and futures accounts. She would have the office wire Woodson a hundred thousand dollars to begin trading when the executives at Nuhoma gave the okay. After getting Woodson on board, she would take the short flight to Kansas City and do the same with the Geeks.

With a sigh of relief that the decision was made, she called room service and ordered a steak with some wine. She was going to eat dinner and then go to bed. It would be another long day tomorrow.

Chapter Thirteen

Marine Sergeant Santana Miranda just wanted to sleep. After four straight days of special ops work with his platoon south of Baghdad, he was drained. Flopping on his cot in the tent he called home, he was instantly asleep, snoring like a tornado, having mastered the art of resting in the arms of Morpheus after years of being on special details that gave little time for relaxation. Two hours later, a corporal entered the tent and shook the sleeping Marine. He grunted for a second, then was instantly alert. Looking around to see who had disturbed him, he spotted the tall and lanky corporal. He noticed that the young man had a terrible case of acne that detracted from an otherwise pleasant face.

"What do ya want, Corporal?" he growled. "I haven't had any shut eye in two days! This better be important or you'll never see the outside of the kitchen until your tour is done!"

The gaunt young man spoke with a hint of a lisp. "Sorry, Sergeant! Captain Larangol ordered me to tell you to report to his office right away, and he said no excuses!"

The profanity that flew from Miranda's mouth would have frightened a seaman on a tramp steamer! It had the same effect on the corporal who jumped with the intent of fleeing but remembered that he had not been dismissed. Returning to attention, he waited to learn his fate.

"Go on; get out of my sight before I have you shot!"

The acne face blanched; then its owner scurried away seeking the safety of distance and of being out of sight.

Sergeant Miranda stood up and attempted to wipe the sleep from his eyes. Looking around, he tried to decide whether to

Chapter Thirteen

put on his clean fatigues or wear the dirty ones he had just taken off. *To heck with it!* He thought to himself, and started dragging on the filthy dust colored camouflage pants and shirt. As he dressed, aching muscles protested the lack of rest. *I'm getting too old for this stuff*, he thought. *I'm thirty and feel like I'm fifty!*

The sergeant carried many scars on his physically fit, hard muscled body. He had already received two purple hearts in his first tour of duty. Now, nearly at the end of his second tour, his body complained more than it used to. Trudging through the sand on his way to the Commanding Officer's tent, he tried to ignore the pain and his muscles screaming for rest. It looked like they were in for a sand storm. He hated these stinking Iraqi sand storms!

When he got to the tent, he entered and stood at attention and saluted smartly. Captain Larangol was seated behind a beat-up desk that looked like it had arrived on the first day of Desert Storm. The captain could have posed for any magazine that wanted to portray the perfect marine officer. His chiseled, deeply tanned face and forceful chin exhibited toughness and strength. Tired, deep-set blue eyes that were once bright and eager were now lackluster; they had seen too much death! They looked out from underneath bushy brows that once were light brown. The strain of battle had taken its toll. His bronze face was distorted by weariness and worry lines.

Larangol looked up as Miranda entered. Returning the salute, he motioned Miranda to take a seat in a chair that did not look like it could support his weight.

"I've got an easy job for you, Sergeant. We need you and your team to take a spook to the Iranian border and insert him into that lovely place!" He smiled without humor. "You may have to take him into the country just a tad; there's a village that he wants to get to, pronto. Wants to sneak around or hide there, I suppose! When you cross the border, you will be on your own; there will be no written orders. No record that your little excursion ever took place. I think they call it deniability!"

"Yes sir, I understand. Is this a first time spook, or has he been around for awhile?"

"I have no idea. It doesn't make any difference. It's up to you to get him where he needs to go. I'll have him check in with you when he gets here. Any other questions?" Not waiting for a response, he said, "Good. Dismissed."

Santana stood and said, "No questions, sir!" He saluted and went out into the gathering cloud of brown, gritty dust.

Aw cripes! he thought. *A lousy CIA puke! They always think God gave them all the brains in the world. All most of them know is how to polish a desk chair with their fat butts! What stinking luck!*

He got back to his tent, closed the flap tight against the weather, and flopped back down on the cot. There was no time to undress; he just wanted to get back to sleep.

Two hours later, a war weary C-130 Hercules touched down on the tarmac and idled over to a hangar that was on the southern edge of the base. Before the roaring engines could be cut, the door opened, and stairs were attached to the fuselage. Tuck scrambled down to the tarmac holding onto his one possession, a gray, soft-sided travel bag that had been designed as carry-on luggage. He had used it as a pillow for most of the eighteen hours he had been in the air. Quick fuel stops had given him a few chances to get out and stretch the kinks out of his legs. He was well aware that he was out of shape, but this flight of torture had made an indelible mark on his brain. He had always avoided exercise whenever possible, but he made a resolution that this would change. The beer belly had to come off and soon!

He was dressed in a ragged casual polo shirt and brown slacks. What had once been a reasonably nice sport jacket was now just protection from the cool air. His shoes were dirty sneakers, one with the shoelace untied. He would have fit in

Chapter Thirteen

well at any homeless neighborhood. His short, unkempt beard only added to the illusion.

Lumbering over to the flight control center, he was met by a young Marine that couldn't have been over eighteen years old. *I bet he's still got peach fuzz,* Tuck snorted to himself.

The Marine saluted smartly and said, "Sir, are you Aristotle Tucker?"

"You've nailed me, Marine. What can I do for you?"

"Please come with me, sir. I'm going to take you to Captain Larangol."

"Okay, chief, lead the way." Tuck still felt as if he was on a plane.

"Oh, I'm not a chief sir, I'm only a corporal," the young Marine stuttered.

"Only a joke, son! Only a joke! Let's go!"

They got into a beat-up Toyota pickup that was waiting for them. Tuck smiled realizing that it was for the sake of his security that they were traveling in something so un-military. Soon, they were on a Baghdad street heading for the Marine base. The sun was just about to set in the west, and its glow made the buildings take on a soft, comfortable look. Crowds of people were everywhere; hurrying to get home at the end of the day. *Sure different from the last time I was here,* Tuck thought to himself. *No doubt we've got the bad guys on the run!*

The dirty Toyota dodged armored patrols that were coming and going on the base and pulled up in front of the captain's tent.

"This is it, sir." the kid said. He wondered what this civilian was doing on the base. He kind of looked like an Iraqi merchant, but he made the decision that this was none of his business and looked forward to getting to the mess tent before the good stuff was gone.

"Thanks, Marine. What did you say the captain's name was?"

"Larangol, sir. Captain Thomas Larangol."

"Got it! Have a good evening." he said to the retreating pickup.

It was very obvious that Captain Larangol was not pleased that his special ops guys had been picked to escort Tuck to the Iranian border. Tuck sat silently as the captain railed about the idiots back in Washington who had no idea how dangerous it was on the border. To them, his men were nothing more than numbers on a sheet of paper. When his rant finally subsided, Larangol asked, "What part of that godless country do you need to get to?"

"Ahyaz. It's about a hundred miles south of Baghdad and ten miles east of the border," Tuck answered.

"Are you nuts, Tucker? That's an awful long way for my boys to travel. Why don't you just parachute in?"

"We wanted to, but a bunch of Revolutionary Guards have been transferred to the area in the last few weeks. They are reported to be conducting a lot of maneuvers and special training. That's about all the information we have been able to find out. We don't have many assets in the area, so we're kind of flying blind. Anyhow, the powers that be did not think I could get past them by flying down out of the sky," Tuck explained, but he knew he wasn't winning a friend here.

"Okay, we'll do our best to get you close, but I'm only giving you four men. Why do you need to get to this place anyway?"

"Sorry, captain!" Tuck replied. "Can't tell you that!"

That was not the right thing to say to this tired warrior. He slowly got to his feet, but he said nothing. Tuck could see that he was about to boil over; his face was getting red and the veins in his neck were bulging like ropes.

"Mr. Tucker, we'll get you where you want to go on your SECRET mission, but my men will not be available again. These men are not going to be the CIA's pack animals! Got it?" He spat the words into the air above Tuck's head.

Chapter Thirteen

"Yes, sir. May I ask when we will be leaving?"

"In two hours. My aide will show you to a place where you can get some shut eye. Good luck!" he said without any pretense of friendliness.

"Thank you very much. I'm going to need a lot more than luck!" Tuck said shaking his head as he walked out of the tent.

The captain watched him and muttered, "You sure are, my friend; you sure are!" He sat back down and resumed working on the stacks of paper in front of him. He felt just a tiny bit guilty for having snapped at the guy the way he did. He knew the guy was following orders and choosing his troops for this dangerous mission probably wasn't his fault. He was going into the enemy's house alone and risking his life to do the job some worthless politician probably thought up. Poor slob!

Chapter Fourteen

Dorri, whose name means "sparkling gem," certainly did not feel like a gem. She had been working for days with little or no sleep trying to re-engineer the DNA in a strain of bacteria that she had isolated. She had been frustrated by the results of every experiment that she had conducted. Her mind was a numb mass of mud taking up space in her head. Ideas had stopped flowing; she couldn't think in a scientific manner. The truth was she couldn't think at all!

She stumbled into a small, cramped room next to her lab, which had become her home away from home, and collapsed onto the little bed. Sleep eluded her as experiments kept rummaging around in her exhausted brain. Just as she was beginning to drift off, there was a knock on the lab door.

"Go away whoever you are! Leave me alone!"

The door opened and Faridoon walked in with Shaheen quietly padding close behind.

"Dorri, where are you?" he called as he looked around the darkened room. He was now becoming used to people jumping when he spoke, and he had to admit that he liked that power. Finally, he spotted the scientist collapsed on her small bed. The professor walked over and kicked it lightly with his foot. He needed her to answer some questions, and he wasn't about to just let her lie there and sleep.

"Come on, get up, I need to talk to you for a minute. You can sleep later!" He had the gift of almost unlimited energy and slept only a few hours at a time, so he had little sympathy for anyone who needed normal sleep.

"Go away; I'm exhausted; I can't think anymore!" she

Chapter Fourteen

mumbled, turning her face to the wall.

Shaheen pushed past Arastoo, leaned over, and grabbed Dorri by the arm and jerked her roughly to her feet. Startled awake, she tried to comprehend what was happening. The black bearded giant was standing inches away from her, and his eyes revealed that they would tolerate no more foolishness. Arastoo's black robed bodyguard had misjudged her if he thought he could terrorize her. She struggled to get out of his grasp and screamed, "Get your filthy hands off me, you big ape! If your boss wants anymore work out of me, you better get out of here and leave me alone!"

Faridoon laughed as he pulled the two apart. "Well my goodness, Shaheen, I think you've met your match! Let's calm down everyone; calm down!"

The giant released his hold on Dorri, but the look on his face was murderous. Now Dorri was in a rage, and she turned on the professor and shouted at him, "Who do you think you are coming in here and manhandling me like that? I'm a scientist, not one of your lady friends from the university!"

She knew instantly that she had made a tactical error. Arastoo was no longer smiling, and it was clear that he would not tolerate anyone talking to him as she had. His eyes glowed with a malevolent glare! He slapped her across the mouth with such force that she saw colors. All at once everything was crystal clear to her. Now she knew what kind of a man he really was, just like all of the rest of them had been, just like her father! Well, she was a survivor. She knew that she had to do the research he wanted if she wanted to stay alive, and she did. But he would never again be that wonderful savior of her country that he seemed to be at first. Now, he was just another dangerous, powerful man. A powerful man that she now hated!

Arastoo smiled at her again as if he was trying to make her forget what had just happened. "Dorri, is your work complete yet? We need the new bacteria as soon as possible. Where are you in the process?"

"You need to understand that this process is not the same as mixing a couple of chemicals in a test tube. We are talking about Recombinant DNA Technology. This work normally takes years, not weeks! It's a good thing I've been working on generating a similar construct for a year before I met you a lot of preliminary research has already been completed," Dorri replied, absent-mindedly rubbing her jaw as she spoke.

The professor nodded. He had to be careful, or she might break, and his desire for a destructive bacteria to be set loose in the United States would be set back for years. He looked deeply into her eyes and said, "Forgive me, Dorri! I had no right to strike you. I guess it's the stress, but that doesn't make you hurt any less. So much is at stake now with the election tomorrow. I took my own frustration out on you. That's no excuse; I am very sorry!"

She almost believed him; almost! "Let's get back to the testing." she growled. "To alter the DNA of a protein we make changes in the Central Dogma, DNA, RNA, by chemical processes. The goal is to change the bacteria's makeup in the protein cell so we can make the bacteria do what we want it to do. What I am working on now is engineering a strain of bacteria that expresses a protein called cellulose, which will breakdown cellulose. We also want this bacterium to have a short replication time which will make it more aggressive."

"After accomplishing that, this dangerous bacteria needs to remain dormant until we are ready to release it. I also need to find a trigger, a chemical reaction that will start the bacteria working, destroying grain or seed. Then there is the problem of transportation. How do we get the bacteria into the country in a stable condition until it gets to the Midwestern United States? Do you understand the complexity of the problem?" she glanced at him to see his response. Then she continued, "We MUST have time to do testing with animals to see if it is dangerous to humans if they happen to eat contaminated

Chapter Fourteen

grain. If we don't and it is dangerous, we could cause deaths in enormous proportions!"

"Yes, I understand," he lied with some impatience! He did not understand, neither did he care to understand! He just wanted results. One thing he did know, she was the most qualified person there was in the country to do the research. *Too bad*, he thought to himself. *Too bad that she will have to be eliminated when she delivers the bacteria! She knows too much!*

"I need a couple more days," she said. "You have to realize that something that has never been done before takes time due to the trial and error process."

"Dorri, take the two days, but get this finished!" He raised his voice, and then said, "The election is tomorrow. We have people in the United States that are ready to put the plan into action. We must have the altered bacteria plus the method to transport it to America. A lot depends on you!" He turned and stormed out, followed by his bodyguard, who turned and shot her a withering glance that made the hair on her neck stand up, then Arastoo was gone.

Dorri was convinced now more than ever that men were stupid brutes who got what they wanted by force or threats of force! In the back of her mind was the nagging thought that she was in danger. Shaking her head as if to discard the thought, she turned her attention to her experiments, forgetting her weariness for the time being. She had made more progress than she shared with Faridoon. She made her way to the incubator, and she withdrew a Petrie dish that contained a new crop of bacteria. She took it over to a "bug bench," a sterile area where she could handle her bacteria and avoid contamination. Dorri carefully picked up her Eppendorf pipette and withdrew a few micro-liters and transferred the sample to a test tube.

Bacteria are so small that light passes through them, so a stain had to be added to her sample so that she could see if she had anything. Then she put the sample in the Lyophilyzer

Speed Vacuum Concentrator to dry it.

Dorri was so weary that she was becoming ill. She walked out of the lab, locked the door, and wandered into the cafeteria. She realized that she hadn't eaten in the last twenty-four hours. She was weak and feared that her mind would begin playing tricks on her if she didn't get some food. In the cafeteria, she went through the line and filled her plate with chicken and vegetables. Finding an empty table in the corner, she collapsed in the chair and began to wolf down her food.

After her lunch or dinner (she wasn't quite sure since she had lost track of time), she walked back to the lab. Her mind was cautioning her that she had overlooked something! But what? As she unlocked the door she had an inspiration! "That's it," she shouted. In all the samples the reengineered bacteria had ignored all materials put in the dish with it. She had to engineer the bacterium in such a way that the bacteria loved grain and nothing else!

She ran to the Lyophilyzer and took out the dried sample, which was now inactive. She took this suddenly precious thing to the safety cabinet. Here, the sample would be protected from any airborne contamination since the air inside this cabinet was filtered through HEPA-filters from above and below. This air was as clean as possible!

Now she was ready for the final test. She took a large sample of her engineered bacterium and put it on several media, such as LB-Agar, Blood-Agar and grain. She hoped it would grow only on the grain. The evidence could be seen by staining the sample, which would make it possible to identify her bacterium on the grain. For two hours Dorri waited, giving the bacteria time to work if it was going to. Finally, she removed the tube and returned to the microscope. "I've done it!" She shouted, laughed, and cried, all at the same time. What she saw through the lens was that the grain was already beginning to spoil. There was absolutely no doubt. Oh, she would run more tests to make sure, but she knew that she was

Chapter Fourteen

right. She had engineered bacteria that would destroy grain! Another important thing she noticed was that the bacteria was replicating more itself! That meant that someone would only have to transport a small amount of bacteria by plane, possibly hidden in a makeup jar in their luggage. Then, upon arrival in the U.S., the agents would only need to have a supply of grain, start the process using the directions she would provide, and they could grow their own unlimited supply! All that needed to be done at this point would be to take a supply of infected grain to an elevator and throw it in. Nature would do the rest! It would take American scientists months to find a way to kill her new super bacteria! Somehow, this thought haunted her.

The emotional release that Dorri experienced sapped her strength completely. She sank into a chair and was instantly asleep. It was, however, a troubled slumber. Her dreams were of hungry, starving people crying out desperately for food, perhaps dying! They did not know, nor did they care that their hunger was happening for political reasons and for power.

She slept fitfully and without rest. When she woke, Dorri knew in her heart that she had to do something. To save her life, she would allow these desperate and cruel men to use the bacterium she had created. But as a scientist she could not turn her back on the consequences of her discovery. An idea fluttered in and out of her mind. There might just be a way out of this mess and stay alive at the same time. Dorri, the beautiful but disfigured woman scientist, could not allow men to hurt her again. *You madmen*! she thought to herself. *I'm not going to let you get away with it. I'll engineer the bacterium so that after the first batch was used, the remaining samples would begin to lose strength. After several batches are replicated the remaining bacteria will DIE! You hot shots will only have limited success.* Sadly, she could not possibly know that this plan would fail, and something far more disastrous was waiting to bring terror upon the United States.

This young woman who had been placed in the center

of a coming worldwide struggle had no illusions about her safety. She would be in danger as soon as Arastoo's men had the samples. She smiled to herself as she thought back to the time in her house when her mother had shown her the poison. Dorri would not go quietly into the night! She would fight to stay alive.

She picked up the cell phone that the dark beast had left. The speed dial connected immediately, and Arastoo answered.

"I've got the materials you want. Your men can pick it up at my lab. I'll teach them how to transport it safely. But there is a problem."

"A problem? What kind of a problem?" he asked suspiciously.

"I haven't quite worked out the on-site replication process," she lied. "When the plan starts, I need to be there to see how it works outside the laboratory. Can you arrange that?"

"It won't be easy, but it can be done. You have done a great thing for your country, Dorri. You will not be forgotten." The phone went dead.

"You've got that right!" she said into the disconnected cell. She smiled to herself and went to bed.

Chapter Fifteen

Professor Faridoon was now officially President Faridoon, leader of the country of Iran, which would soon be transformed into the new Persian Empire. The popular election had been much more than a landslide; nothing like it had ever happened before. He had received an astounding ninety-five percent of the vote. The Iranian people, weary of years of oppressive government, had pledged their full support to him.

The day after the election dawned bright and sunny, providing a promise of another day of warming temperatures. Arastoo's personal items were moved into the Presidential Office at the same time Vice President Bahram's belongings were being moved out. Unsure of what his role would be in the new administration, Bahram was anxious to meet with Arastoo and discuss his future. He ran into Faridoon as the new president was walking into the building. Instinctively he reached out to shake his hand and offer his congratulations. As he extended his hand toward the new president, someone grabbed his arm with such ferocity that it almost dislocated his shoulder. Shrieking in pain, he looked up into the fierce eyes of Shaheen who was suddenly between the two men.

"In the name of Allah, please, you're tearing my arm off!" he pleaded.

"It's all right my friend," Arastoo said to his gigantic bodyguard.

Shaheen released Bahram's arm reluctantly. There was no doubt, however, that he was prepared to inflict further suffering if there was even the slightest provocation.

"What do you want Mr. Bahram?" Arastoo emphasized the Mister as he spoke.

"Please sir; I am unsure what my role will be in your new government. Even though I lost the election to such a worthy opponent, I am still vice president."

He was humiliated to be groveling like this. He hated Faridoon passionately, but like all bureaucrats, his biggest concern was that he be allowed to continue his employment by the government, where if he were careful, he could disappear into the crowd of civil servants for the rest of his life.

"Bahram, you're a remnant of the Niloufar government that was taking our nation blindly down a path of certain destruction. Persia will no longer have the office of vice president, and I have no intention of allowing you to spread ill will anywhere in my government. Get your belongings moved out and leave this building immediately. You are not welcome here!"

Arastoo pushed past him, and the president looked like he had just brushed against something foul! His hulking black robed protector moved immediately between them and served notice through his menacing black eyes that the conversation was over and Bahram had better get moving.

When he got to the president's office, Arastoo was immediately on the telephone barking orders to subordinates. He called the office staff together for a meeting on how he wanted things to function and to instill in them a sense of urgency and of purpose. Those that had worked on the president's staff were already replaced by new and younger people who were wild supporters, thrilled with the opportunity to be working in this great man's administration. They were filled with the idea that now they were the ones in power! Many of these had been recruited from students who were in his classes at the university.

The strict Islamic dress code had already been somewhat relaxed by the new Chief of Staff Rustam although men and

Chapter Fifteen

women were still working in separate areas. The men wore light weight business suits, but in deference to the heat and the humidity, most had removed their jackets and had their sleeves rolled up for comfort. For women, the traditional hijab headgear was no longer mandated; instead they wore Western style business suits and dresses. Faridoon was interested to learn that the hijab was not mentioned in the Koran; it was actually invented by Mussa Sadr, an Iranian Mullah, in the 1970s.

Arastoo poured on the charm as he smiled and looked each one in the eye while shaking hands with the men, bowing politely to the women.

"Well, my friends, I am afraid you have fastened your star to a new constellation. We all will be learning as we go and, no doubt, making some mistakes. That's all right! No one will be in trouble for making an honest mistake. There is so much to do and very little time to do it. I'm afraid that the eight hour day has just been voted out of the office. We will work long, sometimes tedious, hours in order to form our beloved Persian Empire. I am well aware that I cannot do this alone. I need your talents, intelligence, and energy. Will you join me on this historic and awe inspiring journey?" He paused to allow the cheers and applause to die down. Many of the women had tears in their eyes; to them he was their savior! They would be willing to give their lives for him if he asked for such a sacrifice. "Now," he shouted, laughing, "get to work you Persian bureaucrats!" The room seemed to shake with their booming response.

Arastoo went into his office, motioning his new secretary, Afsoon, to follow him. Her name meant "charm," and she certainly was a beautiful charmer.

"Find my new Prime Minister, Hooshmand Teymour, and get him here as soon as possible. You can probably still reach him at the political science department at the university." She nodded and hurried away.

While the others were sleeping, Arastoo created a list of things that needed to be done quickly. Recalling all of Iran's ambassadors was high on that list. He would demand the immediate resignations of those not deemed loyal and replace them with men who had opposed President Niloufar. These men were career opposition politicians that could be quickly trained as diplomats. The vacant ranks would be filled with older graduate students. He smiled to himself. He would love to be present to see the faces of some of the world leaders who believed that gray hair was a sign of experience when these young people presented themselves and their credentials.

Grabbing the phone, he said, "Please find General Parvin and have him come to the office immediately."

He studied the list of men he had appointed to serve on his cabinet. This would be his true "inner circle," and they were critical to accomplishing his secret goals, goals that he had been careful not to share with the country or to people in government. No, these objectives would be carefully guarded secrets even after some of them had been implemented. His phone rang and Afsoon's soft, demure voice began speaking.

"Mr. President, there is a man here that says it is urgent that he speak with you right away. He does not have an appointment, nor will he give his name."

"It's all right; he is an old friend. Send him in."

He stood as the familiar benefactor strolled in. This mysterious man looked around the office and said, "Well, Arastoo, you are doing quite well for yourself. How does it feel to be the president of a country?" The dark glasses hid the man's eyes, as always. He took a seat across from the magnificent desk.

"It feels great, many thanks to you! Can I offer you something?"

"No, I want to get down to business. Is your new cabinet trustworthy?" he asked.

"Yes, completely trustworthy. They will perform any task

Chapter Fifteen

assigned to them with discretion and expertise," Faridoon responded.

"Good. Now, how do you feel about the army; will they follow your directions explicitly and control the country when things get a little dicey?"

"General Parvin will be here in a few moments. I will be demanding his complete submission to my authority. I'm a pretty good judge of character, and if I have the slightest doubt about his loyalty, he will be replaced," the new president responded.

"What about the Revolutionary Guard? Have they completed their re-indoctrination? I have always enjoyed watching such classes. I found them most entertaining some years ago when they were being held in Viet Nam!" The smile on his face was humorless and sinister.

"Most of the Guard will be useful. They have been trained as the private army of the president, regardless of who that person is. Some have already chosen to be transferred to the regular army, while others, perceived as trouble makers, will be held in camps near the northern border."

The visitor nodded slightly but remained silent. Arastoo was always uncomfortable in this man's presence and felt that he could not continue under the present arrangement. He was determined to find out this fellow's name.

"Sir," he stammered, "may I ask you a personal question?"

The smile instantly left the handsome face and the square jaw seemed to become harder. He leaned slightly forward in his chair and said, "What kind of a personal question?"

"Well, this is very awkward, but I don't even know your name. The great destiny of the new Persian Empire will become a reality because of you. Without your help, I would still be teaching at the university. But now, thanks to you, look where I am! I'm the president of the country and I don't know how to address you." He looked at the floor, averting those eyes.

The man stood up and smoothed his expensive jacket. His smile was like the wind blowing over a glacier. Then, abruptly, his whole demeanor changed. He turned to face Faridoon and said, "Of course, how rude of me. I should have told you the first day we met; people call me Mr. Diablo."

"Diablo, is that a Spanish name?"

"You can be assured that it is an ancient name that is held in high esteem by millions," The smile returned slightly. His eyes seemed to take on a glow behind the constantly adorned dark glasses.

"I have never worried about nationalities. My business takes me all over the globe; borders are meaningless to me, a minor nuisance!" Diablo turned to leave; the lights reflecting off his highly polished shoes. "I will be back tomorrow for a progress report and to make sure the plan is ready for implementation. I know you will not disappoint me." The sinister smile returned as he left the room.

"Everything will be ready, Mr. Diablo," Faridoon bowed ever so slightly.

What a strange man, he mused to himself. *Strange and just a little frightening!* There was a knock on the door, and the rotund General Parvin was ushered in, sweating as if he had just left a Swedish sauna. He brought himself to attention and saluted smartly. Arastoo stood and reached out to shake the general's hand. Parvin was startled. The former occupant of this ornate office had never treated him with courtesy. He bowed slightly and warily shook hands.

"Please be seated, General. Would you be so kind to tell me how you view the election?" He said, fairly gushing with sweetness.

Parvin was instantly cautious. He was not stupid and knew all the proper things to say to those in authority over him. He had survived this long by not letting himself to be tripped up by saying the wrong thing. He thought for a moment, then said, "Sir, the people have spoken loudly and very clearly

Chapter Fifteen

that you are the one they want as their president. I agree with that choice and stand ready to serve you to the best of my ability."

Faridoon smiled and continued. "What about your army, General? Will they be loyal to this administration?"

"Yes, sir, they will be loyal and serve you as military officers. You are our Commander in Chief," Parvin responded.

"What about the Revolutionary Guard? Where does their loyalty lie?" His eyes were now fixed on the general in such a way that he became uncomfortable, perspiring so furiously that his uniform was being stained with moisture.

"As you are surely aware, the Guard was called away on maneuvers a short time ago, although I was never able to find out who gave the orders. Since that time, the Revolutionary Guard has been undergoing intensive retraining. Their commanding officer assures me that they are prepared to resume their duties acting as your personal security force." The overweight officer was continuing to perspire under the unwavering stare of the new president.

"That is a good report, General. I want you to study the deployment of your troops carefully, particularly along the border. There is an old American saying, good fences make good neighbors!" Faridoon smiled and stood up to dismiss the general. Parvin saluted smartly and scurried out the door.

As Parvin was heading out the door, the new Prime Minister, Hooshmand Teymour, entered the room. Teymour, a middle aged man with premature graying of his dark hair around his temples, was painfully thin. His suit jacket appeared to be hanging on coat hangers as the bones of his shoulders protruded starkly. His dark eyes were bright and alert and testified to his wisdom. He extended his rather large hand toward his new boss while smiling broadly. Arastoo came around the desk and hugged his old friend and kissed him in the Eastern fashion.

"My friend, we have very little time to accomplish our

goals. You will be my representative on the cabinet. There can be no dissenters, and above all, no leaks! The cabinet meetings are to be held in complete secrecy," he said, emphasizing his last words.

"I understand. May I ask, Mr. President, where does the Supreme Leader stand on the plan that we are about to put into action?"

"I have been assured by a close friend that he is supportive of what we intend to do. Actually, the eighty-six clerics in the Assembly of Experts have become very quiet, and I believe they will also be in agreement with the goals we hope to accomplish. They are the same ones that backed that fool Niloufar with his plan to destroy the United States as a world power and to destroy Israel." he said with eyes blazing.

"Now, my friend, we will go into our first cabinet meeting with my Council of Ministers and tell these unsuspecting gentlemen how their lives are about to change! I have hand-picked all eight of the vice presidents and the twenty two ministers." He laughed and pounded Teymour on the back as they walked to the cabinet room.

Neither man noticed a rather plain looking young woman working on a computer at the far side of the staff room. If they had been closer, they might have noticed that she was not entering data on the computer but was actually text messaging on a Blackberry.

Chapter Sixteen

Sgt. Miranda walked to the tent where Tuck was getting a few hours of shut-eye. To the untrained observer, it would seem Miranda was a soldier ready to go into the field fully equipped. What most did not notice was that there was no sound as Miranda walked; no clicking, clanging or jingling of metal against metal. All equipment carried by a special ops soldier is carefully designed not to make noise that could give away their location in clandestine combat missions. Being quiet was normal and automatic for the sergeant, who was already planning in his mind how to carry out this mission.

As he entered the tent, his eyes quickly adjusted to the gloom, and he found Tuck sleeping on a cot with his back turned to the tent opening. Miranda walked quietly over to the sleeping CIA operative and grabbed his shoulder to shake him awake. Suddenly, there was an explosion of movement, and he was shocked to find a Browning M9 3D 9 MM with silencer pointed right between his eyes. The hand that held the gun was rock steady, and the eyes that peered past the pistol were unwavering and deadly.

Miranda, a seasoned combat veteran, had looked death in the eye many times. He froze. Frightened, he shouted with a quavering voice, "What the …easy, Mr. Tucker, easy! Hey man, I didn't mean to spook you!" He instinctively held up his right hand to show that he was unarmed.

"You have to be the dumbest guy on earth," Tuck shouted. "Are you trying to get killed? I thought you were special ops. Well, if you are, you're awful stupid!" Tuck spat out furiously as he lowered the weapon and swung his legs over the edge of the cot.

"You're the genius who's going to get me inserted into Iran?" Tuck continued. "Forget it! Get me somebody with some brains!" He blurted out as he tried to calm himself down.

"Hey, take it easy will ya? I said I was sorry didn't I? Why are you so jumpy? Criminey, you're in a friendly camp!" Miranda was beginning to get over the shock of looking down the barrel of the Browning, and now he was getting mad.

"Okay, okay, it's all right! You're probably here to tell me it's time to leave," Tuck said, now under control.

"Yeah, we need to hit the highway. It's just getting dark, and we have a couple of hours drive ahead of us. I want to be at the border around midnight. That will give us time to get you across the border and into your village. I'd like my team back in Iraq before dawn," The sergeant said as he tried to regain charge of the situation.

"Sounds about right, let's get moving." Tuck said. "How many men are going with us?"

"Four, including me. They are loaded and ready to go."

"Can they be trusted to keep their mouths shut?" Tuck asked.

Miranda was instantly furious. "Listen, company man, my men and I have been together for a couple a years, and we've been on plenty of secret missions. Don't you dare question my men; they're risking their lives so you can play secret agent in Iran."

"You know what, Marine? Some real good spooks have died pretty awful deaths because the insertion team shot their mouths off. So, don't get your tail in a wringer if I ask if they can be trusted. Who knows, we might all get killed trying to pull this thing off!" Tuck didn't like this Marine, and the Marine obviously didn't like him or the mission.

Tuck gathered up what little gear he had, and they silently trod outside and climbed into the Humvee. There were no

Chapter Sixteen

introductions. They didn't want to know him, and he didn't want to know them. It was better that way; it made it easier if someone died! The engine roared to life, and they sped out of the camp in a cloud of dust as the sun was vanishing below the horizon.

An hour and fifty-five minutes later, they were off the road plowing through sand and brush as they moved towards the dangerous border of Iran. The driver killed the engine, and Miranda checked the satellite to verify their location. Tuck was glad the bumping and banging in the Humvee was over. He was exhausted from holding on for dear life. During the drive, Sergeant Miranda had shared with him how much they all loved this old war machine. He, his men, and this ol' gal had survived a roadside bomb last year, so the banged-up old bucket was held in high esteem that bordered on reverence. It was considered to be a lucky vehicle.

"We're here, men," he whispered. "From now on I don't want any talking! Follow me; we're going down this little ravine that leads right to the border. Remember guys, we've been here before, so there's no excuse for getting lost. We're going to be heading due east to the border. There's a little dry creek there that might have some guys from the Revolutionary Guard nosing around, so be careful. Our assignment is to take our new friend here about five clicks into the country, near a little village called Ahyal, where he wants to set up shop. Everybody ready?" He looked around the group. A stranger would have seen four military guys in heavy camouflage and one sloppy looking Iranian civilian.

As they moved out, they were met by a light but chilly breeze and a very bright half moon. Tuck quickly saw that these guys were experts in utilizing what little cover the desert provided. As they moved through the scrub brush, he thought he could hear things that dwell in the sand scurry away from these unwelcome intruders.

In about twenty minutes, they were across the dry stream

bed. Miranda signaled for the point man to probe the other side of the border. The man slithered through the sand as silently as a sidewinder from the American deserts. In a few minutes, he crawled back to the group and whispered to the sergeant.

"It's clear straight ahead, but I heard some voices a couple of yards to the northwest. Sounds like a couple of very bored border guards. There shouldn't be any problem," he reported.

The small band moved out without a sound, with Tuck following behind the last Marine. He had his little bag over one shoulder which contained some clothing and some electronic gear for communications. His Browning was tucked in the small of his back, under his light jacket. After several hundred yards of slow going through rocky ground, they skirted around sandy areas where their boot tracks could be easily seen.

Suddenly, the point man held up his hand as a warning for the group to stop. Through the light of the half moon, they could see a man coming directly towards them. There was little doubt that this guy was a member of the Revolutionary Guard, and every man there knew these men were the best of the best. They were well-trained killers and Miranda would rather not tangle with the man shuffling towards them. The team spread out on either side of the path the man was walking along. In the moonlight, four knives gleamed for an instant as they were removed from sheaths, ready to bring instant death. It was possible that he would walk right on past them as they remained frozen behind whatever cover they could find, but that was not to be. Just as the man was opposite the point man, he tripped on some unseen brush and fell to his knees, grunting and swearing quietly in Farsi. As the soldier started to stand up, his eyes spotted the Marine huddled behind a small bush. He sprang to his feet and swung his rifle around to take a shot just as Sergeant Miranda's knife sliced through his throat, severing his jugular vein. The man dropped without a sound, blood pumping from the deadly wound. His mouth

Chapter Sixteen

and eyes were open wide, staring in disbelief as his last breath escaped from his lungs.

Miranda motioned for his men to drag the body off to one side where they worked furiously to bury it in a shallow grave. With the swiftness of the defensive action that was carried out without a sound, Tuck was now gaining confidence that he might make it to Ahyal after all.

The killing and disposal of the soldier had taken less than two minutes. After a quick look around in the moonlight to make sure that the evidence of the struggle had been removed, the marines moved cautiously toward their destination. An hour later, they stopped just outside of the little village with the strange sounding name. Miranda crawled over to Tuck and whispered, "This is where we say adios. Do you have a place where you can hide in there?" he asked.

"You bet I do; there's a friend here that I've stayed with on occasion. I know how to find the house. You guys take off. Good luck and thanks!" Tuck said with some emotion.

"Okay, mister spook. Good luck to you," he said as he turned to leave. He had a little more admiration for this CIA guy because he wasn't sure he would want to be walking into that place alone. The special ops team moved out heading back the way they had come.

Tuck made his way carefully to the outskirts of the village, which seemed to be deserted. An occasional bark from an unseen dog, and the snarling of a lonely camel were the only signs of life. The sun would be up in an hour, so he quickly walked in the deep shadows down the filthy street looking for the familiar building that would become his safe house. It took only a few minutes to locate the small building, which was little more than a shed. A muffled knock on the door caused it to open slightly, and he disappeared inside. He was now inside Iran and ready to start his mission.

Outside, someone moved in the shadows near the shed where Tuck had just entered. It might be something as innocent as an early rising shepherd. But, if Tuck had seen this person moving in the darkness, he might have thought the mission and his cover were blown before it ever got started!

Chapter Seventeen

President Faridoon and Prime Minister Teymour entered the cabinet room to find the rest of the newly appointed vice presidents already seated around an oblong, teak conference table. The ministers were seated in rows behind the vice presidents. All of them immediately leapt to their feet as the president came in and took his seat in a beautiful red leather chair at the head of the table.

The room was a pleasant, comfortable room with walls covered in exotic African hardwoods. The large windows could be opened to welcome a cool breeze or closed and then covered with deep blue draperies embroidered with gold along its borders. One large chandelier held hundreds of small, candle-style bulbs that were surrounded by cut crystal which reflected the light into tiny rainbows of color. Gold wall sconces gave off a soft, glimmering light that was for effect, not to give light to the room. Gold lamps adorned with maroon glass shades were perched on the table in front of each chair. These lamps provided light that was more intense than the sconces, designed for reading.

"Be seated, gentlemen," the president began. "I believe that you have all been introduced to each other, so let us begin."

He gazed around the room. The men present were bursting with pride for having been chosen to serve the new government. A quick, but thorough, background check had found them to be clever and intelligent people from a variety of career fields. Of course, the review also disclosed at least one secret weakness in each man's character that might prove useful should the need arise.

Arastoo's eyes were bright with excitement. He cleared his throat and began to speak. "Before we begin, let me advise you about the changes I have made in the cabinet. I know that it is against tradition, but I am giving the vice presidents a new title. They will now be ministers who deal with global issues. The rest of you will be known as advisors to the president, responsible for domestic policy."

"Now, gentlemen, let me begin by presenting what the new empire is striving to accomplish. These details have not been given to the public and will remain known only by the men in this room and a few other advisors who answer directly to me. Of course, the Supreme Leader has been briefed and will continue to receive updates on a regular basis. Should there be a security breach, you will be the natural suspects," Arastoo could see that this news pleased but also concerned them.

"First, our goals. We plan to disrupt the economy of the United States of America to such an extent that it falls into a deep recession, or better yet, a deep depression, causing it to become a second or third rate economic power. For a short time, Europe will take the leadership role, followed by China and to a lesser extent, Russia. However, we must never lose sight of our primary goal, that of the new Persian Empire becoming the world's leader in trade, manufacturing, and oil production."

The room became silent as the men sat in stunned disbelief, unable to comprehend what they had just heard. Several thought to themselves, *This plan is just as dangerous to Iran as President Niloufar's threatening the United States with nuclear war.* They were glancing around the table to see how others were reacting when Faridoon began speaking again. He was smiling broadly because he knew exactly what they were thinking, and it amused him.

"Have I made you nervous?" he asked playfully. "Well, bear with me until you have heard the entire plan. Through a secret, surrogate company we are going to immediately start

Chapter Seventeen

buying as much American wheat, corn, and soybeans as soon as possible. Our bid on the commodity markets will always be at least five percent greater than anyone else's bid. We are not playing the option game; we want the grain. Our company will begin buying immediately after we send the go ahead signal. In addition to buying commodities, the company will be making arrangements to lease every available bulk grain transport vehicle, such as trucks or barges operating on the Missouri and Mississippi rivers. We are also leasing grain cargo vessels to begin transporting the commodities out of the country. Agents in the Midwest of America will began contacting farmers to offer them contracts for their grain at a higher price than they can get from their usual sources, such as Con-Agra. To sweeten the deal to farmers, who are always looking for ways to make more money, we will offer to finance their seed and fertilizer needs at two percent less than their local banks can offer. Of course, crop insurance will be available to them from us at a considerable savings. All in all, the American farmer should absolutely love us, except they will not know whom they are really dealing with!"

Some of the men around the table were beginning to settle deeper in their chairs and allowed the beginnings of a smile to creep onto their faces.

"On another front, the new ethanol plants being built in America are changing the markets in several ways. As part of the new Persian initiative, we are going to announce to the United States and the world that we want to provide the financing to help build these plants. It will be our gesture of goodwill to help the Americans break their dependence on foreign oil. This will give us a tremendous boost towards favorable world opinion. We will be furnishing the world's press with the details of the plant financing and our benevolent goals. Our main objective, however, is to be sure that more land is planted in corn to supply these plants, leaving less for food consumption. This will drive commodity prices to unknown heights. Because of higher prices, farmers will continue to take their land that used to grow wheat, soybeans and other crops, and plant corn for the ethanol market. For example, a few days ago, the price of wheat went up three hundred percent in one day! Imagine the impact that will have on the country's food prices if it stays that high. We intend to see that it does! To guarantee the high food prices, we are going to quietly purchase as many of these ethanol plants as we can even though they are really not financially profitable. We will be financing publicly and purchasing privately. Do you see how this works? The result of our commodity purchases will cause the huge grain surpluses that the United States had always enjoyed to be greatly reduced."

"In addition to what I have just shared with you, we have a secret in-country operation that will take care of the surpluses that are left. I am afraid that this is so secret that only Intelligence Minister Payam will be involved on a daily basis. The final results will be that food prices will sky-rocket out of control. Cattle and hog producers will be unable to pay the high cost of feed, so herds will be reduced by seventy-five percent in just a few months. Those that raise chickens will feel the same impact, and many of the farmers will go out of business. Unemployment will rise by at least twenty percent, and with most of what the wage-earner makes going to buy food, other businesses will also fail, spreading the recession nationwide." He finished speaking and took a drink of water from a crystal carafe while examining the faces of the men gathered in the room. These men would soon become party to the destruction of the strongest economy in world history.

Interior Minister Javaid timidly raised his hand to speak. Arastoo nodded his permission.

"Mr. President, how are all of these projects going to be funded? Has anyone made a financial forecast to estimate the cost of these enterprises?" The withering stare from Faridoon made him regret asking the questions.

Chapter Seventeen

"Do you really believe that I would go into such earth-shaking projects without knowing the cost? Are you such an idiot that you would think that I, a professor of economics, would not be intelligent enough to make a forecast?" he asked, glaring at the unfortunate Javaid.

"Please, Mr. President, forgive me for asking foolish questions. It is just that this plan is so stupendous, it is difficult to grasp! I am sure, with your background, that you already know that the United States produces millions of tons of corn each year, and sixty-four million tons of wheat, which does not even take into account the production of soybeans and barley. No fleet in the world could move that much grain in a short time, and as far as destroying surpluses, they would just import from Europe and countries of the former Soviet Union! How would their economy be destroyed or even damaged?" Javaid sank visibly deeper into the soft chair, trying to disappear from sight. He was immediately sorry that he had spoken up and that he had pointed out perceived weaknesses in the grand plan.

Faridoon's anger subsided slightly, and he continued, "The question has been raised concerning how we intend to pay for these complex, many faceted plans. The answer is that we are going to do two things at the same time. First, we will immediately reduce the uranium enriching processes that are costing us billions of rials a year. Since we are talking about impacting the United States, let's convert that into dollars. We are spending well over one hundred billion dollars on making nuclear weapons. Can you grasp that? A HUNDRED BILLION DOLLARS A YEAR! We will reduce that expense by fifty billion, freeing up the other fifty billion to fund our plan's different facets worldwide."

"Second, I am ordering the expansion of our oil and natural gas production facilities. In addition to that we are going to put pressure on OPEC to increase the price of oil to at least a hundred and fifty dollars a barrel within one year. This will put unbearable pressure on the American economy. They won't be able to afford the oil but will not be able to live without it! Even if we do not achieve that high a price, we will use the sale of oil to the United States to pay for the plan. Ironic, isn't it? The Americans will pay for their own destruction!"

Now the ministers were no longer smiling, they were laughing! They were beginning to visualize what the president was saying and see that it really could work. They had been riveted to Arastoo's every word for over two hours but were still sitting on the edge of their seats. The room was electric with excitement!

"You all know that this is an election year in the United States. We will send millions of dollars to the Political Action Committees supporting candidates who continually use the word recession in their speeches, and openly express their desire to raise taxes. This would be deadly to any economy on earth. The press will pick up on this emphasis and will trumpet the same words on their newscasts and in their papers. The more the American people see and hear this word, the more they will begin to believe that they are in a recession even though all economic indicators show that they are not. And, of course, their horrendous problem with illegal aliens causes a terrific strain on the country's social services and prisons," he exclaimed as he looked around the paneled room. Just as he had held the rapt attention of his students, he now held the attention of the men seated around him.

"Please allow me to continue; there are still several parts of my plan to be explained, and I think you will be pleased. I am now instructing our new Minister of State to recall all ambassadors immediately. Everyone is to be closely examined to verify that they will obey our instructions. The ranks will be thinned and will be replaced by people from the former opposition parties and political science grad students from the university. They will be dispatched to every third world or economically deprived country in Africa, South America, and

Chapter Seventeen

South East Asia and those that were part of the former Soviet Union. They will carry with them my offer to join an alliance with the New Persian Empire. If they agree to join us, we will guarantee that we will supply them with grain at thirty percent of the going world market price, using the grain purchased in the United States." He stopped and glared at Javaid, who withered visibly. Javaid could not know that this was his last day on earth!

"Try and understand, minister, I only want to control enough grain to impact the Third World countries until they join our alliance. I don't want all of America's grain, just enough to impress these countries that we can keep them fed! I am also going to offer the alliance oil at a substantially reduced price." He paused for effect, and to wipe some perspiration from his brow.

"You may ask how these poor countries can pay for these things even at such greatly reduced prices. The answer is simple—they can't! My plan is to allow these countries to pay by bartering their nation's raw materials. This will give us enormous leverage in selling needed raw supplies to the manufacturing nations of the world at higher prices. We will be the world's distributing country for lumber, iron, bauxite, lead, gold, diamonds; the list goes on and on!"

Now, they were on their feet applauding. This plan was brilliant! No one seemed to notice that it was no longer "our" plan. It was now Faridoon's plan, and he am going to do this. Any one paying attention would have glimpsed the rise of a giant ego, perhaps even larger than his distant relative Cyrus.

"One more thing needs to be explained. I agree with one of the old strategies of former President Niloufar. His plan was to drive the Jewish State of Israel into the sea! I don't want them to go into the ocean. I would rather have them as servants of the Persian people, just as their ancestors were to my ancient ancestor Cyrus. The state of Israel must disappear! I will force them to join our alliance as an impoverished little third rate country. You may ask yourself, how I am going to be able to accomplish this. My plan is that when the United States falls into a deep recession or depression, hundreds of thousands of people will be out of work. Tax revenues in their treasury will fall to pre-World War II levels. That means there will be little money, if any, left over for foreign aide. Currently, billions of dollars in aide goes to Israel every year. With no American money flowing into their coffers, and our plan of reducing their ability to import raw materials to supply their industries, they will be forced to look to someone else for needed support. Just think of it, we will conquer Isreal again!" Arastoo was beaming but held up his hand to indicate that there was still more to come.

"One more thing concerning the hated Israel; we will increase our funding of Hamas in their war against the Zionist. We will supply more rockets to help them in their struggle as well as any additional arms they might need. At the same time, we will continue to fund Hezbollah in their war against Lebanon, which will spill over into Israel. Both of these areas of attack are important to our goal against the hated Zionists! These programs will cost the Israelites billions to defend themselves against, further draining their financial resources and increasing their demands on the United States for additional help with military supplies and money."

Minister of State Shahriyar timidly raised his hand to speak. He was considered to be an authority on Persian history as well as world history.

"Mr. President, may I ask a sensitive question?"

Faridoon was suspicious, but said, "Of course, questions are welcomed."

"Sir, you mentioned how your ancestor Cyrus had the people of Israel serving him as conquered people. In fact, sir, he treated the Jews with great kindness and actually freed them to return to Israel and rebuild their temple. In addition to that, he paid all of their expenses and provided protection

Chapter Seventeen

for the journey. Bible commentators all seem to agree that no other king in history did as much for the Jews as your ancestor Cyrus the Great. Now, you are declaring that they are an enemy that must be destroyed. How is this to be reconciled with your own ancestral history?"

There was complete silence in the room except for the nervous shuffling of feet by the stunned cabinet members.

Faridoon was stone quiet. His grey eyes burned with fury as he glared at his hapless minister. He spoke so quietly that everyone in the room strained to hear what he said.

"Minister Shahriyar, surely you can understand that after thousands of years, old friends can become enemies, and old enemies can become friends. Israel has publicly declared their hatred for us, and it is they that have declared that if provoked, we must be destroyed, or do you have a problem reading the daily newspapers?"

"No, Mr. President, I understand the present political situation in the world. I just noticed the historical differences and felt that you might have been misinformed," he responded. He seemed to have finally realized that he may have gone too far and that he might be in some political peril.

"No minister, I have not been misinformed, and I know my ancestral history very well. You need not trouble yourself with reciting history for me, but thank you for your concern about accuracy." The venom in Faridoon's voice was unmistakable and did not go unnoticed by the Minister of State. Had he known what awaited him, he would have been trembling with fear!

"Now, if we might continue, I will address the last part of our secret plan, and I warn you, that this must remain secret at all costs. Any leaks will have come from this meeting, and that puts anyone in great peril if they are the one talking. My friends, I want to emphasize what I told you earlier; we are going to continue to develop missiles capable of carrying a nuclear warhead as part of our national defense. When

Edge of Disaster

developed, they will allow us to attack Israel if that is an option we choose when the global political position is favorable. We can also export them to another country where they can be used by groups like the Hamas or the Hezbollah. We are going to continue to expand our nuclear research with the intent of harnessing the atom for our domestic power needs in addition to enriching uranium for the manufacture of nuclear weapons. This will give us membership in the world's nuclear community, which by the way, we believe includes the state of Israel. It is my intent that Persia will become one of the most powerful nations on earth!" The applause and cheering was deafening.

President Faridoon sat down and accepted the adulation coming from the men seated around the room. He was now certain they would serve him without question regardless of what he demanded of them. He was glowing with the feeling of absolute power. He rose, shook hands warmly with each of them, and walked back to his office where Shaheen was waiting for him.

"We did it, my friend; we have won the country!" The huge man in black said nothing, he simply nodded his head. He stood up, looked deeply into Arastoo's eyes, and sauntered out of the office. He had already been given his assignment.

Chapter Eighteen

Late in the day, the Empire International Bank in Road Town, British Virgin Islands, received a large wire transfer from the Crescent Grand Dubai Bank. Since it was such a large amount, it was not put in the stack of transfers waiting attention but went directly to the wire transmitting department. The bank officer in charge of transfers determined that everything was in order, and according to previous instructions, wired the money, in U.S. dollars, to Western Nations International Bank in New York. The first thing in the morning, Western Nations encoded the transfer with the proper encryption codes for the Office of Foreign Assets Control (OFAC) and Society for Worldwide Interbank Financial Telecommunication (SWIFT), forwarded the amount to the Des Moines Central State Bank in Des Moines, Iowa. Both Western Nations and Des Moines Central had on file the appropriate memo from OFAC with the proper unique encryption coding. Wire transfers, in various amounts, were then sent to six branch banks with Nuhoma accounts. Within hours, $100,000,000 had traveled around the globe until it arrived in Des Moines. Nuhoma was suddenly cash rich without having done one dollar's worth of business!

Mrs. Knapp was sitting at her desk in the Des Moines Central State Bank in Sioux Center. She was processing a few small wire transfers, transferring them into the recipient's accounts. Suddenly, she was startled to see an encryption coded message from the SWIFT communication system. She was fascinated to actually see one of these messages come in. She had a copy of the memo from OFAC giving authorization to honor the wire transfer, so that was not a problem. She was just excited to actually see the real deal, A SWIFT 103 payment advice to credit the customer's account. Then she saw the amount! She gasped, swallowed hard, and then looked again. $10,000,000 designated for the Nuhoma Corporation.

Picking up her phone, she dialed Mr. Ebbits. He answered almost immediately.

"Yes, Mrs. Knapp, what is it?"

"Mr. Ebbits, I think you will want to look at this wire transfer. Can you come to my desk?"

"For heavens sake, Mrs. Knapp, don't be so melodramatic. What are you so stirred up about?" he asked.

"Please, sir, just come and look at this transfer," she pleaded.

"I'll be right there." Ebbits hung up the phone and wondered what the commotion was all about. He didn't like surprises. Without realizing it, his head began to nod a little bit. He walked rapidly out of his office and proceeded directly to Mrs. Knapp's desk, moving beside her to be able to see the computer screen clearly. As he read the message displayed on the screen, his jaw dropped a little, and his head nodded up and down more rapidly. He swallowed nervously, causing his protruding Adam's apple to bob up and down like a cork on ocean waves.

"Great Scott!" he exclaimed. "Am I reading that right? Does that say ten million dollars? Is it for that new company in town, what was its name, new something?"

"Nuhoma Corporation, sir. Mr. Windgate was here setting up the account and told us that they would be receiving wire transfers from overseas. Well, here is the first one, and it's a whopper!"

"Are the codes in order?"

"Yes, everything seems to be as it should be. I'll transfer the money into Nuhoma's checking account right away."

"Good deal." Ebbits walked back to his office. He wanted to get his bottled water, which was secretly spiked with quite

Chapter Eighteen

a bit of vodka.

Mrs. Knapp made the entry into the checking account just as her phone rang. She picked up the receiver and discovered Mr. Windgate was on the line.

"Good morning, sir; how are you today?" she answered pleasantly.

"Oh, I'm fine, thank you for asking. I am expecting a wire transfer today, and I wonder if it has come in yet."

"Yes sir, the money is here and in your checking account," she replied.

"Very good, thank you." He hung up without waiting for her to respond.

On a muddy side street in Sioux Center, Nuhoma had rented a small, vacant building and turned it into one of their field offices. It was sparse by any stretch of the imagination. The walls were a dingy white that was peeling in two corners. Windgate had hired some day-laborers to add some inner walls so the room now contained two offices and a larger meeting area. Scattered around the office space were used couches and stuffed chairs along with two desks and some rather surprisingly decent office chairs. The bathroom was painted in a depressingly dingy green and obviously had not been cleaned in a very long time! A couple of telephones and three computers completed the electronic connection to the headquarters of the new, international corporation.

In the room with Windgate were three men in jeans and heavy shirts wearing obviously new boots that looked like they could withstand anything the weather could throw at them. They moved to a large map table near a big, rather dirty window in the office. Everyone gathered around a map of six counties that surrounded Sioux Center. The map was divided into grids that parceled it into twelve pieces.

"Okay guys, here's the deal. I want you to each take four sections shown on the map. The farms located in your sections are your assignment. I want you to contact every farmer and get him to sign a contract to sell his wheat, corn, or soybeans to Nuhoma." Windgate looked closely at each man and continued talking.

"The company is not interested in excuses. Don't take no for an answer. Remember the five percent markup we are offering; we'll beat any price they are offered. Make sure you talk to them about financing their seed and fertilizer cheaper than they can get from these little "podunk" banks around here. Then, finally, when you have them on the dotted line, offer to insure their crops, cheaper, of course, than they can get anywhere else. Keep in mind that farmers are greedy, and these things I have mentioned can mean a lot of money in their pockets." He looked around to see if there were any questions.

"Oh, I almost forgot, if these guys have grain stored on their farm while they wait for a better market, buy it from them now! Put the pressure on and get that grain. Offer them two percent higher than current market price; you can go as high as five percent." He was emphatic as he spoke.

"What happens if we can't make a deal? Do you want us to wait awhile and try again?" one of the salesmen asked.

"No, just let me know who they are. We'll try something else to encourage them to sell," he said. "Okay, guys, hit the bricks, or should I say mud puddles?" He smiled at his little joke. There was polite snickering from the men as they went out of the door. They got into brand new leased pickup trucks and roared off in different directions heading for the country. They did not know that this new business plan was being duplicated in five other Midwestern towns and fifteen more salesmen were also driving away in new leased pickups. In a few days every farm within a hundred miles would be contacted. Phase one was underway.

Hundreds of miles away in Kansas City, Missouri, Dakota Winters hung up the phone after talking to a superior in Des Moines. She had been told that Nuhoma had rented empty

Chapter Eighteen

grain elevators in Chicago and St. Louis, and they were now ready to start receiving grain. In Chicago, they had rented the Lake Michigan Grain Storage Company, located on Lake Michigan. In St. Louis they now controlled the Erickson Elevators, which is positioned on the banks of the Mississippi and could accommodate a large amount of barge traffic. In New Orleans, the grain would be transferred from barges to ocean-going dry bulk freighters.

Dakota was also told that the company would wire five million dollars to each of the brokerages that she had hired to buy commodities and futures contracts. *Things are sure moving fast!* She thought to herself as she picked up the phone to give the orders to start buying wheat, corn, and soybeans, and August and November futures. Minutes later she had confirmed that both brokerages had received the wire transfers and were ready to start buying. They wanted to know where she wanted to take delivery and she gave both of them the names and addresses of the elevators. She requested that all paperwork be sent to her office in Des Moines. Her instructions were to get the grain even if they had to pay higher prices.

Hanging up the phone, she found that she was breathless, and she was beginning to perspire. She had never been involved in anything that moved so quickly and involved so much money. Dakota gathered up her luggage and headed for the lobby to check out. She had to get to Des Moines as soon as possible.

At the Des Moines headquarters of the Nuhoma Corporation, Roshan Norwall, the President and Chief Executive Officer, was reading a message that had just been received on his fax machine. In this message, he was instructed to begin two different initiatives for the company.

First, he was to have a news conference and announce that his company would soon begin financing the construction of biofuel refineries. Nuhoma considered this a natural progression of their commodity business, and it showed their enthusiasm for the future of this type of energy.

Second, not for public consumption, was a directive to begin negotiations to purchase biofuel refineries that were near to, or already in production. To fund these new programs, a wire transfer of $100,000,000 had been received and deposited in the company's account.

Norwall immediately called a meeting of his staff and instructed them to begin the necessary planning and make applications for the compulsory state and federal licenses. The staff was also instructed to research refineries that were having financial difficulties causing them to be more receptive for help with financing or outright purchase by Nuhoma.

As Nuhoma's president put the fax down on his beautiful red cherry desk, he sighed and thought to himself, *This was going to get so hectic and complex that he might not see his home for weeks on end!*

Chapter Nineteen

Tuck finally arrived in Tehran after taking a beating for hours on an old, dilapidated excuse for a bus, fighting for his share of the seat with a huge old woman who smelled of goats!

Finally, his ordeal on the bus was over. He gathered his bag and strolled down the street looking for a taxi. As he walked, he was careful to utilize his training to make sure he was not being followed. To the casual observer, he looked like thousands of other men, probably unemployed, shuffling along the street with a shoe untied. This, in fact, was intentional. The untied shoe gave him an opportunity to stop on the street while seeming to tie the delinquent lace and check the crowd for a familiar face. No one that he observed seemed to be the slightest bit interested in him. He was unable to find a taxi, so he continued to walk aimlessly along, pretending that he had no place in particular to go. He listened intently to people he passed in the markets. They seemed to be unable to talk about anything other than their new president, and with even more excitement, the New Persia. Open criticism of the former president and his government could be heard everywhere. There could be no doubt; the people of Iran were thrilled and optimistic about their future.

As he hiked the streets of the Iranian capital, Tuck realized he had not brought enough warm clothing, so he walked on the sunny side of the street. Cold and dirty, he longed for a hot shower. He was on his way to a company safe house where he intended to meet with some of the people gathering information on Faridoon and his new government.

He stopped to grab a bite to eat at a small, three table café. He spent an hour there reading a paper and eating his sandwich. The proprietor was less than enthusiastic about this unwashed vagabond taking up valuable table space and perhaps driving other people away. After an hour of listening to the man "harrumph" every five minutes and receiving threatening glares, Tuck got up, paid the bill, and sauntered out onto the sidewalk. He needed to wait until well after dark before going to the meeting place, so he plopped on a bench and spent some time people watching. He needed to check his email and text messages on his LG Voyager touch screen cell phone, but he knew that it would be very out of character for him to use it in public.

Suddenly, while tying his shoe for the fourth time, he noticed someone that looked like a person he had seen earlier. He was a big man with a scruffy black beard, wearing casual clothes that were dirty and well worn. He was also wearing a red and white checked ghutrah commonly worn by Arab men. The hair on the back of Tuck's neck began to rise, a sure sign for him that danger was close by. Turning his back to the man, he watched him in the reflection of a store front window. The man seemed to be watching him while trying to be careful not to be noticed. *Idiot*! Tuck thought. *You don't want to be noticed, but you wear that billboard?*

Dusk was approaching, and it would soon be impossible to keep an eye on this character, so Tuck stood up, wandered down the street, and quickly jumped on a bus that was pulling away from the curb. It was too late for billboard to follow even if he wanted to be so obvious. He glanced out the back window and was surprised to see that the man seemed oblivious to what had just happened, and he was still watching the area around the bench Tuck had just left. *Hmmm.* he thought to himself. *Maybe I'm getting old and jumpy!* He casually touched the back of his jacket and felt the reassuring steel of his trusted M9 3D Browning tucked under his belt in the small of his back.

Chapter Nineteen

He hopped off the bus with a crowd of people heading home for the evening. He sauntered beside a group of men walking away from his destination, but it was better to be on the cautious side before going to the safe house. Tuck stepped down the darkened street then turned suddenly into an alley. Halfway down the alley was a doorway that had a dull green door covered by Islamic graffiti. The sight of the door brought back memories of an old song that had a verse that said, "Green door, what's that secret you're keeping?" *I really am getting old*, he thought to himself.

It was getting cold and the slight breeze was becoming stronger. He ducked into the doorway, crouched down, and waited. He found his heart was pounding, and his breathing was rapid, almost short gasps. *Good grief*, he thought to himself, *I'm really out of shape. I don't think I could fight my way out of a paper sack!* He listened for footsteps coming down the alley, but he heard nothing. He waited for a few minutes before he felt that he was not under any threat of being followed. Slowly, he moved down the alley, turned left, walked to the corner and turned left again. Everything appeared to be okay, so he began to circle the block where the safe house was located, stopping often to look and listen. After an hour of watching, he moved to a side door in the house, knocked twice, waited, and then knocked twice again. The door opened, and he slipped quickly inside.

He was greeted by several people who had been on his team the last time he was in Iran. The men and women laughed and pounded him on the back, telling him that they were happy to see him back in harness. He couldn't keep his voice from getting a little husky due to all of the warm greetings. He said hello to the people that he knew and was quickly introduced to several new operatives that he had not met. They began to brief him, but even though they were in this safe place, they did not use their real names.

"Hi, sir! Everyone calls me Lemon!" The smiling young

man who spoke was rather short in height, slender, with no distinguishing features, except for his long, slender hands. This secret operative had the gift of being able to open any safe or lock devised by man. He had tangled brown hair and a few scattered chin whiskers that he laughingly called a beard. His appearance suggested student to everyone who saw him.

"I've been hanging around the university for awhile, just trying to see what I might pick up. Something that seemed odd to me was the transfer of a woman biochemist from the chemistry department to the Ministry of Agriculture building downtown. Her name is Dorri Golnessa and from what I hear she is a genius in the field of re-engineering bacteria, whatever that is! I tried to access records at the university to get a look at her file, but no luck. Everything about her has been destroyed."

Tuck was very impressed by the thoroughness of the report and asked the young man, "Anything else about this mysterious chemist?"

"One thing that was pretty interesting. A week before he became president, Faridoon paid her a visit at the Ag department. They were together for quite a long time, and, of course, I have no idea what they talked about. They came out of the building together and took a cab to one of his favorite hang-outs. They stayed for awhile but left in separate taxis. The big guy that always follows Faridoon around showed up a little later. He wears black robes, and brother, the scowl on his face would scare a dog off a gut wagon!" That produced a few snickers.

"Nobody has ever seen the big guy speak to anyone. He does, however, whisper to Arastoo, but I think that he is more than just a bodyguard. To me, he looks like a black ops guy even though I have never seen one," he laughed as he finished talking.

"Does he have a name?" Tuck asked.

"Oh yeah, sorry, his name is Shaheen. It means 'peregrine

Chapter Nineteen

falcon' in Persian."

"Sounds harmless enough. We have anything on him?"

"Can't find a thing."

"Anybody know anything more about either of these people?" Tuck asked, looking around the room. His question was met with silence and shrugged shoulders.

"Let's get back to the lady for a minute. Do we have any idea what she is working on, or what Faridoon may have asked her to do? It seems kind of unlikely that a guy who is going to be president of the country in a few days would take the time to meet with an old college buddy," Tuck said as he rubbed the stubble on his chin. He hated wearing a beard.

"Well, not really," an older woman in the group spoke up. "He is using a lot of his former grad students in his administration. They are almost as radical as the former regime. I've heard that he has even made some of them ambassadors! In fact, all of Iran, excuse me, all of Persia's, ambassadors are in town for a big powwow now," she said.

"How do you know that?" Tuck asked.

"We have a lady doing computer work in the president's office. She saw the coded messages go out a few days ago. A baggage handler at the airport said government big-shots began arriving yesterday morning," she continued; her voice betrayed the excitement she felt with the news.

Tuck was quiet for a long time, mulling over in his mind the information that had just been given to him. It sounded like something big was in the works, but he didn't know what it was. He wondered if this scheme would be a threat to the good ole USA!

"How many assets do we have on the ground now?" he asked no one in particular.

"Not many, I'm afraid," Lemon spoke up again. "You have the people in this room and ten more, scattered around the country. Recruitment is going nowhere. There just are not many disgruntled people that we can draw on, except the clerics who have been kicked out of power. I don't think they like us enough to help, though."

He found out that the woman who had been giving much of the briefing was called Peach. She was very tall and had an aristocratic bearing in the way she stood, and in her facial features. Graying temples only added to her mature and successful demeanor. Tuck asked her, "Is there anything else the lady in the president's office might have for us?"

"Oh yes, one little item. They were sent an email that the president would be out of the country for a few days in a couple of weeks, speaking at the United Nations in New York," Peach said, showing almost no interest in the news.

Dog Bone, another member of the team, spoke up. He had the good looks of an NFL quarterback, except for his teeth; several were missing and the others were a dirty yellow.

"This guy could charm the devil out of his eye teeth! I predict that whatever his speech is about, those monkeys in the UN are going to eat it up and proclaim him the new pope. He really is that good! He has great charisma in person, on television, and on radio. He doesn't do so well in the local press, though, because not many reporters have the vocabulary to describe him."

"Do we have any idea what the speech is about?" Tuck asked, looking around the room.

"No idea about the speech, but it's billed as an opportunity for the world to meet him and hear his ideas for bringing his country into the world arena. I predict that he will be the darling of the world's losers; the guys that hate us and anyone that calls us a friend!" Dog Bone said with more than a little passion.

"Tell me, guys, what we really know about this character? Who is he? Where did he come from? Who are his friends? More importantly, who are his enemies? How can a professor of economics become the president of a country that, until a short time ago, was an Islamic theocracy? What happened

Chapter Nineteen

to the ruling clerics? What happened to President Niloufar? Until he disappeared, he had most of the world quaking in their boots!" Tuck was becoming exasperated with all of the things that they did not know about Faridoon.

"Well, we do know a few things," Lemon spoke up after being silent for a long time. "We know, or should I say, we think we know that he came from a rural area where he grew up on a farm. Hard labor and an exceptional mind worked together to get him into the University of Tehran where he excelled in Political Science, Mathematics, and Economics. In a short time after graduation from grad school, he became professor of all three colleges," he stopped talking for a minute, and then continued.

"We got most of this information from his official biography published by his office. His students are fanatical followers, and it is believed that their demonstrations in the street campaigning for him to become president are what assured his political victory. But as to where the clerics went, and what happened to the former guy, is anybody's guess. We just don't know! Another interesting point is that during the time just before the election, the powerful Revolutionary Guard was mysteriously transferred to the Iraqi border for special training."

Lemon finished speaking when another thought struck him. "Oh, by the way, there is one more thing. The guy says he is a descendant of Cyrus the Great."

"Who did you say?" Tuck asked a little incredulously.

"Cyrus the Great. You know the guy that put the first Persian Empire together twenty- five centuries ago. If you study him in history, you'll find that he was a tremendous leader. Think about this, if you don't already know, he's mentioned in the Bible twenty-three times. God mentioned him by name and said that he was His shepherd a hundred and fifty years before he was born!"

"Who said he was his shepherd?" Tuck asked, suddenly

very interested.

"God did!" Lemon was getting a little exasperated.

"How do you know all this?" Tuck asked.

"Good grief, it's in the Bible. Haven't you ever read the Bible?"

"No, never have. Never found the time." Tuck was deep in thought with his brow looking like a newly plowed field. There were just too many unanswered questions. But in the back of his mind, a little voice kept bringing up the biochemist. His gut told him that she was important, but he couldn't, for the life of him, figure out why! And, this Bible stuff made him nervous.

"What are the chances of getting a tail on the chemist?" He peered at them through sleep deprived eyes.

"One of our people can watch her. Do you want to have her followed everywhere she goes? What if she is sent out of the country? We'll need some cash!" Someone in the group replied.

"No problem," Tuck opened his bag and threw a pile of rials on the table.

"I'll take care of it," Peach said.

"Okay, guys, let's get all of this info back to Langley by secure satellite tonight. I've had a long day, so I'm heading for some local flophouse to catch a few winks," Tuck yawned as he finished speaking. He was drained!

"Why not stay here; it's a lot safer than some flea ridden cheap hotel?" Peach asked, just a little worried that Tuck was going out into the night alone.

"Nah, I'll be okay; don't like keeping all of our eggs in this little basket, safe or not. I would suggest that you guys take off and land somewhere else too."

"Okay boss," someone said as they all got up to leave. "Be careful out there!"

"I think I heard that on a TV police show sometime." He laughed because the young ones didn't have a clue what he

Chapter Nineteen

was talking about.

The lights were turned out and as standard procedure; they left one at a time and out of various doors. Tuck was the last to leave, waiting just outside of the door for his eyes to get accustomed to the darkness. He saw nothing that caused alarm, so he began walking north to the corner, turned and headed for an old hotel that he remembered seeing as he was walking around earlier. There was a dim street light on the corner of the block, but the entrance to the hotel was hidden in semi-darkness. As he approached the building, the little voice in his brain began to whisper to him not to go in there. But he was exhausted and his desire to put his head on a pillow outweighed his normal caution.

Just as he approached the door to the hotel, something hit him with a wicked blow on the back of the head, and an unseen fist delivered a vicious jab to his kidney, driving him to his knees. The attack was so sudden, and from behind, that he had no chance to defend himself, or draw the Browning. As he started to lose consciousness, his mind told him that the next thing he would feel would be the blade of a knife! He thought he heard the noise of a terrific struggle and cursing in Farsi.

"My God," he murmured quietly, "Is this how it ends?" Then he blacked out, collapsing in a heap on the dirty sidewalk; blood oozed from the back of his head.

Chapter Twenty

Dorri Golnessa was on the final leg of her circuitous plane trip from Tehran. She had flown to Budapest, then on to Zurich and finally she was about to land at Roissy-Charles de Gaulle airport in Paris. The trip had been uneventful, but grueling! In her luggage was a cosmetic case that contained an eight ounce glass jar which had once contained face cream, but now contained a large sample of the new strain of destroyer bacteria. Her final experiments had shown that the bacterium was indeed engineered to actively destroy grain, but she still worried about not having time to conduct tests to determine if infected grain was dangerous!

The part that she was playing in Arastoo's grand plan weighed heavily on her heart. She held no hatred for the American people or their government. From television programs and smuggled DVD's, she thought that the people on the street wanted the same thing that she wanted: to be happy and live their lives in peace.

Now, her talents and training were being used by an egomaniac to spread suffering, not to help people. Her longed for goal in life was to use her knowledge of bacterium to eradicate disease and suffering. Perhaps she would find a way to make food last longer and be more nutritious.

She had no illusions about Faridoon now. He was a pure politician. He would say anything, do anything, to remain in power. Yes, he was the hero of her country, but they had not seen him as she had seen him! Dorri also knew that her life was in grave danger. Once she had trained the agents in the United States how to grow their own supply of the bacteria and how

Chapter Twenty

to apply the bacteria to grain storage facilities so that it would do its destructive works, she knew that her services would be no longer needed. She was expendable. While alive she was a liability, one that could bring the whole plan to a halt, causing embarrassment to Arastoo and his government. Dead, no one would have ever heard of her or known what she had created. The thought that she could end up as an unknown body in an unmarked grave galled and frightened her. Faridoon was just another man trying to use her, then destroy her. She wanted to make a positive impact on the world, not harm people. She was not a terrorist!

In her mind she was trying to formulate a plan that would enable her to escape the clutches of Arastoo. Surely her cultural exchange privileges with the University of Illinois in Chicago could work to her advantage, but she just could not see how. She was just too tired to think properly. She would work on a plan once she had rested. Dorri had no doubt that she was being watched, so speaking at the university seemed to be her only hope.

As her plane taxied slowly to the gate, the other passengers did not notice the young woman sitting alone wiping a tear from her eye. If they had been watching, they would have noticed that she suddenly sat up straight in her seat. There was a new determination in the set of her chin. Her scarred but attractive face now seemed to regain color from some inward source. Her mind was made up! Dorri had a plan in her heart about how she could destroy Arastoo's heinous scheme. She would play the game until the time was right and then ask the American government for political asylum.

As Dorri deplaned and walked through the massive terminal, she watched to see if she could spot anyone following her. After making some stops at kiosks and shops, she observed a serious looking man imitating her steps. *Ah, there you are!* she thought to herself. Unfortunately, she did not see the plain looking middle aged woman, dressed in drab, dark clothes.

She was lost in the crowd of intent faces hurrying to make connecting flights or scrambling to find their luggage. The woman used her anonymity to her advantage and was able to stay relatively close to Dorri as she walked to the gate where her plane to the United States waited.

Two hours later, the Air France 747 climbed to its cruising altitude as it headed west towards the American continent. Dorri was settled in, determined to read most of a new novel she had purchased. It would help her practice her English to read in that language. Sleep had eluded her for the past week, and she was desperately tired. But now, with her mind made up with a course of action, the emotional release was beginning to show, and she succumbed to slumber.

On this big jetliner were two people who had been assigned the task of following the young scientist who had already been marked for death. Neither agent knew of the existence of the other; both were alert to anything suspicious. However, on the plane, they both took the opportunity to relax and get as much sleep on the eight hour flight as possible.

A little less than eight hours later, the giant plane was flying into the setting sun as it passed over the island of Manhattan on its way to the Newark Liberty International Airport. Dorri looked out of the window and was struck by the magnificence of what she saw below her. The skyscrapers reached toward her and seemed to be offering a welcome. It was a beautiful sight!

As the plane touched down and worked its way in line to approach the gate, Dorri gathered her unread book and put it in her handbag. She had slept soundly most of the way across the Atlantic and now felt refreshed and ready to face whatever was before her.

Dorri presented her passport and visa that declared that she was in the United States on a cultural exchange program intended to improve relations between the two countries. The customs officer behind the glass window reviewed her papers,

Chapter Twenty

checked to see that she was not on a wanted list, or a notify at once list from the FBI or Interpol. He discovered that she was on the notify at once list but gave no indication that he recognized her, waving her through with the customary "enjoy your stay" that he said to everyone. She proceeded down the concourse looking for someone assigned to meet her from the Russian Consulate.

Standing behind the barrier holding a sign with her name on it was a middle aged man dressed in a dark suit with a muted colored tie. He had the ready smile of a diplomat, but his eyes were non-committal and not exactly friendly. She went over to him and said she would meet him at the luggage carousel. They both used very broken English because he did not speak Farsi, and she did not think it was a good idea for other passengers to hear them talking in a language that might be Arabic.

The two Persians from very different agencies advanced separately through customs without any difficulty and moved to where they could see Dorri retrieve her luggage. The woman noticed that the Russian made no effort to grab Dorri's bags for her but stood to one side glancing at his watch every few minutes. He knew that he was routinely followed by agents of the FBI, so as he looked at his watch he was really using that as a cover to see if he could spot a familiar face.

The scientist quickly recognized the man who was following her and made a mental note that she would have to get out of his sight when the time was right. She smiled to herself because she was beginning to think like a spy and thought that was kind of exciting! As Dorri was leaving the terminal, the woman that she did not know was following her met a young girl dressed casually. She spoke briefly to the younger woman, giving her what appeared to be an iPhone; then she returned into the terminal and immediately booked a flight back to Paris. The young woman recorded the number of the Yellow cab as Dorri and the Russian got in the back seat. She climbed into a Chevy Malibu that had been parked at the curb and rapidly sent a text message on her iPhone while her car was taking some shortcuts that would get it to the Russian Consulate before the cab if they were lucky.

At the FBI headquarters in New York, Alan Clarendon, the agent in charge of the internal security desk, received a text message that included a cell phone picture of a young woman who had arrived on the Air France flight from Paris. He noted that the woman would have been quite handsome looking if not for the large scars on her face. Having worked around the criminal element all of his adult life, the agent knew that the scars had been caused by a knife in the hands of an unskilled attacker. The text message identified the woman as one Dorri Golnessa, an Iranian scientist from the University of Tehran, here on a cultural exchange program with the University of Illinois in Chicago. *CULTURAL EXCHANGE PROGRAM!* he exclaimed to himself, *You've got to be kidding!*

"Well Miss Golnessa," he mused quietly to himself. "What in the world brings you to New York, and why are the Russkies meeting you at the airport? And why, my dear, did you fly from Tehran to Budapest, then on to Zurich and Paris, and now here? Could it be that you didn't want to be followed?"

He smiled to himself and typed an email report that would go to the Bureau Chief for his routine review. He would soon have her visa and passport information, which along with Dorri's picture, would be sent to all FBI offices, as well Homeland Security, the National Intelligence Agency and the Central Intelligence Agency. Clarendon was a good officer, and he intended to put out an inquiry to Interpol just in case they knew anything about this lady scientist. Prior to 9-11, this airport meeting of two foreign nationals would probably have gone unnoticed. Now, however, because of Homeland Security, everyone was interested in people coming from countries that expressed their hatred for the United States.

Chapter Twenty-One

Unknown to Dorri, Arastoo was landing at Kennedy Airport in New York at nearly the same time that she was landing in Newark. The man who had been a professor at Tehran University just a few short weeks earlier was now the president of the country of Iran, currently known as Persia.

A few days previous, he had held a super-secret meeting with Zio Payam, his Minister of Intelligence. Payam was briefed on the most important details of the plan to corner the commodity market in the United States. A new wrinkle in Arastoo's scheme was that if it was successful, he intended to strike Australia. Should that also be a promising enterprise, the plan would be extended to Asian countries to include their rice crop. The professor displayed some scruples, however, when he told the minister that the vast Russian grain production would be left unscathed because of Russia's friendship towards Iran when the rest of the world was considering them to be a pariah.

Payam was taken aback when Faridoon began to outline this amazing gambit in world political power. Soon, he was a radical believer in his president and proclaimed to himself that he would do everything and anything to see Faridoon succeed.

The president gave him three immediate assignments. First, find out how many operatives Persia had working in America. He knew that many of them were students attending American universities. They were to be trained to do work of vital importance to Persia. When trained, these men could be dispatched to the Midwest farmland and start the sabotage of stored grain supplies, especially if something went wrong and they were unable to get local men to help. Arastoo did not want female operatives doing his bidding, fearful that they could become too emotional. Payam reminded the president that women could be some of the deadliest terrorists and might, perhaps, attract less suspicion should the Americans began to suspect that something was amiss. The president thought about that for a minute and then hesitantly agreed with his minister. This was one of the rare times that he had reversed a decision since becoming the leader of Persia. They then discussed the meeting Dorri would have with them in Chicago where she would demonstrate the rather simple process of growing more bacteria and how to safely transport these tiny weapons.

Second, Payam needed to have his agency make the necessary arrangements for Dorri's trip to the United States. He was to enlist the help of the Russians in getting her accommodations and transportation while in the country.

Third, the minister was instructed to have this brilliant young scientist followed at all times, starting when she boarded the plane at the airport. Faridoon finished speaking for a moment, then leaned closer to Payam and said, "If you lose her, you will have lost your life!" His eyes bored into the soul of his minister which caused extreme discomfort to the hapless man.

"I understand perfectly, Mr. President. Everything will be done exactly as you wish."

"Satisfactory. You had better get moving; you have a lot to do and vey little time to do it," Arastoo said.

Now, days later, Arastoo was finishing a transatlantic flight in a luxury government jet and preparing himself for his speech to be given to the members of the United Nations. He asked the pilot to circle Manhattan once before landing. Seeing this huge, glittering symbol of American wealth, he visualized in his mind that a city like this would one day exist in his beloved Persia, and it would be considered the center of

Chapter Twenty-One

the financial world.

Shaheen was sitting quietly across from Arastoo watching him closely. He did not look down at the island of Manhattan. He was seemingly uninterested, continuing to watch his boss. The president felt the giant's gaze upon him, turned, and said, "Did you enjoy the flight, my friend?"

The fierce face displayed no emotion. The giant shrugged his shoulders with indifference.

"I imagine the crowds will be small when I enter the general assembly hall. Hopefully, when I am finished it will be a different matter, and I want you close to me. I may need your help getting through the people," he said. The giant just nodded. Faridoon returned to his own thoughts while staring out of the window at the great city.

The plane was directed to a gate designated for private jets, both domestic and foreign. He deplaned and was slightly discouraged to find that there was no press waiting for him; neither were there crowds of well-wishers that he had become so accustomed to in Persia. Well, he was confident that this privacy was about to change.

Arastoo was escorted to a waiting limousine and was startled to find Mr. Diablo sitting in the rear seat, smoking a very expensive cigar, and wearing his customary dark glasses. After regaining his composure, he settled in the rear seat next to his benefactor. Then, surprisingly, he had an unflattering outburst of temper.

"Would you please put that thing out; I detest smoking!" he said rather loudly. Diablo ignored him and continued puffing happily away, smiling all the while.

"I'm on my way to Las Vegas to watch the losers flock to the casinos, fighting for the chance to gamble away their hard earned money! It gives me some pleasure. Tell me, Arastoo, you won't be a loser today, will you?" Diablo asked.

The president did not like surprises and was quite taken aback by the sudden appearance of this mysterious and powerful man who was rapidly beginning to control even more of his life, control that he did not wish to give up! He began to sulk for just a moment and made a big production out of rolling down the window to allow the horrible cigar smoke to escape.

"Answer my question, Arastoo! Are you prepared to present your speech to the U.N. today? I will be listening on a special frequency and looking forward to your brilliant oratory delivered with passion and emotion," he said as he turned in the seat to face Faridoon. The handsome face and raven black hair seemed sinister, somehow. "I ask you again, are you ready?"

"Yes, yes, I'm ready, but quite frankly, you're causing me to doubt myself. Why are you questioning me like this?" he asked with some embarrassment.

"Don't worry about it! I'm not trying upset or distract you. I just wanted to be sure that you are ready for what may be the most important speech of your life. Do you need anything?" Diablo asked, eyeing his companion closely.

"No, thank you. I just need a few minutes to arrange my thoughts," he lied. This surprise meeting had a strange negative effect on him emotionally. He was disconcerted and felt out of control, a disarming feeling that he didn't like.

"Good! I'll see you again." The limo had not moved during the back seat question and answer time, so Diablo got out of the vehicle and strolled to another private jet parked nearby, a jet that was much larger than the one Faridoon had flown in. As he climbed to the top of the stairs, he turned, the picture of power and strength, and gave the slightest of waves directed at the president. The hint of a smile on his lips did not translate as a sign of friendship but resembled a superior dismissing a subordinate.

As the limousine moved into traffic heading for the United Nations building, Arastoo tried to regain his composure and concentrate on the speech he was about to make. His intention

Chapter Twenty-One

was to turn the delegates into positive supporters of him personally and the New Persian Empire globally. Suddenly, the limo was surrounded by police motorcycles with sirens screaming at traffic to move over and let this important person past. Arastoo wondered where this escort came from and who arranged it. Within twenty minutes, they pulled up at the U.N. building. The Persian president emerged from the limo dressed elegantly, but simply, in a light tan business suit and white shirt. He chose to forego the traditional red power tie and substituted it for a beautiful royal purple tie with light tan stripes. There was a subtle difference in this immaculate wardrobe from the one he wore on television; he now wore a conspicuous gold bracelet with a brilliant diamond that changed sunlight into thousands of miniature rainbows of color.

Stepping into the bright sunlight, he recoiled slightly from the odor of the traffic exhaust all around him. That held his attention for only a split second because before him was a sea of reporters and cameramen. Everyone was screaming for his attention, with the pleasing cry of "Mr. President, can we have a preview of what your speech will address?"

Arastoo was thrilled and energized, immediately turning on his extraordinary charm and working the media like a true politician. Instead of smiling and forcing his way through the throng, he stopped, shook hands with reporters, joked with cameramen while pounding some of them on the back and shouting, "Make sure you get my good side!" He absolutely charmed them!

Amazingly, the black bearded Shaheen was tolerant of the mass of people surrounding his master, standing in the way of the most forceful of the crowd, startling them when they glanced up into his fierce face. He moved the press slowly towards the entrance of the building where the world came together to work on common problems, such as finding ways to stop wars, but failing miserably in all attempts to be a relative force in world politics.

Entering the building he was met by a phalanx of United Nations officials offering welcoming handshakes; faces were masked with identical diplomatic smiles that offered no sign of friendliness. They were shocked to realize that Arastoo paid little or no attention to them, stopping instead to speak with ushers and office workers. The secretaries standing in the entrance hall visibly swooned when he shook their hands and looked deeply into their eyes.

Uniformed security guards rushed in to attempt to clear a path for the president to escalators that would take him to the General Assembly Hall. When these armed men came too close to Arastoo, the black robed hulk magically appeared between them, blocking any access to the president. The uniformed men looked at him and involuntarily backed away.

The enormous hall was already full of delegates and staff members, many in the colorful dress of the countries they represented. They quietly admired him as he moved with grace and authority down the center aisle to the platform. He was politely seated on the right side of the platform by an usher who was overwhelmed when this foreign president reached out and put his arm around his shoulders and thanked him for his help.

After being seated, Arastoo ignored those in attendance and calmly ordered his thoughts as he prepared for his coming speech. Again, he would not be using any notes, relying on his superior memory and his gift of ad-libbing when he wished to stress an important point. He reviewed in his mind the need for the proper use of gestures throughout the presentation.

There was an audible rustle as members took their seats and adjusted translation devices as they prepared to listen to this unknown man who had burst on the global political scene. Body language of some members of the audience already revealed a good deal of boredom, and they were ready to dismiss this man as being a person of no importance. The

Chapter Twenty-One

president of the United Nations was a tall, distinguished looking man in his sixties with long, wavy grey hair that gave him the polished look of a diplomat; he ascended to the platform and walked with long, measured strides to the podium. The giant hall rapidly became quiet and expectant! The president made a very polite, unemotional introduction, devoid of the usual platitudes that diplomats love making to one another. Instead, after only a few comments, he motioned Arastoo to come forward. There was a smattering of polite applause as the new Persian president walked to the front of the platform and shook hands with the weak and ineffective leader of the world body. A slight murmur wafted across the room as some delegates realized that Arastoo was not carrying a sheaf of notes. Now, for the first time, the former professor took notice of the somewhat expectant crowd in the very large General Assembly hall.

As Faridoon took his place at the podium, he smiled broadly, displaying perfect white teeth. He unleashed all of his immense charm and began to speak, so softly at first that there was a shuffling sound as translators raced to increase the volume on their receiving instruments. This technique had worked very effectively when he gave his speech to the nation of Iran, and he believed it would have the same reaction here. He made a mental note to remember to make adjustments for the short time lapse between his comments and the translator's efforts to change his words into the language of each individual listener.

"Good morning, ladies and gentlemen. I feel privileged to be allowed to address this august body. I tell you truly that I will be speaking for just a few minutes, so you can relax and get comfortable!" There was a smattering of polite laughter.

He continued, "I must tell you that I have something that is somewhat unusual to mention before continuing. May I say to the ambassadors from the United States, Great Britain, France and Germany, please feel free to leave! I have no interest in speaking to you; I want to address the rest of the world!"

There was a collective gasp from the delegates, with many people adjusting their electronic translators to make sure they were hearing correctly. The delegates mentioned by Arastoo were shocked into inaction, disbelieving what they had just heard. Others became angry and began to shout that this upstart should get off the platform. The former professor paid absolutely no attention to anything happening in the hall. When the uproar subsided, he continued speaking.

"Excuse me if I have offended anyone, but I grow weary of listening to your politicians telling the rest of the world how to live, how to think, and how to follow your lead like the proverbial lemmings rushing to the sea! Be assured that my country of Persia has no intention of continuing to bow to your faulty and misguided leadership. May I give an example of this Imperial thinking? Pakistan, India, and Israel have nuclear power plants. So does France, Germany and England. Oh, I almost forgot, so does America! But the United States, in its infinite wisdom, declares that we are not allowed to have the benefit of this cheap electrical power, because they do not like our government. THEY DON'T LIKE US! EXCUSE ME, BUT WHO APPOINTED THEM GOD OVER OUR REGION OF THE WORLD?" He raised his voice and gripped the podium tightly with his slender fingers. Now there was a smattering of applause and a few 'hear, hear' murmurings. Diplomats were now sitting straighter while nodding in agreement. Because of the audacity of the last few sentences, they were paying close attention to what he was saying. He continued speaking with even more passion and using enhanced gestures.

"I think I am speaking for a number of ambassadors in this room when I say we CHOOSE to think for ourselves! We will grow our own economies! We will protect our own heritage; we have no interest in yours. And frankly, Mr. and Mrs. America, we don't want your sordid money!" Faridoon smiled slyly to

Chapter Twenty-One

himself remembering that he had no qualms about accepting the American's sordid money in payment for the crude oil he sold them every day. Cash from the United States was the same money that would enable him to accomplish the elaborate agenda he planned to implement immediately.

"You attempt to buy our friendship and our allegiance while at the same time you treat us like cheap prostitutes, assuming that we will do anything for MONEY!"

Arastoo was interrupted by delegates cheering like football fans after their team scored a touchdown! He knew that his immense oratory skills were mesmerizing his audience and causing them to suddenly want to align themselves with him. The ambassadors from the U.S., Britain, France and Germany were livid, probably thinking that this would be a convenient time for an assassination. The Russian and Chinese delegations were smiling and nodding in agreement although they were not classifying themselves as third world countries. They just absolutely loved hearing someone give it to the Americans.

"Ladies and gentlemen, I have no intention of standing here wasting hours of your time and mine, reciting the list of offenses we have against these rich and powerful countries. They honestly believe that money can buy anything. Well, as far as I am concerned that STOPS NOW! I speak for the great nation of Persia; you may remember it as being called Iran." He whispered here, leaned over the podium slightly, smiled and winked mischievously.

The crowd exploded with laughter and applause. Arastoo waved and laughed with them. He was exhilarated! He believed that most small and third world countries were now in his camp. Now, he braced himself for the clincher.

"My friends, I am proposing a new alliance of nations between those of us who do not have the powerful threat of nuclear weapons that we can use to frighten or persuade others into marching in lock step with us. We must band together and share our natural resources with each other. We will come to the aide of any alliance member that finds itself struggling economically. But, WE WILL NOT MEDDLE IN THE INTERNAL POLITICS OF OUR FRIENDS!"

For a split second he was afraid they might rush the platform. The response was beyond description. The great hall was filled with ecstatic people, laughing and crying and shouting, "Yes!"

"I am suggesting the idea that you may wish to join the new Persian Empire! Let's forge our alliance together to make this world a happy place for our families and a successful place for our businesses. Join me as we walk into the sunrise of a new day together." He waved his arm toward the east. "Tomorrow, I will dispatch ambassadors from my country to yours, to meet with your governments and share with them our plans for creating this great, new world alliance where everyone enjoys the advantages of peace and security! Thank you for your time and attention." Then he laughed mischievously and asked, "Are the Americans still here?"

The roar of approval was deafening, and there was now a real danger of people rushing the platform in an effort to touch him and shake his hand. Shaheen appeared out of nowhere and proceeded to block their approach. His fierceness stopped the first line of cheering fans dead in their tracks, causing those behind to stumble into them. Several collapsed in a heap on the floor, and people worried that some might be trampled. Security guards rushed to form a circle around Arastoo and lead him off stage while he laughed, waved, and reached between guards to shake hands with people who now could legitimately be called worshippers.

The president had actually forgotten that the speech was broadcast on local television as well as being shown around the world. Nothing in recent memory could compare to the reaction to this unknown man's speech. The little countries of the world were cheering his audacity and courage in telling the big guys to get lost. They felt that this was the dawning

Chapter Twenty-One

of a new era, and they wanted to be a part of it. Governments around the world were placing calls to the Persian Embassies trying to arrange for their ambassadors to meet with them and disclose this wonderful, but mysterious plan for a new alliance. In some nations, Persia did not even have an ambassador in the country yet, forcing the new Minister of State Alborhim to work frantically to get students and former opposition leaders trained in a quick course on how to conduct diplomacy. These excited and anxious people needed to get up to speed to become a Persian ambassador. The response to Arastoo's speech could not have been better!

Chapter Twenty-Two

As Tuck managed to open a slit in his eyelids, his gaze fell upon a little yellow light bulb hanging by a cord from the ceiling. He couldn't comprehend where he was. His vision began to clear slightly, and he was starting to recognize that he was in a dingy, depressing room, and there was someone else in the room with him.

Slowly he started to remember what had happened to him, but just as he was coming out of the fog, the awful pain in the back of his head exploded in his skull, nearly causing him to black out again. The dirty pillow beneath his head was covered with blood even though someone had wrapped a makeshift bandage around his pounding head.

"Oh my God!" He moaned as the room swam before his eyes. It had been a long time since he had experienced such severe pain, and that time he had nearly died.

"Don't move around Tuck. You might have a concussion, we're not sure," someone said.

"We need to get you to a hospital for an x-ray. Hold still, I'm going to give you a shot of morphine to help ease the pain," a voice spoke from somewhere.

He couldn't see who was talking, but at least they sounded like they might be a friend and not an enemy. He flinched as the needle entered a vein in his right arm. Just then searing pain from the blow that had been struck to his left kidney hit him, causing another groan to escape from his dry and cracked lips. Tuck was happy to lie very still while trying to remember what had happened to him. In a few minutes, the drug began to win the battle against the pain, and he could think with a little

Chapter Twenty-Two

clarity. As the aching subsided, his brain scrambled to clear itself as he tried, but failed, to raise himself on one elbow.

"Can somebody tell me where I am?" he asked through clenched teeth. Fear was beginning to gnaw at his consciousness, and the nerves from the small of his back told him that his Browning friend was absent.

"You're back at the safe house, but you may not be out of danger!" the same someone said.

"What happened?" he asked between stabs of pain.

"You got mugged while going in that flea bag hotel you wanted to sleep in," the voice answered.

Now his memory started to kick in, and he recalled some of the events he had just lived through. During the pain and violence of the attack that struck him so suddenly, he recalled hearing a desperate struggle. Tuck began to concentrate on getting his eyes open and get orientated. As he labored to get eyelids that seemed to weigh five pounds open, an image began to form, but he rejected it because he knew it was impossible, couldn't happen! A thumb pushed one of his eyelids open further and a face peered closely to see if his eyes were dilated. But that face; it just couldn't be…!

The bearded face smiled and said, "Hello, Tuck, I'm glad to see you are awake. You worried us for a couple of hours."

Tuck tried to sit up but the pain forced him back on the bed. "Great Caesar's Ghost; it can't be! You're that guy from the Brothers Clinic, what's the name, Abbey something?"

"Abisha, Tuck, the name's Abisha Davidson," he said while smiling, but the smile also revealed his great concern. The cool touch of his hand on Tuck's forehead seemed to bring welcomed relief.

"But, this is impossible! You're that hippie that was always praying. What are you doing here, and how in blazes did you get here? What in the world is going on?" Tuck sputtered. His bulging eyes resembled ugly, red saucers.

"I just happened to be in the neighborhood when those

guys jumped you. It's a good thing I know a little karate; I inflicted a little suffering on their miserable bodies." Abisha seemed to be genuinely embarrassed.

"You just happened to be in the neighborhood? Are you kidding me? I don't gamble much, but what are the odds that you would just happen to be in Tehran, Iran, in the same part of the city, at the same time as I am, so you can come to my rescue? Are you out of your cotton pick'n mind? The odds of that happening are incalculable!" Tuck was exasperated. He lapsed into a fit of coughing from talking with a throat that was as dry as the desert's dust.

Lemon reached around Abisha and offered Tuck a bottle of water. Peach was leaning against a far wall, positioned so she could see out the window and scan the street for danger.

"Tuck, let's just say that I have a few friends working here that I wanted to visit and make sure they were doing okay," Abisha said. Tuck couldn't shake the feeling that when this guy spoke to him, he felt better.

"You've got friends here? Are you crazy? You're Jewish, for crying out loud! These people want to kill you!" he was getting exasperated again.

"Don't worry, Tuck; people have tried to kill me before. In your business, you must know that Israel's Mossad has agents in this country working to protect their homeland. Some of these guys are my friends and I wanted to see them."

"But you're a volunteer in a Virginia rehab clinic for heaven's sake! How the heck can you be involved in world politics, and how in blazes did you get here?" he demanded. Tuck's head was spinning. He was unable to grasp what was happening.

"Why don't we just concentrate on getting you better, and we'll try to answer your questions later, okay?" Abisha asked.

"Yeah, okay, but you're not brushing me off. I want some answers."

Chapter Twenty-Two

"That's fair enough. I'll be glad to answer all of your questions. But right now, Lemon needs to talk to you." The bearded face moved back into the shadow of the single light bulb. Lemon moved closer to the bed.

"How are you, Tuck? Is the morphine working?" Lemon asked.

"Yeah, I'm okay. What happened anyway? Did I get mugged or is my cover blown?"

"I honestly think it was a plain old, down home mugging. You were just in the wrong place at the wrong time," Lemon responded.

"But how can you be so sure? How do we know that VEVAK isn't on to us? They are a superbly trained intelligence service. I thought I saw someone watching me earlier in the day, but I was sure I gave him the slip."

"I really believe that if they were agents of VEVAK, they would have been a lot more professional, and you wouldn't be alive now! These guys didn't seem to have the brains to pour water out of a boot that had the directions on the heel. They were probably druggies!" Lemon reassured him.

"But how did I get here?" Tuck asked with doubt creeping up in his voice.

"Abisha and one of his friends carried you here. They think that they were careful enough to prevent anyone from following them. We still have people out on the streets patrolling just in case. If not for them, this could have been a very deadly calamity."

"But my dear young man," Tuck said sarcastically, "How did they know about this supposedly safe house?" he asked. There was no answer.

"Don't think I'm not grateful, but I just can't get a handle on this thing! Lemon, you need to get in touch with the agency and bring them up to speed on things happening here," Tuck instructed.

"Sho nuf!" Lemon mimicked a Southerner as he activated

his iPhone to get a secure satellite hookup to Langley.

Tuck glanced around the room to locate the inscrutable Jewish guy. He had a bunch of questions to ask him. But Abisha was nowhere to be found. *Now what?* he thought to himself. *This guy really is a spook!*

At CIA headquarters in Langley, Virginia, Herb Worthington was holding his head in his hands. This was turning into a really lousy day. His big hands kneaded his eyes until they became blood-shot and red-rimmed. The day had started by his being told that his old friend and secret operative in Iran, Aristotle Tucker, had been attacked in Tehran. He had no information about how serious the attack had been; what condition Tuck was in; or even where he was. Herb just knew Tuck was alive, but he didn't know if he was safe or if his cover was blown. *Was the attack by VEVAK, the Iranian Intelligence Service?* he wondered to himself.

Another question that haunted him was what had happened to the rest of the operatives that had been staying at the safe house?

This was a nightmare, a severe setback for their efforts to get information out of this very dangerous country. The old Marine was seething inside. He would have loved to have been with Tuck, wading into the attackers with his fists and inflicting the terrible damage that he was capable of delivering. Instead, he was beating himself up for sending his old friend into harms way especially since he was just out of rehab and certainly not in great physical shape.

His phone rang; it was a direct, secure hookup with Tehran and the young operative known as Lemon.

"Lemon, for heaven's sake, what's going on over there?" he shouted into the phone.

"Sir, we're all okay. Tuck's got a bad headache, but otherwise he seems to be all right. We think it was a random mugging and not an attack from the bad guys, but we've beefed up our security around this place just to be on the safe side.

Chapter Twenty-Two

Hang on a minute, the man thinks he's well enough to talk for a few minutes...here's Tuck!"

Tuck took the iPhone and spoke quietly. "Hi, boss; we're all okay and holding our own. My old skull is still harder than a blackjack. I'm grateful that Abisha was there to save me from something much worse."

"Abisha, who's Abisha? Is he one of your guys on the street over there?" Herb asked.

"It's just too complicated to go over now; I'll give you a heads up when I see you. Did you get all the stuff we sent you on the new president and this lady scientist?" Tuck asked quickly.

"Yeah, we got the stuff and sent it out to all the proper people. It came just in time; the FBI got a hit on Dorri as she came into the country yesterday. They're going to keep an eye on her. One interesting thing, the Russians met her at the airport and took her to their house. Do you have any more information about what she may be up to?" Lucky asked.

"No, but I think this could be really big. I hope the G-men stay close to her. We have information that Iran has recalled all of her ambassadors immediately. Something is up over there; we'll try to get as much information to you as soon as we can."

"I think we know what that is all about. The big guy spoke to the UN yesterday and he really wowed 'em." Herb took a few minutes and filled Tuck in on the speech and the way it was received by the assembly.

"Great Scott, Herb! The guy is forming a new Soviet Union! How does he plan to pull that off?" Tuck asked incredulously.

"I have no idea. But you know, Tuck, there is something familiar about this guy when he is making a speech. I can't put my finger on it, but I've seen his style someplace before. He sure can address a crowd and he hooks 'em in no time!"

"Thanks for the head's up, Herb. Gotta go."

"See ya Tuck, take care." The chief of the Iran desk at the agency hung up the phone and rubbed his ham of a hand over his face, opened a drawer, and took out a bottle of aspirin. *This job is killing me!* He groused to himself while popping pills.

Chapter Twenty-Three

The young woman from Iran arrived in Chicago and was met by an unsmiling, casually dressed man who greeted her coldly and escorted her to an old Toyota Camry parked a long way from the terminal. It did not go unnoticed by the scientist that he made no effort to help her with her luggage. He took nearly thirty minutes to drive through bumper-to-bumper traffic and bring her to a dilapidated warehouse near the docks. She couldn't keep from thinking to herself that her life was really going downhill since leaving the university. Now, she was expected to work for her country in a seedy place like this! She wasn't particularly impressed by the men she met upon her arrival at the storage building either. She could tell that these men were surely not scientists; most of them appeared to be professional criminals. They reminded her of those that controlled certain areas of Tehran, a fact that was never publicized by the press or the government.

Dorri was extremely unhappy to learn that there were no women present; she was alone! Here was another occasion in her life where men, all of whom she distrusted and disliked, would have control over her. There was a slight frown on her scarred face as she was shown a small, depressingly shabby room where she was supposed to live while working in the dilapidated warehouse. She was instructed that she was not to leave the building alone under any circumstances.

Dorri got settled in her little room as best as she could, unpacking what little luggage she had brought with her. After freshening up a little, she was told that she would be taken to what was going to be her laboratory. While walking to the lab, she noticed that all but two of the unsavory group of men that had been present before were now gone. She was pleasantly surprised, however, to see that the lab was fairly well equipped and would meet her needs quite nicely. Dorri got right down to business.

"Gentlemen, who will be the scientists working with me?" She asked, grateful that she had been able to learn some English during her years at the university. Even the clerics had agreed that it would be a good idea since most of the world's academic and research work was conducted in English. Now, she could communicate almost flawlessly in this second language.

"We will be using first names only here," a man named Steve stepped forward and spoke up. He apparently was in charge of this portion of the total operation. He was a rather tall man, and seemed to be physically fit and well groomed. He wore a brown business suit that had obviously been tailor made to fit his muscled frame. He kept his light brown hair cut in the military style, which gave him the overall appearance of having just stepped out of an Army recruiting poster. Dorri had no doubt that this man would keep Tehran informed about her work and its progress.

"That is acceptable to me," Dorri said, sounding very formal, but she was nervous and she was trying to be careful. She wanted to let these people know that this project depended on her, and her alone.

"Two people will be assisting you in your work, Ellis and Vic," Steve pointed towards two guys slouching near a work table, eyeing her cautiously.

Ellis was a man whose age was probably on the losing side of fifty. His receding, uncombed hair was gray and dirty. He looked at her over wire rimmed granny glasses that hung on precariously to the end of his thin, slightly hooked nose, causing him to be continuously tipping his head back to see through them. A two day growth of stubble gave his jowl covered face a grayish color. His dirty lab coat was a failed

Chapter Twenty-Three

attempt to hide his weight problem and the unkempt way he was dressed.

Vic, on the other hand, was very tall and slender. He proclaimed his Irish heritage by having bright, almost fluorescent red hair that exploded up from his head like a highway flare. He had pleasant features and a ready smile that displayed perfect white teeth. His lab coat was spotless and bright enough for a laundry detergent commercial. Dorri learned another distinguishing feature about him when she shook his hand; the index finger on his right hand was missing.

Steve gave her a quick tour of the lab and then suggested that they get right down to business.

"Do you have a supply of wheat, corn, and soybean that we can use to begin the replicating process?" she asked Steve.

"We have a five gallon plastic container of each that we can use for starters. We have a truck load of grain in these cans, and we can get greater quantities if you need them. How long will it take for the bacteria to begin spreading?" he asked.

"The bacteria will begin to work when it is mixed with the grain. It will infect all the kernels it touches; they will in turn infect all of the kernels they touch, and so on. The process becomes faster as the bacteria spread so that your five gallons should be full of the bacterium in about one hour." She secretly hoped that she was right. There had not been enough time to completely test her experiment.

"Good deal, let's get started," Steve said as he guided her to the bench that contained three white plastic containers full of grain. Dorri took the glass makeup jar from her coat pocket. The little jar contained about three ounces of white, sterile and uncontaminated granules that would act as 'mules' and carry the bacteria onto the grain. She shook about one third of the granules into each container. Her hand shook just a trifle as she returned the lid to the jar and slyly put it back into her coat. She hoped no one would notice that she kept the jar; it would play an important part in her survival when the right time came if it came! Tiny beads of perspiration appeared on her upper lip as she casually glanced around the room. Dorri relaxed just a little as she noticed that no one was paying the slightest bit of attention to her; they were absorbed with watching the grain buckets.

"What are the visible signs that the bacterium is working?" Vic asked, glancing over his shoulder to look at her.

"The color of the grain will have a slightly bleached look," she answered.

"Gentlemen, because this project has been on such a fast track, adequate testing has been impossible. We need to conduct immediate experiments with rats to see what, if any, danger exists when contaminated grain has been ingested." She looked at Ellis and Vic. "Can you gentlemen take the lead on that project?"

Vic smiled his perfectly white smile and said, "Sure thing. We thought you might want to conduct some tests, so we already have some animals here and we can begin testing as soon as the grain is ready. We might have some results as early as tomorrow evening, especially if the bacteria laden grain proves to be deadly."

"Very good," Dorri said, smiling back at the scientist. However, she had her doubts that either of these two men were actually degreed in anything. There wasn't anything she could do about that, but she prayed a silent prayer to any god that might be listening that eating the grain would not prove to be fatal! She knew in her heart that Arastoo would not be having the same concern. If large numbers of Americans died, he would probably think that was an unexpected bonus.

Then she said, "If you will excuse me, gentlemen, I am going to my room and take a little nap. It has been a long day, and jet lag has set in. Please wake me in two hours so I can check on the progress of the replication process."

She entered the little room and was horrified to discover

Chapter Twenty-Three

that there was no lock on the door. Thinking for a moment of a way to protect herself, she propped a chair under the doorknob, like she had seen people do in the movies. Collapsing on the bed, Dorri was instantly sound asleep.

Steve went to an office, closed the door, and made a phone call, dialing the international access and country codes for Iran. The two men portraying themselves as scientists were busy putting cages together and getting water for the rats. They wanted them nice and hungry for the tests. After thinking for a few minutes, Ellis suggested that maybe they shouldn't give them water now because they might want to see what effect water would have on them after eating the infected grain. Vic agreed, and they took the water away from the scurrying little beasts.

At the same time, in another part of the warehouse, the rest of the men were in a meeting to learn what their jobs were going to be. A large man with a pockmarked face was talking to the group, referring often to notes held on a clipboard.

"Okay, you guys, listen up. All of you have been hired to do a little job for a large company that doesn't want its name known to every Tom, Dick and Harry. Got it? Okay! You will each be paid $5,000 in cash, half now, the rest when you've finished your work. The job is simple. You are going to travel to grain elevators all around the Midwest and spread a little more grain on the top of the pile. You're going to do this at night and without anyone seeing you. We chose you guys because we know that you're efficient and trustworthy." There was a murmur of laughter over the trustworthy remark.

"Now, we don't want any trouble, so if you run into anyone, get out of there and try to finish the job on a different night, but get the job done! Any questions?" He looked around the room. One man raised his hand.

"Yeah, what do you want?" he snarled

"I got a question; what the heck is a grain elevator?" The room exploded in laughter, but the pockmarked guy was nearly purple!

"We'll show you a picture, now shut up!" He shouted furiously while he wiped his face with a dirty blue handkerchief.

"Okay guys, after you get your money, you'll be given an address in Des Moines, Iowa, where you will meet some people who will give you more details about the job. Be there by tomorrow night. If you're late, the deal is off, and we will get our money back!" There were no doubters that this guy would do just what he said. "If you've got cars, drive down there; otherwise, take the bus, but get there by tomorrow night." Pockmark scowled at the men and motioned for them to get moving.

Exactly two hours from the time she closed the door, there was a knock that brought Dorri instantly awake.

"Yes, what is it?" she asked while stifling a yawn.

"It's time to get up. We're anxious to see how the bacterium is doing," Vic said quietly.

"Thank you. Give me a minute and I'll be out."

"Sure, we'll be in the lab," Vic said as he turned and walked away.

Dorri hated sleeping in her clothes, but she had been so tired that she didn't take time to change. She grabbed her lab coat and fussed with her hair as she examined herself in the mirror in the little bathroom. She suddenly was horrified! What if there were cameras in the room watching her every move? She had hid the little cosmetic jar in a pocket inside her suitcase. Going back into the room, she examined all the walls and corners. Dorri was not a spy, and she certainly was not trained in the art of where to look for such things, but she didn't see anything that even resembled a camera. Calming herself she walked out of the room and went immediately to the lab. Steve, Ellis, and Vic were waiting for her arrival with anticipation.

"Well gentlemen, let's take a peek at how our little friends

Chapter Twenty-Three

are doing."

Approaching the first of the white containers, she gently removed the lid and peered inside. The three men nearly knocked her over as they strained to see the results of the experiment.

"Easy, guys, easy! They're not going anywhere," she said.

Looking inside, she found herself excited but fearful at the same time. The grain was SLIGHTLY DISCOLORED! It was working! She took a little scoop and dug deeply into the container. She discovered that all the grain had already become infected. An examination of the other two buckets gave the same results; the test was a success! The men were laughing and whacking one another on the back.

"Now my friends, all you need to do is get the number of containers you expect to use, fill them with grain, and add some of these kernels. By the time you load them onto a truck and deliver them to Des Moines, they will be ready to spread to additional containers. But while you are processing more grain, continue to feed some grain to the rats. It's very important that we know whether the grain is dangerous for human consumption," Dorri gave the instructions with the detached air of a scientist speaking to students.

"We'll take care of everything from this point on. You get some more sleep, and we'll give you a detailed report in the morning," Steve said.

"Thank you, I'll take you up on that one. I haven't had enough rest in a very long time. Good night!" she said as she walked back to her little room.

Inside, with the chair back in its place to provide her with some security, she sat on the bed and held her head in her hands for a moment, quietly weeping. *If there is a god, what must he think of me?* she asked herself.

Steve went back to the office and dialed the number to Iran again. He gave just one code word in Farsi and hung up. Ellis and Vic assembled a crew of men to begin filling containers with grain. They went to each one and added the infected kernels and fastened the lid closed. As an afterthought, they fed some of the grain to the rats. It had no bearing on their jobs if the rats lived or died. They were just responsible for getting a truckload of infected grain to Des Moines by tomorrow night.

The cadre of men left the warehouse and entered the descending darkness which nearly obscured an old Ford F 150 pickup parked in an alleyway between two other warehouses. An elderly man was behind the wheel, and he appeared to be sleeping contentedly. None of the rough men noticed this old gentleman; even if they had they would have assumed that he was drunk, or perhaps a night watchman catching a couple winks. But this white haired man was not sleeping at all. He had been carefully watching the warehouse and had recorded lots of video of this gathering of undesirables. In truth, this man was an undercover agent for the Federal Bureau of Investigation, named Rance England, working out of the Chicago office. He had been with the bureau for over thirty years and now found that his age has actually become an asset. Few people, especially dangerous people, rarely give elderly people a second glance.

Rance had been originally assigned to locate Dorri Golnessa at O'Hare International when her plane landed. Finding her as she came into the terminal was no problem; the scarred face identified her immediately. Following the car and the man that had picked her up was a little tougher in the afternoon traffic on I-55. He was really confused when the car turned north on Lake Shore drive and drove to Lawrence Avenue where they stopped at the run-down warehouse that he was now watching.

There obviously was something going on in the old building, but he had no idea what it could be. One thing was for sure, there were a lot of guys from the criminal element going inside. What would this foreign scientist be doing

Chapter Twenty-Three

associating with these birds?

Shortly after nine p.m. he observed a Penske 22' rental truck capable of carrying 9,000 lbs, back up to the loading dock. The workers started loading white, five gallon containers into the truck. After loading, there appeared to have been 150-200 containers of something that appeared to be of some value, according to the way the jerks handled them. Just before ten o'clock, the truck pulled away heading for the interstate. It was too dark for him to get a license plate or truck number without giving himself away, so he made a note of it in his report. One thing he was going to document for sure; Dorri did not leave with the gang of street thugs!

Shortly after ten o'clock, he spotted on old Chevy Bel Air moving down the street towards him. Two blocks away, the old car turned right and disappeared down a side street. Five minutes later, he noticed it moving silently next to an abandoned building across the street from where he was parked. The car was driving without headlights until it reached the darkest spot on the block, where it stopped and the engine was turned off. No one could be seen in the old car, but after a few minutes there was a dim light from a cigarette lighter for a split second, then the car was again in complete darkness. This was Rance's signal that his relief was here, and he could head back to the office. He carefully started the old Ford and quietly moved onto the street and headed towards the downtown section of the city. It had been a long day, and he was thinking of how good it would be to get home and rest. But first he had to get the video and his report to headquarters. He couldn't imagine why the lady was so important that he should be assigned to watch her, but she sure must be special. What in the world was she doing in that dump with all those creeps?

Chapter Twenty-Four

Business at the Woodson House Brokerage in Chicago was so brisk that it threatened to throw them into overload mode. Their newest client, the Nuhoma Corporation, was submitting buy orders nearly faster than they could be executed. Woodson had been directed to buy grain at whatever the price, and Nuhoma would take delivery at a location they specified. For a brand new client, this company was spending money like there was no tomorrow. Thousands of tons of wheat were already being shipped via rail to the Lake Michigan Grain Storage Company's elevator on Lake Shore Drive in Chicago. The grain was being transported from storage elevators in Iowa, Kansas, North and South Dakota, Nebraska, and Missouri. The executives at Woodson were ecstatic! They were making huge commissions on Nuhoma's insatiable desire, not only for wheat, but for corn and soybeans as well.

This frenzy caused by Nuhoma's decision to pay high prices was forcing other bidders to compete, which drove the prices even higher. Future contracts were selling for prices that were fifty percent higher than the previous week. This was having a ripple effect of raising other futures, such as live cattle and pork bellies. Stock prices for giant agri-business conglomerates were spiraling downward without any hope of seeing an end soon. The price of bread, eggs, beef, pork and chickens was rising, sometimes as much as twenty-five percent per week.

The same scenario was being played out in Kansas City, Missouri, with the Commodity Geeks, except they were buying grain for immediate delivery to the Erickson Elevators

Chapter Twenty-Four

in St. Louis, in addition to futures contracts. As planned, Nuhoma was paying a higher price than other bidders, causing the trading in the pits at the Board of Trade to become so feverish that it resembled a war zone in some South American country. The Geeks were also buying surplus wheat, corn, and soybeans from storage facilities around the Midwest and as far south as New Orleans. The word on the street was that Nuhoma was taking delivery and then making arrangements to ship the commodities overseas.

Like Woodson, the Geeks thought that they had died and gone to heaven! Their commissions went through the roof and were heading higher! Nuhoma had millions in their account, so no questions were asked about this new corporation that just arrived on the commodity scene. Life was good!

On the Anderson farm, located six miles due west of Sioux Center, a new red Dodge Ram pickup drove into the equipment yard where Joel Anderson was working in preparation for the rapidly approaching spring planting season. The driver of the Dodge got out and approached the farmer, waving and smiling like they had known each other for years. He was dressed in a green plaid shirt, jeans, and work boots that appeared to be brand new. The guy wore a broad, dentist whitened smile that shouted salesman to the world.

Shoving his right hand forward he asked, "Hello, are you Mr. Anderson?"

"You've got me nailed," the friendly farmer said. He took off his right glove to shake the proffered hand, noticing it was soft to the touch against his calloused paw. A big man with a kind face that said welcome to everyone, Anderson had been farming for thirty years, through good times and bad.

"My name is Ted Garner. I represent the Nuhoma Corporation. Can I talk to you for a couple of minutes?" He asked as he gave the farmer a business card that was simple in design but had gold embossed lettering.

"Sure, come on in the shed. I've got a pot of coffee brewing.

What are you selling?"

"I'm selling financial prosperity! Are you expecting a good corn crop this year?" He asked the question without waiting for the answer. "As you saw on my card, I work for the Nuhoma Corporation, and I am authorized to make you an offer to purchase your crop this fall."

"Nuhoma, never heard of it. What business are they in?" the farmer inquired.

"You may not be familiar with us now, but you will be in the future. We are in the commodities business buying and selling to overseas markets. We also are in farm machinery and bulk grain transportation. Our headquarters is located in Des Moines, and we buy grain on the Chicago and Kansas City markets."

"Sounds very impressive, but how does that affect me?" Joel asked cautiously.

"Mr. Anderson, we can make a major impact on your profitability this year. We believe that a hard working farmer, like yourself, deserves to get the highest dollar possible for his crop. If you can give me a couple of minutes, I can outline our plan for you," Garner said.

"I'm always glad to hear about new ways to make money!"

"Great, here's the deal. Nuhoma would like to have you sign a contract to sell your corn to us at harvest time. Here's the best part; we guarantee to pay you five percent above the current market price at harvest. I said guarantee!" He paused to gauge how his proposal was being received by the farmer.

"Another very important part of our offer to you is that we can sell you crop insurance at five percent below any other offer you might receive—guaranteed!" Again he paused to see the reaction to his proposal. The smile was still there, but his eyes were looking hard at his potential customer. He intended to make this sale!

"Mr. Anderson, I'm not finished yet! Nuhoma will

Chapter Twenty-Four

completely finance your seed and fertilizer expenses. Our finance charges are guranteed to be two percentage points below anything any bank can offer. Nuhoma is a large company with over one hundred million dollars in liquid assets. They want your business, and they are willing to back these offers with written guarantees," Garner finished his pitch and went for the closure.

"Mr. Anderson, that's the deal. You can see that it makes complete financial sense to sign up with us to ensure that this year's crop is a big success. What do you say about joining the Nuhoma family?"

He was supremely confident that he had made a great presentation and this farmer would sign on the dotted line. He smiled smugly, waiting for Anderson's answer.

The farmer sat in silence for several minutes, quietly sipping his coffee, his piercing blue eyes gazing at the salesman. Joel had been working the land all of his life, and he had already heard about every sales pitch that promised to make him rich. That experience made him skeptical.

Finally he spoke, slowly and carefully. "Mr. Garner, my answer is no."

"No? You have got to be kidding! Didn't you hear how we are going to beat all competitive prices? We are guaranteeing that you will make more money than you ever have! Why would you say no?" he asked incredulously.

"Well sir," the big farmer said as he stood, signaling that the presentation was over, "for one thing, only the Lord provides a good crop, and He is the only one that knows what it will be like this year. Another thing is the deal sounds too good to be true. It's been my experience that when something sounds that good, run! Thanks for coming out to see me, but I need to get back to work. Have a blessed day!" He smiled and offered his hand to his guest.

Suddenly, Garner's smile was gone, replaced by a somewhat menacing leer. "You're making a very serious mistake, my friend. I'm going to give you a couple of days to think this over. I'm sure you will realize that this hasty decision is not the right one. Nuhoma is signing up farmers all over the Midwest who are convinced their offer is wonderful; you don't want to be left out, do you?" Garner asked, getting up to return to his truck.

"I've made my decision. You'll be wasting your time coming back. Goodbye." The big farmer turned and walked away.

Garner was dumbfounded! He hadn't encountered anyone this stubborn. He started his truck and jammed it angrily in gear and roared down the driveway. This was his first refusal, and the men at headquarters had said that they wanted the name and address of anyone that did not sign an agreement. He didn't know why they wanted the names, some kind of an exit poll or something, he supposed.

Late that night, a dark figure could be seen moving in the equipment building. Soon a yellow and orange glow was radiating from the building. A short time later, the building was completely engulfed in flames. Anderson tried to fight the fire as best he could, even sustaining some burn injuries, but everything was a total loss. This kind man, along with his frightened wife, knelt and prayed giving thanks to the Lord that their house and lives had been spared. He also asked for help in rebuilding.

The dark figure lurked in the shadows near the farm. When he got to his car that he had left parked about a mile down the country road, he made a call on his cell phone and said, "The job has been taken care of!"

Chapter Twenty-Five

Tuck had met with the rest of the team the night before in a new safe house. Everyone was too nervous about the old one having been compromised. Attending the meeting was a woman who went by the name of Mango. She was at the upper end of middle age and a little overweight. She was dressed in clothes that could have been taken off the rack at a Salvation Army store in the United States. Her dark brown hair and brown eyes attracted no attention, which was exactly why she was a very successful operative. Tuck had assigned her to follow Dorri wherever she went. She was the unseen person on the plane as Dorri flew around Europe before finally heading west on a 747 bound for the United States. The trip had been uneventful and upon arriving at Newark, she had returned to Iran knowing that the agency would have a person watching Dorri while she was in the United States.

"Is there anything else you can remember that might be helpful?" Tuck queried her.

"When I was walking down the aisle to use a restroom, I passed her seat while a flight attendant was talking to her. I think I heard the scientist say that she was going to Chicago to do some teaching at the University of Illinois. That agrees with the information the agency got from her visa application," Mango replied.

"Hmmmm. Well gals and gents, there's something about this woman that has got me spooked, no pun intended. She starts out as the head of the Biochemistry Department at the University of Tehran. Then, apparently she was astounded to find herself unceremoniously removed from the setting that she loves and shoved into the bowels of the old Agriculture building. Next, we find the new president of the nation of Iran paying her a personal call. They go out to lunch, and then she disappears from sight until we follow her to the United States. Why would the president of the new Persia send his chemist friend to the United States to lecture a bunch of college kids in Illinois? What's the connection?" he asked no one in particular.

"Do you think anyone else on board was following her?"

"I didn't see anyone that raised my hackles, but it would be a safe bet. She seems to be too important to let her run around the world on her own," Mango said.

Tuck thought silently for a moment and then asked Dog Bone, "Do you think our lady scientist is working for VEVAK or the Pasdaran?"

Dog Bone thought carefully before replying. "I don't think she is with the Pasdaran. They are mainly a terrorist organization operating overseas, and they have the added duty of being thought police here, making sure people follow the theocratic rules. These people are really dangerous, but she just doesn't seem to fit their objectives. VEVAK, as you know, is the intelligence gathering arm of the government. They are tough cookies, and you don't want to cross them if you can help it. But I can't see what use Dorri would be as an intelligence gathering operative. Although a lot of their people pose as students in foreign colleges and universities, which might be a reason for going to Chicago."

"No, people, there is more to this than just plain old country style espionage. I'll bet a Bud long neck that something else is going on. I have this awful feeling tugging at the back of my puny little mind that if we don't stop this, the United States will be in real danger!" Tuck exclaimed.

"Then we better get moving!" Lemon was almost shouting.

"Okay guys," Tuck said. "I think it's time for drastic

Chapter Twenty-Five

measures. We've got to get into that Ag building and poke around and see what we can find. We'll go in tonight. Lemon, I need you to go with me and take care of any alarms and safes that we might find. The rest of you will act as lookouts. Any trouble when we're inside, call the cell phone; we'll have 'em on vibrate. Now, how do we get in that fortress?"

"I have a friend that works as a janitor there, and he really likes money. I think I can get in touch with him and have him leave something open for us to crawl through. Give me five minutes and I should know something," Lemon said. In a couple of minutes, he was back and reported, "The price has gone up; he wants five thousand rials. He'll give us blueprints, but he will not open any door or windows for us. He says it is too dangerous. He was scared out of his mustache, just thinking of the idea. I guess we'll be on our own!"

Later, the rest of the gang of conspirators gathered around a blueprint of the building, studying the layout of rooms and halls, carefully mapping out routes of escape in case of trouble. The lab, of course, was not located on the blueprint because an office had been modified for Dorri's use. The friend had indicated where it should be and the quickest way to get there. They committed this information to memory.

"Well, our patriotic friend sure didn't put himself out for us, did he? How do we know that he isn't calling the police right now?" Tuck was getting grumpy. He was tired, and he hadn't been able to shake his headache since the attack. He also had noticed blood in his urine which worried him.

"I think we can trust him. He has always come through for me in the past. He is one of those guys that go from one government building to another, doing whatever janitorial work is needed. He says the best way to get into the building is by using a second story window at the southwest corner of the building. It's not supposed to be wired in the alarm system since it is above the first floor, but we'll still need to be careful. We get to the window by climbing a conveniently located tree.

"Pretty neat, huh!" Lemon exclaimed. He was young enough to still get excited about breaking into a secretive building by climbing a tree in the dead of night.

"Phooey!" Tuck harrumphed. "I'm too old to play Tarzan."

"Who?" Lemon asked.

"Never mind kid, you're too young to remember the guy. Okay team, here's the plan. We need as much time as possible to look for something we can use, so we are going in as soon as it's dark. I need all of you lookouts to be completely out of sight. Now, let's go over everything again," Tuck said, kneading his back where he had taken the wicked punch, which did not go unnoticed by some of the team.

"Are you going to be okay, Tuck?" Lemon asked. "You took a pretty bad beating, so it's okay if you are not up to hanging from trees! Peach and I can handle this little job with no sweat!"

"Nah, I'm okay," Tuck lied stubbornly. "The night air will do me good."

"You da man, boss!" Lemon chided playfully.

The team split up to get ready for a big evening the next night.

Night shadows were beginning to engulf the streets that surrounded the large Department of Agriculture building in downtown Tehran. Traffic was beginning to get lighter as most of the city had made their way home for the evening. Lemon was sitting on a bench at a bus stop one block away, glancing at a magazine that some transit rider had left behind. The young spy turned to the back of the publication to drift through the ads for assorted services available on the internet. These black market ads had a code of their own which only the well informed would know where to find what they were looking for, items such as perfumes, cosmetics, specialty wines, western DVD's, anything that the government had deemed forbidden for the people of Persia.

Chapter Twenty-Five

Lemon was not really interested in obtaining any black market articles, but he was interested in something forbidden. He and Tuck were going to do the unthinkable; they were going to attempt to break into this protected government building and try to obtain any data they could on what Dorri Golnessa was working on in its laboratory. They had learned that it had been especially equipped for her use. Now, they intended to get inside and find that lab and look for any documents that might give them a lead; they desperately needed something to go on.

Everyone was in place and waiting for Tuck's signal to go. Lemon saw an old, shabbily dressed peddler ambling slowly up the sidewalk in front of the Ag building. He carried a large roll of bread under his left arm, the signal for Lemon to meet him at the tree. The leaves of the tree were faintly reflecting the low light from the distant street light, giving it a distinctively sinister appearance as it seemed to rise up out of the darkness. Lemon glanced carefully around. He saw nothing that raised an alarm, so he rose, and walked casually across the street while pretending to read the magazine. Dog Bone was able to gain access to the roof of a building directly across the street from the Ag building, and from his vantage point, he could observe pedestrian and vehicle traffic on three streets. Peach was sitting in a dilapidated parked car on the street that Dog Bone could not see. Everyone was in place with their cell phones switched to vibrate so that their presence would not be betrayed by the sudden ring of an incoming call.

Tuck shuffled in the darkness ending up under the huge broadleaf tree and disappeared into the gloom where he could survey the windows of the building. Everything was dark except for an office in the basement at the southwest corner of the building. Since the lab was thought to be on the northeast corner of the second floor, he made the judgment call that the risk was worth taking. He activated the phone just long enough to make the other team's phones jump, then moved even further into the shadows waiting for Lemon, who appeared out of the gloom in less than a minute. Both of them studied the tree and the access that it gave them to the second floor window.

"I sure do hope you brought a glass cutter!" Tuck exclaimed quietly.

"What kind of burglar do you think I am? An amateur?" Lemon asked jokingly.

"Okay, my young friend, let's get up this tree and see how easily and quietly you can get us in that window."

Good fortune was smiling on them to some degree because there were lower limbs growing out of the now friendly tree that enabled them to climb effortlessly. Reaching the window, Lemon took several minutes to carefully examine it. The window was in two parts, with twelve small panels of framed glass in each section. Using a mini Maglite that he held in his mouth, the young spy looked for any wiring of an alarm system, but found nothing. The locking mechanism was very old and would be easily unlocked when a small pane of glass was removed.

While Lemon was removing the small plate of glass, Tuck was still struggling up the tree, grunting in pain every time he lifted himself up on one of the limbs. He hadn't wanted to admit it, but that kidney blow he had received was really causing him unbearable pain. Just as he got even with the window, Lemon removed the glass, unlocked and raised the lower half of the window, and stepped easily inside. Tuck followed as quietly as he could, but he still made more noise than either of them thought was helpful.

Inside the room, they quickly put their flashlights to work examining the entire space, being very careful to never let the light come close to the window. It seemed that the blueprints were not exactly accurate; the room's only purpose seemed to be storage. The chamber had the smell that all such places have: the smell of dust, decaying paper, and very little stale air. It

Chapter Twenty-Five

held a large number of locked metal file cabinets which needed examining. While Lemon went to work on them, Tuck opened the office door to look down the dark hallway. He listened for a few seconds and heard only the usual sounds of an old building, small creaks and popping sounds as the structure cooled from the heat of the day. Tuck was rather pleased that he did not hear anything else. He padded over to the nearest door and opened it to discover that he had stumbled onto the very room they were looking for. They found a very well equipped laboratory. He noted that this place was windowless, so he felt reasonably safe in turning on a small desk lamp. The light blinded him momentarily, but he was soon able to peer around what seemed to be a well stocked lab. The equipment held little interest for him, but he examined it closely. What Tuck really wanted to find were files that contained some notes or drawings, anything that would help them in their investigation. He saw nothing! On closer examination, the room looked as if it had been recently cleaned. *Rats!* he exclaimed to himself. *The devils are way ahead of us.*

As he continued inspecting the equipment, the tables and benches they were sitting on, and the floor underneath, he couldn't see anything that resembled a clue. Carelessly, he leaned against a plain looking box, which, yielding to his weight, scraped across the floor, moving a few inches from the wall. On a whim, he aimed his flashlight behind the box and saw what looked like kernels of grain, and a dead mouse. He failed to detect anything unusual about an old building having mice, so he continued his explorations. Tuck made a thorough examination of the room, which failed to yield even one scrap of paper. There were no logbooks, no computers or computer disks; nothing.

He finally decided that this whole caper was a waste of time and walked carefully out of the lab back to the file room, hoping that Lemon was having better results with his lock picking. Suddenly, he quietly snapped his fingers in frustration while shaking his head and went back into the lab and shut the light off. *You idiot, you're going to get us all killed!* he berated himself. Then he froze; all of his senses were alerted! He thought he had heard something. He listened intently, holding his breath, trying to hear over the pounding of his heart. He rushed back into the file room with a speed that surprised him, and charged right into a vicious chokehold and was thrown to the floor with a hand over his mouth. Fear and surprise paralyzed him for just a second while he frantically tried to grab his Browning as he used his other arm to try and break the grip around his throat.

"Dang it, Tuck, will you be quiet? Someone's coming down the hall," Lemon whispered in his ear while slowly releasing him.

Tuck was instantly furious! He could only see a shadow in the dark, but he was going to give this kid the thrashing of his life. He stopped suddenly when he heard what sounded like panting in the hall and the faint squeaking sound of rubber soles on marble.

"It's probably a night watchman making his rounds. Get over here behind this cabinet," Lemon's whisper could barely be heard.

They crouched down and held their breath while at the same time preparing themselves to attack the intruder if he came into the room. It sounded like someone was rattling doors to make sure they were locked. Tuck's heart skipped a beat; *Did the door to the lab have a self locking mechanism, or had he left it carelessly unlocked?* The footsteps meandering down the hall toward them abruptly stopped. They could hear the rattling of a doorknob, then nothing. Tuck was cursing himself because the silence could only mean that he had left the door unlocked. Unexpectedly, the man continued on his rounds, walking toward the room where the two agents were hiding. Tuck let his breath slowly escape.

The footsteps and the loud panting came closer. Without

Chapter Twenty-Five

warning, the door to their hiding place was thrust open and the beam of a flashlight swept the room. It looked like they were going to be safe since the intruder did not raise an alarm. Suddenly, as if by accident, his flashlight swept over the window, which was closed. The glare of light stopped on the missing pane of glass. The watchman walked carelessly into the room to examine the window closer, looking intently at the windowsill. Suddenly, he knelt on the floor and used an old policeman's trick of holding the flashlight beam about an inch above the marble floor. This technique has been used by generations of cops to see footprints in the dust, and it was just as effective tonight. Their shoeprints were now plainly visible! This guy was obviously an ex-cop who now had the scent of a criminal in his nostrils. He moved in the direction of the cabinet where the two operatives were cowering. Tuck had his Browning in his hand ready for instant use while Lemon crouched like a lion stalking game. He remained without a weapon, but you could almost hear his muscles coil; ready to spring. Lemon suddenly exploded into action, charging the dark figure advancing toward them, hitting the man with all of his weight, knocking him to the floor where he began pummeling him with punches. The watchman crashed to the floor, knocking the air out of his lungs. Gasping for breath, he tried to defend himself from the flurry of blows raining down on his head. Lemon tried to regain his feet, just as Tuck arrived to deliver a blow on the man's head with the barrel of the automatic. The watchman tried to scream, but grew silent, lying completely still; his breathing shallow and hesitant. Their lights revealed that he was bleeding profusely where Tuck had hit him just above the left temple. Tuck silently gave thanks to someone that the blow had missed the temple, which had saved the man's life.

"God in heaven, thank you for helping us!" Lemon prayed with great emotion.

"Well, we've stepped in it now!" Tuck exclaimed. "We've got to get out of here right now!" Tuck exclaimed as he reached over and checked the guy's carotid artery and found a pulse. "Thank you," he whispered a prayer to no one in particular.

He just wasn't in the mood to kill somebody so he was glad the guy was alive. After all, the poor slob was innocent, just doing his job. He grabbed his Voyager and asked, "Clear?"

"Clear," came back immediately.

They were out of the window in less than thirty seconds and walking down separate streets. They would meet at the new safe house in about hour and go over this botched break-in. Tuck was shaking and his kidney was planning a revolution; the pain was about to take him down. What a lousy mess! Someone was probably alerting the authorities this very minute, and they didn't have one single piece of evidence to help their investigation.

An hour later, they were all gathered in the safe house going through their own debriefing.

Tuck looked at Dog Bone and Peach and asked, "Do you think anyone saw us going in?"

"No evidence of it; no lights came on and no cars pulled up outside," Peach said, somewhat sadly.

"I didn't see anything either," Dog Bone added.

"Lemon, tell me you found something in those files," Tuck urged. This young man had risen immeasurably in his eyes after the dust up in the office.

"The few files that I was able to look at had absolutely no information. It kind of looked like everything dealing with the lab in the last six months has been destroyed. Sorry, my friend." He was acting like he was blaming himself for the failure of the mission.

Tuck would have none of it. He walked over and put his arm around the young man and said, "Hey, don't be so hard on yourself. It was just plain ole bad luck!"

"Yeah, I know, but I sure feel lousy."

"Well I didn't find anything either, just a little grain in a corner along with a dead mouse," Tuck exclaimed, absent-

Chapter Twenty-Five

mindedly rubbing his rebelling kidney. The pain was a nine on a scale of one to ten.

It was quiet for a minute. Lemon raised his head and looked at Tuck and asked, "What did you say?"

"What?" Tuck asked, not really paying attention.

"What did you say about a mouse?" Lemon inquired again.

"I said that all I found was some grain in the corner and a dead mouse. Why?" Tuck was looking at him with a quizzical expression on his face.

"Labs are kept super clean all the time. They even have cabinets with HEPA filters that cleanse the air where they store their testing materials. Where did grain come from?" Lemon was sitting up straight and was obviously excited.

"Good point, my friend, dang good point," Tuck agreed.

"We've got to go back in and get that grain and the little ole mouse!" Lemon raised his voice as he got up and started for the door.

"Wait, wait!" Tuck shouted as he tried to grab Lemon, but dropped instead to his knees in agonizing pain that brought a moan from his lips and tears to his eyes.

Lemon rushed back to kneel by Tuck and asked, "What is it, Tuck?"

"This lousy kidney, I'm afraid I'm done for tonight. Besides, you can't go back in there after all this time. They must have found the watchman by now, and the place will be crawling with cops!"

"Maybe he was the only guy in there, and he is still sleeping quietly. We can go back and just take a look. We have to, Tuck! This might be our only lead," Without waiting for Tuck to respond, he motioned for Dog Bone and Peach to follow him as he hurried out of the door.

Tuck tried to protest, but before he could get a word out, the door had closed behind the team. He looked outside, and thankfully, it was pitch dark, so his people would still have some cover. He crawled to a bed and yowled with pain as he struggled to lie down. He put his automatic on a chair and reached for his Voyager LG and entered the secret codes on the touch screen that would hook him up to a secure frequency from a spy satellite and connect him to Langley. He had no idea what the time was in the United States, but Herb answered almost immediately.

"Tuck, for crying out loud, what the heck is going on over there? Have you guys lost your minds?" Herb shouted into the phone making Tuck winch with this new unpleasantness.

"Easy, Herb, easy. We're all okay, except for me. My kidney has got me down, but the other guys are out getting us some evidence."

"Evidence? What kind of evidence?"

"A dead mouse," Tuck responded, smiling wickedly. Nothing came over the secure line except silence, but in his mind's eye he could see Herb's face, which he imagined was beet red.

"Tuck, I want you to come home right away. You've obviously lost your pea pick'n mind!" Herb was exasperated, and Tuck could hear him wheezing like a steam engine.

"Take it easy, will ya? We think we might have found something. The lab was super clean except for a little grain in a corner and a dead mouse. My guys are going to try and get back in there and retrieve the grain and the mouse. Then we can have your staff analyze it in the lab and see what we've got. It may be nothing," Tuck informed his superior.

"What do you mean you're going to try and get the mouse? Why didn't you get it when you were in the building?" Herb asked.

"Sorry, Herb, but we ran into some trouble and had to beat a hasty retreat."

There was silence again, and then Herb said very quietly, "You don't mean to tell me that your guys are going back in there? The place will be crawling with cops!"

Chapter Twenty-Five

"Sorry again, ole partner, but I couldn't stop them. They should be there now. If you are a praying guy, Herb, it would be a good time to send one up for protection. These people are as brave as any I have ever worked with."

"When you see 'em, tell 'em Semper Fi for me!" Tuck could hear a small catch in the big guy's voice. "Call me the minute they get back," he said, and then he added, "If they get back!" The line went dead. Tuck closed his eyes and tried to relax, but the kidney kept telling him that he had better get to a doctor as soon as he could.

About the time that Tuck broke the connection to Langley, Lemon and Dog Bone were back at the Ag building, carefully watching for any sign of movement inside the building. All was quiet, and there were no signs of anyone around. They had to hurry since dawn was only an hour away. Lemon went up the tree to the second floor like a cat chasing a bird. Dog Bone struggled to keep up with him, but he was not as agile so he battled from limb to limb.

Lemon got to the window and found it still open. He tumbled inside, and fell on the body of the watchman, who was still crumpled on the floor where they had left him. When Dog Bone came through the window, he stumbled over the body and lurched back, pushing a desk, which made a horrible screeching noise. They listened expectantly, but there was no sound of danger or an alarm. The man moaned pitifully, but they ignored him and moved towards the lab.

"Stay here and keep a sharp eye out," Lemon said to Dog Bone, who wasn't all that excited about staying in the room with the guy on the floor who might wake up at any minute.

Lemon was out the door and into the lab, moving like a shadow. A quick search of the corners revealed the little pile of grain and the dead mouse that was suddenly the center of attention for people spanning two continents. Pulling a plastic bag from his jacket, he scooped up the hopeful evidence and the deceased rodent, sealed the top, and headed back out of the door. In the hall, he was frightened by a door slamming somewhere in the building. Rushing into the file room, he motioned Dog Bone to get out the window pronto. He dived out the window head first, catching the first branch that hit him and slid to the ground. They wasted no time by looking around, leaving the scene in different directions.

In a few minutes, they were back at the safe house, pausing to catch their breath. They searched for Tuck, finding him on a bed, moaning like the man in the Ag building.

"Oh dear Lord, what is it, Tuck?" Lemon asked as he kneeled by the bed. "How can we help you?"

"Did you get the stuff and Mr. Mouse?" Tuck asked grimacing with pain.

Lemon held up the plastic bag for Tuck to see. Tuck smiled and said, "Get that bag to the border by courier and on the diplomatic pouch to Washington as fast as you can," He mumbled and then promptly passed out.

Dog Bone grabbed the bag and headed out the door. "I'll make it to Baghdad by morning, and our sample should be in Langley by tomorrow evening."

Lemon stopped him, and looked deeply into his eyes and said, "Godspeed, my friend."

Dog Bone smiled and winked, gave the thumbs up sign, and was promptly gone.

Lemon went into the bedroom where Peach was mopping Tuck's brow with a cold rag. "He's burning up with fever. We've got to get him to a doctor, and I mean right now!"

Lemon called a friend on his cell by giving a coded message that informed the person on the receiving end to bring a car to the safe house. While they waited, he got a secure line and called Langley. He gave Herb all of the information that they had and when to expect the mouse to be delivered by diplomatic pouch. He also gave him an update on Tuck. He tried to sound positive, but he knew he wasn't fooling Herb for one minute. He hung up the phone and knelt on the floor

Chapter Twenty-Five

and prayed, "Dear Lord, please protect Dog Bone and Tuck. They both are going to need you in the next few hours." Then he went into the bedroom to keep a cool cloth on Tuck and wait for the car.

Chapter Twenty-Six

Dorri was brought instantly out of a horrendous nightmare by someone pounding on her door. It took her several seconds to remember where she was, so the pounding began again.

"Yes, what is it?" she demanded sleepily.

"It's Steve. Come on, it's time to get up. We have to get you over to the university and make the arrangements for you to get settled in," he said without any hint of friendliness.

"Give me half an hour to get cleaned up and dressed."

"Okay, but hurry as fast as you can, we've got to get out of here," Steve grumbled as he walked away from the door.

Dorri got slowly out of bed and tried to get oriented. The nightmare was still rolling around in her mind and was hindering her concentration on the things she needed to do. She took a quick sponge bath, ran a brush through her hair, and applied her limited makeup. As she looked at her image in the mirror, she noticed that the scars on her face were scarlet. This always happened when she was upset so she took an extra minute to apply more makeup to make them less noticeable. *Less noticeable; that's a laugh! Thank you, my dear dead father!* she thought to herself bitterly.

Even though she was now in America, she thought it best to dress in flowing clothing in case Steve decided to report her as going Western in her dress. She had no doubt that Steve was the person who had been assigned to watch her during this part of her trip, and she didn't want anything to happen that would cause the Pasdaran to descend on her and drag her back to Persia.

Chapter Twenty-Six

She went out into the warehouse and looked out the windows and noticed that the weather outside was rainy and blustery. Having been born in a desert country, it naturally felt awfully cold to her. She found Steve waiting for her at the makeshift laboratory. She hesitated as she noticed that everyone else seemed to have left. There was not another person in sight, and she was disappointed since she wanted to talk to Ellis and Vic regarding the experiments with the rats.

"Where is everyone?" she asked without looking at Steve.

"They've already left to get started on the plan. Come on, let's get to the car and get out of here," Steve said.

"Please, wait a minute. I need to check on the experiments with the rats. It will only take a minute. I hope they're still here," she muttered as she went to the section of the lab where she had last seen the rats. Spotting the cages, she walked quickly up to them. As she looked inside, she could not stifle the scream that rose in her throat.

"They are all DEAD!" she shrieked.

Steve, who was waiting about fifty feet away, was startled by her scream and came running up to her and yelled, "Who's dead?"

"The rats, you fool! The rats! They're all dead! What happened to them?" she bleated.

"I dunno, I think they ate some of the treated grain and just kicked the bucket!" Steve exclaimed.

Dorri had no idea what he meant by the rats kicking a bucket, but the sight of these dead animals made her stomach coil into a knot. Something had gone terribly wrong. She should have run tests on animals, but there just hadn't been enough time. There was a very real danger that if any of the treated grain got mixed somehow with grain for human consumption, thousands of people could die! The horror of it was more than she could cope with, and she collapsed on the floor, weeping uncontrollably.

Steve thought that this strange woman had lost her mind and

instantly was considering what he was going to do with her.

"What's the matter with you, have you gone crazy?" he yelled at her.

"Shut up, you fool! Do you have any brains at all, or are you as stupid as you look? If people eat that grain after it's been treated, THEY ARE GOING TO DIE!" Dorri screamed at this mindless oaf that she had been sentenced to work with.

Steve was now in a rage and would have killed her, but he was unsure how that would be received in Tehran. He was not going to let a woman call him a fool, so he rushed at her with the intent of giving her the beating of her life, and, as he looked at her on the floor with her clothing revealing that she was indeed a shapely woman, he decided he might do more than just hit her. As he reached her and turned her over so that he could smash his fist into her disfigured face, she sprang to her feet with the fury of a tigress. In her hand she held a small but a very deadly looking knife that she had taken from her purse when she thought that Steve was going to kill her. Steve had not noticed her small purse, and was completely surprised by the steely coolness of his intended victim. He slid to a stop and then jumped back out of her reach.

"If you touch me, President Faridoon will have you tortured in ways that you have never imagined!" Dorri hissed with the calm finality of a cobra preparing to strike.

"Okay, okay, take it easy, will ya? But you had better stop calling me a fool, or I just might want to try to take that knife away from you. This is Chicago! I could always tell the president that you got mugged and killed, and he would never ask any questions. What are you getting all worked up about anyway? Who cares if Americans get killed? Good riddance, I say." Steve was trying to stall for time so that he could figure out what he should do.

Dorri was consumed with hatred for this filthy minded imbecile. She knew what he was thinking as he charged at her; she had seen that look in a man's eyes before, and she was

Chapter Twenty-Six

determined that she was not going to be hurt by another man without him paying an awful price for his indiscretion. She had to get out of this terrible place and get where there were people that could help her. Dorri was so frightened that she couldn't think logically, but she knew that she had to get her bluff in, as she had heard Americans say on the television.

"Call me a taxi, I'm going to the university immediately," she demanded.

"You don't need a cab. I'm not supposed to let you out of my sight; I'll drive you."

"You're not driving me anywhere. Follow behind the taxi if you want, but I am not getting into a car with you under any circumstances. Now, call me that taxi!" she yelled at him as she advanced toward him with the knife aimed at his gut.

"Okay, okay, take it easy," Steve gave in. He walked back to the room that had served as his office to make the call. Dorri was two paces behind him watching every move he made. He glanced at the phone book and made a call, giving the address of the warehouse. He hung up the receiver and turned to her and said, "They'll be here in about twenty minutes."

Dorri was not sure how she was going to get her luggage, but she certainly wasn't going to turn her back on this man that was seething with anger.

Finally, Steve said, "We had better wait outside so the cab can see us, or he will probably not stop. This isn't the best neighborhood, you know."

"Lead the way, oh, and let's go by my room so you can get my luggage and carry it out like a good boy," Dorri said and immediately regretted her spurt of courage. Steve's eyes were blazing, deadly pits, and she feared that she had pushed him too far. Instead, she followed him to her room, and he grudgingly gathered her luggage and carried her things to the door. It was a swirling rainy morning. The porch gave them some shelter, but she was glad to see a blue and white Lakeside taxi turn the corner and pull up in front of where they stood.

She got in the back seat while the driver, a big, but friendly looking man, put her things in the trunk. As they drove away, she told the driver that she wanted to go to the University of Illinois on Roosevelt Road off I-90. She sank back in the seat and began to cry softly as the tension slowly left her body. Turning and looking out the back window, she saw that Steve was following them. What she did not notice was an old Chevy Bel Air that pulled out of an alley following both cars.

As they wove their way through the heavy traffic, Dorri's mind was numb with fear for her safety. She also worried about what could happen to thousands of innocent people because of the research she had conducted for her country and its president, who she now felt had betrayed her. There was no doubt that Steve was reporting in on his cell phone, and she could only imagine the orders that he would receive on how to handle her. *What was she going to do? How was she going to get out of this alive? If she turned herself in to someone, surely the Americans would kill her for what she had inflicted on them.* While she was wallowing in self-pity, she did not notice that the driver was glancing at her in the rear view mirror.

"Are you all right, lady?" he asked quietly.

"Yes, I'm fine, thank you. It's been kind of a bad day," she replied.

"That guy back there giving you a hard time?" He asked with what sounded like genuine concern.

"Well, he's not the finest example of manhood that I've ever met," she said with venom.

"Want me to take you to a police station? He won't bother you there," the cabbie asked.

"No, thank you, I'll be safe at the university. But I do appreciate your concern," she said with genuine gratitude. She noticed his kind, light blue eyes looking at her from beneath shaggy eye brows. He probably was a very good husband and father.

"No problem!"

Chapter Twenty-Six

As they moved onto the interstate, neither of them paid the slightest bit of attention to a convoy of three bulk grain haulers heading for the docks.

When they arrived at the university, the driver stopped in front of the administration building. Getting out, he got Dorri's luggage from the trunk and carried them in for her, which pleased her immensely. This cab driver was the first gentleman she had met in weeks. As they walked up the sidewalk, she noticed the cabbie turn around and look long and hard at Steve in his car while he was pulling to a stop behind them. While this lady was in his care, no creep had better try any funny stuff, and that was exactly the impression that Steve got when he looked at the cabbie's face. He pulled away and parked in a nearby lot to watch what was going to happen.

Inside the office, Dorri took out some money and placed it in the big taxi driver's hand while looking him in his eyes and said, "Thank you so very much for your kindness to me today."

"You're most welcome, little lady," he said as he took her hand and pressed it gently. He touched the brim of his cap, smiled, and was gone.

She looked around the offices and was taken aback by the grandeur of the building. It was beautiful, full of wonderful wooden panels, pastel colored ceilings, brass sconces that radiated a soft yellow glow that made the room seem warm and cozy in stark contrast to the rainy weather outside. The young woman at the reception desk smiled warmly and asked her if she could be of help. Dorri gave her name, stating that she was from Persia, here to take part in a cultural exchange program.

"Why, that's absolutely marvelous!" the young woman gushed. "Please take a seat and I'll let the Dean of Student Affairs know that you are here," Dorri sat in a plush red leather chair and continued to admire the beauty of the room. In a short time, a tall, gray haired woman with a pleasant, patient

Edge of Disaster

face walked towards her.

"Miss Golnessa? Hello, my name is Ellen DeFry. I am the Dean of Student Affairs and the cultural exchange program is my responsibility. We are so very proud to have you with us for the next few months, and we can hardly wait to hear about your work in biochemistry. We have a nice apartment for you in the married student's dorm; I think you will be very comfortable there. I'll have someone take you to your room now, so that you can rest and freshen up a little, then I will give you a personal tour of the campus."

"Thank you for your kindness. I'm sure the arrangements will be most agreeable," Dorri said. She was impressed by the warmth of her reception from this place that her country was intent on destroying.

Outside, the old Bel Air pulled out of the parking lot and headed off campus. It only had one windshield wiper working so even if anyone wanted to, looking at the driver was impossible.

Chapter Twenty-Seven

International transmissions of secure diplomatic traffic between Persia and its embassies around the globe increased to such a high level that those working in the communication offices were rapidly approaching burnout. The world had never seen such an urgency to form global alliances as it was witnessing now. Agreements that normally took years of negotiations were completed in a matter of days. President Faridoon's diplomatic corps were working at a frenetic pace, fueled by the youth of the diplomats and their total disregard of how things have traditionally been done.

The young diplomats had been instructed concerning the details of the alliance and the many benefits to participating nations. First was a continual supply of commodities such as wheat, corn, soybeans and barley. These commodities will be priced at 30% of the prevailing world market prices. The second was that crude oil will always be supplied at rates lower than current OPEC prices. Third, payment for these commodities can be in cash or in raw materials; however, all of the interested nation's raw materials must be shipped exclusively to Persia. There were two requirements for a nation to join the alliance. First, there had to be a signed agreement between the two nations, detailing which commodities were needed and how payment was to be made. Second, each nation joining the alliance would pledge to support the nation of Persia in all world political decisions, including any and all issues that might be brought to a vote in the United Nations.

There was also a very unique requirement that Persia's ambassadors were instructed to follow. They were to negotiate only with the president of the country, circumventing the normal processes of dealing with the nation's State Department. If there was any resistance to this unusual diplomatic process, President Faridoon interceded personally by calling the president or, on several occasions, by flying to the country and meeting with their leader face to face. In all of these meetings, Faridoon's charisma prevailed, and the country fell into line by happily becoming members of the alliance.

The world looked on in amazement as country after country joined the Persian Alliance. In the first two months, seven African nations signed agreements: Western Sahara, Mauritania, Mali, Senegal, Guinea, Sierra Leone and Sudan.

Guatemala, El Salvador, Honduras, and Costa Rica joined from Central America. They were followed by Haiti and the Dominican Republic from the Caribbean, and Laos and Cambodia from Southeast Asia. This brought a total of fifteen nations agreeing with the Persian president and his design for the future of the world.

Before the ink was dry on the latest agreement, giant freighters with cargoes of grain were already at sea with courses set for western African ports for off loading. More freighters were being loaded on Lake Michigan and New Orleans destined for Central America and Southeast Asia. President Faridoon was fulfilling his part of the agreements reached in forming the new Persian Alliance, which would very soon be described as the new Persian Empire.

President Faridoon was busy getting ready to implement another part of the grand plan, convincing the members of OPEC to cut production and raise prices. That meeting was scheduled for the next day in Zurich, and he had asked permission to address the heads of state from the world's oil producing nations. He would have reams of documents supporting his ideas, but he was putting emphasis on what he felt would be a common thread among nations: their love of American money, but their public or private hatred

Chapter Twenty-Seven

of the United States.

The intercom on his desk buzzed, demanding immediate attention.

"Yes," he responded. He loved hearing Afsoon's voice almost as much as he loved seeing her. He believed that he was falling in love with her, and their secret trysts convinced him that she would make an excellent queen someday. She was particularly skilled at stroking his ego and making him feel like she worshipped him.

People worshipping him now seemed to be a perfectly natural thing. Perhaps he would make it mandatory someday when he controlled the world. But the intercom again interrupted his daydreaming.

"Your Excellency, there is a Mr. Diablo here to see you. He says it is very important," Afsoon, his private secretary, said with just a hint of concern in her voice.

Arastoo was irritated. The constant acclaim and near worship by millions of people around the world had certainly enlarged his ego and his feeling of superior self importance. He believed that he no longer needed to rely on this overbearing man who had helped him gain his current exalted position. "Send him in," he responded gruffly.

The door opened, and the familiar tall man with the looks of a TV star walked in and sat down in a maroon leather chair across from the huge, new desk that Arastoo had recently installed. His office had been completely remodeled into the most opulent office in the Middle East. Diablo was dressed casually in a light blue polo shirt and tan slacks with light brown shoes. This manner of dress was considered by the president to be a personal affront to him and his office, which caused his mood to darken even more. He forced a smile and asked, "What is the reason for this pleasant surprise?" He purposely refrained from the little bow that had become his custom when meeting this man.

"I wanted to inform you that I have taken steps to

ensure that your ideas are well received tomorrow. Are you comfortable with the data you have?" he asked.

"Thank you for your assistance in this very important meeting. Yes, I am prepared to make the presentation of my proposal. Actually, I feel quite good about how it will be received. Since the invasion of Iraq, world revulsion for the tactics of the United States has continued to climb," Arastoo responded. He had not noticed his slip of the tongue saying it was his proposal, but it had not escaped Mr. Diablo, whose face darkened ever so slightly.

"But this is an election year in America and both of the leading candidates are promoting their determination to remove all troops from Iraq on the day they take office. Why wouldn't this cause OPEC leaders to take a wait and see attitude?" Diablo inquired.

"The leaders that I have spoken with consider all of the American presidential candidates to be weak and unimpressive. This will give them even more reason to be emboldened to agree with my plan and join us in removing the United States as an economic world leader." There was the error again.

"I am sure that you are right in your assessment. I would like to bring up a point for you to consider when meeting with these leaders. Except for that oaf Chavez in Venezuela, most of the people you will be meeting with are kings of their countries and are used to being treated as such by others. They have a disdain for those who have been elected by popular vote of their people. Nothing causes them more horror than the thought of a popular, free election by their people. My advice is this; do not treat these kings as if they are equals; treat them with reverence and they will be more likely to listen to your presentation." Diablo sat back in his chair smiling, and made a great show of lighting a huge Cuban cigar, knowing the reaction this disrespect would generate.

The president of the Persian Empire leaped to his feet, his face red and contorted with rage. "What do you mean, treat

Chapter Twenty-Seven

them with reverence? They are not gods to be worshipped! I shall treat them as equals and nothing more. They will listen to me because my plan is commendable, one that will make them even richer than they already are," he fumed.

As he had done before, he referred to *my* plan instead of *our* plan. This had not escaped the attention of his guest. His visitor rose slowly and moved around the desk, stopping when his face was inches from Faridoon's. He took a long draw from the expensive cigar and blew it into the president's face, flicking some ash on his desk. Then he did something that he had never done before in Arastoo's presence, he removed his sunglasses. Persia's president was shocked to see blazing yellow eyes staring at him in such a manner that it made him desperate to find a way of escape! Any religious man in the world would have gone screaming into the night if they had been confronted with those eyes. But Arastoo, with no religious training of any kind, had no idea who or what he was dealing with.

"Sit down, Faridoon!" Diablo ordered menacingly while replacing the Oakley glasses.

"Yes sir, Mr. Diablo," the president responded with a shaking voice. Both hands exhibited a noticeable tremor.

The tall visitor, who had just put the president of Persia in his place, seated himself once again in the soft maroon leather chair.

"You seem to want to break off our arrangement, and push me out of our plan for world economic power. You need to listen to me and have a perfect understanding about something. Do I have your undivided attention?" Diablo asked with a humorless smile on his lips.

"I assure you that I am listening to every word you say."

"You need to remember that it was my power and finances that have changed you from an unknown economic professor, in a sub world-class university in a third rate country, into the president of a growing global power, adored by millions.

Can you possibly be so dense as to believe that you no longer require my help, nor want me by your side? Well, my friend, be assured that I can, and will, replace you in an instant if I so choose! And if I do replace you, your soul will be required of you immediately. Let me rephrase that since you are not a spiritual man, you will die! Now, do you finally realize the magnitude of what you are involved in?" he asked.

"Mr. Diablo, I do understand and I beg your forgiveness. I offer you my thanks and gratitude and pledge to you that I will never forget my place again!" Arastoo said with downcast eyes.

"Excellent! You have used good judgment. Now, I know that you have more preparations to get ready for your trip, so I will leave, but I remind you that I have prepared the members to be receptive to our ideas. If they become unsupportive there can be only one reason: you made a mess of things!" He stood, smiled and walked across the luxurious blue carpet to the door and left, leaving the door open as a final gesture of indifference.

Arastoo sat at his desk and reviewed what had just happened in his mind. *Who in the world am I dealing with? Who is this Diablo?* he asked himself. One thing he did know was that this man was dangerous. But to his folly, his ego kept him from fully understanding just how dangerous the man really was. Instead, in his brilliant mind, he began to ponder ways of getting rid of the problem. He would spend some time with Shaheen and see what they could come up with. Things were going too good to be spoiled now by a turf battle with a guy with deformed eyes!

Chapter Twenty-Eight

Roshan Norwall, the chairman of the Nuhoma Corporation, was sitting at his desk in Des Moines reviewing spreadsheets on his computer. He could not help smiling at his good fortune. He had this great job that paid him a small fortune, and all he had to do was spend money! He filed reports on a headquarters web site in Zurich. He had never met anyone involved in the upper echelon of Nuhoma. All of his communication was via the Internet or the telephone, and those contacts were just reporting that they were sending him the money he was requesting to further the business.

Nuhoma's commodity brokers were buying wheat, corn, and soybeans daily on the Chicago and Kansas City Boards of Trade and their constant purchases at higher prices were already producing a ripple effect of higher prices for commodities and meat products. This practice did cause Norwall to wonder privately why anyone would want to keep paying higher costs for a commodity when their own buying practices were behind the rise in prices. But this mystery did not cause him to lose any sleep, nor was he disturbed that many businesses throughout the country were beginning to suffer. He couldn't possibly care less!

Roshan had a business reputation of being a slash and burn artist. He and his partners made a fortune by breaking up a company while he made a vast salary for himself. When bankruptcy or the sale of a company mercifully ended the hemorrhaging, he and his partners simply stepped in to buy up the parts of the company they wanted dirt cheap. The business world considered him to be a takeover speculator, often buying into a company under the guise of saving it, but that was never the intention. The sole purpose was to make him rich! The fact that thousands of people had lost their jobs and retirement benefits meant nothing to him. That was their problem. He considered such people to be stupid and there for the fleecing, so to speak.

Now, this new, rich, fat plum had come into his life, begging to be picked! In his second week on the job, he had seen the tremendous possibilities. He quickly set up dummy transportation companies that began billing Nuhoma for the hauling of nonexistent grain to the company's elevators. He paid confederates at both elevators a tidy sum to adjust the books to show receiving the shadow shipments and include them on their statements. His greed required a never-ending increase in ill-gotten gain. He was putting the final touches on a plan to have his shadow companies include barge traffic on the Mississippi. The opportunities for huge profits was amazing, due to the tremendous additional tonnage that could be shipped by barge verses truck. It would not take much to work out a scheme to cheat on the grain shipments by rail, which could be the mother lode of them all. Yes, he certainly was in high cotton!

Norwall was certainly classified as a genius in profiting from a company's financial problems, but this new company was different somehow. No one seemed to be running the business or paying attention to the cash outlays. Just the thought of taking this lamb to the slaughter caused him to perspire badly.

Roshan was a genius in money matters, but socially he was a loner. Being in his early thirties should have made his life an example of success, but it was not. He had no friends and didn't mourn the loss. After money, Roshan worshipped his god at the dinner table. Relatively short in stature, he tipped the scales at more than three hundred and fifty pounds, and he was still gaining. Sparse bristles of hair were scattered on his

Chapter Twenty-Eight

head, above two small sunken light gray eyes and great falling jowls gave him a distinctive porker countenance. Adding to his unpleasant looks was his problem with perspiration. His clothes were continually wet and great beads of sweat flowed down his face in such quantities that only a constant wiping of his face with a towel allowed him to see at all.

The phone on Norwall's desk buzzed him out of his mental counting of the money he was going to embezzle.

"Yes, Miss Lattel, what is it?" he snorted into the phone.

"There is a call from Zurich for you, Mr. Norwall," she reported. She hated her boss, but her age and her handicap of requiring a cane to walk made finding work very difficult. So she kept working in the office while praying that she would not have to see him much during the day.

Mashing a button on the desk phone, he attempted to smile and sound pleasant on the phone. He failed miserably. "Hello Zurich! How is everything on the continent?" It irritated him that he never knew whom he was talking to; no introductions had ever been made.

"The continent's fine. We have questions about the report that you posted. There seems to be a problem getting farmers to sign contracts with us. Why is that?" the caller asked bluntly, without emotion.

"Well, sir, these farmers are an independent lot, set in their ways. Many prefer to remain with companies who have bought their grain for years, sometimes generations," he responded while mopping his face with a soaked handkerchief.

"We're not particularly interested in excuses. Part of your job is to see that we get those contracts. What plan do you have for increasing productivity in this area?" the voice asked.

"We are going to raise our purchase price another percentage point as an additional incentive."

"Raise it ten percent if necessary, just get those contracts!" the voice was beginning to sound harsh, which made Roshan nervous.

"Sir, that's a lot of money wasted if we don't need to offer that much," he squealed.

"Just do it! I hope I don't have to call again and tell you how to do your job. Make it plain to them that refusal might not be in their best interest. Do you understand?"

"Yes, I understand perfectly. Retraining of the sales staff will begin today." He was blinded by sweat.

"There's one more thing. How is the sensitive project coming? Have the starter seeds arrived?"

"They are here, and our lab is in the process of making more batches. But, sir, I have never been given a heads up as to the purpose of this grain. What do you want me to do with the stuff?"

The voice was now shouting at him, "We don't want YOU to do anything. There will be a man named Smith there tomorrow; he will be in charge of the program. All you have to do is to have enough cash on hand to pay the special workers $2500 each. They have already been paid the same amount, and this will be their final payment. Pay 'em and get rid of 'em!"

"Yes, sir, I'll take care of it, don't worry. Is there anything else?" he asked.

"I have nothing else; goodbye." The phone went dead.

Norwall was furious! No one talked to him that way. Who did these Europeans think they were anyway? Smith indeed! Something illegal was coming down, and he wasn't sure that he wanted any part of it. But as he cooled down, he began to think more clearly. If the company is up to something illegal, there just might be a good opportunity for a little extortion. His god of lucre was getting his attention again. This just might end up being something very good indeed!

Roshan dialed his sales manager's office and gave him the instructions he had received from overseas, and added, "Listen Jack, light a fire under your men. Headquarters is not happy with the small number of contracts you're getting and they're

Chapter Twenty-Eight

not interested in lame excuses, now, get it done!" He shouted into the phone and slammed down the receiver. He wiped his face again and grabbed the phone and made another call. This time no names were used.

"How many farmers have you had to encourage to join with us?" he asked.

"One and it didn't do anything but make him mad," a very husky voice said quietly.

"Just one? Are you kidding? I've told the sales staff to strongly suggest that refusal might not be a good idea. If that doesn't encourage them to sign up, then get your crews to work and set some examples! Got it?" he yelled into the phone. The line simply went dead; there was no response. Now he was beside himself with anger. People didn't seem to appreciate the fact that he was the boss. His clothes were soaked, and the odor of sweat permeated the room as he mopped his vast brow.

Unknown to Norwall, the mysterious Mr. Smith was already in town and was currently in the Nuhoma warehouse meeting with the men who had arrived from Chicago. He examined the starter seed supply and was satisfied that it was growing rapidly. He estimated that a gallon of infected seed spread on top of a full silo of grain would contaminate the whole silo in about two days. It really was remarkable!

He got on a bullhorn and called the rough looking group of men from the Chicago streets to gather around him. They slowly moved closer, reluctant to yield to even this small amount of authority.

"All right you guys, listen up," Smith said while eyeing the group moving toward him. He was glad these men were on his side because they were as tough as they come.

"Here's the deal. You are going to be given containers of grain, and…" then he had a sudden thought that caused him to panic. "Wait a minute, can you tell the difference between wheat, corn, and soybeans?" There was scattered nervous laughter from around the room, but no one said anything.

Then someone from the back spoke up and said, "Grain is grain, what's the big deal?"

Smith rubbed a big mitt of a hand over his face, unable to believe what he was hearing. If he didn't get this straightened out, the whole thing could go terribly wrong. He turned to a couple of his trusted lieutenants and whispered, "For crying out loud, get some samples together to show these idiots the difference!"

"Now listen you guys. We're going to show you examples of the different types of grain. Once you see what they look like, you'll realize that there is no comparison; they are all very different from each other. Let's move on for now; here's the plan we want you to follow. Each of you will be given a supply of seed grain. It's designed to destroy stored grain and your packet of information will show you which elevators to stay away from! These elevators are storing our grain, so leave them alone!"

"Sounds illegal!" someone shouted from the group, which caused everybody to roar with laughter.

"Naw, come on. You guys know that we are as pure as the wind driven snow," Smith joked with them; then he got back to business. "Come on, pay attention! Everybody's going to get a map that shows where the grain elevators are located. Your jobs are very simple, and remember, you're being well paid. Find a way to get inside of each elevator at night and climb to the top and sprinkle about a gallon of seed on top of the pile. Remember, don't get caught! If you see anyone, get out of there and come back later. You are each expected to spread the seed in as many elevators or storage buildings as you can. Any questions?" he asked.

From the side of the room a man stood up and asked, "What does the red circle around some of these places mean?"

"Good question! Boy, I'm glad you asked that because I forgot to mention it. The circles are elevators that have our

Chapter Twenty-Eight

company's grain stored in them, so we sure don't want you to put the starter seed in those silos. Leave them alone," he replied.

Another comic shouted, "Any women in these things?" The place was consumed with laughter.

"No, you idiots, there shouldn't be anybody there, let alone women! Now get out there and get busy!"

As the men moved to the storage facility where the starter grain was creating its infected supply, they milled around trying to pass the time until midnight. Since it had been decided that they should work in teams of two, the men began to find someone to partner with for the next few days and nights. After darkness enveloped the region, rented pickup trucks were loaded with plastic containers holding the infected kernels of grain that were intended to ruin one of the staples of human life, and perhaps something even more sinister!

Lefty and Ralph had decided that they would become a team and climbed into a truck to head for the countryside. As they were driving out of Des Moines heading for the area they were to canvass, Lefty was becoming more uncomfortable because it had been a long time since he had been able to have a shot of whiskey. The thought of waiting until they had finished their work was almost unbearable to him. They were assigned to treat ten elevators scattered over two hundred square miles. This might take several nights of driving and hard work packing these heavy packages of seed up who knew how many stairs!

As Ralph drove towards rural Iowa, Lefty sat gloomily watching nothing in particular when he spotted a potential haven for a few hours. He instantly revived when he saw the green and blue neon light alerting him to the presence of a tavern.

"Hey, Ralph. What say we pull in here and tip a few before heading into the country? You know, spend a few hours while we wait for it to get really dark!" Lefty remarked hopefully.

Ralph thought about it for a minute, and then said, "Yeah sure, why not?" He jerked the wheel to the right and steered the truck into a parking space on the gravel lot surrounding the tavern. Both men poured out of the truck and eagerly headed for the door of this place of refreshment. Inside, they grabbed a booth and began waving at anyone that looked like they could be part of the wait staff. The multi-colored neon signs inside proclaimed the availability of Bud Lite, Miller Lite, Coors, and many others beverages promising to quench a thirst and provide certain happiness! Ralph ordered a Coors while Lefty wanted a Miller with a whiskey chaser. When their drinks came, Lefty forgot the order of consumption; he downed the whiskey first and told the waiter to bring another one.

"Better take it easy, Lefty. We've got a long night ahead of us," Ralph commented.

"Yeah, yeah, I know. Quit worrying, will ya? I get depressed out here in the sticks. I wish I didn't need the money so bad; I wouldn't have left Chicago," Lefty quipped.

"What's the matter, a bookie after ya?" Ralph asked.

"You got it. I'm down ten grand and had to get out of town. The guy has people who have a reputation for inflicting pain!" Lefty responded as he waived for the waiter to get another beer.

Two hours later, they wobbled and weaved out of the bar, wondering where their truck was and trying to remember what the fool thing looked like! After a haphazard search, they found the truck and made it inside of it without incident. Ralph was again in the driver's seat because it was obvious that Lefty had consumed too many chasers. Pulling out of the lot after pausing to see if there might be a cop in the area, they headed for the farmland on dark highways. The inky blackness of a cloudy night was unbroken by any illumination from street lights.

Lefty was given the assignment of giving Ralph directions

Chapter Twenty-Eight

on how to reach the first elevator without realizing that he was holding the map upside down! With almost no traffic on the country back roads, their weaving down the highway went virtually unnoticed.

Fifty other teams of men were fanning out over several states with most of them beginning their journeys with the same liquid lubrication as Ralph and Lefty while the targeted concrete giants towered in the darkness awaiting their fate.

Chapter Twenty-Nine

Tuck lay moaning and thrashing about restlessly on a small bed in a little room that hadn't seen a coat of paint in generations. The rising heat outside was turning the makeshift hospital into a Turkish bath. Lemon was asleep on the floor, exhausted from getting Tuck to this safe building and staying with him while they waited for a doctor that could be trusted. The visit from the medical man did not provide much encouragement in helping to relieve Tuck's terrible suffering. He reported that Tuck's kidney had been severely damaged by the mugger's blow on the streets of Tehran. He suspected that there was internal bleeding, and it was probably infected. The doctor provided some antibiotics for the infection, but he said that Tuck must get to a real hospital soon where he probably would need surgery to repair, or perhaps remove, the damaged organ.

The door to the clandestine room quietly opened, and a figure moved into the darkened chamber. The shadowy figure proceeded to the bed and looking intently into Tuck's burning face. A hand was gently extended and began to dab the forehead with a damp cloth that was lying on a side table. Miraculously, the desperately injured secret agent became quiet and seemed to be resting peacefully for the first time in many days. The visitor gently reached under the light sheet covering Tuck, working a hand to the area of the damaged kidney. A few minutes later the visitor placed his hand on the damp forehead, leaned over and whispered in Tuck's ear, "You're going to be fine, my friend. Rest easy. I'll see you again soon."

Turning to leave, the mysterious visitor reached down and

Chapter Twenty-Nine

softly touched Lemon's arm and smiled, saying quietly, "Rest well, young man; you deserve it." Tuck's friend left; closing the door silently behind him.

Two hours later, Lemon leapt to his feet, instantly awake and feeling guilty for having fallen asleep. He moved to the side of the bed and was relieved to find the patient sleeping peacefully. Tuck's forehead was cool to the touch even though he was covered with perspiration from the heat in the room. Lemon slipped out of the room and went to what supposedly was a kitchen area and found Dog Bone and Peach sitting there drinking tea.

"How's the patient?" Peach asked.

"He seems to be doing better. The drugs the doctor gave him appear to be doing the job. He's sleeping quietly instead of thrashing around like he was earlier," Lemon reported.

"Did Abisha talk to him?" Dog Bone asked while pouring some more tea for Peach and waving the pot at Lemon to see if he wanted some.

"What?" Lemon queried the Bone.

"I asked if Abisha talked to Tuck while he was in the room a while ago," Bone responded.

"Abisha was here?" Lemon asked incredulously. "When was that?"

"A couple of hours ago, I guess. What's the matter with you?" Dog Bone was getting a little irritated.

"I dozed off for awhile and didn't know that he was in the room. Did he say anything to you guys? I wonder why he's still in the country?" Lemon asked the two agents.

"No, he didn't say much. He just said he would see us later and walked out the door."

"Well, for crying out loud!" Lemon exclaimed. He was going to say something else when the bedroom door opened and Tuck walked slowly into the room and took a chair.

"Tuck, good grief, should you be walking around?" Peach asked as she rose to help him to a chair.

"To be honest, I feel a lot better. I think the fever is gone, and the kidney pain is much better. Boy, that doctor really knew his business!" he exclaimed to the group, all of whom were grinning like Cheshire cats. He took the proffered tea and drank it greedily.

"Tuck, these guys say that Abisha was here. I must have been napping. Did you talk to him?" Lemon asked.

Tuck nearly jumped out of his chair. "What in the blooming blue blazes is that guy doing here, and how in the heck could he possibly find this place? Have we thrown security out the window?"

The group sat in an uncomfortable silence trying not to look at each other. Dog Bone finally said, "No, Tuck. We searched the city very carefully and chose this place as the best one we could find. It's been abandoned for years, and no one lives in the area."

Tuck calmed down a little and quietly changed the subject. "What have we heard from Langley? Did they get our precious mouse?"

Lemon responded, "They got him. He is undergoing an autopsy as we speak, and the grain kernels are under the microscope. Herb said the FBI followed Dorri to a warehouse in a seedy district of Chicago. It seems she attracted a lot of unsavory types. A truck was loaded with something and left in the early morning hours, but Dorri spent the night in the dump. Pretty weird! She left later and is now at Illinois University getting ready to teach some classes in biochemistry."

The injured agent sipped his tea quietly, thinking about what he had just been told. "That has got to be the strangest way for a chemist to act in a foreign country. You know what? I'm beginning to think that I should get back to the states and meet with this woman. Who knows, maybe she's tired of the new Persian Empire. I've just got this feeling that something is not right with her. What do you guys think?"

All of the American agents in this dangerous country

Chapter Twenty-Nine

were quiet for a few minutes as they carefully thought about what Tuck had said. Finally Peach spoke up and assumed the position of speaking for the group. "Well, I'll tell you, Tuck. The search of the Ag building didn't turn up much evidence, and you've almost gotten yourself killed, so maybe going back home and getting some medical care would be a good thing. If you think that talking to the lady scientist might pay some dividends then it would be silly, if not dangerous, to wait too long before confronting her."

Tuck nodded silently, seeming to agree with what Peach was saying. He couldn't see any benefit of staying any longer in Iran. Shaking his head as if he had made a decision, he said, "I think I can do more good now back at Langley and in Chicago. But we need you guys to keep on trying to get more information out of the president's office and anywhere else that will help us find out what this guy Faridoon is really up to. He sure is on a roll politically, and his idea of forming this alliance with third world countries seems to be working faster than anyone thought possible. But I think this guy's ego is growing as fast, or faster, than his empire. I'm no shrink, but when you watch this guy on the television, you can almost see his head swell. You know, seeing him kind of reminds me of watching the old newsreel clips of Mussolini when he was in power. He would fold his arms, and stick his chin out smugly, accepting the adoration of the crowd."

Lemon looked at Tuck sheepishly and inquired, "Mussey who?"

"Great gobs of gopher grease, Mussolini! Mussolini! Don't you remember the history of World War II?" Tuck shouted with exasperation.

"Hey, what can I tell ya? I'm Iranian, and we were taught a pretty carefully controlled history!" Lemon replied with humor.

"Oh well," Tuck sighed, "forget it. Anyhow, I think this guy is heading for world domination. We already know how he feels about the United States, and I think he has a plan on how to cripple our country; I just can't figure out what it is!"

"We're going to keep up the investigation of the people in his government. Something might pop loose anytime. We are approaching a secretary in the cabinet who is disgruntled by the way she was treated by a supervisor and by the lack of respect the new student leaders show everyone. It seems like they're acting like a bunch of teenagers at a party."

"Good deal. Well, you know it's critical to dig up any information, no matter how insignificant it seems. But remember, this government is very, very dangerous! Triple check everything you plan and for goodness sake, watch your back. It's possible that we are being watched. By the way, are there any cabinet members that might be induced to talk if we grease their palms with a little cash?"

"That won't be easy. These guys seemed to be genuinely thrilled to be a part of the new government, plus we know VEVAK is watching everybody like eagles!" Lemon said.

"Hawks!" Tuck corrected him.

"What?" Lemon asked with some confusion.

"Watch them like a hawk, not an eagle," Tuck pointed out.

"Who cares, they're all being watched very carefully!" Lemon responded with a little indignation.

"Okay, forget it. Well, let's split up and get to work. I'll call Herb and tell him I'm heading back to base. Now, you guys be good spies and disappear into the woodwork."

They hugged Tuck and wished him the best and cautioned him to be careful getting out of the country. As each one slipped out, they turned and waved goodbye. Tuck was getting sentimental because he had to wipe a tear from his cheek each time one of his new friends went out into the darkness. He immediately called Herb and gave him the details regarding his trip home. Herb agreed wholeheartedly and said he would make arrangements for a military flight out of Baghdad

Chapter Twenty-Nine

whenever he got there.

Tuck was the last to leave the room. Glancing around the area, he saw nothing that might signal danger. Unfortunately, he did not see the people watching the building from a corner room in a run-down two-story house across the street. They had taken night vision videos of each person as they left and teams of two people fell in behind each agent, following them from a safe distance. Everybody was oblivious to the danger!

Chapter Thirty

Arastoo's new, super luxury private jet touched down in Zurich just one hour before the start of the OPEC meeting. As the president waited for a huge umbrella to shield him from the gentle rain, a casual observer would immediately note a dramatic change in the way the Persian president was dressed. His tailored lightweight dark blue suit was now covered by a dark maroon and white robe that was bordered with gold and worn in the Middle Eastern tradition. This beautiful outer garment was made of the most expensive silk and woven in such a light, airy weave that it resembled clouds painted with sunset colors. His crisp, white shirt bore huge ruby cufflinks at the wrists. His wardrobe's palette of colors was made more stunning by a bright orange and red silk tie, secured in place by a huge, multi-carat matching ruby that was surrounded by twenty perfect diamonds. A massive diamond encrusted golden Rolex watch, which fractured the sunlight into many miniature rainbows, adorned his wrist. Topping off his wardrobe ensemble were his shoes, black with a shiny finish that were as reflective as mirrors with a gold, diamond-encrusted chain draped across the arch of the shoe.

Some would call his wardrobe dapper and modern, perhaps even suave. Others would label it as garish and tasteless. But whatever the description attached to him, it was obvious that he wanted to blend in with the world's super-rich.

The press tried to mob him as he descended the stairs, causing the man in charge of security to nearly have a coronary. He screamed at his uniformed officers to get between the Persian president and the reporters who were

Chapter Thirty

rushing forward like a herd of American buffalo. The fierce giant, Shaheen, was in his customary position of clearing a path for his president. He was effective because his ferocious and grim appearance automatically caused people to back up and get out of his way.

Arastoo waved and smiled at the press, even stopped to shake a couple of hands, which made him the journalists' darling. It was apparent his walk had changed because he now moved with a regal step, which was slow and measured. His back was ramrod straight with his head held high, which gave him a somewhat haughty look. As he prepared to enter his limousine, he turned for one last wave to the crowd, which brought a roar of approval from the people huddled in the rain.

In the big, black vehicle that was taking him to the Hotel Leoneck for the OPEC conference, he congratulated himself on the warm welcome and show of affection that the crowd of journalists had given him. Arastoo loved adulation from any array of people, but he knew that he needed the world press's support if he was going to be able to properly promote his ideas. The sirens from the police escort were clearing traffic as he reviewed what he intended to say in various meetings during the two day convention. He knew he would have to contend with a group of leaders made wealthy beyond imagination by selling oil to the United States and the real possibility they would oppose his proposals. He was not worried. He was absolutely secure of his belief in his oratory prowess and his ever-expanding ego prevented him from even considering any difficulty in winning these men over to his point of view and his ultimate goal of damaging the economic power of America. But, perhaps more importantly, he was going to begin talking about the danger the state of Israel presented to these important oil-producing countries. This would be touchy, and if the press picked up on it, there could be worldwide consequences.

Arastoo's limousine pulled up in front of the Leoneck to

crowds that were pressing against the satin ropes, which were straining to keep a clear path open to the entrance of the hotel. Police were making a concerted effort to give him enough protection to be able to walk inside, but it appeared impossible. As he rose to leave the automobile, the driver signaled for him to remain seated. The driver mashed the accelerator and the limo lurched forward in grave danger of running over some of the human masses. Apparently the driver had received a radio call to take the president to a back entrance to protect him from the throng. The vehicle careened around a corner of the hotel and stopped at a back door entrance. There were no crowds and no press; Faridoon was livid with rage! He screamed obscenities at the driver and demanded that he be taken back to the front of the hotel. He was the president of the Persian Empire, and he would not tolerate being treated as a truck driver delivering groceries! The driver was shocked and confused. Unsure of what he should do, he began calling on his radio trying to get instructions from someone in charge, when Shaheen, who was riding in the back with Arastoo, jumped out and charged around the limo and got in next to the driver. In one fluid motion there was a knife in his hand, pressing against the throat of the terrified driver. The man looked into the eyes that spelled death with unmistaken clarity and jammed the pedal to the floor. The limo leaped forward then squealed around a long turn in the parking lot and headed back to the front of the hotel. Fifteen feet of dark smoking rubber appeared on the asphalt, brakes screaming in protest, as the two-ton automobile slid to a stop. People and police dove for cover; running in every direction trying to escape from this roaring black machine!

Arastoo's entrance as an important world leader attending an OPEC conference had become the worst calamity imaginable. The president of the Persian Empire had been bounced around in the back seat like a passenger in a small plane flying in turbulence. He was screaming his rage at the

Chapter Thirty

top of his lungs! The once perfectly attired president was now disheveled; his face was nearly purple and the veins stood out on his neck to the point of bursting!

The hotel official who had the given the order to the limo driver was horrified at the result of his failed attempt to protect the Persian president. He wept in shame and was unable to be consoled. He would have wept even more had he known that this was his last day of life. The murderous Shaheen was already seeking him out. The end would be swift, sure, and undiscovered.

For now, the huge bodyguard had another priority. He leapt out of the limo and rushed to the crowd of television cameras trying to regain control of the situation and get back on the air when the black robed giant stood in front of them. He said nothing, but his demeanor shouted loudly that no pictures would be allowed! The crowd picked up on the dangerous atmosphere surrounding the entrance and became quiet and subdued.

In the back seat, Arastoo was attempting to regain his composure and was frantically trying to straighten his clothing like a teenager caught in the glare of a policeman's flashlight shining through the window of a parked car. Hotel officials rushed out in an attempt to help the president recover his dignity. They actually formed a shoulder-to-shoulder cordon around the humiliated leader to enable the president to reach the hotel lobby unscathed. He was met by OPEC officials who attempted to offer their condolences while some privately chuckled at the absurd entrance of this prima donna.

Arastoo smiled and shook hands with many gathered there but whispered to Shaheen to get him a room along with a change of clothes. The whole catastrophe had caused his clothes to be soaked with perspiration, and he refused to meet any more dignitaries until he was showered and dressed in a new wardrobe. It was necessary that he hurry since he was scheduled to speak to the members in less than an hour.

In forty minutes, Faridoon walked into the conference center calm, clean, and dressed just as elegantly as he had been earlier. He walked to his seat with confidence, smiling, and shaking hands with the delegates. The staffer that showed him to his seat was ignored, unlike Arastoo's meeting at the United Nations. The members sat waiting for him to begin, aware that the president of Persia was going to be speaking without notes.

Clearing his throat, Faridoon began speaking in English, starting with a quiet voice as he always did. He quickly realized that he was uncomfortable speaking while seated, so he abruptly stood, waiting as harried staffers scurried to locate a floor microphone for his use. He continued from where he had left off.

"Gentlemen, I appreciate the opportunity to address this group of distinguished world petroleum producers. My comments will be short, relieving you of the necessity to constantly check your watches, wondering how much longer the speech will last." There was a murmur of chuckles around the room, and many made a great show of looking at their watches in jest. Arastoo was relieved and convinced that the crowd was under his spell as all crowds typically were.

"As an oil-producing nation, Persia is interested in protecting the wealth created by our natural resources, but it is also in our best interest to protect our reserves for future production. I believe that we, as the world's oil producing nations, need to be more aggressive in controlling the price of crude on the global markets. Oil is presently selling for nearly one hundred and fifty dollars per barrel, with the price at the pump in the United States consistently staying over four dollars per gallon."

"As you know, I was the head of the Economics Department at the University of Tehran. I am, therefore, familiar with global economic conditions, which remain very strong. The issue before us is production levels. Do we continue to deplete

Chapter Thirty

our national wealth in order to satisfy the seemingly insatiable American appetite for oil so they can waste the world's raw materials making them richer and lazier? The third world countries have little to eat, which, by the way, the Persian Empire is busily working to remedy. You may not be aware that Americans spend more for dog food in a month than many people around the world earn in wages for a year!" The group began to applaud and nod in agreement with Faridoon. He found it highly amusing that the richest men in the world were upset with dog food sales in the United States.

"My friends, I wish to propose to this group that we stop depleting our oil reserves so that Americans can have three cars and a power boat. We should increase the price of crude to two hundred dollars per barrel," Arastoo said. The men around the room gasped and started to rise from their chairs while looking at him angrily.

The delegate from Saudi Arabia jumped to his feet and shouted, "Do you want to destroy the whole global economy? That represents a twenty-five percent increase, which would push us into a worldwide recession, crippling our own revenues and economies! I think your proposal is outrageous and dangerous."

Arastoo smiled and waited for the tumult to subside. "I fully realize that this plan can be a little frightening when first embraced. But I encourage you to think about the robust economies of China and India. Their oil consumption will soon rival that of the United States, and they are quite willing and able to pay the higher prices."

"Think about it for a minute. Raise the price of crude by twenty percent, and you force most of the world's consumption to drop in roughly the same percentage. What happens then? You sell less oil, but at the higher price giving you the same amount of revenue. You are now protecting your reserves for the future!" The president was experiencing a new phenomenon. This crowd was not worshipping at his altar, and he felt a tinge of apprehension that for the first time in his career he might not get his way in something.

The delegate from Qatar rose to speak. He was a quiet and intellectual man who was greatly respected by the other delegates. "President Faridoon, I find your proposal to be provocative and treacherous. Do you not realize that the United States is already beginning to seriously explore sources of alternative energy? They are producing greater quantities of ethanol; wind farms are growing; bio-diesel is being produced; and oil exploration is expanding. All of the presidential candidates shout to cheering crowds about their plans to make the United States less dependent on foreign oil. Raise the price of crude, and all you accomplish is to force America and other nations to seek relief by using alternate fuels. I believe your real goal is the economic destruction of the United States because of your country's long-standing hatred for America. Well, speaking for my country, we are not going to agree to anything that uses the price of crude as a weapon of war. We depend on the global economy remaining strong and robust. Reducing the production levels to increase the price by a few dollars may be acceptable, but not twenty percent!" The delegates rose and applauded the speaker.

Arastoo was not familiar with humility and even less with humiliation, but he got a dose of it from the Qatar speaker. He realized that attempting to continue would be fruitless and degrading, so he smiled, waved, and sat down. He remained quiet during the rest of the meeting, fuming inwardly about the first defeat of one of his ideas.

The meeting continued for another two hours with a large number of items debated until the agenda was completed. As the gavel fell and Arastoo rose to escape the room, he was approached by the delegate from Venezuela. Mr. Carlos Santos shook hands with him and asked if he could speak with Faridoon for a few minutes. Arastoo agreed, somewhat reluctantly. They took a seat in the corner of the room, trying

Chapter Thirty

to speak quietly even though there was a din of noise as the busboys went about their tasks clearing tables.

"Mr. President," Santos began, "I can assure you that my country's government shares your dislike of the United States of America. I believe we share the same delight in using their own money from the sale of crude to further our agenda for their demise."

The Persian president began to perk up and pay attention to someone who was obviously a comrade in arms. "It does give me some amusement, I admit," he said.

Santos continued, "Mr. President, my government believes that you may be actively involved in attempting to ruin the American economy," he paused looking at Faridoon with the sly smile and hooded eyes of a co-conspirator.

He continued, "There has been a spike in the price of commodities brought on by greatly higher commodity trading prices, coupled with building more ethanol plants that require increased quantities of corn. Food prices have already risen about thirty percent and all indications are that they will be going higher. Our intelligence services report that you may be behind this move in commodity prices. Are our reports accurate?"

Arastoo was taken aback and averted his eyes for a moment. Recovering, he said, "I am always happy to see the American economy suffer, but quite frankly, I am more interested in expanding the Persian Empire through alliances with other nations," he lied.

Mr. Santos smiled, giving Arastoo a knowing glance. "A thought, Mr. President, that is all it is, a thought. More damage could be done to the United States by getting some of your brilliant former students to hack into their banking systems and destroy all of their financial records. The same could be done to corporate America, perhaps even to the Federal Reserve. But think for a moment what chaos this would create; investments wiped out, retirement savings gone, 401K plans demolished, just by someone intelligent enough to hack in and destroy files. Nothing could compare with the damage that would be done. It would take time to overcome this loss, and in the meantime, the United States would be crippled for a generation!"

Faridoon was awestruck as the possibilities became obvious to him. He was irritated with himself that he had not considered this method of potential destruction. A side benefit would be that with the United States crippled for years, the fall of Israel would soon follow.

"Yes, I understand. Thank you for your input and I am going to give this much thought," the president said, as he rose, shook hands, and moved quickly towards the front exit. The limo, with a different driver, was waiting for him and as soon as he was in the back seat he grabbed his cell phone and dialed Tehran.

The departing president did not notice that several delegates were gathered together in the far corner of the meeting room where Arastoo had just left in disgrace.

The Saudi delegate spoke quietly to two other delegates and their staff personnel.

"If you can get by his arrogance, his idea has some merit. A slow increase of twenty percent over the period of a year or eighteen months could be beneficial to us, but I just couldn't bear agreeing with Faridoon in a public way. Sooner or later that would be leaked to the press. What do you think about polling the members privately and getting a sense of how the numbers were received?"

The delegate from Yemen joined in by saying, "I think such a proposal would be received with some enthusiasm by my government. Along the same line of thinking, we have been considering reducing our investments in American treasury bonds and moving our money to China and India."

"We are also considering this strategy, but again, I couldn't bear giving Faridoon the credit for such an idea. We all know

Chapter Thirty

that he is out to destroy the economy of the United States to further his own political goals. Perhaps a little recession would be good for America; make them stronger in the long run," the Saudi envoy mentioned.

"If the president was less narcissistic, he would realize that everyone can see what his Persian Empire is really about. He wants to be the most powerful nation on earth, and he plans on conquering the world by buying countries off with cheap food and cheap oil. He gives oil away for a third of the world price and expects us to raise the price for our oil to the rest of the world." the man from Yemen commented.

"I wonder if a private word to the American ambassador might be in order. They may not have picked up on the giving away of grain to create a new empire. Well, gentlemen, it will be an interesting year," the Saudi delegate said as he strolled away.

Chapter Thirty-One

Stanley Grizzell, known affectionately by his colleagues as Grizzly, was pawing through papers on his desk. He hated paperwork, but as FBI Bureau chief in Chicago, it became his lot to be drowning in the stuff most days. He always roared with derision when someone told him that computers would reduce paper usage. What a crock!

Grizzly preferred to be out on the streets where the action was. The typical FBI man he was not; he was too big, too strong, and too hairy. He had the mussed appearance of an old bear that had just crawled out of its winter den. His hands were massive and did indeed, resemble bear paws. His temperament was a stark contrast to his behemoth size. He spoke quietly and politely to everyone, crook or king. But God help the hapless wretch that endangered his agents! Harm or attempt to harm one of his people, and he became like his namesake, a terrible mass of roaring strength who knew no fear. Many gangsters had been misled by his quiet demeanor and spent days in the hospital recovering.

Today, Grizzly was trying to find the report filed by agent Rance England, who had been watching the Iranian or Persian, whatever they called themselves these days, scientist Dorri something. He finally located the sheaf of papers and sat down to study the report. After reading the report thoroughly, he buzzed for his most trusted agent, Duke Lessing, to come into his office.

Duke looked more like a college professor than an agent of the Bureau. He was short and slender, with a shock of blonde hair that was continually dropping into his blue eyes. His

Chapter Thirty-One

sharply jutting chin betrayed an unshakeable determination to finish everything he started. He was good with numbers, but lousy with firearms! Grizzly always found it necessary to go with him as he tried to qualify on the annual practical pistol course. It sometimes required Grizzly to make a slight adjustment on the official score sheet that went into Duke's personnel file.

"What do you think, Duke? There sure seems to be something funny going on in that old warehouse. What's this Persian babe doing in that dump with all of those gangster types?" Grizzly queried his friend.

"Well, most of them left during the night, preceded by a Penske rental truck that was loaded with something. Since she is from an official terrorist nation that doesn't like us, I think we should go in and do a little snooping around!" Duke responded.

"We need to get a search warrant first since we might find something that could become evidence," Grizzly exclaimed as he reached for a phone to call a district judge for the warrant. They certainly had enough probable cause that something was happening in the warehouse that might be a threat to the United States.

One hour later, Grizzly and two cars full of agents arrived at the warehouse. Boiling out of the vehicles, several agents pounded on the front garage door while three agents headed for the back of the building. After receiving no response, the ham-fisted agent took a sledgehammer and pounded a hole in the door large enough for them to gain entrance. Once inside, they fanned out to cover the interior of the building and look for anyone trying to make an escape. As they made their sweep of the huge room, it was obvious that no one was home, and there was not much left behind as evidence. Nothing except dead rats in wire cages, and that evidence was already starting to smell!

"Looks like some kind of experiments took place here,

and these poor little fellas were the subjects." the big agent sneered. "Okay guys, let's bag up some of these rodents and take them to the lab for analysis to see what killed them. Take some of the food bowls along too; it might give us something to think about."

When he got the results from the lab, Stanley Grizzell planned to make a little trip out to the University of Illinois and have a chat with this Persian scientist. Hanging around a warehouse with criminal types certainly was not included as duties of her cultural exchange program.

Chapter Thirty-Two

Tuck caught a ride in the back of a vegetable truck to Ahyal. A short message to Langley alerted them that he was coming in, and that he needed a Marine escort from the little village in Iran back to Baghdad. He was to meet them sometime after two in the morning at the same location in the village where they had deposited him a few weeks ago. He hoped that the marines wouldn't have Sergeant Miranda with them. He wasn't up to the guy's macho stuff tonight. There wouldn't be any sleep until he was aboard the Air Force jet headed for Germany, which would then take him to the good old USA.

The old truck trundled into the village right at the stroke of midnight. Tuck thanked the driver and slipped him some rials for his trouble. He could go to the safe house and maybe get an hour's shuteye, but his brain told him that this might not be a good idea. Moving silently in the shadows, he headed toward a stable near where he was supposed to meet the military guys. His nose directed him to the little barn. The CIA operative crept inside and swung his Maglite around to see if he was alone. He wasn't even close to being alone. The barn was full of dirty, smelly sheep that were bleating up a storm because he had frightened them when he came in the door. He stood still, hoping they would quiet down before their owner was aroused from slumber because of all the commotion. Tuck found a corner to lie down in, and the sheep followed his lead and settled down in the straw to continue their snooze that this unwelcomed human had interrupted. Well, at least he would be warm while he waited. He desperately wanted to sleep but knew that was impossible. If he missed the signal, he would be on his own because the Marines wouldn't stay around to find out if he was waiting for them or if he was dead.

At ten minutes before the hour, Tuck moved into a position where he could watch for the expected signal. He took a minute to scan the area around the little sheep barn looking for anything out of the ordinary. His senses were straining to alert him of danger as he waited for the flash of muted light that would signify friends were close, ready to move him out of this dangerous country.

The digital readout on his watch told him that the time had arrived, but he saw nothing to indicate the marines were in the area. Glancing around, he thought he saw movement on the street behind where he was hiding. He studied the area carefully; his nerves screaming danger in his brain! Tuck felt he had to get out of there now; something was wrong and he needed to get moving. He crawled around the fence bordering the sheep pen and started to move in the direction where the marines had dropped him weeks ago.

Suddenly, fingers like steel talons grabbed his shoulder. Tuck exploded into action, striking out at his attacker with his left arm while tripping him at the same time with his left leg. The blow struck the guy in the throat causing him to hit the ground with a grunt and whispered cursing. Tuck's right hand had already found the comfort of the Browning's grip, and he was pulling it into position to fire a silenced bullet into the eye of the man on the ground. His brain stopped his trained response to danger, seconds before pulling the trigger. *What was it?* He thought to himself. Then he knew; the cursing was in English! The dim moonlight revealed that the man on the ground was wearing desert fatigues, and he was struggling to get away from the barrel of the automatic held so close to his left eye that it blocked the soldier's vision.

"For God's sake, take it easy, will ya?" the man whispered angrily. "I'm here to get you out of here!"

Chapter Thirty-Two

Tuck knew that voice. "Miranda, is that you?" he demanded.

"Yeah, it's me. Now get that gun out of my face before one of us gets killed! You're making enough noise to wake up the whole Revolutionary Guard," the Marine said as he struggled to his knees, moving toward the scrub brush in the distance.

Tuck was bristling with fury as he followed the Marine into the brush. "You're still the dumbest guy I've ever met! What's wrong with you? Have you got a death wish or something? You must enjoy sneaking up and grabbing me like that!"

Miranda turned and faced him in the dim moonlight. "Shut that stupid mouth of yours, spook! This place is crawling with bad guys, so let's get out of here."

Three other marines were waiting along the path. Tuck couldn't see them well enough to determine if they were the same bunch that had brought him into the country earlier, but he was willing to bet that they were.

They moved silently down the path, heading for Iraq with the point man signaling that it was clear. Tuck's heart was beginning to beat normally as they moved through the sand and gravel. "Thank you," he said quietly to no one in the group. He had come within a whisker of killing the young sergeant twice, and he was grateful it had not happened. He was also thankful that his trusted Browning did not have a hair trigger!

After a little over an hour, they came out of a draw and found the lucky Humvee sitting patiently waiting for them. They all clamored inside while the engine roared to life and her wheels clawed the sand for traction. The trip back to Baghdad took longer this time because of an unusual number of trucks heading into the capital before dawn. It looked like business was good and getting better, based on the loaded vehicles they mixed with on the highway.

Arriving at the base, the Marine at the wheel drove to a cluster of tents and stopped.

"This is where we get off, spook." Miranda exclaimed. "I can't say I'm sad to see you leave. I'm tired of checking to see if you have cleaned your lousy automatic."

Tuck couldn't help smiling. The sergeant was a tough Marine, but Tuck was beginning to like him in spite of his scaring the life out of him twice. "Sorry we got off on the wrong foot. I appreciate you guys risking getting shot while keeping me safe."

"You're welcome, I think. I hope you got what you wanted in Tehran," the big Marine said.

Tuck smiled again and absentmindedly rubbed his kidney that had been damaged so viciously. He didn't say anything; Miranda knew he wouldn't. Miranda waved goodbye as he walked toward his tent. Tuck smiled and returned the wave with some emotion.

A young Marine walked out to the Humvee and removed Tuck's gear and transferred it to the old Toyota pickup that he had ridden in before. They climbed in and started to drive out of the compound, heading out on the freeway, bound for the airport. The agent was glad he was not going to meet with the captain again.

In a very short time, due to the marine's driving at a reckless speed, weaving in and out of traffic, and running a number of red lights; they arrived at the base. Orders were shown at the gate, and they were waved through without comment. The old Toyota pickup stopped by an old, battle weary C-130 that would take him on the first leg of the journey back to Washington. The old girl's props were already spinning on the two inboard engines as Tuck struggled up the steps into the bowels of this dependable war machine. It began moving immediately down the taxiway; ready for a quick and uncomfortable takeoff. Tuck strapped himself into his seat, thrilled at the power the engines produced as they left the ground, climbing at an extraordinarily steep angle towards the heavens. Five minutes later, he was in a deep, dreamless sleep.

Chapter Thirty-Two

Fourteen hours afterwards, he was driven to CIA headquarters in Langley, Virginia. Going through a rear entrance, he quickly walked with one shoelace still untied into Herb's office. Herb rose from his desk to greet him, but he could not hide the sadness on his face.

"Good grief, Herb, what in the world's the matter?" Tuck asked with concern.

"Sit down Tuck. I'm afraid I've got some bad news." Herb muttered with averted eyes.

As Tuck collapsed in a chair, Herb looked at him through blood-shot eyes. It was obvious that he was having a hard time speaking. Finally, after trying unsuccessfully to find just the right words, he gave up and just blurted out, "Lemon's dead!"

"What?" Tuck asked incredulously. "What did you say?"

"I'm afraid it's true, old friend. His body was found dumped in a shallow grave outside of Tehran. It's obvious that VEVAK grabbed him. There's no doubt that he was tortured before he died a very unpleasant death. We've got to assume that he cracked under the torture and probably gave the names of some, if not everyone, on the team, and maybe some of our other operatives. We've lost a great young man, and our operation is no doubt blown. We're trying to contact the others in the team and get them out of there if it's not already too late!"

Tuck was unable to do anything but sit with his face in his hands and weep silently. Others in the offices on the same floor were walking around dabbing their eyes and fighting back tears. None of them had known Lemon, or even met him, but they had heard about his great courage. They knew he was talented and devoted to his work as he tried to save his country from even further ruin. Some had heard of his simple, but great faith, and his sense of humor and positive outlook on life. Now, this fine young man was gone!

Aristotle Tucker was a CIA secret agent who had been

close to death a number of times, but he could not stay in the office. He got up and shuffled slowly, painfully, out of the office and headed for the nearest exit. He had to get out into the air; he couldn't breathe. He was consumed by grief. He walked slowly outside and moved to a bench in a park-like section of the Langley campus. He admitted to himself that in the short time that he had known this splendid young man, he had come to love Lemon like a son. He hated this business that put brave young people into places of tortured death. He couldn't contain his grief any longer; putting his head back he groaned and shouted his anguish and heartbreak!

"God," he shouted, "How could you do this to my friend Lemon? He believed in you. He trusted you, and look what you gave him, a vicious and horrible death!" His sobbing was uncontrollable, and he continued to rail against a Deity who he publicly claimed did not exist.

When he calmed down, he was startled to find someone sitting next to him, and he was embarrassed that a stranger might have heard his screaming and crying. "Sorry," he muttered, angry that this person had rudely pushed into his private space.

"That's okay, Tuck, I understand." The voice was familiar. Tuck looked up incredulously as an arm gently encircled his shoulders and squeezed lightly.

"You! Is it Abisha or something like that? What in the world are you doing here?"

"I just wanted to be your friend. I think you could use one about now," Abisha said.

"I cannot understand how you get around the world and turn up at the strangest times!" Tuck gasped. "Don't you have a job?"

"I know that you are really hurting because of Lemon's horrible death," Abisha responded, ignoring Tuck's last question.

Suddenly, Tuck's anger boiled to the surface again and he

Chapter Thirty-Two

turned on Abisha, shouting, "You pray a lot to your god, so did Lemon. Tell me, what good did it do him? When he needed him, his god wasn't there!" He shrugged off Abisha's arm as he vented his deepest feelings.

"I can tell you, Tuck, that Lemon was not alone. God suffered terribly throughout the whole messy ordeal. If Lemon could be here, he would say the same thing," Abisha did not elaborate on his comments although he could have done so.

"Tell you what. You stay away from me and I'll stay away from you, okay?"

Tuck got up and stormed away without looking back. If he had, he would have seen how sad and hurt Abisha was and the tears that fell gently into his beard. Tuck felt lousy and wished he hadn't been so hard on the young man who was only trying to be a friend. He finally glanced back, but Abisha was gone.

Chapter Thirty-Three

Lefty and Ralph had finished spreading the infected grain in a huge elevator just outside of Des Moines. It had been easy to gain entry to the giant structure, but it had been anything but easy to get to the top of the fool thing! Since the elevator was basically divided in half, with 30 silos on each side of a central core housing stairways and augers for filling and emptying the silos, they each worked on a side.

Spreading the infected grain had gone well, and they were finished at 3:00 a.m., heading back down stairs to the ground floor. They needed to rest and get moving to their next target, which was thirty miles away.

Lefty was leading the way down the last flight of stairs, shining his flashlight around in front of them as they descended from the gloom of the dark interior. He was antsy because he found the darkness and silence of the massive concrete structure spooky, and he was anxious to get outside where he could breathe some fresh air. He was mildly claustrophobic, but he didn't know it; he didn't even know what that meant.

Suddenly, a light flashed on above the stairway, and someone shouted, "HEY, WHAT THE BLAZES DO YOU THINK YOU'RE DOING IN HERE?" The light and the shouting terrified them, and actually drove Ralph to his knees in shock! As their eyes became accustomed to the bright light, they saw an older man with a red and black checkered cap and matching jacket standing at the foot of the stairs holding a wicked looking baseball bat in his right hand. In his other hand, he was holding a cell phone.

"Take it easy, old timer!" Ralph shrieked with a voice

Chapter Thirty-Three

that was awfully high pitched. "We were just looking around, never seen one of these things up close before. Boy, this thing is big!"

"You're looking around at this time of night? Do you think I'm crazy? Who gave you permission to be in here?" The older man eyed them warily while backing up a step. "You guys get out of here, or I'm calling the cops!"

Ralph moved slowly down the stairs toward the man with the bat, Lefty was right behind him. They both had the same idea; they had to prevent this guy from making a call. As they moved closer smiling broadly to make him think there was no danger, the stranger moved backward trying to keep distance between them while he tried to get the phone working. Suddenly, he stumbled and fell crashing to the floor. Instantly both men were on him, pummeling his head and body with wicked blows. The stranger screamed at the top of his voice and fought back gamely, but he was without hope. Ralph grabbed the bat out of his hand and delivered one killing blow to the head. In the silence they could only hear their own panting and the pounding of their hearts. They had to get out of there. Both men dove for the door, wrenching it open and exploding outside, running toward their hidden pickup.

Suddenly, Lefty slid to a stop, grabbed Ralph, and forced him to stop. "Wait a minute Ralph, we've got to go back and get that grain. We can't let anyone get their hands on the stuff." Ralph knew this was true, so they both turned and raced back to the elevator. They found their backpacks where they had left them on the stairs. Grabbing both, they bolted outside again, jumped in the truck and roared out of the parking lot heading to the highway. Unfortunately for them both, a car was just turning into the lot and had to swerve quickly to keep from hitting the fleeing pickup. The driver, who was half asleep when making the turn, was startled awake by the truck bearing down on him. He was alert enough to get the color of the truck and the last three digits of the license number. In less than five minutes he would be in the building, finding the murder victim and calling the police.

The two vandals were now murderers, and luck was running against them. Lefty said, "Man, I got to find a drink!" His hands were shaking badly.

"Where are we going to find a drink at this time of night?" Ralph snarled. "Right now, we've got to get to the other elevator and finish the job and then get the heck out of here!"

Lefty heard him and understood, but he didn't feel any better. He had to have a drink and he needed it now!

The pickup roared into the darkness, heading in a northerly direction, where another elevator was waiting for their visit.

The dispatcher at the Des Moines County Sheriff's Office received a call at 3:17 a.m. from an excited man saying that there had been a murder at the Olson Grain Elevator. A pickup with two people in it had nearly hit him when he turned into the parking lot. The red pickup was heading north on County Road 217 at a high rate of speed. Deputy Wilson immediately dispatched a patrol car to the scene and broadcast an alert about the pickup to local law enforcement agencies and to Louisa County Sheriff's Office just north of Des Moines where the pickup might be heading. Lefty and Ralph were now hunted men!

Chapter Thirty-Four

Peach was huddled in a darkened vacant house on the south side of Tehran with her iPhone, trying to get a connection to the secure satellite and then on to Langley. She was afraid her battery was getting so low that she would not be able to make the connection.

This experienced agent for the Central Intelligence Agency had been in virtual hiding since Lemon's capture and terrible death. Although she had never seen anyone who she thought was following her, she had to believe that she was in danger. Hungry, thirsty, and dirty, she would often think of how she was going to survive in this treacherous city. VEVAK was everywhere, and the team was effectively out of business for the time being; it was just too perilous.

Hiding had not stopped her from thinking and planning what she should do next. She could request that the agency pull her out of Persia and use her at headquarters or perhaps in another country. But lurking in the recesses of her mind was the desire to inflict misery on the people that had tortured her friend. If they thought she would be too frightened to continue in espionage, they were sadly mistaken. Her contact in Arastoo's office was quietly picking up bits and pieces of data that was slowly forming a picture of what the president might be planning. One piece of information was not really kept secret. It was almost as if the president was proud of what he had ordered his minions to do. Persia was sending millions of rials to hand-picked people in Washington, D.C., who were funneling the money into the campaign coffers of those running for president that were promising to raise taxes on the American people if elected.

Peach thought that sending money to an American political campaign was more than just a bit odd. She wanted to send all the information she had as soon as possible, but she had to find another battery. Attempting to buy one in a store would bring suspicion upon her. Her only choice was to get one on the black market, and to do that she had to get out of this rat trap! She made up her mind and moved to a darkened window in the back of the building. She spent a full ten minutes watching the buildings that were adjacent to where she was hiding. Seeing no danger, she slipped out into the darkness and moved quickly down an alley, heading to an area of town where she could buy anything if she had enough money. She wanted to be there as soon as everyone opened for business.

Three hours later, Peach had her new battery and was looking for a safe place to make her uplink. She climbed up to the roof of an old apartment building where women were hanging up their laundry on lines strung all over the place. They were gossiping and laughing while working, and children were playing and squealing, making a grand cacophony of background sound that would prevent anyone from overhearing her conversation. She was dressed as a peasant and no one paid any attention to her as she took out her cell and called Washington.

To her surprise Herb Worthington answered. "Oh Lord, it's great to hear your voice, are you all right?" he asked.

"You bet I'm all right. It takes more than these thugs have to put me out of business!" she replied with forced cheerfulness.

"That's great, but come on, Peach, let's gets you out of there. It's just too dangerous!"

"I'm thinking about it, but I need to pass on some info and get off this roof before someone puts me to work washing clothes. Herb, Faridoon's government is sending millions to the United States to help fund the campaign of candidates that say they're going to raise taxes. I find it kind of unusual for a foreign government to be so interested in an American election."

Chapter Thirty-Four

"That is interesting, but I wonder if it is part of a bigger picture. Do you have anything else that might give us a clue?" he asked.

"I think the Persian Empire that the president is pushing is the key. Providing cheap grain and cheap oil to third world countries is very expensive, that's for sure. So far, these countries seem to be fighting for the chance to climb on board the bandwagon, but this business of taking raw materials in payment is ludicrous! We don't have a manufacturing base here, and acting like a global dealer of raw goods doesn't make sense to me. But I didn't major in economics, so I may be missing something," Peach responded.

"Believe me, our guys have been watching that situation. We think he is definitely building his empire by using the money we pay him for his oil to finance his scheme. Anything else?" he asked.

"One more thing, then I've go to get out of here before someone picks up on this transmission. Where is he getting all of this grain?" she asked and then shut the phone down.

Herb put down the receiver and ran his hand over the stubble on his chin while he glared at a cold cup of coffee that warned him that his stomach couldn't handle it. Grain! What's the deal about grain? It keeps coming up over and over, and where is this guy getting all the stuff he's giving away? He thought he would pass everything he had on to the FBI and see if they had any ideas.

He dialed a number and was connected immediately to the office of Roger Ansley, Director of the FBI's New York office.

"Hey, Roger, how you doing? This is Herb Worthington."

"Hi, Herb, what's happening in the spook department?" Roger asked laughing.

"Roger, we have been talking a lot about this new Persian Empire that President Faridoon is organizing with third world countries. We don't know what he is really up to, but we sure don't think that he is a friend of the United States. The question is, if he is trying to hurt us, how is he going to do it?" Herb queried.

"Well, we've been talking about this lady biochemist who's here on a cultural exchange with the University of Illinois. Why would a woman from a country that hates us want to come and teach for a few months at one of our universities?" Roger inquired. "And why in the name of all that's holy did the State Department approve her trip here?"

"It's a mystery, that's for sure. You may not know, Roger, but we lost one of our best agents in Iran. Real nasty affair and we don't have many people over there to take up the slack. But before his death, the agents made a raid on the office where this lady used to work found that it had been cleaned up, obviously by experts. What they missed was some grain, and a dead mouse."

"Mouse?"

"Yeah, a dead mouse. We have it at our lab for testing. No specific data yet, but it appears that the poor little guy died from eating the grain! One of our other agents seems to think that the grain shipments Faridoon's sending all over the world play a part in his grand scheme of things." Herb responded.

"Grain, you say! Funny, I saw a note somewhere that was commenting on a bunch of overseas money coming in and seems it was going to a company that was trading in commodities. I wonder if there could be a connection," he wondered aloud while making a note on a yellow tablet on his desk.

"Well, Roger, I just wanted to pick your brain and pass on what little we have on our friend in Persia. Hope it helps," Herb said.

"Thanks, Herb. You've put the little gray cells to work. I'll keep you advised," he said as he hung up the phone. *Grain!* he thought to himself. *Where is this guy getting all the grain he is giving away?*

Chapter Thirty-Five

Fourteen giant bulk freighters had transported thousands of tons of grain to members of the Persian Alliance with three more en route and six waiting to be loaded in Michigan and New Orleans. Oil tankers that were prepared to deliver millions of barrels of crude oil were at anchor in the few ports that could accommodate these behemoths. It seems no one had stopped to consider that these countries had limited refinement and storage capabilities, which prohibited them from rapidly off loading this precious commodity. Persian oil company officials had stopped any further shipments until someone could figure out how to get the crude refined into gasoline or kerosene. Two tankers had actually been rerouted to the United States where their cargo would be quickly offloaded. Loaded tankers sitting at anchor cost thousands of dollars per day, so this part of the Empire's altruistic plan was not going well.

A far more serious problem had arisen while the first grain ship was being unloaded. In some countries armed gangs, rival war lords, and corrupt military leaders took possession of the grain and proceeded to extort huge sums of money before they would allow the grain to be delivered to the people throughout the country. Adding to the corruption on the docks was the rampant theft of grain as it was being transported throughout the countries. By the time this commodity arrived in the hands of the people, there was much less of it, and it cost a lot more. Adding insult to injury, the leaders of the countries receiving grain shipments were demanding that Persia increase the tonnage to make up for the losses due to corruption!

Ambassadors from Persia were still actively signing nations that wanted to belong to the new Persian Empire, particularly in Southeast Asia, which created more transportation problems getting the grain to the West Coast of the United States and then finding bulk freighters to transport it across the Pacific. The Persian economic plan was putting a huge strain on the shipping industry, which was already filling the needs of other nations around the world. Trying to accommodate the need, some shipping companies were actually taking smaller bulk freighters out of mothballs and beginning to refurbish them to put them back into service. All of these expenses were being passed on to the customer—Persia.

In Tehran, Vice President Behruz, who was now responsible for the Interior Department, clutched his head in his hands, demanding that someone bring him some aspirin. He was convinced that this grand scheme of President Faridoon to create a new Persian Empire through alliances with third world countries had not been planned properly. It should have had months of study, not days! Gigantic problems were beginning to disrupt the whole process, and the costs were going through the roof. He had not forgotten the meeting when his predecessor had questioned the cost of the president's plan, nor had he forgotten that the man disappeared and was never seen again. He now believed that no one had foreseen the corruption, or the transportation dilemma they were facing, and he dreaded facing President Faridoon with the issues he was confronted with.

Arastoo was in his new palatial home that had recently been constructed using the most skilled artisans in the country. Constructed of light yellow sandstone, it was surrounded by flowering gardens that filled the air with glorious fragrances. The palace dominated a hilltop just outside the city and was now considered a tourist attraction. Its thirty-foot entrance was flanked by light pink marble columns that seemed to soar out of sight. Massive teak doors with gleaming brass hardware

Chapter Thirty-Five

opened into rooms that had various pastel colored walls that shared the room with ten foot windows of beveled glass, which welcomed sunlight into the building. White gossamer panels wafted gently in the light breeze, providing the gold trimmed rooms with the feeling of coolness and ballet-like movement.

The president had summoned Intelligence Minister Payam to meet with him and give a progress report, particularly about grain purchases. Payam entered the room, bowed from the waist and waited until he was given permission to be seated.

"Come in, my friend," Arastoo instructed him. "Let's sit in these most comfortable couches instead of the stuffy conference room. I am most anxious to hear your report."

Payam seated himself and took some papers from a briefcase that always accompanied him. The president noticed that he seemed a little distracted but decided to let it pass. "Your highness, I must tell you that it is possible that the American Central Intelligence Agency may have compromised our plan to destroy grain stored throughout their country."

"Why do you think they know about the plan?" Arastoo asked.

"VEVAK captured one of their agents a few days ago. They used some very imaginative techniques to encourage the young man to talk. He gave us some names of other agents that are working in Tehran as well as in other cities in Persia. We are tracking them down and arresting them as we speak. I believe they will all be in custody by tomorrow night."

"But why do you believe they have discovered our grain destruction operation?"

Payam hesitated a moment. He was beginning to experience a very dry throat. "Might I have some water, Your Excellency?"

"Certainly." Arastoo clapped his hands and a servant in pure white robes appeared as if by magic, carrying a carafe of water and two crystal glasses. He poured both men a glass of water then silently disappeared. "Now minister, please continue."

"VEVAK agents were tipped off that someone might be about to break into the Agriculture building. Everyone thought that this might be a decoy since there is nothing of value in such an old government structure. Then one of our agents remembered that the lady scientist Dorri Golnessa worked there for a number of weeks. After she left for America, our people gave her office and laboratory an agency cleaning that is designed to eliminate any clues that might have been left," Payam remarked.

"Then, what is the problem? What could an agent find after such a cleaning as you have described?" Arastoo asked, watching Payam intently.

"It is what he said, just before he, ah, expired," Payam was now visibly nervous.

"Well out with it, man; what did he say?"

Payam cleared his throat as he looked furtively around the room, before glancing at Faridoon. He quickly took another swig of water then said, "He said, 'We've got the mouse!'"

The room was filled with absolute silence. Perspiration began to form on Payam's forehead as he waited for the president to say something. Finally Arastoo leaned forward and his eyes testified that he would brook no further nonsense, and he said, "Would you repeat that please?"

"He said 'We've got the mouse.'"

"And just what does that mean? Is it some kind of code?" the president asked.

"We have absolutely no idea what it means. But he was in terrible distress when he said it, so we believe that it has some importance." Payam was squirming on the couch.

"Are you telling me that the agents of our intelligence organization could get nothing out of a foreign spy but something about a mouse?"

"Well, Your Highness, there was one more thing, but we believe it was just his delirium."

Chapter Thirty-Five

"Please be so kind as to enlighten me. What else did he say?" Faridoon's voice was replete with danger.

Payam referred to his notes, his hand noticeably shaking. Clearing his throat, he said softly, "His exact words were, 'Oh, dear Yeshua, you've come for me!' He smiled; then he died."

Faridoon was quiet for a long time; then he asked, "Who is Yeshua?"

"Our men did some research. They think it is the Hebrew name for Jesus."

"Was this man, who we are assuming was a spy, a Jew?" Arastoo asked quietly.

"It may be so Your Highness, he had certain physical ... characteristics."

Arastoo ignored the comment. He grew very serious and looked closely at his Minister of Intelligence. "Are you telling me that this man was a member of the Israeli Mossad?"

"No, sir, I am not. There is no evidence that he was anything other than an agent for the United States."

Faridoon's brilliant mind was processing ideas at a tremendous speed. The information given him today was troubling, and he felt it might have serious consequences. A young spy is tortured and all they get out of him is some veiled reference to a rodent and a reference to Jesus while he was in a hallucinatory state. What could all of this mean?

Changing the subject, Faridoon asked, "Have your agents kept Dorri under constant surveillance?" he asked, watching Payam closely.

"Yes, Your Highness. We followed her to America where Pasdaran agents took over watching her. She went immediately to the warehouse without stopping or talking to anyone. Our man at the warehouse reported that she performed the grain experiments properly. She then went to her room where she stayed until the next morning. The infected grain reproduced exactly as predicted and was immediately transferred by truck to Des Moines, Iowa, wherever that is! The next morning she took a taxi to the University of Illinois, where she is preparing to begin teaching at the beginning of the week. She is doing everything according to plan." Payam finished speaking and waited for Faridoon to say something.

"Was the warehouse given the same careful cleaning to eliminate all clues?" the president asked. Something was bothering him, but he couldn't identify what it was.

"It has been cleaned and locked up."

"You're telling me that no evidence was overlooked after Dorri and the men left the building." He asked as his eyes bored into Payam; searching for any sign that he might not be telling the complete truth.

"The warehouse was sanitized professionally. Anything left was put in the trash several blocks away," Payam recounted carefully.

"What do you mean; anything left was disposed of. What was left?" he demanded.

Payam was now obviously nervous. "The usual things found in an abandoned warehouse, Your Highness, dirt, trash, rats, things like that."

Faridoon was still uneasy, but he couldn't pin the worry down to anything of substance. "Is the plan on schedule?" he asked.

"Yes, Your Highness. Everything is taking place exactly as you planned."

"What about the treatment of the elevators?"

"About one hundred elevators have been treated, and their contents will be completely contaminated by tomorrow evening. The few remaining elevators should be treated tonight." The president's questions were beginning to make him nervous, and he hoped that they would end soon so he could escape back to his office.

"Fine. That is a good report. Please make sure that your agents watch Dorri at all times. We may want to pull her out of the country quickly. Before you leave, what progress are we

Chapter Thirty-Five

making in funding Hamas and Hezbollah?"

"We have sent them about ten million dollars each, plus providing them with surface to surface missiles, a thousand AK 47's with thousands of rounds of ammo. Their attacks on the Zionists have been happening often; however, the accuracy of the homemade rockets Hamas uses is less then inspiring. They do cause Israel to respond with attacks in Gaza and the West Bank, which the world's press views as unprovoked attacks. Many nations condemn the responses which work in our favor," Payam reported happily.

"Thank you again. You are excused."

"Yes sir, everything shall be as you wish." Payam rose, bowed from the waist, turned and left the room hurriedly.

Faridoon watched him retreat with a smile on his lips. It pleased him to cause his staff to squirm on occasion; it was good for them, kept them in their place. He was beginning to think like a monarch and that also pleased him. He was formulating a plan now on how he was going to inform the people of Persia that he needed to be their KING if he was to govern the growing alliance properly.

He rose and rang for his secretary to come into the room. Afsoon came in with all of the feminine grace given to her gender. The averted eyes, the hint of a smile, and impeccable grooming made her alluring, and it did not escape his notice. When he was king, he was convinced that this delightful creature would be a good choice for a queen.

"Get in touch with Minister Behruz and have him come here at once. Tell him to bring all the data he has concerning the grain shipments around the world," he instructed her. She nodded silently and glided out of the room. As she left, Shaheen came through the door. She carefully avoided this menacing figure and hurried back to her desk. She was unable to control a slight shudder as she thought of the man with such dark features. He was frightening!

"Well, old friend, everything seems to be going well with

our new alliance. Countries are signing with us almost every day," he exclaimed, pleased with himself. The giant did not respond, he simply bowed slightly and waited. He knew there would be instructions.

"Payam has just informed me that everything is going as planned in America. But something about his story of the cleaning of the warehouse bothers me. See if you can get any more information about the things that were cleaned out. He said that there was just trash, rats, and dirt; it is possible that there is nothing to worry about, but I need you to look into it." He nodded, dismissing the great hulk of a man, who bowed and strode out of the room.

Arastoo moved to his desk and prepared to meet with his new Minister of the Interior. He imagined the man would be nervous and would want to talk about money. The sales of crude had brought in more revenue this past month as the price per barrel had climbed over one hundred dollars. He angrily thought of his humiliation at the OPEC meeting. The fools! Speculators were going to drive the price up to where he suggested. He would prove all of them to be idiotic lap dogs of the Americans.

Chapter Thirty-Six

Lefty and Ralph spent the night in a fleabag motel on Interstate 35, just outside of Ames. They had located an all night liquor store and bought two bottles of Jim Bean to get them through the night. The killing of the old man made them want to get out of the state as soon as possible, but they elected not to travel in the daytime. In addition, they still had another elevator to treat before they could get the rest of their money. There was a Taco Villa across the freeway from their motel; Lefty was chosen to hike across and get them some food since the whiskey on an empty stomach was making them a little ill.

When Lefty came back, they sat at the little table eating, drinking, and trying to figure out what they should do.

"Why don't we just throw the rest of the stuff in the garbage and get out of here?" Lefty asked, downing a taco in two bites.

"I don't think we should cross these guys. This deal is really planned out to the last detail, and I think they would find out and track us down. I worry more about the people that we're working for than I do about the cops!" Ralph said.

"Well, what are we going to do?"

"Why don't we go and treat the elevator that's circled in red. It must be really important! We do that one and the guys will really be pleased, maybe even give us a bonus!" Ralph said proudly. He liked his new idea.

Lefty looked at the map and nodded his head. "The place we were supposed to hit is way back the way we just came; a place called Knoxville. But the red circle is right on our way out of this cruddy state. It's called Waterloo, and it's just off of Highway 20 which heads us back to Illinois." He was feeling pretty good about his reading of the map and figuring a way out of the state.

They congratulated themselves on being very clever. Deciding to leave after dark, they settled back and looked forward to a day of drinking and trying to think of how many women they would be able to buy with five thousand dollars in cash, giving no thought to the debt one of them owed to a very dangerous bookie in Chicago. Soon, they were snoring loudly, oblivious to anything happening outside of the room.

A state police cruiser was just getting ready to turn into the motel's parking lot to check for the wanted pickup when the dispatcher sent the patrolman to work an accident back towards Des Moines. He made a fast u-turn in the parking lot throwing gravel and dust in the air and screamed down the freeway with its siren yowling with blue and red lights flashing.

At six o'clock the conspirators were awakened by a cheap, screeching alarm clock. They woke slowly; both of them were hung over from all the whiskey they had consumed. Their mouths tasted like the floor of a chicken coop, and their throats were desert dry. They checked out of the motel without washing or changing clothes. They found out from the desk clerk that they could find a liquor store about a mile up the highway, and there were also some restaurants in the same area.

They found the liquor store and bought a couple of six packs and sat in the truck drinking a couple of beers while they tried to decide where to eat. The vote was for Kentucky Fried Chicken, which was next door. They got their order and returned to the pickup to eat and drink more beer. The two mental giants finished eating, wiped their hands on their clothes, and threw the trash out of the window. Lefty gunned the truck into life, and they headed to their red-circled elevator.

Chapter Thirty-Six

In two hours, they were parked in the dark next to the concrete silos of their target.

"Man, I hate to drag this stuff to the top of this thing! What do they think we are—mules?" Lefty groused.

"Aw shut up, will ya, this is the easiest five grand you've ever made, so quit your belly aching," Ralph snarled. "Let's get it over with and get out of here."

They soon had a lock broken off of the door to the office and were inside, flashing light around to see if there was anything to worry about. Seeing nothing unusual, and no one around, they proceeded up the never-ending stairs. In an hour, they had made their way to the top and had spread the infection. On their way down, about two stories from the ground, they heard the rumbling of a diesel engine outside. Ralph looked through a window and was startled to see a long string of grain hoppers being backed up to the rail siding by the silos. It looked like they were going to be shipping a lot of grain in the next day or so. But what worried him more was the fact that there were a couple of pickups parked outside. One guy was walking around with a clipboard counting cars and recording their numbers.

"We've got trouble Lefty! There's a train backing in here and there's a couple of guys checking the cars," Ralph said.

"What the heck are we going to do?" Lefty asked worriedly.

"I guess we just sit tight until they take off."

"Nuts to that! They could be here all night. We've got to get out of here now!" Lefty exclaimed way too loudly.

"Be quiet you idiot, do you want them to hear us?"

"I don't care if they do; I'm getting out of here. This place gives me the creeps!"

"Okay, okay, take it easy will ya! We've got to think of a way to get outside without those guys seeing us." Ralph reasoned.

"There's got to be a back door to this dump. We'll find it

and sneak out to the truck," Lefty said, desperately needing a drink.

The two burglars found a side door that they had to force open; it obviously hadn't been used in years. They were creeping up the side of the silo towards the truck when a bright flashlight blinded them.

"Where you going, boys?" someone asked. They didn't answer.

"Come out here under the light so that I can see you better," the voice demanded.

"Why should we?" Lefty asked as he prepared himself to attack the light. Years on the streets of Chicago had made him a very dangerous opponent in a fight.

"Because my rifle here wants you to, now get moving!"

Suddenly someone shoved both of them forward toward the man that was speaking to them. "Get moving, you creeps," the voice behind them shouted. "Keep your hands where we can see 'em."

Lefty and Ralph moved toward the light warily, looking for any chance to wage an attack. When they got to the light, Ralph could see that these were the two men who were checking the train. One of them held a rifle that was pointed right at them, and they could see that the guy meant business.

"What were you guys doing in the elevator?" the man with the rifle asked.

"We were just looking for a place to sleep; got tired of driving," Ralph lied.

"You're a liar!" the man with the rifle shouted, as he spat out some tobacco. "You two are just a couple of thieves; we're calling the cops. Hand me your backpack, so I can see what you've swiped."

This was the chance the Chicago street fighters were looking for. Ralph carefully took off his pack and slowly handed it to the guy with the rifle. Just as the man reached for the pack, Ralph let it drop, causing the man to automatically

Chapter Thirty-Six

react and try to catch it. That was his last and fatal mistake. In one rapid motion, Ralph had his flashlight crashing into the man's skull with all the force he could muster. The big man dropped to his knees, then fell flat on his face, without making a sound. He was dead before he hit the ground. Lefty knew the drill and waited until the man behind them tried to come to his friend's aid. He stuck out a leg, tripping the unsuspecting fellow, who fell to the ground yelling at the top of his lungs. Lefty jumped on him and began to beat him mercilessly with his own flashlight. In a moment, it was all over. Ralph could tell that both men were dead. Without exchanging a word, they raced for their truck. Ralph started it, jammed it into drive and boiled out of the lot heading for Highway 20. What both of them had forgotten was that they had left their backpacks behind. Both of the packs still contained a little of the infected grain. But the two men could not have cared less. All they cared about was getting out of state, pronto!

When the state police arrived several hours later to investigate the double homicide, the backpacks were taken as evidence and placed in the evidence locker at headquarters. No one bothered to examine the grain.

Chapter Thirty-Seven

Nuhoma Corporation was continuing to make a huge impact on the American Commodity exchanges with their immense purchases of wheat, corn, soybeans, and some barley. Because speculators quickly learned that when Nuhoma entered the bidding for grain, the price was guaranteed to go higher; they bought future contracts knowing that the price was going to hit the limit for daily trading. It was a sure thing. These professionals were making fortunes as were all commodity-trading firms.

Roshan Norwall, Chairman of Nuhoma, was in his office in Des Moines having just been notified by the bank that another one hundred million dollars had been transferred into the company's bank account.

Norwall believed that he had died and gone to heaven! He was skimming millions from false grain hauling charges, funneling money into his phantom companies. He was also playing the commodity trading futures contracts because he knew that the price would only go up as Nuhoma bought everything it could bid on. The fact that American food prices were going sky high and people were having a hard time paying for their groceries meant absolutely nothing to him.

The phone on his desk rang, interrupting his delicious thoughts about how rich he was becoming. He was so excited he was already on his second towel of the morning.

"Yes, what is it?"

"Sir, there is a call from a gentleman that works for us in Chicago, and he says that he needs to talk to you right away.

Chapter Thirty-Seven

His name is Steve Smith."

"Smith! I'll bet his name is Smith. Okay, put him through."

"Hello, is this Mr. Norwall?" the voice on the phone asked.

"Yes it is, Mr. Smith, what can I do for you?"

"I need to advise you that the program dealing with stored grain is nearly finished. About one hundred facilities have been visited, leaving at least another hundred facilities, which could be visited and would make a much bigger impact on surplus supplies. Do you want us to continue or stop the program?" Smith asked.

Norwall thought for a moment. If he took the initiative and authorized the expansion of the elevator program, and it was successful, he would look like a genius to headquarters. If it went bad, he could be in a world of trouble. He was flush with the success of his personal illegal activities, which may have been influencing his judgment. Nonetheless, he said, "You have my approval to expand the program to at least another hundred additional facilities. Just make sure that the training program is continuous so there will be no mistakes. Got it?"

"Got it! We'll get more raw materials growing now, so we'll be ready to travel to the facilities tomorrow. There are a lot of elevators in Kansas, Minnesota, and in North and South Dakota that have been bypassed. We'll target those facilities first and then smaller facilities later."

"Good, is there anything else?"

There was silence on the line for a few seconds. "There is one small thing that you might be interested in; a watchman in a facility in Des Moines was found dead today. The press is not saying if it was murder or not, but it is a strange coincidence. That elevator was on our list and should have been treated the night before they found the dead guy. It may be nothing; just thought you should know," Smith said as he waited for a reply.

"Is there anything that could link this unfortunate happening to us?"

"I don't see how. None of the people working for us even know our corporate name. They're paid in cash, so there is no paper trail of any kind to link Nuhoma with the men; all of them came from the streets of Chicago and they are only interested in money," Smith reported.

There was a nagging thought in the back of Norwall's brain warning him to be careful, but his greed swayed his thinking, and he said, "Okay, go ahead, but verify that the training is thorough, and the men do not know we exist."

"Okay. Goodbye."

Norwall did not respond. He just hung up the phone and returned to examining spreadsheets regarding the company's financial status. In his mind, the business was doing lousy! They were spending vast sums of money while bringing in no revenue. The investments in ethanol plants that had cost millions of dollars were not making a profit. They had ordered thousands of tons of corn to fuel these refineries, which were now either on site, or enroute. The few farmers that had taken the company up on financing their seed purchases and buying the crop insurance brought in hardly any cash. Even though those that did not agree to the plan were victims of special encouragement in the form of fires in their outbuildings, the number of farmers accepting was small. This special encouragement terrified Norwall. This enforcement program could really backfire on them if it was ever discovered.

He checked shipping reports and found that two more bulk freighters had just left the Chicago docks heading for sea. Three more were at anchor, waiting for their turn at the elevator to load their grain cargo. He noticed the cost of keeping these freighters at anchor was outrageous, thousands of dollars per day. He needed to talk to someone at headquarters and have them stop hiring so many ships at the same time. People at the

Chapter Thirty-Seven

main office needed to schedule these things more carefully.

If Roshan knew what was happening with his independent contractors Lefty and Ralph, he would have listened more carefully to the nagging thought in the back of his head. They had been stopped near the Illinois border as the result of an all points bulletin sent to all police agencies and were now being questioned in Dubuque by the Dubuque Police Department. The Iowa State Police, working closely with the police department, had sent out requests for all information or evidence concerning the three murders. Their clothes and their flashlights had been sent to the crime lab for forensic investigation. Lefty and Ralph were being interviewed separately, but the street-wise thugs were not talking. They just grinned and said they wanted an attorney and went happily back to their cells. The weak one of the pair was certainly Lefty because of his alcoholism. He was now beginning to have the shakes and occasionally see pink snakes. This had not escaped the notice of the jailers, who passed the info on to the detectives. They let him sit for a couple of hours; then pulled him back into an interrogation room to corroborate his story one more time.

Detective Tim Zorovich looked at the shaking Lefty and said to him, "Man, you look really rough, are you going to be okay?" the detective, nicknamed Zorro, asked.

"I will, if you'll give me a drink," Lefty replied.

"You know I can't do that, but I can get you some medication that will make you feel better, but first we need to get these killings behind us. What can you tell me, my friend?"

"Man, I'm sick. Get me some of the stuff you said would make me feel better."

"Not so fast; we need some information that will help us. You're going away for a long time. We've got your rap sheet man; it's four pages long. You're going down on the habitual criminal act. Cooperate with us, and I'll put in a good word for you with the District Attorney. Maybe it can help with where you do your time; no promises you understand, just maybe. Now, my friend, what were you guys doing around those grain elevators? Were you trying to steal equipment or something?" Zorovich asked.

"Naw, there's nothin' to steal in them places! We were just spreading a little grain around," Lefty replied.

"Spreading a little grain around? Are you kidding me? If you're trying to make jokes, we can arrange for you to spend more time waiting for the drugs!" Zorovich was angry and was about to end the interview and send the guy back to his cells.

"No, wait, I'm not kidding. Some guy hired us, along with a bunch of other guys, to spread grain that they gave us on top of the stuff in those big whatever you call 'em," Lefty squirmed.

"Why were you asked to put grain on top of grain? What's that supposed to do?"

"Don't ask me, man! I got no idea. All that we had to do was put the stuff on top of the grain in them concrete things, and we got five thousand bucks for doin' it." Lefty was getting desperate and wanted to throw up.

Zorro changed the subject abruptly and asked, "Why did you kill those guys at the elevator?"

"Man, we didn't want to; they jumped us when we came out the back door. We didn't have a choice, man; they had a gun. What else could we do?" His complexion was pasty white, and Zorovich thought this guy was really going to be sick.

"Tell you what, old friend. I'm going to get your statement typed up so you can sign it. While we're doing that, I'll get the medicine coming and have a doctor take a look at you, okay?"

"Whatever! Just bring me some help." The detective misjudged how bad Lefty was getting; the gangster vomited

Chapter Thirty-Seven

all over the room and the furniture. Zorovich swore and yelled for a jailer to get the guy out of there.

Later in the day, the detective questioned Ralph, but this time he had Lefty's confession as ammunition. Ralph listened, shrugged his shoulders, and said, "Okay, we did it, but you haven't got it all; there was also a guy just north of Des Moines. We killed three all together. But if I tell you about the grain, I want a deal!"

"You've been around long enough to know that I can't promise a deal. I'll take your information to the District Attorney and tell him you cooperated with us, he might go a little easier on both of you."

"Don't you lump me in with that idiot, Lefty. He's just a worthless drunk; he don't know nothin'!" Ralph shouted.

"Okay, we'll give the District Attorney your stuff. Now give us the statement and I'll get the paperwork going."

Zorovich rushed back to his office and began making phone calls to other departments. When he found out that the State Police had the backpacks in their property room, he got a subpoena to transfer the backpacks to his department and then get them to the lab as soon as possible. He had no idea what they might find, but he had a hunch it was going to be important.

Chapter Thirty-Eight

Herb Worthington called Tuck at his apartment and asked him to come to the office as soon as he could. "Things are poppin' around here and I need you to come in to the office now!"

Tuck grabbed a cab and headed for Langley. As soon as he arrived, he made a beeline for Herb's office. When he walked into the glassed-in outer office, Sally, Herb's secretary, smiled, jumped up, and gave him a hug. "Glad to see ya, Aristotle! Go on in, the old man's waiting for you," she gushed while snapping her gum loudly.

Tuck hated it when she called him by his real name, but she was a nice lady, so he didn't make a big deal of it. Herb waved him to a chair and started talking before Tuck could hit the seat. "Tuck, we've got a chemical breakdown on the grain you brought back from Tehran, and we have an autopsy on our good friend, the mouse. First, the grain has been genetically altered. We're not sure why, but it has been. The boys at the lab are still running experiments, and we should find out the results pretty soon. This is where the biochemist, Dorri Golnessa, comes into the picture. This must have been the project she was working on for Faridoon, and I can't believe that his motive was for the welfare of mankind. We need to talk to her and see if we can get any information out of her while she's in Illinois. We can use your help because you speak her language. I need you to fly to Chicago and see what this lady has to say. At the very least, we'll get her deported so she can't do anymore damage here."

"Sure, I'll get on the next plane to the windy city, but let's

Chapter Thirty-Eight

hold off on kicking her out of the country. I've got a feeling that she might be easier to talk with than we think. Lemon found out," he couldn't help choking up a little at the thought of his young friend, "that she has had a rough time in life, and that has always been at the hands of brutal or powerful men. Maybe we can use that information to our advantage when we talk to her."

"Okay, get going and I'll keep the information coming to you as soon as we receive it. When you get to Chicago, you need to contact Stanley Grizzell, the FBI Bureau Chief. This whole thing is in his court now." Herb said.

Tuck got up to leave and as he passed Sally's desk, she handed him an American airline ticket to Chicago. It always amazed him how the government could do things very efficiently when they put their minds to it.

Four hours later, he walked out of the bright sunshine and into Grizzell's office and introduced himself. He noticed that his hand disappeared in the bear's big paw. J. Edgar Hoover would roll over in his grave if he could see the size of this agent. He didn't fit the cookie cutter dimensions that the former Director preferred.

Grizzly motioned Tuck to a chair in his rather stark office equipped with plain furniture and the requisite venetian blinds covering the only window. The only thing unusual Tuck noticed was that the Bureau Chief had his own water cooler, and there was a pitcher of the stuff sitting on his desk.

"So you've just come back from Iran, huh? What's it like over there?" he asked.

"It's pretty crazy right now. The people are madly in love with their new president, and he is doing just about anything he wants, especially with their money. The agency thinks this alliance scheme of his has anti-American overtones, particularly because of the speech he made at the United Nations. We have heard some of those notions in public, but I think there is a lot more we don't know about," Tuck explained.

"We think you might be right, but we don't have enough hard evidence to complete the story. One link might be this Dorri Golnessa. We've been watching her, thanks to you guys giving us a heads up. She has been acting pretty weird," Grizzell said while rubbing his chin with his giant paw.

"Like what?" Tuck asked.

"This lady flies all over Europe before coming to New York. She immediately gets on a plane for Chicago where we followed her from the airport to an abandoned warehouse down by the docks. This place was full of about a hundred thugs off of the streets. You wouldn't want to meet any of these guys after dark! After a few hours, a rental truck was loaded with something and takes off, and a little later, the creeps take off in their own vehicles. For a few minutes, the traffic was like it is after a Cubs game! But this lady of the world stays in this dump all night! The next day she calls a cab and goes to the University of Illinois where we understand she is going to do some teaching in a cultural exchange program. I sure would like to know what American politician puke put that deal together!" Grizzly was puffing and blowing as he got himself worked up about the stupid things politicians conjure up.

"You guys are following her, but is anybody else watching what she is doing?" Tuck asked.

"Yeah, somebody was on the plane with her, and a big guy met her at the airport and then followed her to the university. Our guy that was observing them thought that the two might have been having a squabble."

"It's probably the Pasdaran, the Iranian foreign intelligence service. You need to warn your guys that these people play for keeps. They probably have agents at the university posing as students. I don't know what you think, Stan, but I think we should go ahead and play the cards we've been dealt and bring her in for questioning. There doesn't seem to be much of a down side," Tuck added.

Chapter Thirty-Eight

"I'm with you. I'll get the okay from the State Department. We don't want to ruffle the diplomat's feathers. They think everyone in the whole world would love us if we would just talk to them. The geniuses at the State Department put together this cultural exchange deal; they probably want us to join the Persian Alliance."

"How long will that take?"

"Couple of hours at the outside. We should be able to get her this afternoon."

"I suggest that we visit with her at the university. It will be a comfortable surrounding for her, and she might be more willing to talk with us, particularly if she thinks that the Persians following her might not see us," Tuck suggested.

"Sounds good to me; I'll get the paperwork going and then maybe we can get some lunch." Grizzly looked hungry, which made him look a little bit fierce. They stopped at a fast food chain where Tuck ordered chili and crackers. Grizzly ordered two cheeseburgers and a salad. The salad was an attempt to appease his wife who was always after him to eat healthy food.

An hour later, they were on their way to the University of Illinois in an unmarked Chevy Impala that had been seized as a result of a drug arrest. As they drove together, the two agents became good friends. They were both working for the same thing—the security of the United States. As they drove, Grizzly stated, "I heard that you took a serious beating in Tehran. How are you getting along; is everything okay?"

"Yeah, I feel pretty good, thanks for asking. I was in pretty bad shape with a damaged kidney from a sucker punch by a mugger. While I was out cold, my team told me that a friend visited me. When I woke up, I felt pretty darn good. I don't really know what he did during the visit, but I sure felt a lot better!" Tuck exclaimed.

"Neat story; sounds like the Lord healed you," Grizzly said without embarrassment.

"I don't know about that; I'm not religious. I don't believe in spirits or a higher authority, so I can't imagine that a guy that I don't believe exists would do anything for me. It just doesn't compute in my little pea brain."

Before they could finish their discussion, they turned into the parking lot of the Administration building. Both men were convinced that the bad guys were probably watching Dorri, so they wanted it to look like university people were calling her to an office for a meeting. An agent dressed like a professor, carrying an arm full of books and a bulging brief case, got out of another unmarked car and went into the building to make the arrangements. In just a few minutes, the agent came back out, climbed into his car, and pulled out of the lot. That was the signal that the meeting had been arranged. Grizzell left the car first and wandered into the beautifully designed structure. Tuck followed in about five minutes. They were shown to an office in the back of the reception area. Dorri was escorted in a few minutes later, and when she saw them, she was stricken with terror. She knew instinctively that these men were from the American government and were probably here to arrest her.

Tuck spoke to her quietly in Farsi and assured her that she should not be afraid. "Miss Golnessa, I work for the CIA and my friend here, Mr. Grizzell, works for the FBI. We are aware of some of your activities. Will you tell us more about your visit to the United States?" Tuck inquired.

Dorri was very quiet; her mind was whirling with what could happen to her in this foreign land. What were her options? If she told these men what she knew, she could never go home again. In fact, she would probably be killed by Faridoon's government. Tears welled up in her eyes. Once again men were deciding her fate, perhaps even whether she would live or die.

Tuck was sensitive to what she must be feeling and reached across the table and touched her hand lightly. He smiled at her

Chapter Thirty-Eight

and asked, "Would you like to have some tea?"

"Yes, please," she said without looking up. Tuck noticed the terrible scars on her otherwise beautiful face. They were a stark, deep purple, due to the stress she was suffering.

The tea was served, and as she sipped the hot brew, she relaxed somewhat and looked at both men closely. She observed the huge man sitting quietly off to one side of the room, but for some reason he no longer frightened her.

Tuck wanted to be very careful interrogating her. He had a hunch that she was a very lonely person and that it would be more productive to be friendly and not try to force information from her. He knew that Grizzly would agree with this approach.

"Miss Golnessa, I have been in your laboratory in the Agricultural building in Tehran. We believe that you were working on something in the field of biochemistry that was designed to harm the United States." He paused and then continued, "Oh, and I need to tell you that we found a dead mouse." Tuck was anxiously waiting to see her reaction, but he didn't have to wait long. She broke down completely, sobbing and wailing that she never meant to hurt anyone.

"A dead mouse? Where did you find this mouse?" she inquired, her voice rising a little higher.

"We found the little guy in a corner of your old laboratory. We also found some grain by the rodent," Tuck responded.

Dorri continued to sob softly. In a few minutes, she regained her composure and said, "Arastoo said that I was doing important research that would help Persia become a powerful nation. He said I was a patriot!" she managed to say.

Tuck was wise enough to be quiet and let her talk. He knew that she had pent-up issues that she was ready to get off of her chest, and he believed she was ready to do a lot more talking. Tuck leaned slightly closer to her and looked deeply into her eyes. He did not see a terrorist. He saw a frightened young woman who was being used by a megalomaniac to further his own goals. The CIA agent quietly whispered, "Miss Golnessa, there may be many lives at stake here. Will you tell us what kind of research you were doing in Tehran?"

Dorri glanced into the agent's eyes and made a decision. "Yes, I will tell you what my research entailed. You are probably not a chemist, so I will try and use familiar terms to describe my work."

"Thank you, you are very kind," Tuck replied gratefully.

"In the simplest of terms, I was working to hack into the DNA makeup of bacteria. The assignment was to make bacteria alter the genetic makeup of grain kernels, so that they would spoil, and cause any other kernels they touched to spoil as well. The bacterium is self replicating, so there is a continuous supply of newly infected grain to be used for Arastoo's diabolical plan." She paused to see if Tuck was following what she was describing.

"What does he want to do with the spoiled grain?"

"He wants to destroy to entire grain surplus that the United States has in storage."

Grizzell couldn't keep silent any longer. "What is going on; what is she saying?" he blurted out. Tuck held up his hand asking Grizzell to wait a minute, and he asked, "Are you comfortable speaking in English?"

Dorri was startled by the big man's outburst; she had forgotten that he was still in the room. She said, now speaking in English, "I'm really not sure. But I believe the destruction of the grain surplus is part of a larger plan that the president is working on. If you heard his speech to the United Nations, you heard him speak out against the United States. I think the real answer deals with his own ego. He wants his new Persian Empire to become the strongest alliance in the world."

Tuck was trying to process all the information they had received when a sense of urgency overwhelmed him. Suddenly he jumped up and asked, "Miss Golnessa, what happened to

Chapter Thirty-Eight

the bad grain? Where is it now?"

Dorri looked at her hands and whispered, "Men were hired to take the infected grain and spread it in storage facilities all over the middle part of America. I'm afraid that much, if not all, of the grain has been distributed already and is now at work spoiling the surplus grain your country has put aside."

"How many guys were hired to spread the stuff?" Tuck asked, on his feet again.

"I think there are a hundred or more going to states in the middle of America with the first batch of bad grain, but I am afraid that they might strike more than once."

Tuck turned to the grizzly with shock on his face. "Man, this could be a big deal! I don't know how much grain the country has in storage, but it must be huge. What I don't understand, is how this helps Faridoon?"

Grizzell thought for a minute then said, "I can get on the wire and see if the Bureau has stumbled on any unusual activity coming from Iran, like an increase in agents, unusually large amounts of money coming in, something like that." As he spoke, he was pawing his cell phone out of a pocket and moved to the side of the room so that he could hear better.

Dorri spoke up and asked Tuck, "What did you find out about the dead mouse?"

"We haven't gotten any information yet. I understand that the agency decided to send our furry friend to the Center for Disease Control in Atlanta, with a request for a priority designation. We have to find out the cause of death."

"I should tell you, sir, that we were conducting an experiment at the warehouse and we fed rats some of the infected grain. We needed to do this because there was such a rush to get the bacteria DNA changed that I did not have time to conduct the experiments that should have been performed before the bacteria left the lab."

"Well, what happened?"

"They died!" she exclaimed while wiping a tear from her eye.

"Why did they die?" Tuck asked.

"I don't know what killed them. I just know that there is something in the bacteria on the grain that has become deadly. I am terrified that it might also be deadly to humans! I was not allowed the time to run experiments on the infected grain to see if it was dangerous; I needed more time!"

Now she was weeping fiercely due to the realization that her work might result in people dying, maybe thousands of people dying! She didn't think she could bear the guilt.

Tuck ran to where Grizzly was talking on the phone and grabbed him by the arm interrupting his conversation. "Hold it, Stan; this is important! Tell your office to send out a flash alert to all police departments, sheriff departments, and state police agencies telling them to get armed guards around all grain elevators in the Midwest. Tell them a foreign power is trying to infect the grain stored in the silos with some stuff that looks like it might be deadly!" Grizzly nodded and got back on the phone.

Tuck grabbed his Voyager and called Langley. When Herb answered, Tuck was trying hard not to shout. "Herb, you have got to get to the CDC and tell them we need to know what killed the mouse now, not tomorrow." He then gave Herb a run-down on their conversation with Dorri.

Herb said, "Don't let that woman out of your sight; get her to an FBI safe house.

"Gotcha!" Tuck said. He turned his attention back to Dorri and saw that she was near hysteria. He stuck his head out of the office and found a clerk working nearby. "Excuse me, we have a medical emergency in here; will you call a doctor, please?"

He knew that they had to get Dorri out of here and into a safe place. Faridoon probably had agents located on campus, so haste was important. He turned to Dorri and said, "Miss, we have to get you out of here and take you to a place where you will be safe. When your president finds out you've been

Chapter Thirty-Eight

talking to us, your life won't be worth a plugged nickel!" She looked at him, puzzled about what nickels had to do with anything, but he didn't take time to explain.

Grizzell came over to them and said, "The word's out. Guards should be surrounding the elevators sometime today. Dorri, what does the infected grain look like? How can we tell without chemical tests if the grain is good or bad?"

"It looks slightly bleached and a little shriveled. Inspectors should be able to see the difference if they look very closely," she answered.

"Okay, that means we have to notify all food producers that use grain as well as the meat and poultry industries. We also have got to get the state health departments in all of these states to stop all grain shipments until every load of grain is inspected. This is going to be a gigantic job and will take some time. Tuck, we need to get out of here so I can get back to the office; I can't work on this stupid toy!" he whined as he jammed the cell into his pocket.

Just then the door opened and a thin middle aged man with blazing red hair and half-glasses poked his head in and asked if someone needed a doctor.

"Yeah, doc, the lady could use something to calm her down. She's had a lot of bad news today."

The doctor came in and examined Dorri's eyes checked her pulse and breathing. He took a bottle of pills from his case and told her they were light tranquilizers. "She should take two now and two at bed time," he smiled and left. Tuck, ever observant, noticed that the index finger on the doctor's right hand was missing. Dorri, nearly fainting, had noticed nothing.

They turned to leave the room; Tuck put the pills in his pocket, planning to give them to her when they got to the safe house. They walked carefully to the parking lot, got in the car and roared toward the freeway.

At the same time the agents drove out of the lot, tractor

trailer bulk grain rigs and trains pulling hundreds of hopper cars were leaving elevators in Iowa and Nebraska, loaded with grain destined for flour mills and cereal producers. Others were rolling for delivery to producers of cattle and poultry feed.

Chapter Thirty-Nine

Arastoo sat at his ornate desk while he put the finishing touches on the speech he was going to deliver to the nation that evening. He wanted to have the largest possible audience, so he scheduled the speech to begin at 8:00 p.m., just at the beginning of the soccer match between Persia and Pakistan. His staff had tried to convince him that interrupting a hotly contested soccer match was not a good idea, but he demanded that it be done. His giant ego convinced him that the people of Persia would much rather see him and listen to an important speech than watch a silly soccer game.

Minister Payam was anxious to meet with Arastoo to discuss some new intelligence information, but the president was distracted by the writing of his speech, so Payam was kept waiting in an outer office.

Arastoo finished his speech and committed it to his incredible memory. He then moved to a full-length mirror to practice the gestures and facial expressions he would use to make the speech more effective. He looked at his image with great satisfaction and anticipated the national reaction he would generate when he told his people that in order to govern the nation and the alliance more effectively, he needed the power of a king! He would ask the 290-member parliament to grant him this title and give him the throne for life! This decision would, of course, have to be approved by the Council of Guardians.

The president had neglected to inform the Supreme Leader Khodadad of his decision, but he was certain that this would not be a problem. Surely the great man would see the wisdom of having a monarchy to control the rapidly growing Persian Empire. He smiled at himself and said aloud, "O great Cyrus, you had to be king when you formed the first Persian Empire twenty five centuries ago. I, your direct descendent, will now do the same in order to govern the new Persian Empire, which will soon be the largest nation in the world."

He did not notice that Afsoon, his secretary had entered the room unannounced and was listening to him. She silently turned and left the room, perplexed at what she had just heard.

Reluctantly, the president returned to his desk and rang Afsoon to send the minister in. While he waited, he mused about what his official attire should be when he became king.

Payam slid quietly into the room, bowed and wished the president good morning and waited for permission to be seated. Faridoon motioned him to take a seat; he was irritated by the interruption.

"What is it, Payam?"

"Your Excellency, we have disturbing news from America," he exclaimed nervously.

Faridoon was now listening intently. "What news?" he asked.

"The American FBI has taken our scientist Dorri Golnessa for questioning. They apparently have been following her since she arrived."

"This is a complication that we all worried about when we sent her to the United States to supervise the replicating of the new strain of bacteria. What is your recommendation Minister?"

Payam was noticeably distressed. "Your Excellency, you were meeting with alliance members all day yesterday, and left word that you were not to be disturbed, so I..." he hesitated.

"You imbecile, what did you do?"

The minister was close to losing his breakfast. He stammered, "I took it upon myself to issue an order for our

Chapter Thirty-Nine

agents to pick her up, or ..."

"Or what? Tell me what you've done. you fool!"

"I ordered them to pick her up or eliminate her!" he said, quaking. He was sure that his life was now at its end.

Faridoon was silent for several minutes, thinking. Then, quietly, he said, "Good! You have done the right thing. Your actions will protect our nation from unwanted scrutiny regarding our plans for the United States. Well done, Payam! Is there anything else?"

"No, sir, nothing else."

"Then you may go. Thank you again for your quick and clear thinking, it will not be forgotten."

Payam bowed and left the room. He was absolutely beaming due to the praise he had just received.

Faridoon spent the remainder of the day meeting with various ministers who were presenting reports on their departments.

Behruz reported that he was alarmed about two problems that had surfaced dealing with the alliance, which caused him some concern. One problem was that members of the alliance had begun shipping raw materials to Persia in payment for food and oil, but there were little or no storage facilities to handle things like iron ore, exotic timber, or bauxite. Further, they were having a difficult time finding buyers for these materials; many nations decided to get their supplies from other countries. The United States, in particular, had boycotted all purchases from Persia, and had, in fact, actually reduced the amount of crude they would purchase. They simply increased their purchases from other OPEC countries.

The second problem, a startling number of the alliances were not making any kind of payment, either in raw materials or in cash. They seemed to consider the food and oil to be foreign aid from Persia rather than from the United States.

Minister Behruz complained that the cost of grain purchases had already exceeded two hundred million dollars, which did not include the cost of shipping and storage. The shipping of oil to the alliance members at a discounted rate had lowered revenues by millions of dollars, increasing the stress on the nation's finances.

Faridoon did not want to hear this kind of news before making such an important speech, so he said that he noted the minister's concern and would address the issues later.

The time for the speech to the nation had nearly arrived. He had made arrangements to have the broadcast take place from his new office located in his palace. Arastoo was behind his desk having makeup applied when Afsoon came in and quietly said, "Mr. Diablo is here and wants to speak with you right away. He is very insistent!"

Arastoo was furious and screamed at his unfortunate secretary that he could not be bothered right before his speech. He roared, "You tell him that he will have to wait until after the speech. I cannot be distracted right now!"

Afsoon withdrew, fearful of Arastoo, but also fearful of delivering his message to the tall stranger that always seemed to appear at the wrong time. She slowly walked to her office where Diablo was seated and found him quietly leafing through a magazine. She went up to him and said, "I am sorry, sir, but the president says he cannot see you now because he is preparing to speak to the nation. He will be glad to see you as soon as he is finished."

Diablo said nothing, giving her a look that froze the blood in her veins. He slowly rose to his feet, walked so close to her that she could smell his breath, which had an unusual odor. She instinctively backed up, but he just moved closer. He finally spoke, "Thank you, Miss Afsoon. Please tell the president that he has made a very grievous mistake because I had some very important information to give to him before his speech. I most certainly will speak to him later." Then he was gone!

Arastoo used great emotional effort to calm himself. Soon the director motioned to him that he would be live in five

Chapter Thirty-Nine

seconds. When the seconds passed, he looked into the camera, smiled broadly, and began to speak. Most Persians had tuned in to watch a soccer game, and they were not happy with the interruption.

"Good evening, my good friends. I am so proud to be allowed into your living rooms tonight to bring you what I believe is a very important announcement."

"You all know that our new alliance with countries all over the world has grown to include over fifteen nations in Africa, Asia, and Central and South America. This alliance is bringing people together from different races, religions, and cultural backgrounds. All of this diversity makes us a better and stronger nation. But, it also means that we are a much larger and a much more important nation."

"It is my suggestion that the countries in the alliance take the next logical step. They should no longer remain poor, independent nations, but join us as states in the Persian Empire!" He was now warmed up, smiling and gesturing with all of his usual fervor. He did not notice that the technicians working in the room and the few staff members watching the speech, were smiling a little as they glanced around the room, but they were not cheering.

Arastoo was not perspiring because he had had the foresight to have a huge air condition unit installed to keep this room cool as he intended to make many speeches to the world in the future. He was purposely speaking with a lower voice, which he believed made him sound wiser. He continued, "Now, my fellow countrymen I want to inform you of an important decision that I have made that will make us even stronger," he paused for effect.

"The running of a rapidly growing world wide nation requires experience and constant attention. It cannot be done by a president that has to run for reelection every four years, or a new person taking the reins who may not be qualified to govern. Therefore, I have made the decision that, for the good of the Persian Empire, I am asking the Parliament to declare me KING for life, and for the Council of Guardians to add their blessings!" He was shouting with both of his arms raised, almost as if he were in worship, praying to a god. He paused to regain his composure while glancing around the room. He was startled to realize that there was no cheering as he had expected there would be, but he, nevertheless, continued with his prepared remarks.

"You will remember that when the first Persian Empire was formed by the Great Cyrus twenty-five centuries ago, he became king in order to provide strength and stability to the largest nation of that time. The same things apply today. It is necessary that I become Arastoo the Great, King of the Persian Empire!" He stood and waved at the cameras while looking like a great, almost divine, somber monarch; he had practiced this for nearly an hour in front of his mirror before he got just the right presentation. He had changed his speech at the last minute because even his giant ego told him it was too much to say that he wanted to be known as CYRUS II!

A few of his staff offered their congratulations and support. Most of them, however, had disappeared. He walked regally out of the office to wait for the television and radio people to remove their equipment.

Throughout the nation, the soccer match filled the television screens and the nation learned that Persia had scored a goal during the speech. In many homes, however, there was stunned silence as people questioned what was happening.

Throughout Tehran, members of Parliament began calling one another asking, "Has he lost his mind?" Arastoo had anticipated that this might happen, so he had made arrangements with General Parvin to have the military take over all of the telephone offices in the country as well as disconnecting power to towers in order to disrupt phone service. Minister Ebrahim, in charge of the media, had people ready to take control of television, radio, and newspapers. Their responsibility was

Chapter Thirty-Nine

to publish only compliments and agreement with the public announcement that Arastoo should be king. The new monarch was not fooled by his own rhetoric. He fully realized that there would be some opposition.

He was prepared to take his limo to the home of the Supreme Leader, Ayatollah Bahman Khodadad, to explain his plan for world power when Diablo burst into the room and roughly pushed Faridoon into a chair. He glared down at him with bulging yellow eyes; the Oakley glasses were gone.

"Well, my friend, you've gone off the deep end!" Faridoon had no idea what that term meant, but he was too startled to object.

"I've done what needed to be done for Persia's benefit. Being king is a logical and natural progression in our history. This country loves having a king," Arastoo struggled to regain his composure.

"If you would have continued with my plan, you would have achieved everything you wanted. Now, the whole world will think you are nothing more than an egomaniac, just like your predecessor. You're on your own and free to do anything you wish, but you'll suffer the consequences!" He turned and stormed out of the room.

Arastoo jumped to his feet and shouted at the retreating figure of his former friend, and screamed, "I don't need you or anybody else!" He was shaking from the stress of the encounter. *How dare anyone talk to him in that way?* he asked himself.

He climbed into his limo and was driven to the home of the Supreme Leader. A servant showed him to a small, but elegant, room to await this important man's arrival. He was kept waiting for nearly an hour, which infuriated him. Finally Khodadad came in the room and greeted Arastoo coolly.

"What brings you here at this hour, Arastoo?"

"Sir, I wanted to explain to you the reasoning behind my speech tonight and to give you an update on how our plan is working to disrupt the economy and strength of the United States. I also want to update you on our progress in destabilizing the Zionists. We are rapidly becoming a world power, and we are growing stronger each day. Our country needs a strong, working monarch. Electing a president every four years is a distraction and makes the people uncomfortable."

"Who told you that, Arastoo?"

The self-appointed king was taken aback and did not know how to respond, so he was silent.

"I think you have disillusioned yourself. Your giant ego, which was a benefit to us before, now has become a detriment. But, we will leave that where it lies for now. I'll give you quiet support for the time being. I'll be watching you closely in the future. I caution you; be very, very careful!"

"Yes, sir, I will make very careful decisions, always planning to do what is best for Persia," Arastoo was very subdued when he answered.

Khodadad rose and left the room without further comment. As Arastoo exited to return to his limo, he began to smile a little. He had just overcome a tremendous hurdle, and his confidence was returning. Tomorrow was going to be a great day!

Chapter Forty

Tuck was sitting in a motel room in Chicago with the television on low while he watched the speech on his iPhone, patched through from a CIA spy satellite uplink. As soon as the speech was over, the phone rang. It was Herb.

"Did you see the speech?"

"Yeah, I sure did, but I'm not quite sure what to make of it, I kind of think the guy is going goofy!"

"You know who he reminds me of? Adolph Hitler! He has the same mannerisms and speaking delivery, and he sure has the same ego!"

"We need to watch him very closely, Herb. He seems to have a huge hatred for America, but is it fueled by jealousy or something else? I doubt if anyone knows how far he is willing to go to cause us harm."

"By the way, what's happening with the Iranian chemist?" Herb questioned.

"She's in an FBI safe house. She's pretty shaken, but a doctor gave her some tranquilizers."

"Good idea. I'm going to call the Center for Disease Control and see what they have discovered about Mr. Mouse. I've got a bad feeling about that little guy, but I can't put my finger on what's wrong."

"Well, Herb, remember Dorri has already told us that she changed the DNA of bacteria so that it would make grain spoil, and that grain would cause other grain it touches to spoil as well. The worst part is that the grain may be deadly to humans."

"That's why we sent out the alert to inspect all shipments

before they leave the elevators. The crazy guy in Tehran wants to ruin all of America's surplus grain and maybe kill us in the bargain. I think he believes that if he can ruin our economy our government will be preoccupied with keeping the country going and too busy to pay attention to his nation building," Tuck said. "Gotta go, Herb, see ya!"

"Okay, see ya." Herb said and hung up. He immediately used speed dial to contact the CDC in Atlanta. He could care less that it was getting late; he wanted some answers from those guys in the white coats. The phone was answered by an unknown person who didn't sound like a receptionist. He was put on hold for a short time, and then a man who identified himself as Doctor Renfro came on the line. Herb introduced himself and got down to business.

"What can you tell me about the mouse we sent you that was taken from a lab in Tehran?"

"He's dead!" The doctor said, trying to be funny.

Herb did not laugh. He sighed and said, "Doctor, the security of the United States may he at stake. Please spare me your humor and give me some information that I can use!"

The doctor cleared his throat nervously and said, "Agent Worthington, our tests show that the mouse died from a strain of bacteria that we have never seen before. The rodent apparently ingested some grain that was infected by this new, perhaps altered, bacteria. I use the term altered because it seems the DNA of the bacteria has been genetically tampered with. We put some of this stuff in a Petri dish with normal grain, and in a few minutes, the whole sample spoiled. We added more, and the same thing happened. The infected grain replicated itself by touching normal grain. It is a mystery to us why someone would want to make grain spoil, but that seems to be what the goal of this experiment was."

"Thank you, doctor. I will need a written report with your signature as soon as possible. But I want to tell you that you guys have got to get busy and find a way to destroy

Chapter Forty

that bacteria and also discover how to stop the spread of the infected grain. And while you're at it, find a way to save the people who have eaten the stuff! We think it could be deadly. Now, how do we get all of this research started? Do I need to call the White House or something?" Herb asked.

"No, have your boss call the United States Department of Health and get an order from the Director. In the meantime, I'll get my staff started working on some preliminary experiments while we wait for the bureaucrats to do their paperwork."

"Thanks, guy," Herb said and hung up and then used his speed dial to contact FBI headquarters in Washington. After a few minutes, he was connected with a man who identified himself as an analyst by the name of Broderick. His job was to share information with other members of Homeland Security. Herb gave him a short briefing of the information he had received from CDC in Atlanta to bring him to speed.

"Agent Broderick, has the Bureau had any information about any foreign entity being suddenly interested in commodities?" Herb asked.

There was a rustling of papers as the agent went through some computer printouts before answering. "I don't find anything that jumps out at me, but let me do some research and call you back. It will probably be tomorrow morning before I can get the information run through the computer and check with some other guys around here."

"Thanks Broderick, I appreciate your cooperation. I would ask you to put a high priority on this case; it could have serious implications for the good ole' USA."

"You've got it. Goodbye," he hung up and began making some inter-office phone calls.

Herb hung up and tried to decide what he should do next. For one thing, he needed to get another memo out giving the latest information from Tuck.

Tuck called Grizzly to see if he had any new data to think about. Grizzly said, "We're working hard on getting snitches to rat on the guys that were in the warehouse, but we are not having much luck. One thing that might be of interest; a couple of bad guys have been grabbed by the Iowa State Police. Know why they got 'em?" he asked playfully.

"Doggone it, Bear, I hate guessing games. I never get the right answer."

"They killed some guys around grain elevators!"

"What? What did you say? Grain elevators?" Tuck asked with excitement.

"That's what I said, grain elevators."

"Goodnight, Bear, that could be the common denominator in all of this. Dorri said Arastoo wants to destroy our surplus grain. These guys could be the foot soldiers doing the dirty work of spreading the infected grain. Who knows how many guys are out there spreading this wicked wheat. I think we need to get Dorri Golnessa out of that safe house and put her to work finding a way to stop the growth of bad bacteria. She's not doing us any good sitting around waiting to see what is going to happen to her."

Grizzell said, "You call your boss and see if there is any more information while I get in my little Impala and pick you up. You know you CIA guys are not supposed to be doing anything in the country. I'd hate to have to turn you in!" he laughed.

"Yeah, yeah, wait until you want to do something in Iran; then we'll see who gets turned in!" Tuck responded playfully.

Tuck indeed was a CIA man who was a long way from foreign shores, but he felt that he could make a difference by talking with Dorri. He called Herb and was given the information about the infected grain the CDC had discovered.

"Great Scott, Herb. What's going on here? Is that egomaniac in Tehran trying to kill us with bad wheat?"

"I'm not sure, but it appears so. The FBI in Washington is checking their records for anything unusual regarding foreign

Chapter Forty

interest in our commodities. I think the lady scientist is our quickest link to solving this bacteria problem. Go see her now!"

"All ready on it! Grizzly is picking me up in a couple of minutes. We'll do our best to try and get her to help us now that she is in custody." Tuck hung up the phone and grabbed his jacket to protect himself from the slow drizzle that was coming down.

As Tuck waited for Grizzell, two more trains with over a hundred grain hopper cars headed out of Hays, Kansas, on their way to New Orleans where they would be off-loaded at an elevator. The grain then would be loaded on a freighter that was making its way up the Mississippi River from the Gulf of Mexico.

Chapter Forty-One

Detective Tim Zorovich was in his office when his intercom buzzed; it was his chief.

"Zorovich, you're working on those grain elevator murders aren't you?" the chief asked.

"Yes sir, I am. We have two suspects in custody, and I think one might cave if we sweeten a deal for him," Zorovich answered. He was pleased that his chief knew what he was working on.

"Detective, this thing is getting a lot bigger than a few guys getting bumped off by a couple of hoods. The FBI is sending an agent to work with us on the investigation. It seems like this thing has some kind of national implication. I want you to cooperate with the feds as much as you can. Let's work together. I don't want even a hint of a turf war!" the chief said.

"Sure thing, chief. I just hope we don't get some frustrated director who wants to shove his college degrees down our throat. Remember the last guy they sent us? He thought he was God's gift to law enforcement!"

"I sure do. Well, do your best, and if the guy gives you any lip, let me know, and I'll chew on his boss's ear!"

"Fair enough, thanks!" Zorovich said, while he closed his eyes. *Here we go*, he thought to himself through clenched teeth. *Here comes another know it all federal creep who will try and take over the case. Rats!*

Almost as if by magic, there was a knock on his office door.

"Come on in," he yelled.

Chapter Forty-one

The door opened and a pretty, petite young woman with bright red hair came in and asked, "Are you Detective Zorovich?"

"Guilty. I'm Tim Zorovich, but guys around here call me Zorro. What can I do for you?"

She stood smiling in front of the detective's desk that was piled high with case files. "Hi, I'm Special Agent Valerie Ruskin. I work out of the Des Moines office and have been assigned to work as a liaison between your office and mine." She stuck her hand out to shake with the detective, who was just a little taken aback by her beauty.

They shook hands and Zorovich motioned for her to take a seat in front of the desk.

"Why is the FBI interested in some punks killing a couple of guys around a grain elevator?"

"Have you been watching this new president in Iran, excuse me, in Persia?"

"Not too much, been kind of busy working through this pile of junk on my desk," Zorro said, waving at the stack of file folders.

"The CIA and the Bureau believe that this guy is trying to ruin our country's surplus grain supply, causing prices to rise, and, he hopes, send our economy into a tail-spin. He thinks that we won't have time to watch his attempt to grab power around the world," the agent said.

The detective was already impressed with this special agent. She was obviously bright and not pushy.

"How is he going to do that?"

"We think his agents stationed in our country hired a bunch of thugs out of Chicago to spread grain that has been infected with genetically altered bacteria in grain elevators. When this contaminated grain touches good grain, it becomes spoiled. The government apparently has no idea how to stop the growth of this bacteria. There is also concern concerned that the infected grain might be deadly to humans if they eat it," Agent Ruskin explained.

"Criminey nuts! What are we doing about it? Do we have people guarding elevators?" Zorro exclaimed jumping to his feet.

"We do now, but it may be too late. We think tons of the infected grain has already left the area and has probably made its way into the food chain. The Bureau is trying to get inspectors on sight, but there are just not enough men to cover all of the elevators in the Midwest. Owners have been notified and asked to check the grain themselves. We have no idea what the impact of this will be. Imagine what the cost to insurance companies would be if they had to pay for millions of tons of spoiled grain. This sure can be classified as terrorist action in my book! A lot of people are going to go out of business if this is as big as we think it might be."

Tim settled down, and said, "It looks like you have a handle on the problem, so what are you doing here?"

"If we can get one of your suspects to give us some names of the other guys, we can start picking them up before they do more damage."

"Let's start with Ralph. Lefty is fighting the DTs, so he's not good for much."

They left the detective's office and went to the interrogation room to wait for Ralph to be brought over from the holding cell. He was ushered into the room where he caught sight of Valerie. A rude, lecherous grin broke out on his face as he leered at the agent. He said, "Well, now we're getting some place! Come closer baby, and I'll tell you anything you want to know and a few things that might surprise ya!"

Valerie smiled warmly and moved toward the prisoner. He had spittle on his chin as he openly lusted after the young woman. Suddenly she sprang at him with blinding speed, grabbing an arm and threw him to the floor. Ralph tried to resist but found her foot on his throat just under his chin. He couldn't speak or breathe, but she was careful not to injure

Chapter Forty-one

him. She growled, "Talk nice to me, little man, or you might fall and hurt yourself. Got it, goat face?"

The agent slowly allowed Ralph to return to his feet. He was furious and embarrassed, but respectful. Zorro loved the confrontation and laughed heartily. He had a real respect for this agent's abilities and was anxious to get to know her better. He pushed a chair at Ralph and commanded, "Sit down before you hurt yourself, Ralphie boy! The three of us need to have a little visit, but this is the last time we'll see your pretty face unless you do some talking."

"I've got nothin' to say to anybody," Ralph snarled, rubbing his throat with a dirty hand.

"You're looking at life in prison, my friend. If you cooperate we may, and I repeat may, be able to convince the District Attorney to settle for twenty-five years," Zorro said.

"That's not a deal! You get what you want and I get nothin'."

Agent Ruskin moved closer and stared into his eyes, saying, "It's life or twenty-five. It's your choice. We don't have time to fool with you. Answer our questions, or you'll never see sunlight again!"

Ralph thought for a minute; his swagger was suddenly gone. "What do you want to know?"

"We want names of the other men that were in this with you and particularly the name of the guy in charge and where the money came from."

Ralph was ready to spill his guts. They recorded all of the names he could remember, including the boss. The only thing he could remember about his boss was that his name was Steve, and he wasn't from Chicago; he might even be a foreigner. Ralph could shed no light on where the money came from.

"Anything else?" Tim asked.

"A woman came to the warehouse and did something to samples of grain that made it go bad. That was the stuff we used. I think she was a foreigner too, a real looker except for the scars on her face. I think she was a scientist or somethin'; she wore a white coat all the time."

"Okay, my friend. We'll see what we can do with the lawyers." He buzzed for a jailer to come and take Ralph back to his cell.

Valerie said, "I'll get these names to the Bureau right away. We might get lucky and find these jokers back on the streets in Chi town. We know about the woman; her name is Dorri Golnessa. She is a biochemist from Iran who was used by their president to invent this new strain of bacteria. We have her in a safe house now. She may be willing to cooperate to avoid being tried as a spy." She got up to leave, saying, "I've got to get back to Des Moines. I think you've got a good enough case to put the creeps away forever. It's been fun working with you." She stuck out her hand to Tim while walking to the door.

"I'll keep you advised on how things are going. If I ever get down to the big city, maybe we could get a cup of coffee?" he asked hopefully. He was thoroughly smitten by the lovely FBI agent.

"Let's do that," she said as she walked out. "See ya later."

"Yeah, right, later." Tim said with some sadness. He wondered if he would ever see her again.

Chapter Forty-Two

Woodson House in Chicago and the Commodity Geeks in Kansas City were beginning to have second thoughts about their transactions for the Nuhoma Corporation. The buy orders kept coming in as did the money, millions of dollars so far. Both traders were making tons of money in fees, and they were not unaware of the historic rise in commodity prices that these unrestricted purchases caused. Food prices throughout the country were at unheard of highs, and there were shortages of meat and poultry as feed grain became too expensive. Many firms were already out of business.

Jim Reynolds, president of Woodson House, was in turmoil over a decision that he should make. He felt that he needed to stop representing Nuhoma on the floor of the Board of Trade. He could no longer convince himself that this all was just good business, and if his firm didn't represent the corporation, someone else surely would. Everyone in the firm was getting rich, including himself, but at what cost? Poor people were having a hard time getting enough to eat because of the high prices of staples, like bread and cereal. Beef and chicken were too expensive to buy. Fish was still affordable, but who knew how long that would last as the giant fish distributors watched others making fortunes. For the last week, the stock market had fallen a thousand points with no end in sight. The dollar was in the tank compared with the Yen and the Euro. Commentators were constantly talking about the country going into a recession, which he knew would be a self-fulfilling prophecy. Most damaging to the country, though, was that unemployment was higher than it had been in the past eight years. He couldn't get all of this out of his mind, and he was certain that he and his firm were playing a large part in this drama.

Reynolds drove through a slight drizzle to meet with his pastor. He had to talk to him and ask for prayer because of this terrible guilt he was feeling. His pastor, a godly man, quoted a passage from a book by Ralph Waldo Emerson, "The ill-suppressed murmur of all thoughtful men...should be heard through the sleep of indolence, and over the din of the routine."

Reynolds asked sheepishly, "What does that mean, Pastor?"

"It means that you can no longer keep operating as usual. Your heart is telling you that you are gaining great wealth on the backs of poorer Americans. Jesus would never agree that what you are doing is right."

"Thanks, pastor, I just needed to hear it from someone else."

As he drove back to the office, Jim made up his mind. He would gather the staff together and give them his decision and the reason behind it. He knew that when you disturb people's wallet, they usually get very angry. Well, that was just too bad. There was such a thing as honor and a good reputation!

Immediately upon arrival at his office, he summoned all of his staff together. There were so many people that they had to gather in the dining room. Everyone was talking, laughing, and wondering what had prompted this extraordinary meeting in the middle of the business day.

"Ladies and gentlemen, I have come to a very difficult decision. Each of you, in your own heart, realizes that the huge transactions we are conducting for the Nuhoma Corporation are having a negative impact on the lives of our fellow Americans. We all know that buying commodities at these ever-rising prices is putting tremendous pressure on the food supply of this country. There is even talk that our great

Chapter Forty-Two

surpluses of grain are nearly gone with much of that surplus being shipped overseas. Foreign nations are getting the grain that our own people need."

"I must tell you that I can no longer, in good conscience, continue to be a part of this. I intend to contact Nuhoma immediately and give them my decision that we will no longer represent them. Any monies still in their account will be returned to them the next business day."

"I know this affects each of you personally. If you do not agree with this decision, I wouldn't be surprised if you decided to leave the firm as a result of the direction I have resolved to take. You do what is best for you and your family, but our getting wealthy on the backs of the American people has to stop, now!"

He braced himself for the angry response he knew he would receive. He was shocked instead to hear a groundswell of applause from the people gathered around him.

"Good for you, boss!" someone shouted. "We knew there was something fishy going on with this deal. I can't watch my 401K grow while my neighbors are starving. This will give us a chance to return to serving our old clients. Let's get back to them; they brought us to the dance!"

Reynolds could not help getting misty eyed. They pounded him on the back and punched him on the shoulder and shouted, "Go get 'em, boss!" He walked directly to his office, wiped his eyes and asked his secretary to get Nuhoma on the line.

In Des Moines, Nuhoma's chairman Roshan Norwall was just congratulating himself on successfully establishing two more dummy corporations to bill his company for services not rendered. That money would flow into his offshore accounts in the Grand Cayman Islands. The thought of it caused him to perspire even more. He would need to change his shirt again. He smiled broadly to himself. Oh, how he loved money!

His phone rang, and Miss Lattel said that a Mr. Reynolds

was on the line. He had to think a minute to remember who Reynolds was.

"Yes, Mr. Reynolds, what can I do for you this fine day?"

"Mr. Norwall, I am calling to advise you that we will no longer act as your broker on the floor of the Board of Trade. Your wild and reckless commodity purchases are having such a negative effect on the economy of the United States and her people that we no longer want to be involved."

"Why, you self righteous creep! You've made a fortune from representing our account. You can't just say goodbye like lovers ending an affair! We've got a contract, and you're going to honor it or we'll sue you for everything you've got," he raged.

"Sue away! That's why we have attorneys. Personally, I would love to have you show up in court and have our attorneys reveal that you and your company are responsible for our economy being in such a mess."

Norwall didn't like to hear that. He loathed appearing in public under any circumstances, but this would be too traumatic to even comprehend. He slammed down the receiver and shouted a string of obscenities while throwing files across the room. Miss Lattel heard the commotion but remained cowering in her chair. This was a time for privacy, she reasoned.

Just as peace was being restored, the door to the office opened, and two very tall and very tanned men walked in. They introduced themselves as Mr. Smith and Mr. Jones, producing a business card stating they were auditors for the Nuhoma Corporation. They asked to speak to Mr. Norwall immediately. Miss Lattel offered them chairs, but they said that they preferred to stand. The secretary walked quickly to her desk and buzzed Mr. Norwall, dreading how he might react.

"Yes, what is it?" he shouted into the phone.

"There are two men here from Nuhoma headquarters who

Chapter Forty-Two

want to speak with you."

These words startled him, causing the perspiration to flow in tiny rivulets down his face and under his collar. "Just a minute, please," he said as he dashed to his closet to get a fresh shirt.

He had just taken his drenched shirt off when the door burst open and the two men strode into the office.

"What do you mean barging in here like this? What is the meaning of this?"

"Shut up, fatso!" Mr. Smith ordered. "Get your shirt on. It makes me sick to look at you!"

Norwall struggled into a clean white shirt while turning his back to his intruders, trying to gain some semblance of privacy. Tucking his shirttail inside his trousers with a great deal of difficulty, he finally collapsed in his chair, wheezing like a steam engine low on water.

Smith got right down to business. He leaned over the desk and looked at Norwall with the smoldering gleam of malice in his eyes. "What do you think you are doing, fat boy?" he asked with a fiendish scowl on his face. "Can you possibly be so stupid to think that we would not catch on to your little scheme of skimming cash from the company?"

Norwall stuttered; sweat poured into his eyes, blinding him so that he could not see his tormentor clearly. "I...I don't know what you mean. I haven't skimmed any money from the company."

"Be quiet, you fool. We have friends that work in a little bank in the Grand Cayman islands. They say that there has been tons of money flowing into your little numbered account, adding up to about $7,500,000 so far. Do we pay you that kind of salary, Piggy?"

The chairman realized that his goose was cooked, and there was no sense in lying about it. "I...uh...don't know what to say. Is there anything I can do? Surely you will want me to resign, but perhaps we can arrive at some solution that benefits all of us."

Mr. Smith turned to Mr. Jones and said, "Did you hear that? He's trying to bribe us. Why, piggy, that's not nice." He came around the desk and slapped Norwall in the face, hard, causing large droplets of sweat to fly off of his face and land on his desk. He wiped his hand on the chairman's shirt then briskly walked to a chair and sat down.

"Here's what you're going to do, Pork Chop. You're going to pick up that phone and call the bank in Grand Cayman, close your personal account, and authorize them to wire the remaining funds to the Nuhoma headquarters in Des Moines. Since Mr. Jones and I have gone to a lot of trouble to track you down, it is only appropriate that you give us all of the cash you have on hand. Oh, by the way, the guys you had submitting false invoices for you; well, they had a little accident. You know how dangerous it can be working around water. Now get on the phone!"

The chairman, who had been so enamored with his own brilliance, was now terror-stricken. He dialed the bank, gave his code identification number and issued instructions on closing the account and wiring the cash to Nuhoma. In the meantime, Smith and Jones were busily stuffing cash they had discovered in the safe and in Norwall's personal briefcase and putting it into large cloth bags. When they finished, they closed the safe and motioned Norwall to get up. "Sorry Lardo, you've been replaced." Mr. Smith opened the door and a small, slender, bald man with huge glasses walked into the room. He had obviously been waiting in Miss Lattel's office while the official announcement was being made. The slim man sat down at the desk, ignoring everyone in the room. He produced a handkerchief from a pocket and began to wipe away the little pools of moisture that had escaped from Norwall's face when he had been assaulted.

Miss Lattel was so terrified she was unable to speak or move. She heard one of the men say, "Come with us, Mr.

Chapter Forty-Two

Piggy. We are going to take a little trip." They walked past her, each man clutching one of Norwall's arms, half dragging him out of the room. No one ever saw him again!

Chapter Forty-Three

Before leaving to pick Tuck up at his motel, Grizzell had been on the phone to the Bureau in Washington. He asked the assistant director to have his men search for any large amounts of dollars wired to banks in the United States from overseas.

"Funny you should ask that," the man said. "One of our analysts has been tracking millions of dollars coming into the country, transferred to a company in Des Moines called the Nuhoma Corporation. We haven't been able to learn where the money is coming from except that it originates in Macao. You know how their privacy banking laws are tight as a tick!" The agent continued, saying, "We do know that someone with a tremendous amount of clout is involved because all of the proper banking codes overriding standard Homeland Security regulations have been used to bypass current banking laws pertaining to the moving of dollars in large amounts."

"What have you got on this Nuhoma Company? I've never heard of it," Grizzly asked.

"It's a new company. Been in business about a year. They're in the commodity business, buying lots of grain on the Chicago and Kansas City Boards of Trade. They take possession of all the grain and ship huge amounts overseas."

That was all Bear needed to hear. Now, it was all falling into place. Persia was using this dummy corporation as a front to purchase American grain and ship it to its alliance members at cut-rate prices. This was what was causing the price of food to skyrocket and the surplus grain to disappear. What Faridoon wasn't shipping overseas, he was ruining with the new strain

Chapter Forty-Three

of bacteria. At last they knew what was going on; now they had to prove it!

He called the Bureau in Washington and the CIA in Langley, providing them with the details he had learned. They would then inform the White House and the Defense Department. There was now no doubt that Faridoon was trying to derail the country's economy. Search warrants were issued for the Nuhoma Corporation headquarters in Des Moines and all records were seized to be held for possible criminal prosecution.

It was vital that all companies using grain in their food production be warned so that they can inspect every railroad car and every truck before permitting any grain to be processed. That was the big boy's problem. Now, he had to pick up Tuck and get over to the safe house on Yorkfield Road. This Iranian woman needed to work on discovering a way to prevent people from dying if they did eat some of the contaminated grain.

Tuck was waiting outside of his room at the motel, trying to keep the cold drizzle from the lake off his head with a newspaper. He climbed into the Impala, and Bear filled him in with all the details regarding the plot that Faridoon was implementing.

When they arrived at the safe house, they hurried inside and searched for the lady who was manning the desk in the old living room.

"Do you know where the lady is we brought in a few hours ago?" Grizzly asked.

"I don't think she has ever left her room. Here's the key if you want to check on her," she said as she handed over the key.

They went to Dorri's room, knocked and waited. There was no answer. They knocked again, listening to see if they could hear anything inside. Still no answer. Tuck grabbed the key, unlocked the door, and rushed inside. They found Dorri on the bed, unconscious. They tried to wake her, but there was no response and very little pulse. Grizzly left to have the woman call an ambulance while Tuck stayed in the room, looking for clues as to what had happened. He remembered that he had only given her two of the sleeping pills the doctor had given them and there were no empty bottles of anything lying around the room.

Bear lumbered into the room. "Any idea what's wrong?"

"None, but she's out cold." He took the bottle of pills from his jacket pocket and looked closely at them. He thought he could barely smell some strange odor, but he couldn't be sure. "I wonder about that doctor. Now that I think of it, he got to the office awfully fast."

"You're right. Give me those pills, and I'll get them analyzed while you stay with Dorri. The ambulance should be here any minute since it's coming from McGrav Hospital, just up the street."

In a few minutes, which seemed like hours to Tuck, the ambulance arrived and loaded Dorri in the back while EMT's worked feverishly on the scientist. Tuck got in with her in case she woke up. At the hospital, she was taken to the emergency room where they pumped her stomach.

An hour later, Tuck and Bear were in the waiting room burning up cell phone minutes as they reported to their offices what had happened. Both of them felt like rookies because they had been so easily fooled into not taking the proper precautions to protect such an important witness. In a little over an hour, a doctor came in and said, "She's going to be okay. We got her stomach pumped before any permanent damage happened. Another half hour and we would probably have lost her. You guys got there just in time."

"Do you know what happened, doc?" Tuck asked.

"She was poisoned. Each one of those capsules had a small quantity of nicotine. The bottle had enough to kill a crowd."

"Nicotine!" the Bear exclaimed. "You mean like in cigarettes?"

Chapter Forty-Three

"You've got it. The stuff is a powerful poison, and people put small quantities into their lungs with every puff! Brilliant, huh!"

"When can we talk to her?" Tuck asked.

"Give her another hour. She's had a real rough time."

Tuck turned to Grizzell and said, "This is all my fault. I knew Faridoon's Pasdaran was dangerous, but it never occurred to me that they would be this effective in Chicago, Illinois!"

"Take it easy, Tuck. No one's to blame. We're just now beginning to get a handle on this thing. Thank heaven that people in the country are starting to wake up and take some steps to defend her from this very clever attack." He got up to leave. "You stay here, Tuck. I'm heading back to the office to keep fires lit under the right people. I'll see you later," he said as he hurried out of the room.

Chapter Forty-Four

King Faridoon was in an ugly mood after being up all night studying reports from various ministers concerning his plan to wreck the American economy. Grain was still moving out of the country, heading to Africa and South America aboard seven gigantic dry bulk freighters, all loaded to the maximum depth their Plimsoll lines would allow. But there was no way of telling how much longer he would be able to get grain out of the United States. Pasdaran agents had reported that the FBI had discovered their plan of exporting all the grain that Nuhoma had purchased and was sending to alliance members.

One of the Persian agents, by the name of Steve, was reporting that the FBI had searched the warehouse used to infect the starter kits. He believed that nearly two hundred elevators had been infected with the bacteria laced grain before armed guards began to appear, stopping all break-ins. A nationwide manhunt was now underway for the men who had been hired to spread the deadly grain, with several men already in custody.

To make matters worse, the American government apparently was aware that the treated grain might be dangerous if ingested. He smiled at that thought! Not only had he very nearly succeeded in depleting the country's grain surplus, the treatments would destroy vast amounts of stored grain that people were unaware of. Thousands might die! Now wasn't that just too bad! It didn't occur to him that thousands of people in his new Persian Alliance might get infected grain and also die. He believed the plan had been foolproof and that

Chapter Forty-Four

his grain would be left untouched. He failed to realize that the plan was dependent on a bunch of unreliable street bums being able to follow simple instructions.

Now, in the early morning hours, Minister of State Shahriyar had just informed him that the United States had filed a formal complaint with the United Nations, charging Persia with an unprovoked attack against the American people. Within the last few hours, the new president had placed his armed forces on national alert. The American Department of State had officially notified Persia that the American government considered the destruction of basic and vital food supplies an act of war, and they would take any steps they deemed necessary to punish Persia.

Arastoo had instructed his Media Minister to go on national television and denounce this threat to Persian sovereignty while claiming this was an unprovoked threat to the people of the Empire. He was also instructed to say officially that the complaint was just a bunch of fabricated lies from an evil nation.

The plan that had originally been given to him by the mysterious Mr. Diablo was designed to wreck the American economy, forcing aid to Israel to be cut back or illuminated. This would permit Hamas and Hezbollah to wage warfare against the tiny, financially weakened nation.

But Arastoo's narcissistic ego had become so enormous that the original plan to sink the American economy was forgotten replaced by his own, grander scheme of world domination through the control of raw materials, commodities and much of the world's crude oil supplies. The fact that Persia's oil production was only a small fraction of the world's daily production did not deter him because of his belief in his own superior intelligence and oratory skills that would be used to convince others to join him.

King Faridoon considered what steps he should take next. The fact that the grain might bring death to anyone consuming it was a surprising but delightful turn of events that he had not considered. It was possible that thousands of Americans might be killed before an antidote could be discovered. The threat of retaliation by the new president of the United States did not frighten him at all. History had proven that most politicians in the United States were cowards and had been devoid of courage for decades. They would talk endlessly, bluster, threaten, and talk some more, but they would never make the tough decision to actually protect themselves. They were absolutely convinced that if they could just talk to their enemies they could make them their friends. *What fools!* he thought. *That was the reason Islamic radicals were not afraid to attack this soft giant! Their only fear was that the Americans would talk them to death!*

The new king did not know anything about the new American President, Philip Somerset. He knew that he was not one of the candidates that had campaigned for the office. He was what the American's called a dark horse. All of the candidates running were roundly disliked by the people, so this man was nominated at a political convention as an independent candidate. The people loved his quiet, simple belief in the goodness of the people and the belief that he would defend the United States from anyone that would harm her.

Faridoon would not have been able to comprehend the fact that defending the country against further attacks was exactly what President Somerset was doing at the moment. Phil Somerset was not very presidential looking. He was fifty-six years old with receding red hair. His plain looking face was covered in red freckles, making him look like someone out of a Norman Rockwell portrait. He was tall and gangly, but he was a terrific speaker who possessed an iron determination when he believed in a cause. More importantly, he did not suffer fools well! Somerset also had a flair for the dramatic; the plan he was discussing with his Joint Chiefs of Staff would certainly fall into that category if implemented.

Chapter Forty-Four

"I just want you gentlemen to tell me that it can be done," President Somerset said quietly.

"Sir, the answer is yes, it can be done relatively easy with the technology we have."

"How long will it take to put the demonstration together?"

"We'll be ready in forty-eight hours."

"I'll hold you to that; no excuses!"

The Joint Chiefs raced out of the war room with a combination of excitement and joy written on their faces. The Admiral of the Navy glanced at the other members, smiled broadly and exclaimed, "Finally, we have a genuine Commander in Chief!"

In Tehran, while the new king was ordering breakfast and gloating over the possibility of thousands of Americans dying, there was a meeting not unlike the American one that was taking place. Prime Minister Teymour, Interior Minister Behruz, and Minister of Intelligence Payam were meeting together in the office of General Parvin. The General had posted extra guards around the headquarters building leaving orders that anyone who did not have a good reason to be around the building was to be arrested. The room was full of tension, and its occupants were very, very nervous. Discovery would mean a swift and unpleasant death.

"Gentlemen, I have asked that you attend this meeting so that we can discuss what we can do, if anything, to stop our nation's slide into certain oblivion." General Parvin spoke in a hushed tone although he did have the room swept for bugs before the meeting.

"I believe that the Americans will not sit still regarding this poisoning of their grain surpluses. They have expelled our Ambassador, as we have theirs, in retaliation. But that doesn't change the fact that they are furious and their press is demanding action," the Prime Minister interjected.

"I am worried that regardless of what the Americans do in

retaliation, we are storming down the road to financial ruin. These programs that give grain and oil away for next to nothing are draining our treasury. You will remember that when Faridoon became president, he originally said that we would stop the process of enriching uranium and the rush towards creating intercontinental missiles with atomic warheads, saving over one hundred billion dollars. Well, brothers, that has not happened. We are still pursuing those original goals that the president denounced in order to get elected. Now, we are not only burdened with the cost of enriching uranium and attempting to build intercontinental missiles, hundreds of thousands of tons of grain are being purchased at the highest prices ever, and then for all intents and purposes, giving it away to countries whose governments could, and were, previously buying their own food. Their thinking is that the grain's free; why shouldn't we take it?" the Minister of Interior stated.

"Well, the president's oratory skill did persuade them!" Teymour stated.

"Isn't the sale of oil paying for all of these programs?" Payam asked.

"Not even half of the cost is being covered by oil sales. We are losing hundreds of millions of dollars a month. Just transporting the grain costs millions! We are not producing more oil, nor have we constructed the new refineries that were promised to our people."

"Gentlemen, we find ourselves in very dangerous times. We have enraged a sleeping tiger. Now, our president has decided that he must be king and has appointed himself to be just that. I have no doubt that his next step will be to make the members of the alliance Persians with him as their king. He will declare that the governments of these nations are null and void, with their peoples owing allegiance to Persia, and Persia alone. In my mind this will create such animosity towards us that the alliance will dissolve. I fear that our new king's ego and vanity will bring us to ruin sooner rather than later!"

Chapter Forty-Four

Teymour stated.

"What can we do? We are a part of his government and we will be blamed along with Faridoon if everything fails or if the United States attacks us," Parvin moaned.

"What will your army do if there is any resistance to the new king?" Behruz asked.

"I fear that they may go so far as fomenting a coup or perhaps a complete revolution taking us back to being an Islamic Theocracy. Right now they love Faridoon and will do anything he asks, including going to war with the United States and Israel. Most of the men believe that he can do anything, and we can conquer anyone. I am afraid that reason has become a casualty of hero worship," the general said.

"It appears to me, gentlemen, that we need action, not more words. Words are what placed us in this precarious position. I propose that we take action before all is lost. We should send a secret envoy to Washington under our own authority, proclaiming our desire to avoid any military action and our willingness to make restitution for damages inflicted upon their nation. This envoy must also say to the American government that we are struggling under the heel of a demented leader, and we are searching for a way of escape. I suggest, if you agree, that this person be sent immediately!"

The Prime Minister spoke carefully and with great emotion. He was well aware that discovery of this secret mission would mean certain execution. There was a murmur of agreement from the others that this plan should proceed.

"Payam, will you be able to control VEVAK? Is it possible that they could provide some kind of protection to prevent the Pasdaran from learning of the secret trip?" someone asked.

"I have a few trusted agents that will do our bidding, but very few. Pasdaran is made up of radicals who care more for killing than diplomacy. If we are able to save our nation, one of our first duties will be to cleanse the country of these dangerous murderers. Excuse me! I got off the subject. I think my most trusted agents can provide the necessary security," Payam responded with some embarrassment.

"Good! Then who do we trust enough to send on this mission? Surely any one of us would be missed and suspicion aroused. History teaches that kings are notoriously paranoid, and I should think that ours is no exception. I have an idea that is radical to the extreme but might work because of the very audacity of it. I suggest we contact our scientist, Dorri Golnessa, and ask her to help the nation that used her so mercilessly. She could be instrumental in saving our nation from the fate it deserves. She is in the custody of the FBI after Pasdaran attempted to take her life. I can only hope that she has the heart of a patriot, not one full of vengeance. Her name in English means sparkling gem. We must pray that she is exactly that, a sparkling gem that has been buried in betrayal but still capable of a beautiful spirit. Is there agreement to having her as our choice of special ambassador?" he asked.

The other men thought long and hard about the suggestion. If Dorri was approached and refused, their plan would fail, and they would die. Unfortunately, no other course of action seemed plausible; they couldn't think of a single person that would be as believable as she was after the foiled attempt on her life. Finally, as if by an unheard signal, each man raised a hand to register his vote. Without realizing it, they had just demonstrated their belief in democracy!

General Parvin asked, "How will we get in contact with her and give her the information that we need to have her relay to the Americans?"

Minister Payam said, "Leave that to me. There is a CIA cell still operating in Tehran, and we can identify at least one of the members. We also know that she suspects we are aware of her activities and she is planning to leave the country as soon as she can make arrangements. We could pick her up, explain what we hope to accomplish, and ask her to contact her CIA handlers and tell them why we are trying to get a message to

Chapter Forty-Four

Dorri Golnessa. We must guarantee that this agent's safety will be assured when she leaves Persia."

Minister Behruz sat at the corner of the table chuckling. "What is wrong with you Behruz?" Payam asked with some irritation. "What do you find amusing in all of this?"

"It's just that here we are leaders of a former Islamic Republic, and we're placing the hope for the salvation of our nation in the hands of two women!"

They looked at each other in stunned silence for several moments. Then, as if by a signal, they all broke out in hilarious laughter. They laughed until tears washed down their cheeks, and they were out of breath.

Chapter Forty-Five

Tuck was in the lobby of the hospital working the phone. There were so many things happening at the same time that it was difficult to keep abreast of events. Inspectors were trying to examine every load of grain before it left an elevator. Unhappily, however, grain stored in metal silos on individual farms was not being inspected. Nuhoma trucks loaded the grain from the farm and hauled it directly to Chicago for export.

Thankfully, some commercial elevators had been spared, so very limited tainted flour, bread, and cereals were produced. Spoiled grain was being transferred to giant landfills that had been hastily dug in desolate parts of Wyoming to be burned and then buried, which caused environmentalists to go ballistic! For the first time in decades, politicians paid no attention to these self-proclaimed watch dogs of the environment. Scientists were adamant that burning would destroy the bacteria and prevent it from spreading. The new President said, "Do it!"

The fear that gripped the nation had not been known in the United States since the bombing of Pearl Harbor in 1941. No one knew how much damaged grain had made it into the food chain. Fear was rising in hearts of citizens because there were reports that children were becoming ill from eating a certain brand of bread. Doctors and scientists were working feverishly to discover a way to protect people even if they had eaten some of the contaminated grain. Up to this point, they had failed, and, tragically, a child had died!

The country now had an additional reason for paranoia. News reports were coming in that told of the deaths of

Chapter Forty-Five

thousands of cattle held in feed lots, and entire flocks of chickens and turkeys had been wiped out.

The same fear spilled over into the financial markets. The stock market continued to fall to levels not seen in decades. The cost of living, especially food, had risen 28%. The dollar sank out of sight while gold rose to dizzying heights. Housing markets, already in a free-fall, hit bottom with sales hovering at zero. Grain surpluses, once the pride of the nation, no longer existed. No one was saying recession any more; now the pundits were reporting that the country was in a full-blown depression. The King of Persia had succeeded in wrecking the American economy to an extent beyond his wildest dreams!

While Tuck worked, he had to force himself to concentrate on what he was doing. His mind kept returning to Dorri, who was now resting and out of danger. While sitting with her, she had shyly told him about the harshness of her life. The story of her father's attack on her and his disfiguring her beautiful face filled him with rage and pity. He wished he could get his hands on this evil man; he knew a number of horrible ways of inflicting pain that he would have enjoyed sharing with this animal!

The story of how she had been used by Faridoon was not much better, and he knew that she was filled with guilt for what she had devised and the suffering she would be causing.

Now, other thoughts were besieging this spy who had spent his life in foreign nations trying to protect his country. For the first time that he could remember, he felt loneliness, and that frightened him. He had been alone all of his life, depending on his wits and intelligence to survive. Suddenly, he didn't want to be alone anymore. Incredibly, he wanted to be with the woman upstairs who had wreaked such havoc on his country. He had to admit to himself that he was in love with Dorri. He was amazed since he had only known her for a few days. Surely love could not happen that quickly! Logic told him that this could lead to nothing but disaster for both of them.

Tuck, the secret agent, wrestled with this problem for a long time and then finally came to a decision. He didn't care what the cost; he was going to ask Dorri to marry him! His mind was made up as he moved to the elevator and punched in the number of her floor. When he arrived at her room, he knocked gently while smiling at the police officer who was guarding her door.

"Come in," she said faintly.

Tuck opened the door carefully and found Dorri lying in the bed, with her face turned to the wall.

"I just wanted to check on you and make sure you are doing okay," he said quietly, his quivering voice betrayed his nervousness.

"Okay?"

"Sorry, it's an American term. It's short for are you all right?" he asked.

"Yes, I am well, thank you for asking," she said while still facing away from him.

"Dorri, I need to ask you something, but I'm afraid I'll say something stupid. I'm not very good with words, but here goes. Dorri, I've been a bachelor all my life; I just never found anyone that I really enjoyed being around until I met you. I'm not sure how to say this, so I'm just going to let it all go and say, with all my heart, that I love you, and I want to ask you to marry me." He said this with more emotion and passion than he even knew he had. For a second he panicked and wondered if he should get down on one knee!

Dorri was shocked and was having a hard time believing her ears. She had been abused by so many men throughout her life that marriage, and the possibility of happiness, had been pushed from her consciousness years ago. She remembered vividly what her father had done to her, but she also remembered the abuse that he heaped on her dear mother for years and years. She couldn't see anything good about marriage, particularly a

Chapter Forty-Five

Muslim marriage.

But now, this American spy was proposing to her, and waiting for her answer. A few weeks ago she would have snarled her rejection to his face. Things had dramatically changed in her life. *Could she love a man?* she asked herself. *Could she love this man? Can he possibly truly love me?*

"Please, Tuck, you can't possibly want to marry me. You know what I look like. I couldn't stand the thought that you're looking at my scars every time you face me!" she said crying softly.

His heart nearly stopped beating. He rushed to her bed, and pulled her to him; hugging her so tightly that she couldn't breathe. "Dorri, you are the love of my life. When I look at you, I don't see the scars; I see a beautiful, wonderful woman!"

"Yes, a woman who most of your people would call a terrorist. I was used by my country to do great harm to your people. How can you look past that?"

"I can see past what has happened to both of us! Remember, I'm no angel. I'm a spy, and I've killed people in the line of duty, and some of them were your people. Doesn't that make us even?" he begged her.

Dorri cried and hugged him tightly to herself. "Oh, my dear Tuck! Yes, I will marry you."

Tuck was so overcome with joy and emotion that he couldn't stop kissing her and holding her close to him. He didn't want to take a chance of letting her go; he was afraid she would change her mind. Gently, she pushed him away and looked into his eyes. "I need to tell you something, Tuck. Something very important."

"Sure, go ahead," he said hesitantly, hoping she hadn't already reconsidered. He sat on the side of her bed staring at her, waiting.

"Tuck, your friend was here to visit me," she said.

"Friend? What friend? Was it Grizzly? How did that big galoot get in here without me seeing him?" he asked with laugh.

"No, it wasn't the bear. He said you know him as Abisha."

"Abisha! You've got to be kidding! What's he doing in Chicago? How does he know about you? How did he get past the guard at the door? That guy drives me nuts! He's always turning up in the craziest places. He's just a half-Jewish, hippy volunteer who works at the Brothers Clinic in Virginia. What is it with this guy?" he kept rattling on and on until Dorri put a finger to his lips.

"He was the kindest person I have ever met, present company excepted, of course. It was strange, but he knew all about me. He knew what my father did to me and how other men have hurt me all of my life. He said his father was very different from mine. His father was full of more love than we can comprehend! He touched my scars and said that he also had scars that were caused by angry men. He showed me his wrists; he carries horrible scars on both of them!"

"Then he looked into my eyes and said that he wanted me to understand that he knew all about my life and the suffering I have endured. He said that he wanted to offer me peace and happiness and eternal life! Then he took my hand and said, 'The Jewish people call me Yeshua. If you will believe in me, all of these things will be granted unto you. I love you, Dorri, and my Father loves you, too.' I was so overcome with the feeling of love and happiness that I confessed that I did believe in him. Then, he stood, touched my face with those wonderful hands, and said, 'My daughter, you will be with me forever!' Then he was gone."

Tuck was speechless. He suddenly remembered that Lemon had told him that Abisha had visited him when he was out cold after the mugging in Tehran. Lemon said Abisha had touched his back around his damaged kidney. He remembered that when he woke up, the pain was gone, and he had felt pretty good. What could this mean? He was confused when suddenly

Chapter Forty-Five

a thought came to him from the distant past. "His Jewish name may be Yeshua, but Christians know him as Jesus!"

Could this be true? He had never believed in God and had never said Jesus except when he used it as profanity. But Dorri's story was so convincing, and what about the way he kept appearing all over the world, exactly when Tuck needed help?

Suddenly, he was struck by something, something amazing! He looked at Dorri and began to laugh and cry at the same time. He pulled her out of bed and began to dance with her. He was filled with unspeakable joy. "Dorri!" he cried. "I've just noticed; dear God, look in the mirror!"

She looked at him as if he had lost his mind. Slowly she turned and looked at her image in the mirror. The sight drove her to her knees. Those ugly, terrible scars were gone! She wept with joy and repeated over and over, "Oh thank you, dear Yeshua, thank you!"

Tuck collapsed with joy; crying and holding Dorri tightly. Then he said, "Well, Yeshua, or Jesus, whichever name you prefer, I'm afraid that if you have Dorri, you've got both of us! I have seen so much evidence of who you really are, but I was too stupid to pay attention. I know that you are not a half-Jewish hippy. You are the Lord! Please take me into Your family so that Dorri and I can be together with You forever!"

At the Brothers Clinic, Abisha was in his customary place praying. He had been talking with an agent of the National Security Agency who was in the clinic for treatment of a drug abuse problem. As he raised his head, tears of joy were again falling into his beard, and he whispered quietly, "Yes, my beloved friends. We will be together always!"

Chapter Forty-Six

Peach found herself standing in the corner of the bus station waiting to catch a bus that would take her close to the Iraqi border. Things were just too hot in the capital. She believed that VEVAK was on to her, and that it was just a matter of time before she was arrested. She would suffer the same fate as Lemon.

Peach was right. VEVAK had identified her as an agent working for the American CIA. They had two male and one female operatives in place, waiting for the right opportunity to move in and make the arrest. The bus traveling to her destination was announced, and she moved into line ready to board. In just a few minutes she would be leaving Tehran for good and start a new life someplace other than this horrid country!

Suddenly, she noted with terror, three people were surrounding her, and vice-like hands grabbed her arms as they forced her towards a waiting car. Screaming would be useless but also impossible, since fear had constricted her throat to such a degree that she was speechless. The American agent was bundled into the car in complete silence and the vehicle roared into the early morning traffic. *Funny,* she thought to herself, *it's a pity to have to die on such a beautiful day.*

The trip through the Tehran streets was noisy and dusty, but the occupants rode in complete silence. Horns honked and men shouted curses at the drivers of other cars, but traffic continued to move slowly; bumper to bumper. The VEVAK driver was no exception. He frequently leaned out of the open window to remind someone that their parents were camels!

Chapter Forty-Six

Peach noted, with some humor, that the most feared people in Persia were just as helpless in Tehran traffic as the lowliest taxi driver.

After what seemed an eternity to Peach, they arrived at a dismal looking grey building with few windows. A vehicle gate was raised to allow them to enter the basement garage. The car was parked, and she was taken to an elevator, which transported them to the eighth floor. She found herself placed in a windowless room that contained a small table and two metal chairs. The door was closed, and the woman agent proceeded to search her without comment or ceremony. Her iPhone was quickly discovered and confiscated along with her passport and identification papers. When the search was complete, the female agent left the room, and Peach found herself alone. There was no doubt in her mind that she was being observed on closed circuit television.

They kept her sitting alone for almost an hour before a fierce looking man came in sat across from her. The man's shirt and jacket bulged with unseen muscles that she was sure could be used to inflict terrible damage. He glared at her for a moment then demanded, "What is your name?" She steeled herself for an onslaught of threats, verbal and in all probability, physical. "The Americans call you Peach, do they not?" She remained silent.

The interrogator slammed both hands down violently on the desktop, which sounded like a small explosion echoing through the room, shocking Peach into a harsh scream. The man leaned across the desk; his face so close to hers that she could smell and feel his foul breath. He snarled, "Tell me the name you are using. I can assure you that your life depends on it."

Peach recovered her composure, thought a minute, and then said, "I have been known as Peach."

The muscled inquisitor said nothing. He turned and left the room, slamming the door behind himself. In a few minutes the door opened and a very distinguished looking elderly man entered the room and sat down across from her. He smiled pleasantly and spoke softly to her, saying, "Miss Peach," he couldn't help smiling. "Miss Peach, you are in a great deal of trouble, which I am sure you realize. I represent some important persons that are, shall we say, disturbed by the direction our nation is taking. We feel that our beloved Iran, excuse me, Persia, is in grave danger of being attacked by the United States in retaliation for some unwise endeavors our president authorized to inflict on their country."

"I am aware of what was done to America," she replied.

"Good. That will save us some time, which we do not have the luxury of wasting. I'm going to get right down to business. We would like you to make a top secret trip to the United States and contact Dorri Golnessa. Are you familiar with Miss Golnessa?"

Peach remained silent. "I understand your silence. She is the biochemist who produced potentially deadly bacteria that was unleashed on the food supply of the United States. She has since been taken into custody by the FBI and is being held somewhere in the city of Chicago. My instructions are to ask if you will hand-carry a sealed letter from high officials in our government. If you agree, you will ask Dorri to hand-carry this same letter to the highest officials in the United States government, preferably the President himself. We believe that the future existence of our country depends on the speedy delivery of this communication. We will permit you to contact people in the CIA or FBI and inform them of the reason for your trip. Either group can meet you at the airport to escort you to Miss Golnessa. VEVAK agents will fly with you acting as your personal bodyguards with specific orders to protect you from anyone wishing you harm, especially if word of this unauthorized communication gets out. I know you have been unhappy with the government, or you would not have become a spy. However, I hope there still might be an Iranian

Chapter Forty-Six

heart beating in your chest. I am asking you to do this for your country. Will you help us?"

Peach looked at this representative of the government that she hated, the same government that had tortured and killed her dear friend. Now they were asking her to help them. Glaring at this official, she asked, "Will I be allowed to stay in the United States without fear of harassment from Pasdaran?"

"Yes."

"Then I accept. I need my iPhone to let the agency know that I'm coming; otherwise, I'll never get past the FBI."

"That is acceptable," he said smiling. "We took the chance you would accept. Transportation has been arranged, and you will be leaving within the hour on a flight to Zurich where you will get a connecting flight to Chicago."

Peach's entire luggage was now on its way out of Tehran on the bus that she missed. She would have to wear what she had on unless her captors would allow her to get some clothes and makeup. What mattered to her most was that she was on her way out of this dreadful nation and she now had the possibility of making a new life in America. Lemon was right; God really does care!

Chapter Forty-Seven

Doctor James Renfro of the CDC in Atlanta had collapsed on a cot in the office trying to get a few minutes of rest. He had been going non-stop since the call from the FBI placing such urgency on finding a way to protect people from this new bacteria strain. Every single scientist on his staff was furiously conducting experiments. Suddenly, he sat upright and raged to himself about being so stupid! He had to talk to Dorri for an explanation of the processes she used in changing the DNA of this strain of bacteria. He jumped to his feet, grabbed a phone, and dialed the FBI in Chicago. In an amazingly short period of time, he was startled to be speaking directly with Dorri Golnessa while she was in the hospital. He was pleased to learn that she spoke English very well.

"Hello, Dr. Renfro; this is Dorri Golnessa. I hope I can be of help to you," she said.

He was surprised to hear a soft, beautiful voice. "Hello, Dorri; we are on a very short timeframe, so we need to get right down to business. Please, go over the steps you took in hacking into the DNA to make this new, destructive bacterium."

They talked for nearly an hour. When they finished, Renfro's stamina and excitement had returned. He had taken pages of notes, and when he hung up the phone, he yelled at his staff to come into his office to discuss what he had learned. Both of the scientists had agreed that the best way to kill the bacteria if it made its way into humans was by using antibiotics. The CDC's job was to find the right one!

Dorri began crying, and Tuck asked what was wrong. She said, "If people die, it will be my fault, and I'm not sure I

Chapter Forty-Seven

can live with the guilt. If only I had been given more time to conduct additional tests. How can God ever forgive me?"

"Well, not being a religious person, I can't answer that question very well. But I can say that Yeshua knew all about what you had been required to do for Faridoon, and He loved you anyway! I believe everything will work out. Maybe you should pray and ask God to show the scientists the answer. I can't believe I just said that!"

The phone rang again, and Tuck answered, "Hello, who is this?"

"Hi, Tuck; this is Peach. Are you all right?"

"Peach, Great Scott! It's wonderful to talk to you, but the important question is are you all right?"

"I'm fine; I'll fill you in on the details later. It's important that I talk to Dorri right away. Is she well enough to speak to me?"

"Sure, here she is." He handed the phone to Dorri while covering the receiver so he could tell her a little background about Peach. He tried to act like he wasn't listening, but he was bursting with curiosity. In a few minutes, Dorri said, "All right, I'll do my best," and with a very puzzled look on her face hung up the phone.

"What was that all about?" Tuck asked.

"Your friend Peach is coming to America on a mission for the unofficial Persian government, whatever that means. They want me to present something to the President of the United States. I need to meet her at Dulles International tonight. Can you arrange for a plane to get me to Dulles at 11:00 p.m.?"

"I'll bet our friend Grizzly can take care of that for us. He's got planes all over the place; surely he can lend us one."

"Good. Now can you please get out so that I can get some rest before I have to leave?" she said as she blew him a kiss.

Chapter Forty-Eight

You could hear Dr. Renfro screaming all over the office, perhaps all over Atlanta.

"You did what?" he yelled at the top of his voice.

The young lab technician by the name of Ellery Snook stood before his boss with his head down, shuffling his very large feet back and forth. The glasses on his protruding nose were in the process of abandoning ship, but he caught them in time and pushed them back up next to his furrowed brow. His brown, close-set eyes darted around the room, pleading for help. Finding none, he confessed again, "I ate some of the grain. I thought it was important to find out how dangerous the stuff was right away, so I ate some to see what would happen. I knew you could help me if anything went wrong."

"Are you completely crazy? Is there a history of mental illness in your family? When did you perform your brave and idiotic experiment?" Renfro raged, eyes bulging from his head.

"I took a couple of mouthfuls of the bad stuff at 5:00 p.m. yesterday afternoon."

"Well, what happened?" Renfro demanded.

"Nothing."

"What?"

"Nothing happened. I feel fine," Snook said.

The doctor stared at the hapless young man for a long time. As his temper came under control, he began to realize that this might be the answer they were looking for. In fact, this guy could be a hero! "I want you to have a complete physical immediately; I mean right now!" As the young man began to

Chapter Forty-Eight

walk away with his head still down from the berating he had just taken, Dr. Renfro stopped him and gave him a bear hug. Through misty eyes he said, "Thank you, Ellery."

Two hours later, the examination was complete, and the results were in from the lab tests and blood work. Ellery was fit as a fiddle! Apparently that wonderful human immune system that God in His wisdom saw fit to put into mankind was working, fighting off an attack from a new enemy. Renfro dove for a telephone and asked a secretary to get the President on the line and to also get Dorri Golnessa on the line. Wisely, he knew that she must be suffering from terrible guilt. His phone rang. "This is Dr. Renfro."

"Phil Somerset, doctor. What do you have for me?"

"I have very good news, Mr. President! One of our technicians took it upon himself to eat some infected grain."

"He did what?"

"He ate some of this stuff, and he is perfectly fine. It appears, without more testing, that our immune system handles the contaminated grain just fine. We may have been worried for no reason. It is possible that those with weakened immune systems may become fatalities, but for once, a human came through a drug test better than a rat!'

"Well, for crying out loud. When this all dies down, I want to shake that young man's hand," the president said. "What's his name?"

"Ellery Snook. He sure can be called a hero."

"Thanks for the call. Goodbye." The president hung up the phone and gave the switchboard a list of people he wanted to talk to right away.

As soon as the Doctor hung up, the phone rang; it was his secretary. She said that Miss Golnessa was on the line; she was calling from an airplane flying somewhere. He picked up the phone and nearly shouted as he said, "Miss Golnessa, I have good news for you. One of our technicians ate some infected grain yesterday, and there have been no ill effects. He's fine.

I think our immune system may be capable of handling the bacteria." he said as he anxiously awaited a response. Silence. Finally a man came on the line and said, "Thank you for calling. Miss Golnessa is so grateful that she is unable to speak right now. Please be assured that you have her complete gratitude, and she asks that you convey her personal thanks to the technician." The phone went dead.

Doctor Renfro stared at the phone then shrugged his shoulders and hung it up. He looked at the cot standing in the corner, hesitated for a moment, then flopped down, and was instantly asleep.

Chapter Forty-Nine

It had been a couple of days since King Faridoon had read all of the negative reports about his alliances. He refused to believe the numbers that were shown to him; he was convinced that his enemies did not want the alliance to survive and prosper, so they were spreading false rumors. He was determined to prove them wrong. Like all kings throughout history, he had become paranoid and believed that his enemies were surrounding him, plotting to invade his kingdom.

He had assigned his secretary Afsoon the task of arranging a video conference call with the heads of all of the nations in the alliance. He was going to address them directly, reminding them that he was king, and he would make sure they prospered as members of the alliance. He was also going to broach an idea with these leaders. His idea was that their countries would be even more prosperous if they became governors of a member-state of the Persian Empire with Faridoon as their king. It never occurred to him that these presidents had egos nearly as large as his own, and that they would never allow power to be given up voluntarily.

Before the telecast, he was in his office preparing to go on the air when King Faridoon had a temper tantrum with his personal tailor. The tailor had just presented him with new royal robes made of purple satin bordered with white trim that was embroidered in gold. His trousers were a soft beige color contrasting with glistening tan Italian loafers.

It was his intention to be videoed while standing so that he could employ his famous gestures during his speech, but he found that the robes did not flow gracefully enough when he lifted his arms to the heavens, leaving too much of the sleeves of his white shirt exposed. The tailor was frantic and tried several different adjustments; all were failures in the king's eyes. The king ordered the tailor out of his royal sight.

Another item had been added to the royal attire for the first time today. It was a single gold band that he wore around his head that would serve as his crown. Looking in the mirror as he practiced his gestures and facial expressions, he was exceedingly pleased with his appearance. He was ready to give the latest in the long list of his great speeches.

The director of the broadcast motioned for him to take his place beside his green leather executive chair behind his desk. The cameras would swing around giving the audience various views of the king. As he cleared his throat and took a quick drink of water from a crystal tumbler, the countdown began. The red light on a camera came on and he began speaking, smiling like a benevolent monarch should with just the smallest amount of his white teeth showing. He made an expansive, greeting motion with his right arm, and began to speak. "Good afternoon, my friends. I send you my blessings! Thank you for giving up some of your valuable time to join me in this telecast. First, it would be helpful to me if we went around the world, so to speak, and have each president or representative introduce himself." This was a small gesture to these men, but he had no intention of allowing them to do much talking.

"Or herself!" the female president of Laos interjected.

"Excuse me, did someone say something?" Arastoo asked irritably.

"I said, 'or herself.' You may not have noticed, but I am a woman, and I am the president of Laos."

"Of course you are! How inexcusable of me. I do beg your pardon, Madam!" he said with some sarcasm.

The introductions proceeded a little awkwardly because many spoke in their native tongue. He interrupted them and

Chapter Forty-Nine

said, "Gentlemen, and lady, there seems to be a language problem that we should have anticipated. Let us all speak in English. Feel free to use an interrupter if necessary." The introductions continued, and it was determined that each member of the alliance was represented.

"I felt it was necessary to call this meeting because I have news that will be of great interest to you all. As members of the Persian Alliance, you have been receiving shipments of grain and crude oil at prices that are well below world market prices. I trust everything is going well, and you are receiving shipments in a timely manner." He smiled into the camera for their benefit, but it gave one of the members a chance to interrupt him by shouting, "We've got so much grain that we are feeding it to our cattle! Can you slow down the shipments a little?"

Faridoon was enraged by this interruption from the president of Guatemala. Forcing a smile, he said, "I'm sure that something can be arranged. Please feel free to contact our ambassador if any of you are experiencing any difficulty with the grain or oil shipments."

The president of Haiti boomed into the microphone, saying, "We don't have any deep water ports, so the ships have to anchor offshore. That means we have to use a fleet of smaller boats to offload the freighter. That's too much trouble! Can't you ship our grain to us in smaller ships, or perhaps barges?"

Faridoon almost lost it with that one. He struggled to keep his composure and said, "I think a little gratitude is in order, don't you?" Haiti was silent.

"Now, my friends, I want to explore a new idea with you and show you ways that together we can become stronger. Each of you governs a small nation that has little impact on the world financially or politically. To coin a phrase, you have no power!" Arastoo failed to notice the reaction his speech was having on the group of leaders. There was some disbelief on their faces as they tried to grasp what he was trying to say.

"As part of the great Persian Alliance, you are experiencing what takes place when the weak are gathered together; they become strong! Here is a clear example which will help you understand." Now, muttering could clearly be heard from the group. They did not like being addressed like school children. Faridoon's condescending attitude was grating on their nerves.

"If you take a single strand of thread and pull on it, it is easily broken. But if you take that same thread and join it with many others, you have a strong cord that cannot be broken." He raised his voice and began to gesture with great flourishes, which caused his satin robe to have the graceful movements of a curtain reacting to a light breeze. He was caught up in the wisdom of his own words.

The king had the smile of a tolerant genius talking to imbeciles. He continued, "I want to show you how we all can be stronger and more powerful than we already are. I propose that each country you represent relinquishes its independence and becomes a state in the great Persian Empire!" He threw his arms wide and thrust his head skyward as if he was caught up in worshiping a god. Shouting now, he continued, "Like the example I gave you, together we will be strong and powerful. As an illustration of how this new nation would be designed, we only have to look at the United States of America. It is a powerful nation made up of fifty individual states that are self-governing but receive many benefits from the nation's government."

"This new nation will soon be as large and powerful as the American example. I volunteer myself to take on the responsibility of governing such a great nation. Each of you will become governors, and I will be your king!" He shouted and moved around the desk in such a manner that the cameras had a difficult time keeping him in the picture.

The reaction from the television audience was one of disbelief and anger; some were shouting "no" or even

Chapter Forty-Nine

obscenities. The word *crazy* could be picked up amid the shouts from these leaders. Arastoo heard none of these exclamations of anger and disrespect. He was caught up in the wonder of his greatness. He continued without realizing that he had lost his audience. "Because we will form a new, greater nation than any on earth, it is important that I, as its leader, have the name and title to fit the responsibility. When the new country becomes a reality, I shall reach back to ancient times, back to my ancestor, whose name and title was perfect for his circumstances as a nation builder. I will become the Great Cyrus the Second, King of the Persian Empire!" Faridoon's face was one of ecstasy! His arms were spread wide to receive the praise and worship he knew he would receive.

At the exact moment that Faridoon was at the pinnacle of his glory, the picture on all of the television sets changed. Instead of these leaders seeing the Persian King, and the Persian King seeing the leaders, they all were startled to see a man with receding red hair wearing a dark blue suit with a yellow tie. Comprehension was slow in coming, but when it did arrive, it was as if they had been struck by a bolt of lightening! It was Philip Somerset, the President of the United States!

He said, "Hello, Faridoon. I heard you were having this little conference, and I thought I would join you."

Faridoon began to rant and wave his arms wildly about. He shouted, "What is the meaning of this outrage? This is a private meeting; you have no right here!"

"Be quiet, Faridoon!" the President ordered brusquely. "You've talked enough. Did you really believe that you could damage the economy of my country and endanger the lives of American citizens without punishment? Did you think we would just grin and bear it? Well, you make-believe monarch, you are going to learn a lesson this day, and we have arranged for all of the nations in your alliance to witness your instruction. Oh, by the way, the people of Iran will see this on their televisions as well."

"If you would be so kind to look out your beautiful window, you will see in the distance a large electrical sub-station that lights the city of Tehran. Have you heard of a smart bomb? If not, you will shortly. You see, one of our B-2 bombers is about to arrive over your city. Oh, don't bother your air force to send jets up to attack it because they won't see it in on their radar, stealth and all that."

"In about thirty seconds, you will witness what we are capable of doing…there, did you see? Your station is gone! I imagine the city is in the dark by now. I know that your emergency generators are keeping you supplied with power, and you can still see me. I hope this little instruction will cause you to think twice before you challenge the United States again. It will not be tolerated! By the way, I also demand that you pay the United States the full amount of the monetary damage you have caused. If you ever try and harm us again, you and your people will experience our terrible wrath. Have a good day!" The screen went black. Sirens were screaming in the distance as emergency workers raced to the sub-station.

Arastoo slumped down in his executive chair and wiped his face with a handkerchief. He was stunned into silence. As a narcissist, he had thought only of himself. He held the belief that he could do anything he wished and get away with it. He was convinced that he was more intelligent than others; therefore, no one could oppose him. His self-centered ego had just suffered the most damaging blow imaginable. The President of the United States had humiliated him publicly in the presence of the entire world.

No one in the room spoke a word. They quietly gathered their gear and left, closing the door carefully behind them.

The presidents of the alliance were also stunned into silence. Then slowly, one at a time, they began to smile, then laugh, then hoot and yell with happiness. They were all thrilled that this pompous jerk had been knocked off of his pedestal; he deserved it! Cyrus the second, indeed.

Chapter Forty-Nine

The students who had been the backbone of Faridoon's presidential election and who served him blindly were confused. Many were ashamed. They were feeling as if they had been violated. How could the man they love behave this way? Most had no idea what the future held for them, but it looked very bleak and hopeless.

Chapter Fifty

Dorri and Tuck were seated in a small waiting room, just down the hall from the Oval Office where President Somerset had just stunned the world with his positive, forceful action. They had watched the event with different emotions. Tuck was thrilled that his nation had finally found the courage to strike back at this snake that had been biting them. Dorri, however, was saddened by the depths that this madman had taken her nation.

The door opened and the President entered the room and shook hands with both of them. He held Tuck's hand for a few seconds, looked into his eyes, and said, "Thank you, Aristotle, for your courageous service to our country. You are a real hero, who will unfortunately never be publicly recognized because of your secret past that must be protected. But I know, and I appreciate you!" Tuck was humbled beyond measure.

Then the President turned to Dorri, grabbed her hand and said, "I understand you have something for me."

"Yes, Mr. President. This envelope was hand-delivered to me to present to you. It is from some members of Faridoon's cabinet."

"Thank you; I will examine it carefully. I fully believe that there are many good people in Iran. We have no wish to harm them."

"By the way, I know you are a gifted scientist. Please be assured that the people of the United States realize that your research was done according to the orders of your president, not from a desire by you to harm us. It is my hope that you will consider staying in America and perhaps teach at one of

Chapter Fifty

our universities."

Dorri smiled at Tuck and then looked at the President saying, "I am very grateful, Mr. President. I would love to become a citizen of this great country!"

They said their goodbyes. Before Tuck and Dorri left, they took a quick tour of the White House. President Somerset went to his cabinet room where his closest advisers waited for his arrival. When he entered the room, the men and women rose as one, cheering the Commander in Chief; some even gave him high fives! He smiled somewhat bashfully and walked to his seat. When they were all seated, they waited expectantly while the President opened the envelope and read its contents.

When he finished reading, he looked up and said, "Ladies and gentlemen, it appears that there are some in the Persian cabinet who are aware that their president, or king, or whatever he is, does not speak for them or the nation. They are asking for our patience as they work on how to resolve the dilemma they find themselves wallowing in."

Those around the conference table applauded with genuine pleasure. "It appears that we might have some allies in Tehran. We will encourage them and provide assistance if they request it. The king may be getting some new clothes!" They laughed again.

Chapter Fifty-One

Several weeks after the meeting with the President, Tuck and Dorri, with her now beautiful face beaming, were standing in the chapel at the Brothers Clinic in Virginia. Tuck felt that this was only appropriate because it was here that he first met this wonderful half-Jewish hippy! This special CIA operative's life had changed so drastically in the last few months that he could scarcely remember all of the things he had done and survived. And now, about to take one of the most important steps in his danger-filled life, he wanted to see his special friend. Tuck glanced around furtively, half expecting to see Abisha in his usual pew praying. He had to admit that he was disappointed that their new friend was not present. What they could not see was that in the shadows in the back of the room, He was there, eyes glistening, while smiling and quietly offering them His blessing.

Their wedding was a small, private affair with only a few friends present. One special friend was Grizzly. He was pleased to serve as Tuck's best man. The couple had grown to love this giant bear of a man and were honored that he flew in to attend their nuptials.

As they took their vows from the chaplain, they heard sniffling and quiet sobs. Tuck glanced out of the corner of his eye, and to his astonishment, it was the Bear! He was wiping his eyes with a giant, green handkerchief, and when he blew his nose, it sounded as if a wounded moose had wandered in!

When the ceremony was finished and Tuck had kissed his beautiful bride, he looked around at those gathered in the chapel and was delighted to see that Abisha was there after

Chapter Fifty-One

all standing quietly in the shadowy back of the room. Tuck laughed and pointed to where their friend was standing so that Dorri would also be able to see Him. Both of them waved their arms in excitement while shouting His name! Abisha's face was one gigantic smile, and He returned their greetings with an excited wave of His own. The small crowd of guests closed in around the couple to offer their congratulations, and when they could free themselves and run to the back of the chapel, they enveloped Abisha in their arms and wept with joy, thanking Him over and over. He laughed and hugged them both, congratulated them, and promised them eternal happiness.

Abisha then turned and spoke to Grizzly, "Hello, my friend, are you going to be all right?" He asked as He put his arm around the fearless crime warrior who was still sniffling and trying to wipe his eyes with his soggy handkerchief.

"Yeah, I'm okay. I can't stop crying; I think it's hay fever!"

"I'm sure that's what it is," Abisha laughed and pounded the Bear on the back.

With a final wave, He turned and was gone! They knew that this wonderful man surely had been called away to help someone in the same way that He had helped them! They were bursting with pride that He had come and blessed the ceremony that He had made possible.

After the service, the couple left for an extended honeymoon in Jamaica. Both of them were happier than they had ever been in their lives.

However, before they could think about enjoying a life together, there was still one unresolved issued that had to be taken care of, the death of the little girl that had eaten some of the contaminated grain which had somehow made its way through the food markets to her table. Tuck had asked the FBI for the name and address of the parents because he knew that Dorri would never be able to have peace in her heart since she was harboring the guilt she felt from this tragic death. She had to face the parents and ask them for their forgiveness.

The parents were Donald and Sharon McMann, and the little girl's name was Ann, but everyone called her Annie. She was nearly five years old when she passed away. All of her little life she had suffered from poor health; she had recently been weakened by a bout with pneumonia.

The McManns lived in Yukon, Oklahoma, so the newlyweds took a plane to Oklahoma City where they rented a new Chevrolet for the drive to Yukon. As they arrived at the street address that the Feds had given them, Dorri was overcome with grief and began to sob quietly. She doubted that she had the courage to go through with meeting the family.

Tuck said, "Let me go in and explain some things before you talk with them." Dorri couldn't respond.

The CIA agent was glad that the FBI contacted the McManns to tell them they were coming and what time they would arrive. Before he could ring the bell, the door opened and a smiling, middle-aged couple met him and invited him inside. After refusing tea, Tuck learned that Donald was an accountant and Sharon was a stay at home mom and homeschooler for two other children, Becky who was eight and Jerry who was twelve. Both children were welcomed into the conversation by their father, who was calm and soft-spoken.

Donald was average height with salt and pepper hair while Sharon was a little on the plump side with a happy face that was lined with the pain they had suffered with Annie. She had light brown hair that she wore in a ponytail.

Tuck carefully shared with them Dorri's life story and the suffering she had experienced in Iran. He told them that her experiments with changing bacteria to destroy grain were against all of her training. She had hoped to find ways to increase grain harvests and help feed hungry people, but her country's president had persuaded her that this instead was her patriotic duty. Tuck recounted how the experiments

Chapter Fifty-One

were done without being given ample time to perform animal testing for assurance that the grain would be safe for humans. Tuck shared what Dorri had done to help the American government in their search for a way to destroy the bacteria, but she couldn't get over the guilt she felt over the death of their beloved daughter.

The McManns listened carefully to Tuck's story. No one in the family said a word; they just sat holding hands or hugging each other. Sharon looked at her husband and her two children, then quietly got up, walked to the door, and went outside to the car where Dorri sat with her head hidden in her hands. Sharon opened the car door, reached in to Dorri, and said, "Hello, Dorri; I'm Sharon. You are welcome here; please come in the house with me."

Dorri hesitated and then took the hand that was offered to her. She got out of the car where she was immediately scooped up in Sharon's arms and given an embrace that nearly took her breath away. This act of love and acceptance caused both of them to start crying; neither was able to move. They were soon joined by Tuck and the rest of the family with everyone hugging someone.

Finally, they moved to the house where they sat in the living room while Sharon made tea. Donald told Dorri about Annie and showed her a picture of the beautiful, but obviously ill, little girl. He explained that their daughter's immune system was non-existent because of her life of sickness. They shared with Tuck and Dorri that they were a Christian home where forgiveness had been received by them and freely offered to others. That forgiveness was now given to her, not just with a word, but with all of their hearts.

Tuck and Dorri spent the entire afternoon with this wonderful family and formed a bond that would last the rest of their lives. When it was time to go, Dorri thanked them and asked if she could keep in contact with them. Everyone agreed that would be a wonderful idea. As they drove away,

Edge of Disaster

Dorri was exhausted but grateful that now, finally, she was guilt-ridden no more. Waving goodbye, both Tuck and Dorri thanked God for the privilege of meeting these wonderful and gracious people. Thousands of miles away in Afghanistan, Abisha paused from treating a wounded soldier, looked to heaven, smiled, and gave thanks, too!

Chapter Fifty-Two

At about the same time as the Tuckers silver airliner lifted off the runway into the bright, overcast sky above Oklahoma City for the flight to the island paradise, Ellery Snook was being presented a plaque expressing the country's appreciation for his courage. President Somerset made the presentation in the Oval Office. He was accompanied by his boss, Dr.Renfro. Snook gave Dr. Renfro a smug look after the presentation, and the good doctor knew that the next few weeks would be unbearable!

The clean up of the spoiled grain was winding down throughout the nation's midsection. Elevators had been cleansed and disinfected and were ready to receive the next harvest. The cost to the nation was running in the billions of dollars, but thankfully, only one death had been recorded: a small child with immune deficiencies.

The sudden death of cattle caused many nations in the Persian Alliance to realize that they had received tainted grain. They were frantically working to track down every bushel and destroy it. Apparently, most of their citizens also had good immune systems although there had been much sickness in some of the poorer villages. Most nations had informed Persia that they no longer wished to participate in the alliance.

The world was returning to a state of normalcy.

Chapter Fifty-Three

Several weeks after the American attack on Tehran's power supply, the Great King Cyrus II was walking in the garden around the palace enjoying a cool breeze which caused his purple robes to billow out from his body, giving him a nearly godlike appearance. His mood was anything but godlike, though.

Power had been restored to Tehran four days ago. His ministers advised him to go on television and reassure the people that they were not in danger and urge them to return to their normal daily life. He refused to do so because he would not be able to look like a powerful monarch since the whole country had witnessed the destruction of the sub-station. No, he had to punish the aggressors before he could regain the respect of the Persian people.

Faridoon spent most of his days fuming at how the Americans had humiliated him in front of the people of the world causing his grand alliance to unravel in less than a week. He was also irritated that not one alliance member had thanked him for the cheap grain or crude. Many had actually complained about receiving too much grain and oil, and that they didn't have the capacity to handle these commodities. They admitted that because of this, much of the grain had been left out to rot! He had spent millions of dollars to purchase their allegiance, and what had he received for his generosity? Laughter and derision!

When he was not thinking about the American attack on his sovereign territory, he was consumed with planning his revenge. He had administered a severe blow to the American

Chapter Fifty-Three

economy; his next attack would cripple them forever. Arastoo spent many hours with General Parvin going over various military options. One option that seemed very attractive was to hire terrorist groups to bomb United States' embassies around the world. That idea had been abandoned when Parvin was able to convince the king that the Americans would be able to determine that Persia was funding this program. The retaliation would be devastating.

Missiles aimed at US military establishments in the Middle East were considered, but the idea was forgotten for the same reason. There didn't seem to be any options that would bring the desired results without causing an all-out war with the most powerful nation on earth.

As Faridoon walked in the garden, he began thinking about Dorri Golnessa, wondering what had happened to her. He would have his Minister of Intelligence find out what her fate had been when the Americans discovered what she had engineered.

Suddenly, a stupendous thought burst into his brain. That was it! Bacteria! He could order that deadly airborne diseases, like Anthrax, be developed in huge quantities and then spread around that hated country. What a wonderful idea!

The Persian king was so satisfied with the idea of mass murder for his enemy that he couldn't wait to talk to Minister of Intelligence Payam. He seemed to be the logical choice to take into his confidence since he controlled the country's worldwide spy network.

He went to his office and ordered Afsoon to call Payam and have him come to the palace as soon as possible. While waiting for the minister to arrive, Arastoo ordered a meal of wild pheasant, rice and a variety of fresh vegetables. He would top that off with a dish of Ben and Jerry's ice cream. He was slightly embarrassed that he loved this American dessert so much that he had a supply flown in each week. The fact that the cost of obtaining the ice cream was more than the weekly salary of most Persians never occurred to him.

When Payam received the call, he was unsure of what he might be asked to do for the king. He hoped the king would be more rational than he had been.

Arriving at the palace, he was shown directly into his office. King Faridoon, or Cyrus, was talking on the phone and motioned for his minister to come in and take a seat. In less than a minute, he hung up and turned to Payam. His handsome face was absolutely radiant! The depression of the past several weeks was obviously gone, replaced by his normal unbounded energy. Arastoo wasted no time in describing his tremendous new plan for defeating the United States, and if it was as successful as he hoped, the defeat of Israel would follow.

He planned on increasing rocket supplies and money for Hamas with instructions to them to step up their rocket attacks. He complained to Payam about the current unproductive use of the rockets by Hamas, citing the relatively small number of Israeli fatalities.

Payam listened with interest and attempted to appear excited about the plan for spreading disease on the North American continent. He believed that the whole continent could be at risk depending on where the deadly diseases were released and the prevailing wind direction.

Faridoon continued to harangue the general for over an hour. It was obvious that he was completely obsessed with destroying the United States and Israel. It no longer mattered to the king that they would be discovered as the aggressor in such an attack; he wanted Americans to die!

The minister was finally dismissed with instructions to get busy finding supplies for diseases such as Anthrax or any other airborne malady that he could find. As he left the palace, he grabbed his cell phone and placed a call using speed dial, saying only "parachute" when the call was answered.

Two hours later, the famous four were again gathered in

Chapter Fifty-Three

General Parvin's office. They all had grim looks on their faces as the general gave them an update on the king's plans.

Prime Minister Teymour began by saying, "The only good news we have is that the American president has read our letter and sent word back to us that he understands our situation and will refrain from any further military action as long as Persia does not threaten the United States again. He stated that Persia must also pay for the damage to their grain surpluses. If Faridoon initiates some kind of a strike against the Americans, the President said, 'All bets are off.' I believe that's an American term that essentially means they will defend themselves."

"Then there is no other choice remaining to us," Behruz said.

"I agree. We act now or put our nation in further peril, both economically and militarily," Teymour said sadly.

Payam was gazing at his folded hands on the table. Finally he said, "If we are all in agreement that Faridoon must be removed from the leadership of Persia, I will make the necessary arrangements. It will take place tomorrow."

They all nodded in agreement and left the room in silence, walking separately to the parking lot where their limousines were waiting. The sun had just set, and the sky was painted in brilliant oranges and reds, a beautiful desert sunset that promised a bright day tomorrow!

Payam arrived at the building that housed the nation's intelligence agency and walked to a deserted parking lot in the rear of the building. Darkness had now descended on Tehran, and the lot was poorly lighted. He stood waiting under one of the dim lights for several minutes, while thinking to himself, *At least the power was back on.* Suddenly, the black robed giant Shaheen appeared beside him, blending in with the darkness outside of the circle of light. Payam quietly whispered a few words. The giant nodded and disappeared into the night.

The black sky was filled with millions of diamond like stars and a bright half moon, which shed some light on the Iranian landscape. The palace stood out vividly in the darkness; with exterior lights that made the palace resemble a brilliant pink and gold jewel against black velvet.

It was 2:30 a.m., and Arastoo was finally asleep after spending the majority of the night working on his plans to release a terrorist-led germ warfare attack on the United States. He would give specific instructions to make sure the President of the United States was infected, so great was his hatred of the man that had publicly reprimanded him.

Unknown to the slumbering king, the exterior lighting suddenly was extinguished. Night lights in the bedchamber also went out, leaving the room in dark shadows contrasted by a minimum amount of moonlight coming in from the huge bedroom windows. A large shadow slithered in the moonlight, stopping at the head of the bed. A huge hand reached over and grabbed the king by the mouth and nose, forcing him on the bed while waiting for the chloroform to calm the struggling monarch. The gold satin sheets were thrown back, exposing the half naked king dressed in purple satin pajama bottoms. The shadow lifted the king's body as if it were weightless and threw it over its shoulder. The duo exited through one of the massive, open windows and moved to a waiting black Mercedes Benz sport utility vehicle. The unconscious Faridoon was thrown unceremoniously in the back.

Three hours later, the same old CH-47 Chinook helicopter was, ironically, carrying another leader of Iran to a rendezvous with his fate. Once again it landed in the Dasht-e Lut region near the small town of Mashhad where its human cargo was lifted and placed in an old Toyota pickup equipped with wide, desert tires. Duct tape kept the trip in relative silence except for the sound of a continuing struggle in the back. Faridoon's hands and feet were bound with the same duct tape, but that didn't stop the victim from thrashing, kicking, and trying to throw his body over the tailgate to escape his impending

Chapter Fifty-Three

doom. Several times the driver braked violently, throwing the victim to the front of the truck.

Finally, the king's journey to eternity was about to come to its earthly finish. The truck pulled alongside the desert wadi that was the final resting place of the previous president. The old pickup screeched a complaint as the large driver got out and moved to the back of the truck. He reached in and grabbed the kicking and wriggling, self-appointed king and dragged him from the truck bed.

Arastoo's face was contorted with terror; his bulging eyes were streaming tears down his face as he sullenly looked at his captor. Recognition caused him to become silent as he stared with disbelief into the dark and pitiless eyes of SHAHEEN! Acting as if he was allowing a condemned man to say his last words, the former bodyguard ripped the duct tape from Arastoo's mouth.

"Shaheen, my dear friend, what are you doing? I am your king! You have sworn to protect me from all harm, and now you are performing this atrocity! What has happened to you?" The scowling face revealed nothing. He remained silent.

"I order you to release me immediately and return me to the palace. I give you my word that I will not require that you suffer too great a punishment. Remember that I am your benefactor; you would be nothing without me. Now, you stupid monster, release me!" The behemoth in dark robes glared at him with eyes that were nearly invisible in the moonlight.

Surprisingly, Shaheen replied. "You are a fool! You turned your back on the one that made you great, Mr. Diablo! He gave you money, palaces, and power. Payment for your ingratitude is now required; he never forgives! To quote from the Old Testament, 'Thou are weighed in the balances and found wanting.' Your fate is certain. The horned viper will be your companion on this last journey!"

The hand of death shot out and pinched the nose of the hapless Arastoo shut while covering his screaming mouth with his paw-like palm.

Smothering is an unpleasant and undignified way to die. After struggling and writhing for several terrible minutes, the former king became quiet. Shaheen dragged the body to the edge of the funeral wadi, glanced down for a brief moment, then threw the earthly remains of Cyrus II over the edge and watched it roll to the bottom where it came to rest in deep shadows. Unlike his ancient ancestor who died in battle surrounded by loyal soldiers, this Cyrus was murdered in the desert, witnessed only by the passing fox or lizard. The new Persian Empire came abruptly to an end!

Chapter Fifty-Four

The Trilateral Commission had reserved the entire Una Hotel Cusani in Milan, Italy, for their annual meeting. This semi-secret organization was formed in 1973 to foster closer cooperation among core democratic industrialized areas of the world. A report posted on the Internet states that there are about 350 members who are distinguished leaders in business, media, academia, public service, labor unions, and other non-governmental organizations.

During a lunch break, a member from Denmark was meeting with a familiar person who was also attending the meetings as an invited guest. He still had the handsome good looks of a movie star. His eyes were still invisible behind the ever-present Oakley sunglasses. Both of the men were smoking very expensive cigars. They were meeting in a small, beautiful outdoor garden area where a few other people were enjoying a brief time to relax in the sun.

"I am sure you will agree that all of our people made handsome profits by buying commodity futures contracts in the United States during the Faridoon administration," the man in the dark glasses said.

"Yes, sir, I think you can say that we made a fortune! Your idea to have the chairman of the commission use his influence to get the proper banking codes to overriding American banking procedures, preventing our funds from being traced by the FBI, was brilliant!" The Scandinavian remarked. "The question is, what do we do now? I am assuming that you already have a new plan ready to be implemented."

The handsome Mr. Diablo smiled and let out a cloud of

cigar smoke. "I think that you and our investors will be very pleased. I anticipate that our profits will exceed those we just realized in the United States."

The delegate asked, "May I ask where we will be going next?"

Again the smile and the cloud of smoke met the delegate's gaze. "I think Hong Kong is becoming very attractive, and it is very pleasant this time of the year. I am presently arranging things there now. I have the right man moving into a place of leadership. He will be as influential in Hong Kong as Faridoon was in Iran. He is brilliant, attractive, and ambitious. Just the kind of leader we need in this rapidly growing region of the world."

"I am honored, sir, that you have included me in your circle of associates. Ask anything from me, and I will do my best to make you proud of me." The delegate fawned and bowed slightly as they both moved to return to the meetings.

"Oh, I shall! You can rest assured that I will be calling upon your talents in the near future," the man in the Oakleys said.

The distinguished delegate from Denmark was listening to Diablo so intently that he failed to notice a giant of a man with a fierce expression on his darkened face, lounging in the shade of a nearby tree. As they were walking away, this mysterious stranger fell in behind them without speaking. Between puffs from their cigars, the commission member imagined he could smell a faint odor of sulfur!

To Contact the Author
Lway@windstream.net